P9-DVI-656

ALL MORTAL FLESH

ALL **M**ORTAL FLESH

Julia Spencer–Fleming

Thomas Dunne Books   St. Martin's Minotaur ✖ New York

This is a work of fiction. All of the characters, organizations, and events portrayed in this novel are either products of the author's imagination or are used fictitiously.

THOMAS DUNNE BOOKS.
An imprint of St. Martin's Press.

www.thomasdunnebooks.com
www.minotaurbooks.com

Library of Congress Cataloging-in-Publication Data

ISBN-13: 978-0-312-31264-0
ISBN-10: 0-312-31264-4

First Edition: October 2006

10 9 8 7 6 5 4 3 2 1

3145 1047
8.07

To independent booksellers everywhere, and especially to:

Crosshaven Books, Birmingham, AL; Capitol Books and News, Montgomery, AL; The Poisoned Pen, Scottsdale AZ; Book Passage, Corte Madera, CA; Fig Garden Bookstore, Fresno, CA; Mystery Bookshop, Los Angeles, CA; Mysterious Galaxy, San Diego, CA; San Francisco Mystery Bookstore, San Francisco, CA; M Is for Mystery, San Mateo, CA; Tattered Cover Bookstore, Denver, CO; Murder by the Book, Denver, CO; Just Books, Old Greenwich, CT; Murder on the Beach, Delray Beach, FL; Prairie Lights Bookstore, Iowa City, IA; The Mystery Company, Carmel, IN; Rainy Day Books, Fairway, KS; The Raven, Lawrence, KS; Kate's Mystery Books, Cambridge, MA; Spirit of '76 Bookstore, Marblehead, MA; Brunswick Bookland, Brunswick, ME; Maine Coast Book Shop, Damariscotta, ME; Books, Etc., Falmouth, ME; Longfellow Books, Portland, ME; Nonesuch Books, South Portland, ME; Aunt Agatha's, Ann Arbor, MI; Schuler Books and Music, MI; McLean and Eakin, Petoskey, MI; Once Upon A Crime, Minneapolis, MN; Uncle Hugo's, Minneapolis, MN; St. Andrew's Bookstore, Jackson, MS; Lee Booksellers, Lincoln, NE; Bookworm Bookstore, Omaha, NE; Toadstool Bookstore, Milford, NH; White Birch Books, North Conway, NH; Book House of Stuyvesant Plaza, Albany, NY; Partners and Crime, New York, NY; Black Orchid, New York, NY; Episcopal Book and Resource Center, New York, NY; Books and Company., Dayton, OH; Joseph-Beth Bookstore, OH; Foul Play, Westerville, OH; Powell's, Beaverton, OR; Malice the Mystery Bookstore, Bend, OR; The Bookloft, Enterprise, OR; Mystery Lovers Bookshop, Oakmont, PA; Trinity Cathedral Bookstore, Columbia, SC; Murder by the Book, Houston, TX; Third Place Books, Lake Forest Park, WA; Whodunit? Books, Olympia, WA; Seattle Mystery Bookshop, Seattle, WA; The Episcopal Bookstore, Seattle, WA; Aunties Books, Spokane, WA; Hastings, Spokane, WA; Creekside Books, Cedarburg, WI; The Velveteen Rabbit, Fort Atkinson, WI; Book World, WI; Booked For Murder, Madison, WI; Mystery One, Milwaukee, WI; Books and Co., Oconomowoc, WI.

Acknowledgments

If every publishing company was as supportive as St. Martin's Press, authors would have nothing to complain about over drinks. Thanks to Ruth Cavin, Toni Plummer, Rachel Ekstrom, Matthew Baldacci, Pete Wolverton, Matthew Shear, Talia Ross, Ann-Marie Talberg, Sally Richardson, and everyone in the art, marketing, and sales departments for taking such good care of me.

Much appreciation to my former agent, Jimmy Vines, enjoying his retirement, and my new representative, Meg Ruley. She, Christina Hogrebe, and the folks at the Jane Rotrosen Agency routinely leap tall buildings in a single bound and make it look easy.

Several people allowed me to pick their brains (mmm, brains!) for this book: Thanks to the Rev. Mary Allen, the Very Rev. Ben Shambaugh, Timothy Lamar, Roxanne Eflin, and Ellen Pyle. My thanks also to Joanne Wetter for suggesting the title.

A writer spends her time alternately avoiding all human contact and relying utterly on the kindness of family and friends. Thank you, Ross, Victoria, Spencer, and Virginia Hugo-Vidal; John and Lois Fleming; Dan and Barbara Scheeler; Patrick and Julia Lent, Calvetta Inman Spencer; Denise Hamilton, Mary and Bob Weyer, Jamie and Robin Agnew, Ellen Clair Lamb, Rachael Burns Hunsinger, and Leslie Smith.

Let All Mortal Flesh Keep Silence
—Liturgy of St. James; para. by Gerard Moultrie
The Hymnal, 1982, The Church Publishing Company

Let all mortal flesh keep silence,
And with fear and trembling stand;
Ponder nothing earthly-minded,
For with blessing in his hand
Christ our God to earth descendeth,
Our full homage to demand.

King of kings, yet born of Mary,
As of old on earth he stood,
Lord of lords in human vesture,
In the Body and the Blood,
He will give to all the faithful
His own self for heavenly food.

Rank on rank the host of heaven
Spreads its vanguard on the way,
As the Light of Light descendeth
From the realms of endless day,
That the powers of hell may vanish
As the darkness clears away.

At his feet the six-winged seraph;
Cherubim with sleepless eye,
Veil their faces to the Presence,
As with ceaseless voice they cry:
"Alleluia, alleluia! Alleluia, Lord Most High!"

ALL MORTAL FLESH

ONE

---

idway this way of life we're bound upon, I woke to find myself in a
M *dark wood, where the right road was wholly lost and gone.*

Clare smelled the smoke first. She came to a standstill, breathing
in the chill and windless air. Pine tar and wet wool and the frozen freshwater
smell of snow. And smoke. She had crammed as many logs as she could into the
cabin's woodstove before she left that morning, but they would have burnt
down into glowing cinders by now, their smoke long vanished into the air.

So. Someone had stoked the woodstove. She wasn't alone. She clutched her
poles and almost—almost—turned back into the woods. She had food and
matches and a blanket and a knife in her day pack. She could escape.

A cold touch on her bare hand startled her. A single fat snowflake melted
onto her skin. As she watched, another fell. Then another. She sighed. There
was no escape. She trudged forward, breaking through the last of the hemlock
and white pine, clambering over a hard-packed wall of snow thrown up in the
wake of the private road's plowing.

Gathering her poles in one hand, she sprung her bindings, stepped free of
her snowshoes, and scooped them up with her free hand. Her legs felt shaky
and insubstantial as she tottered toward the cabin.

Thank God, thank God, she didn't recognize the SUV parked next to her car.
It was a clean, late-model Scout, anonymous in this area where everyone spent

the winter in a four-wheel-drive vehicle. She supposed it could belong to a relative of the cabin's owner. Mr. Fitzgerald had offered the place when she told the congregation she was looking for a post-Christmas retreat, but he was into his early eighties and perhaps had forgotten promising the space to a grandkid.

She mounted the steps to the uncovered front deck and hung her snowshoes and poles on two of a row of pegs jutting from the log wall. *Please, Lord, let it not be someone from my congregation.* Anyone making the hour-and-a-half drive from Millers Kill would have to be hurting bad. *I don't have it in me to minister right now.* She opened the door.

The man rooting beneath the kitchen counter stood up and up and up before turning toward her. "Ms. Fergusson. Finally. I confess, I was beginning to feel a bit concerned."

Clare blinked. "Father Aberforth?" She looked around, as if there might be someone else who could explain why Albany's diocesan deacon-at-large was standing in the kitchen on a Monday afternoon holding a battered teakettle. The open floor plan didn't leave much scope for hiding, however, unless the presiding bishop was lurking in the bathroom. "What are you doing here?"

Father Aberforth plunked the kettle into the sink and twisted the tap on. "Making tea." He gestured behind her. "You might want to shut the door before you let all the heat out."

She kicked the door closed without turning around. "I've been on retreat." Her voice sounded shaky, as if she were excusing her absence from her parish. Willard Aberforth was known as the bishop of Albany's hit man, a scarecrow in black who dealt discreetly and firmly with problem priests. And she, they both knew, was a problem priest. Or at least a priest with a problem.

"I hadn't forgotten that," he said dryly, shutting off the water and swinging the kettle onto the stove. "I spoke to Father Lawrence before driving up here. To see how everything went. He said you had called him and told him you were coming back early?"

"Tomorrow morning."

"You had Wednesday to Wednesday, you know."

"I know. I just . . . I did what I came up here to do. Now I think getting back to work will be good for me."

Aberforth raised his eyebrows, unfurling an expanse of sagging skin. "Do you have concerns about Father Lawrence's abilities? I'm the one who approved him as your supply priest for the week, you know."

"Ah. No. No worries. He seemed quite"—*geriatric*—"nice. When I briefed him. Experienced. Very experienced."

"He was a good friend of your predecessor."

The late, lamented Father Hames, who had become St. Alban's priest around the time Betty Grable was a pin-up girl.

"I believed he and your parishioners would feel quite comfortable together."

She had thought, after the events of the past night, that her reserves of grief and dread were plumbed out, but she felt a fresh upwelling of fear at his words. "Are you . . . is the bishop suspending me?"

Father Aberforth looked at her. He had once been a younger and heavier man, and his face fell in deceptively drooping folds, but his black eyes showed that inside he was still all hard lines and angles. "Does that thought distress you?"

"Yes!" She was surprised how much. Over the past four months, she had been praying for some sign that she was in the right place, that God intended her to be a parish priest rather than a social worker or a chaplain or a helicopter pilot—her old, easy calling. God had remained resolutely silent on the matter. Maybe now He was talking to her, in the sick clench of her gut.

Father Aberforth nodded. "I thought it might. The answer is no, the bishop is not suspending you from your duties."

The last of her energy left her body with her breath. Clare let her day pack thud to the floor and collapsed into a nearby sofa without bothering to remove her parka. She heard the click-click-clicking of the burner as Aberforth turned on the gas and a whoosh as his match lit the ring into flame. "I know you're a coffee fiend, but there must be tea here somewhere," he said.

"In the pantry. In one of the Tupperware boxes." She listened to Aberforth rummage around, the clink and clunk of mugs and spoons and the sugar tin, and she could hear her grandmother Fergusson chiding her to get up and act the hostess, but for once she couldn't bring herself to care about Doing the Right Thing. She sat there dully, rubbing her hands over the smooth twill of the sofa cushions.

The kettle whistled shrilly and cut off. "Do you take your tea the same way you do your coffee? Ridiculously sweet?"

"Gosh," she said. "You remember." She waited without expectation as he crossed the floor and set a mug on the table in front of her. He folded himself into one of the leather Eames-style chairs opposite the sofa. It wasn't meant for

Aberforth's storklike six and a half feet, and he struggled to get comfortable for a moment before snatching a kilim pillow off the companion chair and stuffing it beneath his knees.

"Idiotic furniture," he said. "Where did you find this place?"

"Belongs to one of my parishioners," she said. "He doesn't use it very much since his wife died a few years ago."

Father Aberforth grunted. "Drink your tea. You look half dead."

She reached for the hot mug with as little effort as possible and managed a few sips. "What are you doing here, Father? I didn't think we were due for another chat until after I had sorted myself out up here."

"My visit has two purposes."

Clare smiled to herself. Who but Willard Aberforth talked like that?

"First, to tell you that the bishop has assigned you a new deacon."

She cradled the warm mug between her hands. "I don't need an assistant."

"This will be a full-time position, salary paid for by the diocese."

Clare looked closely at the old man. "St. Alban's isn't large enough or prosperous enough to warrant a full-time deacon."

"Nevertheless."

The penny dropped. "I'm getting a babysitter."

"Consider her more of a guide. To keep you on the straight and narrow."

"Emphasis on the straight." It had been her celebration of a gay union the year before that originally brought her to the bishop's—and Aberforth's—attention. She had broken her vows of obedience and flouted the bishop's policy toward homosexuals, both faults she had admitted but failed to repent of. She had been waiting for the bishop's reaction since last November, but the flaming car crash that was her personal life had kept her distracted. Now she tweaked to something else Aberforth had said. "Her?"

"The Reverend Elizabeth de Groot. She was raised up from St. James in Schuylerville. Since you'll be back tomorrow, I'll let her know she can report for duty as of Tuesday."

"Is she transitional?" That is, on the road to priesthood, which would give Clare some chance that the woman would be shuffled off to another parish within a year.

"Oh no. She's a career deacon. She was ordained over a decade ago after helping build St. Stephen's into the church it is today as a volunteer and a vestry member and a warden."

Clare translated that to mean *old enough to be your mother and has already seen it all twice.* "What's she like?"

"An elegant lady. Dignified. She has a lovely sense of tradition."

Clare translated that to mean *so high church she makes the archbishop of Canterbury look like a guitar-strumming folksinger.* She sighed. It wasn't as if there were anything she could do. As a response to her transgressions, it was fairly mild. "So that's the one thing," she said. "What's the other?"

Father Aberforth fussed a bit with his tea. "I came to check on you. To see if you needed to talk. Having found myself in the position of your confessor."

Clare smiled faintly. "You can't take confession." Despite his honorary title of "Father," the deacon was not eligible to act as God's intermediary when people spilled their most painful secrets. Still, he probably believed more wholeheartedly in the rite than did Clare, who forgave sins on a weekly basis.

"It wouldn't do you any good if you weren't prepared to repent and mend your ways," he said. She could feel her cheeks coloring. "Yes, I thought this retreat had more to do with your situation than with some post-Christmas and Epiphany exhaustion. Have you figured out what you're going to do with this married man of yours?" He craned his neck, trying to peer over the edge of the upstairs loft. "He's not staying here with you, is he?"

She didn't know whether to laugh or cry. "No. No, he isn't."

He pierced her with his black eyes. "I'm not here to judge you, girl. You think you're the first sheep to wander out of the fold because greener pastures beckon?" He reached for his tea. "At least you show some originality. Most priests who dabble in adultery go for the music director or one of the warden's wives. The town's chief of police—that's novel. Not too bright, but novel."

"Don't hold back. Please, tell me what you think."

"Straight talking is exactly what you need at this point, Ms. Fergusson."

He was right, and she knew it. The deacon made for a strange confidante—he didn't approve of women priests, he was formal to the point of eccentricity, and, most damning of all, he reported directly to her boss. But there was something about his dry, unsentimental demeanor that had made it easy, over the past two months, to tell him everything. About how lonely she had been, a stranger in a strange place, looking out onto a sea of faces waiting expectantly for her to either fail miserably or to walk on water. About making friends with the only person in town who looked at her and saw plain old Clare Fergusson instead of a bundle of assumptions in a dog collar. About walking farther and farther away from the narrow, well-lit path with Russ Van Alstyne, talking and laughing and ignoring the signs screaming DANGER: OFF TRAIL and ENTERING UNPATROLLED LAND and GO NO FARTHER THIS MEANS YOU and then being surprised—surprised!—when she looked around and found she was utterly lost.

Something of the wilderness must have shown in her face, because Aberforth leaned forward awkwardly against his Eames-spindled knees and said, "I haven't said anything to the bishop yet, but you're going to need to come to a decision soon, Ms. Fergusson. Not for him or for me or for the people in your parish. For the sake of your own soul."

She nodded mechanically. "I know, Father. And I've . . ." Her voice faded off. How could she describe the past few weeks? Days? These last terrible hours? "I've taken steps."

She picked up her mug of tea, watching with a clinical interest as her hand shook. "Unless something extraordinary happens, I do not expect to see Russ Van Alstyne again."

TWO

Meg Tracey wasn't the sort of woman who had to keep tabs on her friends. She enjoyed her own privacy too much to intrude on others, and she frequently quoted the phrase "An it harm no one, do what you will," which she had picked up in a book on Wicca she bought at the Crandall Library's annual sale for a buck.

She liked to think of herself as a neo-pagan and threw an annual winter solstice party with lots of torches and greenery and drinking of grog, but she wasn't interested enough to dig much deeper into the philosophical underpinnings. It was enough for her that it annoyed the hell out of her intensely Catholic family (she had been born Mary Margaret Cathwright) and that it distinguished her from the vast majority of her neighbors in Millers Kill, a town she frequently described as "three stop signs east of Nowhere."

It was a mutual loathing of the poky little burg their husbands had brought them to that first threw Meg and Linda Van Alstyne together. On the surface, they had nothing in common. Meg was the full-time mother of three, while Linda, childless, was busy starting up her own business. Meg's husband was a former peace activist who taught at Skidmore College; Linda's husband "retired" to run the Millers Kill Police Department after a twenty-five-year career in the army. Linda was a meticulous homemaker whose two-hundred-year-old farmhouse was a showplace for her decorating skills; Meg's house, like her, was careless and eclectic, filled with child-battered furniture and dog hair. Linda guarded her space, inviting few people into her sanctuary; Meg's family room was always filled with sprawls of teenage boys, her kitchen overrun with giggles of girls.

At an estate auction in Glens Falls, Meg (scouting out the Adirondack cedar chairs) overheard Linda (examining the hand-forged iron trivets) cracking a joke about Millers Kill (the punch line had something to do with dairy farmers and cow insemination). She introduced herself. Their discussion led to lunch, which led to an invitation to Meg's for a blender of strawberry daiquiris, which led to an impromptu dinner invitation since Linda's husband was working late. As Linda's husband frequently worked late, dinners together became a more-or-less regular thing until Linda's custom curtain business began to take off in a serious way. Still, Linda touched base with Meg by phone if not in person almost every day. Especially since her husband dropped the bomb on her. Which was why, a full forty-eight hours after their last conversation, Meg was worried.

"I haven't heard from her since Saturday afternoon," she said into the cordless phone tucked beneath her chin.

"Maybe she's at the Algonquin Hotel. Didn't you say she's spending a lot of time there on the renovation?"

"Not all weekend."

"Honey, the woman does have a life. Give her a break." In the background, she could hear the sound of rattling file-cabinet drawers and footsteps. Instructors in anthropology didn't get large, soundproofed offices. "Maybe she went out Saturday night, picked up some young stud, and has been holding him hostage ever since."

"I wish. That's what I'd be doing. And don't you forget it."

He snorted. "I believe you."

"So if you think you can get away with any private counseling with one of those nubile young hotties you have floating around campus . . ."

"Please. I value my equipment too much to risk losing it." She could hear Deidre slamming through the front door. "Mo-om! I'm home!"

Meg lowered her voice. "Get home early tonight and I'll show you how much *I* value your equipment."

Jack laughed. "I'm going to start paying all your friends' husbands to misbehave. I'm going to find Russ Van Alstyne and plant a big wet sloppy one on him."

"What? What?"

"Ever since he told Linda he was having an affair, you've been a total tiger kitten. Rrowr."

Meg giggled. "Just reminding you how good you've got it."

"Mo-om! I need a ride to piano!"

"I gotta go," Meg said. "Deidre's bellowing. Hold that thought."

"Faster, pussycat! Faster, faster!"

She could hear Jack laughing as she hung up. He was right, she thought, gathering up her coat and car keys. She had been keeping very close tabs on him since the morning Linda, ping-ponging between fear and rage, had told Meg about her husband's infidelity. It wasn't that Meg thought she had anything to worry about. On the other hand, Linda hadn't thought she had anything to worry about, either.

Despite the steadily falling snow, Meg drove to the piano teacher's with only half a mind on the road. Deidre, plugged into her MP3 player in the backseat, didn't say a word until a quick "See ya later, Mom," punctuated by a slamming door.

Now she had an hour to kill. Meg tried Linda one more time on her cell phone. The number rang and rang, until a recorded male voice clicked on.

"You've reached the home of Russ and Linda Van Alstyne. Leave a message." Meg hung up. Without consciously deciding, she switched on her headlights and turned left out of the piano teacher's driveway, headed toward the Van Alstynes'.

Linda lived on an old country road halfway between Millers Kill and Cossayuharie, dotted with houses that had been farms in the nineteenth century, widely spaced, with quarter-mile-long driveways. Good business for Meg's son Quinn, who had kitted out his 200,000-mile pickup with a plow to earn extra money, but way too remote for Meg's taste.

The Van Alstynes' house was set back, high on a treeless rise that gave them sweeping views in the summer but looked desolate and wind-scoured in the winter. The long, long drive hadn't been plowed anytime recently. Meg drove up as far as her Saab would take her, riding in the ruts left by the last vehicle to brave the hill, but around the halfway point she slowed, skidded, and slipped back several feet. Admitting defeat, she yanked on the parking brake and got out to walk the rest of the way.

Despite the gathering twilight, there weren't any lights on that Meg could see. On the other hand, she would have to circle around to the west side of the house in order to spot the windows in Linda's upstairs workshop. She banged on the mudroom door. No answer. Maybe Linda was out? Meg crossed the end of the drive and peered through the barn windows. No, there was her station wagon.

It was turning back toward the house that she noticed the odd blot in the snow near the doorway. She recrossed the drive to look at it. The falling snow was beginning to cover it, but she could see it was pink and slushy, as if someone had plunged a spoonful of spaghetti sauce into the snow and stirred vigorously. At the sight of it, something cooled in the back of her brain, and she suddenly noticed the rhythm of her heartbeat making its way to the very edge of her skin.

She couldn't think what it might be. But she really, really didn't want to consider it.

She almost went back to her car. She would have to leave soon, to pick Deidre up on time. She examined the door, the granite step beneath it, the spotless bronze handle. Nothing out of place. Nothing odd. She took hold of the handle and turned it.

The mudroom was dark and cramped. "Linda?" she called. There was a thump and a rumble, like a subterranean beast waking up hungry, and Meg jumped in her skin until she realized it was just the furnace kicking in. "Oh, for God's sake," she said, impatient with her imagination. She wiped her boots off on the bristly mat and opened the door to the kitchen.

She saw what was on the floor there.

For a moment, none of it made sense; then the reality of what she was seeing slammed into her and her lungs and throat filled with a scream that would have torn her voice clean out of her—

—and she heard a creak. Beyond the kitchen.

Ohmygod he's still here he's still here whoever did this is still here.

Meg tumbled backward out of the mudroom door and ran, slipping, rolling, slopping through the snow, catching herself on her car's hood, flinging herself behind the wheel. She twisted the key so hard in the ignition the starter motor ground its teeth, then threw the stick into reverse and gunned down the drive, one arm twisted across the seat back, the other barely keeping the wagon from sliding into the snowbanks lining the narrow way. She backed straight into the road without looking in either direction and slammed on the brakes, blocking both lanes of traffic.

She stared up the driveway. There was nothing stirring. No hand or face appeared at the open mudroom door. Then, with a suddenness that made her flinch, an orange-striped cat darted through the open door and bounded over the snow toward the barn.

Meg's head fell forward onto her steering wheel. The cat. She had forgotten the cat. Linda had visited the shelter the same day she gave her husband his walking papers. She had told Meg his allergies kept her from owning a cat for years, but they weren't going to hold her back one minute longer.

Her whole arm trembling, Meg reached for the phone on the passenger's seat. It was almost too heavy for her to lift. She dialed 911.

"Nine-one-one Emergency Services. Please state your name and the nature of your emergency."

"I'm . . ." Meg took a breath. "I'm Meg Tracey. There's been a—someone's been killed."

"Where are you, ma'am? Are you safe?"

Was she safe? Oh, God. Meg smashed the door lock button.

"Ma'am? Are you okay?"

"Yes. Yeah. I think so. I think I'm safe. I'm not in the house. I mean, I was, but now I'm in my car. Across the road. Please, you've got to send someone."

The dispatcher's voice was both calm and authoritarian. "I'm already alerting the police and ambulance service, ma'am. Tell me where you are."

"398 Peekskill Road."

There was a crackle over the phone. Then the dispatcher again, this time alarmed. "Did you say 398 Peekskill Road?"

"Yes! For God's sake, hurry."

"Stay right where you are, ma'am. The first car will be there within five minutes. Don't go back into the house." The dispatcher sounded shaky now, like someone reciting a well-worn prayer during a moment of crisis.

"I won't. I—"

The dispatcher hung up. Meg stared at the phone. Weren't they supposed to keep her on the line until someone got there? Inside her warming car, she shivered. She wrapped her arms around herself and settled in to wait for someone to deliver her from this nightmare.

THREE

There are moments in life that are between: between the blow and the pain, between the phone ringing and the answer, between the misstep and the fall. One that comes to everyone is a moment, or three, or five, between sleeping and waking, when the past has not yet been re-created out of memory and the present has made no impression. It is a moment of great mercy; disorienting, like all brushes with grace, but a gift nonetheless.

Russ Van Alstyne was floating in this moment.

He rolled over and emerged from a dreamless sleep like a diver floating to the surface of the ocean. The room he was in was dark, tiny, not his. He had never made up stories about the cracks in the plaster ceiling, and he had never tried to replace the lopsided overhead glass light. The room was neither dark nor light but thick with shadows, and he lay in the comfortable bed with quilts rucked up beneath his chin and wondered if it was day or night. Was it summer or winter or spring or fall? His hand moved between thick, thousand-wash sheets. Was he alone or was . . . ?

That thought tumbled him back into his life.

He pressed his face toward the feather pillow, desperately reaching for the last handhold on the vanishing train of sleep, but that car was gone, and he was well and truly awake. In an upstairs bedroom at his mother's house. He eyed the small windows in the kneehole wall, where gray light leaked in around the brittle green shades. Probably late afternoon. He should call the station and get a status report from Lyle MacAuley. Things had been dead quiet since New Year's, thank God. The only open case they had was the death of Herb Perkins's border collie. Somebody had lured the dog out of the barnyard and butchered it. Gruesome but not urgent. Lyle was checking out the extremely long list of people who might have disliked the foul-tempered Perkins enough to give him the Millers Kill equivalent of the horse's head between the sheets.

He dropped his hand over his eyes. He could identify with the poor dumb dog. Get tempted out of your home by a forbidden treat and next thing you know, your guts are steaming in the snow next to you.

No. He wasn't going to start feeling sorry for himself again. He had too many things to do. Empty the woodstove ashes and restock the bin. Get a head start on shoveling out the driveway. Offer to help his mom with dinner.

He wondered how he was going to manage any of these when he couldn't summon the will to get out of bed. He checked his watch, holding his arm out straight and squinting to bring the face into view. It was three o'clock on Monday. And he was still alive. Not doing much, but still here. That was something, wasn't it?

He heard the stairs creaking, quiet footfalls outside his door. He shut his eyes and let his hand fall relaxed over the quilt, putting off for a little more time the minute he would have to emerge in the land of the living again. The steps retreated downstairs, and he sighed. Christ, here he was, fifty years old and hiding from his mother. Could he possibly be any more pitiful?

With that, he tossed off the covers and swung out of bed. He was completely clothed, except for his socks, and as he pulled them on he tried out his game face. Capable. Stable. A guy who can Deal with Things. He stood and checked himself out in the dresser mirror. Okay. No stains. No bad bed head—although if he didn't get to the barber soon, he might as well start wearing a ponytail like one of those idiot downstaters in the throes of a midlife crisis.

He did not meet his own eyes.

He opened the door onto an upper landing masquerading as a miniature hallway. In the bedroom opposite, twin beds frothed with pink gingham and lace and heaps of stuffed animals, ready for his nieces to sleep over. He shuffled down the first flight and paused on the turning. He could hear voices from the kitchen. His mom and . . . he eased down a few more steps . . . his sister.

". . . yet?" Janet was saying.

"No. He got in a little before lunchtime, looking like death warmed over. He went straight to bed. I didn't ask."

"What's going on with Linda?"

"I don't know. I'm trying not to interfere."

"Has he talked to a lawyer yet?"

"As near as I can tell, he doesn't want to consider it."

"Oh, for chrissakes."

"Janet . . ." His mother's warning tone. God help the child who swore or blasphemed in front of her. Even if that child was a forty-six-year-old mother of three.

"Sorry." A chair scraped the floor. "But really, Mom. She could be clearing out their accounts while he mopes over here."

"If she does, he'll have to deal with it. I'm not pushing him into a divorce, and I'm not telling him to go back to his wife. I'm keeping my mouth shut."

He was about to stomp down the rest of the stairs and announce himself when Janet said, "I can't believe you! When I was thinking about splitting up with Mike, you were falling all over yourself with advice!"

Russ stopped, one stockinged foot poised over a stair tread. Janet? Almost left her husband? Didn't anyone tell him *anything*?

"Sweetie, you know I love Mike like he was a son. Any advice I gave you was meant to help the both of you. It's not the same with Russ and Linda. It's no secret I never really took to her."

No shit, Russ thought.

"If I start bad-mouthing his wife, who is it fixing to get hurt when they get back together?"

"You think they're going to get back together?"

"I'd like to think . . ." Her voice trailed off. Even with the last turn of the stairs and the living room between them, Russ could hear his mother sigh. "Your brother is the closest thing I've ever seen to a real-life Horton the Elephant. He meant what he said and he said what he meant . . ."

"An elephant's faithful one hundred percent," Janet finished the quote.

Great. His entire personality could be summed up by Dr. Seuss.

"So you think this is just the middle-aged crazies?" Janet sounded relieved. "Well, he won't be the first guy to get the urge to dip his wick into a much younger woman when the clock starts tolling fifty."

His hand tightened around the banister until his knuckles showed white and his arm shook. To hear all his pain, all his teeth-gritting self-control, all his astonished joy dismissed as a midlife crisis was almost more than he could bear right now. He knew his sister and his mother loved him, but they didn't know him. Nobody knew him.

Except Clare. Who was lost to him now.

He let his next step come down loudly, then thudded the rest of the way down the stairs. His mom's tiny living room opened directly onto an even tinier dining room, where the two women were sitting, folding single printed sheets of paper into thirds.

Margy Van Alstyne looked up at him with the face of a worried chipmunk, well-padded cheeks between frown lines above and a little wedge of a chin below. That, combined with her short, beer-keg body, gave her a misleadingly harmless appearance. "Hey, sweetie. We were just talking about you. Did you have a good nap?"

He cleared his throat. He could at least try to sound normal, even if he couldn't feel that way. "Yeah, I was out like a light. What's this you two are working on?" He picked up one of the pamphlets. "An antiwar rally? Aw, Mom, not again." One of his mother's proudest possessions was a photo from a 1970 *Time* magazine showing her in a screaming match with the then-governor of New York at a peace demonstration.

"Just because the corporate war machine doesn't have you in its clutches this time doesn't mean I'm not going to shout out against this blood-for-oil idiocy."

He scowled at his sister. "Are you in this, too?"

Janet, like him, had gotten most of her features from their father, and they shared a rangy build and bright blue eyes. She used to have his almost-but-not-quite-brown hair until a few years ago, when it mysteriously went blond overnight. From fright at turning forty, she claimed. Now she stretched out her long legs beneath the table and cracked her arms over her head. "Don't look at me. I'm just the hired help."

"You'd be singing a different song if you had sons instead of daughters," their mother said.

"I did all the singing I intend to do back when I was a kid," Janet said. "I'll help you fold your mailers and I'll take 'em to the post office and I'll even drive you to Albany to picket at the statehouse, but I have yet to see that anything an ordinary person does has any effect whatsoever on the powers that be."

"And this would explain why you drive your old mother batty by refusing to vote?"

O-kay. At least they were off the topic of him and his marriage. Or him and Clare. "I'll see if there's anything I can make for dinner," he said, beating a retreat into the kitchen.

He was head-deep in the pantry, wrestling out a sack of potatoes, when he saw Janet's jeans in the doorway.

"What are you going to make?" She moved out of the way as he hoisted the twenty-pound bag onto the table.

"Potato soup," he said. "Mom's on one of these all-protein, no-carb diets. All she ever has for supper is this freeze-dried wild salmon or turkey sausages."

"So of course that makes you crave bread and rice and potatoes."

"What can I say? I guess I'm the type to want what I can't have." He tried to smile, but from the look on Janet's face, he didn't succeed.

She dropped her voice, in deference to their mother's presence in the next room. "How are you doing? Really?"

"Really?" He stared at the potato sack. He was numb, that's how he was. Cauterized. He knew that soon he'd smell the stench of burned flesh and all those nerves that had been seared in half would come screaming to life and he would be in a world of pain. He knew that if he took his concentration for one moment off the here and now and started thinking about the future, he would probably pull on his boots, leave his mother's house, and jump off the conveniently located bridge—just a two-minute stroll from her front door—into the rocky, ice-rimmed waters of the upper Hudson River.

"I'm okay, I guess," he said. "Considering."

Janet looked at him skeptically. "O-kay. And how's Linda?"

He felt his lips draw tight together. "Busy. She's redoing all the drapes and stuff she originally did for the Algonquin Waters Spa and Resort." Pretentious name. Although, having met the owner, he wouldn't have been surprised if the place had been called the Peasants Stay Out Hotel.

"When's the last time you saw her?"

"What's with you and Mom?" *Time to change the subject, little sister.* "You two don't usually wrangle over her causes."

She pulled a face that said, *I know what you're doing, but I'll play along anyway.* "That's because she's been sticking to the save-the-earth stuff since . . .

well, since the last Gulf War." She dug several potatoes out of the bag and dropped them into the sink.

"Stop the development, stop the war—what's the difference?" He stooped to retrieve the colander from one of the lower cabinets.

"Easy for you to say. You were in Vietnam."

He snorted a laugh.

"You know what I mean. You weren't the only freshman in Millers Kill High whose mother was arrested for throwing cow's blood on the Armory." She opened a drawer and got the peeler out. "I went to all those sit-ins and lie-ins and marches with her, and it didn't mean squat."

"C'mon. You know Nixon was quaking in his boots at the thought of Mom."

Now Janet was the one who snorted. Russ turned on the tap and unhooked the wooden cutting board from beside the kitchen window. As his sister rinsed the potatoes and began her rapid-fire peeling, he threw open the freezer door. "Mom! You got any salt pork?"

Her voice floated over the sound of running water. "That stuff will clog your arteries, sweetie. Never touch it."

"How about some real bacon, then?" He withdrew a package of 100% Lean Turkey De-Lite Bacon and waved it in Janet's direction. "Look at this crap," he said.

"Nope. What you see is what we've got."

He swung the freezer door shut. "I'm going to the market. I can't make potato soup without pig fat." He stepped into his boots, waiting on the soaking board next to the back door. "Try not to tear each other's hair out while I'm gone."

Janet smiled at him. "Watch yourself, smart-ass. Mom believes she can fix anything if she just tries hard enough. If you don't sort things out, and fast, she'll make you her next cause."

Russ was clearing off his windshield and headlights when his cell phone, plugged into a wall socket in the kitchen, began ringing. He was carefully pulling out of the drive when it let off a series of sharp beeps, indicating he had a message. And he was well down Old Route 100, absorbed in his wipers beating away the fast-falling snow, when his mother got up from the dining room table to answer her own phone, ringing off the hook in the living room.

FOUR

L ater—much later—Officer Mark Durkee would wonder what might have happened if he hadn't gotten the phone call. It wasn't a foregone conclusion. He often popped in a video and turned off the phone about an hour before Rachel got home from her shift as a surgical nurse at the Washington County Hospital. Maddy, their five-year-old, was like a crack addict getting a pipeload when it came to her Disney Princess tapes. She wouldn't budge until her mother arrived, and by then he'd be an hour into his evening nap, soaking up enough sleep to make it through another eight-hour overnight in his squad car.

Or he might have been stretched out in the crawl space beneath their kitchen, stuffing yet more insulation in an attempt to protect the pipes from freezing up yet again this winter. There were always, always leaks and blown fuses and foundation cracks to be repaired in the old house. Mark had probably spent more than the place was worth on making it as solid and square and tight as it could be, but he had seen how the chief had transformed his old farm-house. Twice a year, they were all invited over, for the Christmas party and the summer barbecue, and damned if every time the chief hadn't done something to make his house sweeter. He was Mark's inspiration.

Of course, he might have been running Maddy to Rachel's parents or to her cousin's or to her aunt's for a sleepover or a birthday or to go sledding. Rachel complained about her family taking over their lives at times, but she hadn't ever been without their wide and generous circle. He had grown up in a family that was neither warm nor close, and as soon as they could, its members scattered to the four corners, connected by nothing more than Christmas cards and a rare phone call. He liked the fact that generations of Bains made Cossayuharie their home. Times were good and bad, businesses grew and died, but they never lost sight of the fact that it was the family, first and foremost, that mattered.

Which was the gist of the screaming fight he was having with his wife when the phone call came.

"I can't believe you'd go behind my back like this!" Mark said. "Christ on a crutch!" He rattled a letter beneath her nose. It was on a heavy vellum, with the seal of the New York State Police on the top. He didn't have to see the body of the letter to know what it said. Since it arrived this morning, he had practically memorized the thing.

Dear Officer Durkee: I very much enjoyed our conversation at the Troy Forensics Conference. Based on the service records you forwarded to me, I'd like to invite you to apply to the NYSP with an eye to joining us here at Troop F . . .

"I forwarded Captain Ireland my service record? *I* did?"

Rachel shut the family room door, closing them off from Maddy, before turning on him. "For chrissakes, Mark. It's an invitation to apply, not a death threat. I knew you'd never screw up the courage to send them your CV without a little push."

"When were you going to tell me about this? Before or after you set an interview date for me?"

She stomped up the stairs. He followed. "What the hell's wrong with the Millers Kill Police Department?" he asked.

She turned at the head of the stairs and glared down at him. "Mark, you've worked there five years now and you still can't get moved off the dog shift."

She disappeared into the bedroom. He trailed after her. She stripped her smock off and tossed it into the corner hamper. "Maddy's halfway through kindergarten. Next year she'll be in school from eight thirty until three thirty. She won't need you at home during the day." Rachel kicked her work shoes off into the closet. "And in case you hadn't noticed, this day-night working thing sucks. Big time. I never get to see you."

"You're right. It does suck. Now explain to me how the solution to the problem is to for me to join the state police and move to Middletown."

She unhooked her bra. He looked away, refusing to be distracted by the sight of her full breasts.

"Cut it out," he said.

"I've done my research, you know. With your experience, you could skip trooper entirely and lateral in as a sergeant. You'd be making more money and actually have a chance to climb the ladder. You could be an investigator."

"I have opportunities right here."

"As what? The town's so cheap they don't even have a detective pay grade. You need to stop thinking the sun shines out of Chief Van Alstyne's ass and to let him know that you've got other options." She hooked her thumbs in her waistband and shimmied out of her bright blue work pants. "Maybe at least then they'd take your requests for a day shift seriously."

Mark flopped back on their bed, feeling like his head might explode. He let out a strangled sound of frustration.

"No one's saying you have to take a job with the state police. But wouldn't it be neat to know you could?" The bed dipped as she knelt next to him, nude except for her bikini underpants. "C'mon. Try it. An application doesn't commit you."

Part of him—the part from the waist down—was telling him, *The gorgeous naked woman wants to have sex! Agree with her, you idiot!* The part of him above his neck noticed that this wasn't the first time Rachel had sidetracked a heated discussion with sex. And, funny thing, he never seemed to get back to the points he had been making before they hit the sheets.

Who cares? His groin howled. *It's sex! Sexsexsexsex!*

He pushed himself up, off the bed. "Rache, we need to talk about this."

"We are talking about it. You don't want to work the graveyard shift anymore. I want you to have the recognition and opportunities you deserve." She kneaded her hands on the bedspread and leaned forward. He had to look up at the ceiling. "You can even take the letter in, so Chief Van Alstyne can see you're being all open and aboveboard." The bed squeaked a little. "Now come on. We're wasting time. *Beauty and the Beast* only has another twenty minutes."

"Rache," he said to the ceiling, "it's not just contacting the staties without telling me."

The bed stopped squeaking.

"It's . . . look, I like the MKPD. I like my work. I like knowing Maddy's five minutes away from her grandparents." He glanced down.

Rachel's face was very still. "Do you remember when we got married? I told you I wanted something more than to spend the rest of my life in Cossayuharie." She rolled off the bed. "I thought you wanted that, too." She snagged her robe off the hook on the back of the closet.

"Rache, when we got married, I was just starting out. I thought what I wanted from police work was all guts and glory. But working with the chief these past five years—I want what he has. A history with the place he's protecting. Roots in the community."

"A girlfriend on the side? A little late-night patrolling action?"

He clenched his hands. "Nobody's got any proof of that. As far as I know, it's a bunch of gossip."

"And that's one of the things that drives me crazy about living here. There's no such thing as privacy in a small town."

"Is this about your sister?" Two months ago, Rachel's sister Lisa had lost her husband in a mill fire. That would have been bad enough as it was, but the guy had been in the mill in the first place because he had decided to try his hand at assault, kidnapping, and extortion.

"Maybe. A little. I can't be sure, of course, because half the time when I come into the staff lounge, everybody else shuts up."

"It'll be old news soon, Rache. Something else will come along and start the biddies clucking."

"It's not just that." She bent over her dresser and swiped it with the sleeve of her robe. "I've been offered another job."

He paused. "Same place as last time?"

"No. With the Capital Medical Center trauma unit." She straightened. "This is the third time I've gotten approached about a job with bigger responsibilities and better benefits. I'm getting tired of saying no just so you can grow up to be Russ Van Alstyne."

He opened his mouth to say something. He didn't know what it would be, just that it would be bigger and nastier and would cut her like she'd just cut him.

Then the phone rang.

"This conversation is not over," she said, pointing a shaking finger at the bedside table.

"It might be the station." He reached for the phone.

"Probably the chief. I'm sure he's got lots of time to devote to work now his wife's thrown his sorry ass out—"

"Hello," he answered.

"Mark? It's Lyle MacAuley."

Mark frowned. Why would the deputy chief be calling him five hours before he was due in? "What's up?"

"I need you to do something. Can you get away from home?"

Mark's eyes flicked toward Rachel, who was hopping into a pair of jeans, swearing under her breath. "Yeah," he said.

"I need you to pick up the chief and bring him to the station."

"Pick him up? Is there something wrong with his truck?" Another oddity popped into his mind. "Hey, isn't this his day off?"

"He's staying at his mother's, up where Old Route 100 crosses the river and heads toward Lake Lucerne. You know the place?"

"Yeah, but it's gonna take me thirty minutes to drive there in this weather. Why—"

MacAuley cut him off. "His mom said he's gone to the market. It could be the local Kwik-mart, or he might have gone all the way to the IGA. I need you to find him, get him into your vehicle, and bring him in."

Mark stared out the window, where the snow was falling relentlessly out of a dark sky. Behind him, Rachel was still muttering baleful comments. "Lyle, what the hell is going on?"

"I'll tell you when you get to the station. And Mark—no lights. Keep radio silence. I mean that. Don't even turn your damn radio on."

"But—"

"I'll see you as soon as I can." There was a click, and Mark was left listening to the angry buzz of a dead line.

He turned to Rachel. "I have to go."

"Of course you do," she said. "What's more important than you being satisfied in your work? Certainly not anything I might have to say." Her words whipped past him like the winter wind, annoying, but not something he paid attention to when he was thinking hard. As he was now.

What the hell was going on?

FIVE

N oble Entwhistle was about as solid and unimaginative an officer as Lyle MacAuley had ever worked with. He was the guy who did the door to door, called everyone on the thirty-page phone list, worked the radar gun. If you wanted leaps of deduction or seat-of-the-pants interviewing, he was no good, but if you wanted methodical, if you wanted organized, if you wanted polite to old ladies, you wanted Noble Entwhistle.

Lyle never in a million years could have pictured him hunched over in the snow, crying snot-faced, unable to speak.

Noble had made it three steps out of the kitchen door of 398 Peekskill Road before collapsing, openmouthed and weeping. He had reholstered his flashlight but forgotten to turn it off, and now a beam of light jerked up and down as his tree-sized back shook with sobs. Fat snowflakes blazed for a moment in glory and then vanished into the deepening drifts on the ground.

None of the three police vehicles parked in the drive had its lights on. Lyle had radioed them to go dark almost as soon as he had gotten the brief from Harlene, their dispatcher. Instead, he had left the mudroom door, open when they arrived, pushed wide. Warm light spilling out. Cold air seeping in.

"Jesus, Noble," he said. "Try to pull it together."

Noble twisted his head in Lyle's direction. "Pull it together," he gasped out. "Did you . . . did you see her? Her face is just *gone*."

Lyle, shadowed against the bright light spilling from the mudroom and screened by the fast-falling snow, knew he was no more than a blur to his officer. And thank God for it. His self-control was hanging by a thread. One wrong word, one tiny misstep, and he was going to lose it as bad as Noble. Poor sonofabitch. He racked up his voice to make a steady shot. "I saw her." Butchered like an animal. "You're not going to help her by falling apart."

He scanned the road. A lone car drove toward them, slowed down, and kept on going. Good. He heard the muffled crunch of boots through loose and packed layers of snow. "Whaddya got, Eric?"

"I completed the friend's statement." Officer Eric McCrea's features emerged out of the darkness as he plodded toward the long rectangle of light. "Are you sure you don't want me to run her down to the station and get it on video?"

"No."

Eric leaned in closer, as if to pierce the shadow cast by the brim of Lyle's cap. "This is not the time for shortcuts. We're going to catch the fucker who did this, and when we do, we don't want him getting off because we were half-assed putting the evidence together."

Lyle drew in a breath to ream McCrea out, but cut it short with a click of his teeth. It wasn't his fault. He was on edge. They all were. And Lyle wasn't going to be able to carry this off by himself. He was going to need one or two others backing him up. Containment—that was going to be the trick.

"Well?" Eric demanded.

A brilliant splash of light broke their stare-off. Another vehicle was churning up the driveway's slope, its headlights bouncing through the billows of white.

"Shit. That's Kevin Flynn's truck." Lyle glared at McCrea. "Did you call him?"

"No. But what if I did? What the hell's the deal, MacAuley?"

The almost-new Aztek looked like what it was, the prize possession of a boy who got his first learner's permit seven years ago. It rumbled to a stop behind McCrea's badly angled squad car, and Flynn jumped out. Kevin, the most junior officer of the Millers Kill Police Department, was finally getting enough meat on his bones to lessen his resemblance to a six-foot Howdy Doody puppet. In an effort to look older than sixteen, he had lately grown a soul patch, a would-be-cool square of facial hair beneath his lower lip. Unfortunately, Flynn's facial hair was the same color as the stuff on top, and he now looked—to Lyle's old and uncool eyes, at least—as if he had an enormous furry freckle on his chin.

"Harlene called me! On my cell phone!" Kevin kicked through the snow, his face open and eager. "I told her I wasn't working today, but she said to get over here. Whadda we doing at the chief's house?" He had gotten close enough to finally make out Lyle's and Eric's expressions. He frowned. "Guys? What's up?"

Harlene called him. Lyle's heart sank. Christ, she was probably ringing up every guy on the force to pitch in. How the hell was he going to manage this now?

Behind him, Noble lurched upright, a messy, tear-sodden bear emerging from its den. Flynn saw him. "Noble?" He turned to Lyle. He looked scared. "Is it . . . is it the chief?"

"No."

The one-word answer didn't do anything to relieve the anxiety on Kevin's face. Lyle breathed in and tried again. "The chief is fine, Kevin. We're trying to . . . deal with a crime scene here without drawing too much attention to our-selves." Out of the corner of his eye, he could see Eric's jaw swing open. "This is what you can do for me. Take your truck and park it at the intersection of Peekskill and River Road. You got your flares?"

Kevin nodded.

"Good. I've called in the state police CS unit. They're going to be sending a van and a couple of techs, and I want you to be on the lookout for 'em. You know how it can be with people from away driving these country roads. You send 'em up here. Can you do that?"

Kevin nodded again. His expression relaxed. The low-man-on-the-totem-pole job; this was familiar territory.

"You need anything, you call Harlene on your cell phone. Don't use your radio."

"I don't have one in my Aztek yet."

"Okay, go."

Flynn fluffed through the snow, intent on his assigned task.

"That's the biggest load of bullshit make-work I've ever seen. There's not a man in Troop G who couldn't find this road in the dark, and half of 'em proba-bly know which house is the chief's."

Lyle nodded. "That's why I put in the call to Troop D."

McCrea stared at him. "Are you nuts? They're down in Amsterdam. It'll take their CS unit an hour to get here." He scrubbed his face with one gloved hand, dislodging the snowflakes that were attaching themselves to his eyelashes and beard.

"Eric," Lyle said. "Stop. And think for a moment. Forget who all's involved. Lay it out like a domestic violence case."

Eric's mouth twisted in disgust. "Domestic violence?"

"Just do it for me."

"Okay." McCrea closed his eyes for a moment. "A woman found dead in her home. No signs of forcible entry. No known history of drugs. No arrests. No known involvement with any suspicious individuals."

"The victim recently separated from her husband," Lyle added. "The husband left the marital home under protest. The husband has access to weapons and is trained in their use."

Eric stared at him. "You can't say . . . Jesus, you don't think the chief had anything to do with this?"

"Ssh. Keep it down." Thank God, this part he had already rehearsed. He didn't hesitate. "Of course I don't think the chief was involved. But if you didn't know him, if you didn't have any stake in this investigation, who would you peg as the prime suspect?"

Eric's mouth worked before he could get the words out. "The victim's husband."

"And if this investigation gets taken away from us and handed over to the staties, who do you think they'll come down on?"

Eric shook his head. "But . . ."

"You don't think we can crack this case without their help?"

"No, but—"

"'Cause I'll tell you what the staties will do. They're gonna tag the chief as it, and the entire rest of the investigation is gonna be devoted to proving them right. If we don't want that to happen, we need to keep this as quiet and low-key as possible. We need to control any information, starting right here and now. Are you with me?"

Eric stared down at the snow beneath their boots, packed by the footsteps of everyone who had already crossed this dooryard and gotten involved. "I gotta tell you, Lyle. I been a cop ten years now, and four as an MP before that. And this . . . this gives me a bad feeling."

"Christ almighty, don't you think I feel the same way? It's making me sick to my stomach. If you think it'd go down a different way if the staties took over, please, convince me. I'd love to hear I'm wrong."

"You aren't wrong." Eric squinted toward the neighbor's house, a good quarter-mile away on the ridgeline. Lights had come on in the windows. Lyle thought he could see someone's silhouette. Watching them. "Okay," McCrea said. "I'm in."

"Good. I want you to run the crime scene. You know to expect the Troop D CS." A mournful yowl wound through the sky from somewhere behind the barn. "For God's sake, get ahold of her cat and get it to a shelter."

"Will do."

"I'm heading back to the station. I'm going to call the ME when I get into town."

"You sure you want to wait that long to get the medical examiner out here?"

"Yes. Control. That's our motto here. Control. I need to tell Harlene to clamp down on the phone calls." His gut churned, acid and fear and regret all mixed together. "And I need to tell the chief."

SIX

Russ Van Alstyne was really, really pissed off. It surprised him; he had figured he had hours, if not days, of leaden, white-noise numbness ahead
of him. Of course, he hadn't counted on getting picked up—picked up!
Like he had a warrant out on him!—by one of his own officers. At the meat
counter of the IGA.

He had to admit, Mark was good. He had hustled Russ out of there and into
his squad car almost before he knew what had happened. It wasn't that Russ
minded getting called in on a moment's notice. Lord knows, that had happened
more than once in his life. Although he couldn't recall a time when he had had
to abandon a half-filled basket of groceries.

No, what hacked him off was Mark's refusal to tell him what was going on. "I
can't say" became "I really don't know anything," which turned to "Your guess
is as good as mine, chief."

Russ knew he was being a pain in the ass, but he couldn't figure out anything that would require Mark to drag him in to the station with zero intel on
the situation. Even if the unthinkable had happened, and one of his men had
been wounded or killed, it would be squawking all over the radio.

The radio. It was part of a nifty computerized information system, currently
dark, mounted below the edge of the dash. The whole computers-in-the-cars
thing still amazed him. Probably more evidence that he was rapidly approaching the age where they could push him out into the open sea on an ice floe.

He started pressing on buttons. Computer, radio, monitor.

"Uh." Mark turned toward him. "I don't think you ought to do that, Chief."

"Keep your eyes on the road. I don't want to wind up in the ditch."

Mark snapped to front, but his attention was all on the small screen, running its boot-up sequence. "Uh. Deputy Chief MacAuley told me to maintain radio silence."

"Did he, now?" Russ unhooked the mike. "Did he say anything about *me* maintaining radio silence?"

"No . . . but I think he—"

"Were your orders to put me under arrest, Durkee?"

Somehow, Mark managed to come to attention while sitting behind the wheel of a moving car. "No, Chief!"

"Then let me explain how it works. Lyle is the deputy chief. That means he gets to tell you what to do. I'm the chief. That means I get to tell *him* what to do." The computer screen was asking for an officer number before allowing access. Russ tapped his own into the small strip of keyboard bolted in beneath the screen. The system happily blipped him in.

He keyed the mike. "Dispatch? This is—" He turned to Mark. "What's your car number?"

"Fifty-four-ten." Mark was either defeated or disgusted. Russ couldn't tell which.

"This is fifty-four-ten inbound. I'd like to know why I'm not at home making soup right now."

There was a long pause.

"Dispatch?" He pulled the mike higher, checking for a loose connection.

"Chief? Is that you?" Finally. Harlene sounded odd.

"Yes. It's me. And I want to know what the hell is going on."

Another pause. "It's . . ." A crackle. "I think . . ." A staticky beat. "Just get here as soon as you can. Dispatch out." Harlene clicked off from her end.

He stared at the computer. Harlene never hung up on him. Never. He keyed the mike. "Dispatch. Dispatch? Harlene?" She wouldn't come back on the line. "Well, if that's not the damndest thing I've ever seen." He frowned at Mark. "Is this some sort of elaborate practical joke? 'Cause if it is, I can guarantee you I won't be laughing."

"Honest, chief. I got the call, MacAuley said to bring you in, and that's all I know."

Christ on a bicycle. Russ prayed that Lyle hadn't taken it into his head to cheer him up. He could just imagine what his deputy—a long-divorced, self-proclaimed ladies' man—would consider a picker-upper. Probably a pair of strippers dressed as beat cops. One word leaked about something like that and Russ would be handing his head to the Millers Kill aldermen on a silver platter.

"We're here," Mark said helpfully, bumping over the strip separating the police department's parking lot from the road.

"Thanks," Russ said. "I might not have recognized it with all the pretty snow."

Mark flushed red and jammed his cap on his head. They both got out. Russ scanned the parking lot as he tromped toward the front steps. He recognized Lyle's Pontiac Cruiser and Eric McCrea's Subaru station wagon. Noble's nondescript Buick and Harlene's Explorer. Nobody who shouldn't be on duty right now, thank God. That ruled out the stripper party. Unless Lyle was planning on wrestling him over to the Golden Banana in Saratoga?

He mounted the unswept granite steps carefully, Mark at his back, and stomped down the hallway toward his office, shedding snow as he went. The Millers Kill police station was state-of-the-art law enforcement construction— in 1880. Lots of granite, marble, and frosted glass. Very few spaces convenient for large electronic dispatch and routing boards. A great big holding tank in the basement, from the days when judges rode the circuit in buggies. A warren of small offices above stairs.

Harlene's communications center had been knocked together from two small rooms and straddled the space between the officers' bullpen (formerly three offices and a storage closet) and Russ's office (original, but with much uglier furniture than his predecessors had a century ago).

"I hope someone has an explanation for me," Russ said, entering the dispatch room. Harlene looked at him, her eyes red-rimmed and puffy. She silently pointed toward his own door like the Ghost of Christmas Yet to Come—if the Ghost of Christmas Yet to Come had had a tightly curled iron-gray perm and a purple MKHS Minutemen sweatshirt on its rotund form.

Sighing, he went in. Lyle was standing there waiting for him. Big surprise.

"Okay, what is it?" Russ crossed to his battered metal desk and plunked himself into his chair. He crossed his arms over his chest and glared at his deputy.

Lyle shut the door. Tested the handle. He bit the inside of his cheek. "There's been—" He stopped. "I have to—" He seemed genuinely disturbed.

Russ leaned forward, bracing his elbows on various pieces of half-completed paperwork. "Just tell me, Lyle."

MacAuley sat down. Russ always thought of Lyle as a contemporary, but in the unkind fluorescent light, Russ realized his friend and sounding board was closer to sixty than fifty. His bushy eyebrows had as much white as gray in them, and the folds beneath his eyes, which normally gave him a deceptively lazy look, were sunken and settled, as if the skin had been pulled away from his bones and left to lie.

"Lyle?"

Lyle ran a hand over his face. "There's no easy way to say this, Russ. Your wife has been killed. I'm sorry. I'm so sorry."

In Russ's head, the usual clatter of thoughts and concerns fell absolutely silent. Everything within eyesight took on an otherworldly clarity: the damp sheen of Lyle's face, the thin coating of dust on the straggly philodendron in the corner, the faded, felted spines of the *Police Gazettes* stacked on his extra chair.

"Linda?" he said.

MacAuley nodded.

Russ snorted. "That's ridiculous."

"Russ, I know it's hard to—"

"Linda's a good driver. A cautious driver. As much snow as there is on the road—that wouldn't throw her. And her car. A late-model Volvo wagon? I can't even imagine how many of them must be registered in the three counties. You guys have tagged the wrong car."

Lyle was shaking his head no, swinging it back and forth like a bell, and the look on his face was the look of something terrible trying to be born. Russ was suddenly afraid. Terrified of what was coming.

"There hasn't been any car accident. Russ, she was killed. Stabbed to death. In your—in the kitchen."

"Killed," he echoed stupidly.

"Entwhistle and McCrea and Flynn are all over there right now, along with the state CS team. We're going to find who did it, Chief. I swear to you, we're going to find who did it. And when we do, he's going to spend the rest of his life regretting he was ever born."

The terrible thing was here. He felt himself crack open, his jaw unhinge, his lungs constrict. His field of vision shrank, and his head filled with a loud, dry-edged shuffle as his mind laid down every card in its deck. Linda relaxing in her favorite chair at the end of the day. The two of them shouting at each other over the hood of her car. A funeral—he had never planned a funeral, didn't know how to do it, didn't know who to call. Oh, God, he was going to grow old and feeble alone, without his wife, his beautiful wife . . .

The way it would feel, his finger tightening on the trigger as he pumped onetwothreefourfive rounds into her killer. Just like that.

Memory. Guilt. Confusion. Self-pity.

Rage.

He held on to the rage. All the rest flapped and fluttered around him, and he knew that if he stopped to consider them he would fall apart. He couldn't fall apart. He had a job to do.

He held on to the rage.

"Harlene! Is the chief's mother here yet?" Lyle's voice, harsh with fear, seemed to be coming from a long way away. "Chief? Russ?" Someone shook his shoulders.

His vision cleared. Lyle was out of his chair, leaning over the desk, his hands tightening Russ's flannel shirt into uncomfortable knots. "Jesus Christ, Chief. I thought you was having a stroke. Are you okay? Do you want to lie down?"

"No." He held on to the rage. He had a job to do. "I want to be brought up to date on the investigation."

"We're not going to be able to put together anything like a coherent picture until tomorrow. The CS team is at the—is at your house right now. The ME ought to be over there as well. I can have Noble and Mark talk to the neighbors, see if anyone saw anything."

Russ tried to snort. It came out a wheeze. "Not likely."

"I know."

"I want to see the scene. I'll need to—to identify anything that might be out of place." It felt as if he were pushing his thoughts, one at a time, down a long, dark track. "You think . . . home invasion?"

"You mean a burglary? Not from what I could see. Nothing missing that jumped out at me, unless you've loaded up on silver or electronics since last summer's open house. There weren't any signs of forced entry. The storm windows were all in place. She"—Lyle swallowed hard and went on—"she always locked the door when she was alone at home, right?"

Russ nodded. There was a noise, outside his door, down the hall.

"I think your mother's here."

"I need to see the scene." He looked up into Lyle's face.

"You will. Just not tonight. Trust me on this, Russ. Not tonight. Go home with your mother." The noises grew closer. Footsteps, and voices. A rap on frosted glass, and before he could answer, the door swung open and his mother stood there, short and squat and beautiful.

"Oh, my darling boy," she said, her eyes filling. Then she was there, beside him, wrapping her arms around him. Sitting down, his head came to her shoulder, and he pressed his face into a purple sweatshirt that would forevermore be the color of grief to him, while she rubbed his back and said, "My boy. Oh, my sweet boy," and wept tears he could not allow himself.

SEVEN

Tuesday, January 15

Clare awoke early to a cold cabin and the realization that she was due to return to civilization today. To meet the new deacon the bishop was saddling her with. The thought should have made her grimace, but even annoyance was too much for her to compass this morning.

She rose; she dressed; she stripped the bed and threw the sheets, along with the napkins and the tablecloth, into the washing machine. Her attempt at morning prayer was flat; she had no words to offer. It felt as if she were kneeling inside a refrigerator box. Finally, she simply read out the Fifty-first Psalm. *The sacrifice of God is a troubled spirit; a broken and contrite heart, O God, you will not despise.*

Well. She might not come up to snuff in any other way, but she had the troubled spirit and the broken and contrite heart down pat.

She pulled on her parka and gloves and went out to shovel her car free. The clouds had shaken out all their snow and moved on overnight, leaving the morning stars burning clear and bright in an indigo sky. Her brand-new Subaru, purchased with a combination of insurance proceeds and what she couldn't help thinking of as blood money from the family of the man who destroyed her last vehicle, was a featureless mound of white. She brushed off the windows, the lights, and the door handles, then attacked the driveway behind the car. She figured two paths, each about ten feet long, would give her tires enough traction to make it the rest of the way down the long, narrow road. She was carrying two twenty-five-pound bags of kitty litter in the trunk and had her own snow shovel wedged in the backseat. Between them, she ought to be able to get out of any deep spots.

By the time she finished, she had stripped off both her parka and her sweater and was working in a sweat-dampened turtleneck. She tossed her coat into the Subaru and went inside to put the wash in the dryer. She packed her clothes and her rucksack, wiped down the kitchen and straightened the stack of old *New Yorker* magazines, knocked the snow off her snowshoes and poles, and had the whole shebang loaded in her car by the time the dryer was finished. She folded the sheets, left them on the end of the bed, and walked out of the cabin for the last time.

The rising sun made Mondrian patches of reddish-orange between the black lines of the trees. She got into the car and watched it ascending in her rearview mirror. She had spent an hour and a half in a continual round of motion. She had not stopped sorrowing for a single moment.

She leaned her head against her hands, folded atop the steering wheel. "A little help, here, God," she said.

She turned the ignition, and David Gray poured out of her big, balanced speakers. *Well if you want it, come and get it, for cryin' out loud. The love that I was giving you was never in doubt . . .*

She wondered what it said about her spiritual fitness that her clearest messages from the Almighty seemed to come from the alternative rock station.

At the rectory, she debated acknowledging she was back on the job by wearing clericals, versus pissing the new deacon off by meeting her in her civvies. She compromised by wearing a black blouse, dog collar, and subdued black cardigan over a pair of old undress-green fatigues.

"Interesting look," Lois said when Clare checked in for a report on the past week.

"It's a clerical mullet," Clare said. "Business on the top, party on the bottom." She took the handful of pink message slips the St. Alban's secretary handed her. "Miss me?"

"If I say yes, will I get a raise this year?"

"You have to miss the vestry and the finance committee for that, I'm afraid. I could preach a special sermon for your birthday, though."

Lois tucked a shining strand of her strawberry blond bob behind one ear. "Please. At my age, my birthday's already a religious holiday. Passover."

Clare grinned, while one part of her head marveled that she could smile at all. She shuffled through the messages. "The Ketchums want to know about baptism—" She looked up at Lois. "Why didn't they bring the kid in on January sixth?"

"They were still vacationing in the Caribbean on the Feast of the Epiphany."

"Well, they'll have to wait until Easter with the rest of them." She laid that one on Lois's desk. "Mrs. Thomas wants a home visit, okay, Mr. Stevenson . . . Mrs. Darnley—what does it say about our parish when half the congregation is either shut-in, at the Infirmary, or in the hospital?"

"It says it's time for a membership drive at the Adirondack Community College?"

"It's scary that *I'm* one of the youngest attendees of my own church." She flipped through a few more. "Abigail Campbell wants me to perform a funeral service for a *lamb*?"

"She said it was the children's 4-H project. Something got into their byre and tore the poor thing up, and the kids were devastated."

Clare waved the slip at Lois. "What was this lamb's fate going to be, before it became coyote chow?"

Lois steepled her fingers. "Easter dinner."

"Which they would have asked me to bless, I suppose." She shook her head. "I'll have to think about this one." She glanced up at the office clock. "Look, if anyone calls this morning, I'm going to be unavailable a little longer. I'm expecting a visitor. Reverend Elizabeth de Groot. She's been assigned to us by the bishop. As our new, prepaid, full-time deacon."

The secretary's perfectly shaped brows rose, and Clare found herself thinking, *No Botox for her! You go, Lois.*

"When is she starting?"

"Uh . . . now, I guess."

"Now? Today? Nice of the diocese to notify us."

Clare wanted Lois to form her own opinion of the new deacon, so she skipped over the reason they were receiving the bishop's largesse. "It was a surprise to me, too."

Lois sat ramrod stiff in her typing chair. "Well, it's not going to be my fault she's not in the new directory. It went to press last Friday."

"Don't worry about it. And think of it this way—she'll be another willing worker. Many hands make light labor, and all that."

A calculating look crept over Lois's face. "You mean she wouldn't just be doing pastoral work?"

"Of course, her focus will be on assisting me with the counseling and the services. But I don't see why she couldn't help out in other ways." After all, a very busy deacon was less likely to have extra time to poke her nose into Clare's business.

Lois smiled. It was not a beatific sight. "Oh, yes. I can think of lots of jobs I could use some help on."

"There you go. Now, before I get sidetracked, I'm going to need—"

"Excuse me."

Clare and Lois both turned around. The woman standing in the office doorway didn't look anything like the mental image Clare had built up of the Reverend Elizabeth de Groot, which ran heavily to Dame Judi Dench. This woman was younger, for one thing, maybe a decade or so older than Clare herself. She was petite—bird-boned, as Clare's grandmother Fergusson would have said. Noticeably skinnier than Lois, who at a size six was usually the thinnest woman in the room. But Lois was close to Clare's height. This woman could have walked underneath both their chins without mussing her beautifully blown-out ash blond mane. She was wearing a little black suit with her collar that looked like Chanel, if Chanel made clerical garb.

Clare could feel the ghost of her own seventeen-year-old self stretching to reclaim her skin. Her wrists, poking out from beneath her sweater, seemed huge and bony. Her hair was already coming out of the knot at the back of her head. She was sure that if she looked, she would see the same grease around her fingernails that had been her permanent badge when she worked on airplane engines with her dad.

"I'm Elizabeth de Groot." The woman smiled pleasantly. No wonder. It was undoubtedly a wonderful thing to be Elizabeth de Groot. Her smile grew more fixed, and Clare realized she hadn't responded.

"Hi! I'm Clare Fergusson." She stuck out her hand—a quick peek proved that no, there wasn't any more grease on it now than there had been fifteen minutes ago—and shook. "This is our church secretary, Lois Fleming."

"I hope this doesn't come as a total surprise to you, Ms. Fergusson. Please tell me the diocese let you know I was going to be assigned to St. Alban's."

"Oh, no, no," Clare said. "I mean—yes, they did let me know. In person. I just haven't had my coffee yet." She made a noise that was meant to convey self-deprecating amusement but wound up sounding like she was clearing her throat. "Why don't we go into my office? We can chat there. Lois, will you hold my calls?"

She ushered Deacon de Groot down the hallway and into her office. The room had the usual accoutrements one would expect of a rector: a bookshelf filling one wall, a large and graceful quarter-sawn oak desk, two chairs flanking a fireplace, and a sofa not far away, complete with boxes of tissues close at hand for people in counseling.

However, there were some unique touches as well. The two chairs were salvage from a WWII-era destroyer's admiral's quarters. The wall behind the desk was hung with framed aviation sectional maps. Interspersed among books on theology and pastoral care were mementos such as a photo of a much younger Clare and her crew in Kuwait, an Apache helicopter clock whose rotors ticked away the minutes, and a flight helmet.

"My goodness," the new deacon said. "This is positively bristling with martial energy. I take it you were a pilot? In the army?"

Clare unscrewed the Thermos of coffee she always brought to work. "Yes." She breathed in the steam as she poured herself a mug. She waggled her clean Virginia Episcopal Seminary mug toward the other woman. "Would you care for some? It's dark-roasted Sumatran. I grind it myself."

De Groot smiled apologetically. "I'm not a coffee drinker. Do you have any tea?"

Clare gritted her teeth. God save her from tea drinkers. Always with the water not hot enough and the soggy little bags dripping. "Let me get Lois on that for you," she said. She picked up the phone and buzzed the secretary. "Lois, will you make a pot of tea for Deacon de Groot?" She hung up quickly enough to avoid Lois's answer.

"So, what were we talking about? The room. Yeah, when I first got here, I just wanted lots of my favorite things around me. But I've come to realize the novelty value helps to break the ice when people meet with me." Clare gestured toward the chairs. "Like now."

De Groot took a seat, her pleasant little smile unchanging as she eyed Clare's DEATH FROM THE SKY! mug. "I realize this must have come as a shock, Ms. Fergusson. Going off for a week's retreat and getting home to a new deacon."

"Please, call me Clare. And are you Beth? Liz?"

"Elizabeth."

"Elizabeth." Of course. "I can't lie, it was a surprise. I didn't hear from Willard Aberforth until yesterday afternoon." She propped an enthusiastic look on her face. "But I'm looking forward to working with you," she lied.

"Oh, thank goodness. I feel just the same way. I've heard so many wonderful things about all the energy and innovation you're bringing to this parish."

I just bet you have. "Since you know more about St. Alban's than I do about you, maybe you can tell me how you see your role here. You'll be helping me out with services and . . . ?"

De Groot beamed. "Oh, there's so much more that a deacon can do besides assist during services! This is a good example of how I believe I can be most of service to you. I want you to think of me as a repository of knowledge. Church culture, church tradition, church law—I'm here to give you the information you need to do the best possible job you can."

Clare set her mug down so the winged rattlesnake would be visible to her new deacon. "I *do* have a master's in divinity," she pointed out.

"And I have a doctorate. But really, what is book learning compared to experience? I'm sure you feel you've learned more in the past two years than you did during your whole time in seminary!"

In the past two years, Clare had been shot at, crashed a helicopter, nearly drowned, and had her car blown up. Oh, yes—and had fallen in love with a man as inaccessible as the moon. "Yeah," she said. "I'd have to agree with that."

"That's what I can supply. The experience. There's at least one advantage to getting to my age!" Elizabeth's laugh was both self-deprecating and musical.

Every possible response Clare could come up with sounded snotty, so she held her tongue. "What else do you see yourself doing here at St. Alban's? Besides being a font of wisdom?"

"Oh, you're funny!"

A kick to the half-open door swung it wide. Lois stood there, balancing a tray loaded with a china teapot, matching cups and saucers, and a silver sugar bowl and creamer. "Tea is served," she announced.

"Thank you, Magenta," Clare said under her breath. She smiled. "Great. Let's put it here on the table—"

Lois was already lowering the tray. She faced Clare directly and whispered, "Don't get used to this."

Elizabeth was exclaiming over the china.

I owe you one, Clare mouthed. With their guest fussing with the tea and the cream, Lois walked backward out of the room. Clare didn't think she had ever seen anyone bow sarcastically before.

"Okay. Getting back to the subject at hand—"

"Of course. What else can I do to be of assistance? Let's see. I have a master's in counseling. I used to be a teacher, so I have a special interest in all aspects of Christian education. At St. Stephen's, I worked extensively in parish development and volunteer coordination. And at Bethesda Church in Saratoga, I led the capital campaign to restore their historic bell tower." She smiled brightly at Clare.

"Wow." Clare couldn't think of what to say to that litany of accomplishment. "I mean that. Wow. Why aren't you a priest?"

For the first time, Elizabeth de Groot looked less than serene. "I've actually been up before the Discernment Committee several times." She fingered her collar. "They seem to feel I just haven't had . . . an authentic call."

Clare felt her cheeks pink up. She had been silently carping at the woman, and now Elizabeth's honesty shamed her. "It seems to me you have been called. To do what you're doing now."

The deacon set down her china teacup. "Well, I'm certainly not going to sit around moping about what can't be." Her voice was brisk. "And I believe it gives me a sensitivity toward—a reverence for the role of priest that will help me help you."

Several alarm bells went off in Clare's head. "Uh, just so you know, I'm not really comfortable with the whole reverence thing. Ordination didn't suddenly make me a better and nicer person."

Elizabeth smiled indulgently. "You remind me of some of the first-time parents I used to meet when I was teaching. They often felt insecure about using their natural authority with their kids. Accepting where you are in the hierarchy takes time and experience."

"I was in the army for ten years. Believe me when I say I don't have any problem with authority. I just don't want to be stereotyped into something I'm not."

"You don't feel you have any problems establishing your control over your parish?"

Control. Good God. "Leadership isn't a matter of control," Clare said. "Leadership is infusing the people around you with trust and confidence and expectations, so that when you move in one direction, they follow."

"What about the bishop?"

"What about him?"

"Do you have any problems with his authority over you?"

"I don't see how that—" Clare was saved from making a rude remark by Lois's appearance in her doorway.

"There's somebody here to see you."

"I'm in a meeting." Clare's voice was tight. "They'll have to wait. Or call for an appointment."

"No, you have to see her now."

Lois's tone caught Clare's attention. The secretary's face was drawn taut, her lips pressed bloodlessly together.

"Okay," Clare said. "Elizabeth, please excuse me." She stepped into the hall-way. "What is it?"

Lois gestured down the hall, to the door leading into the sanctuary. "Just . . . go." She retreated into Clare's office. Clare could hear her asking de Groot how the tea was.

Clare walked toward the church with a rapidly coalescing mass of dread fill-ing her stomach. It had to be bad news. But not a parishioner. She had had parishioners sicken, be injured, die. Lois would have told her the details. She wouldn't have been so shaken. It had to be something personal.

Oh, God, what if it was her father? He owned a small aviation business, he flew nearly every day—what if something had gone wrong?

No, that didn't make any sense. Her mother or one of her brothers would have called her directly. Who else did she know who might be—

Then she realized. There was someone else whose job exposed him to danger.

She pushed open the door to the sanctuary and spotted a figure standing in the dimness of the north aisle. "Is it Russ?" she said. "Has anything happened to Russ?"

Anne Vining-Ellis, Clare's closest friend among her congregation, turned. Her face, usually gleaming with a sly sense of humor, was grave. "No," she said. "It's his wife. Linda Van Alstyne was murdered yesterday."

EIGHT

It was more like a wake than a meeting. Six o'clock Tuesday morning. Mark's shift was officially over, and he had been awake since Monday morning, but he looked like an ad for Sealy Posturepedic next to the chief.

They sat in the bullpen, everyone who was working the investigation. Eric McCrea kept glancing between the chief and Lyle MacAuley, like he was watching to see which one would be the first to crack. MacAuley was at the whiteboard, writing down what little information they had. Noble Entwhistle sat in his usual spot, his notebook open on the desk in front of him. He looked the same as always, and different. Like someone had taken a drawing of him and rubbed out some of the edges with a gum eraser.

Kevin Flynn, who usually rattled all over the place talking and asking questions, sat silently. He was still in his civvies, although at some point he had put on his Day-Glo orange POLICE vest. Once in a while he looked as if he might say something, but he'd just drop his head and crack his knuckles instead.

And the chief . . . Mark wasn't a religious man, but when he saw the chief come though the doors in the predawn darkness, he thought, *God, don't ever let me come to that.*

". . . just bring us all up to date," MacAuley was saying. "Eric?"

McCrea stood. "The state CS techs didn't find anything that leaped out at them. There were some hairs and a variety of prints. We'll see when we get the report. The neighbor destroyed any tracks there might have been in the snow when she drove up to the door and then ran in and out."

"Friend," the chief growled. He was sitting in his usual place for a meeting, atop the sturdy oak table near the whiteboard, his feet resting on a chair.

"Uh . . . I'm sorry, Chief?"

"Meg Tracey isn't a neighbor. She lives on Dunedin Road. She's—she was Linda's best friend."

Lyle wrote her name and *BEST FRIEND* on the whiteboard. "What do we know about her?"

The chief blinked. "Know about her?"

"Chief, she found the body. We should at least eliminate her as a possible." Lyle's voice was gentle. "Eric, you took her statement. Anything?"

McCrea flipped open his notebook. "Her husband teaches at Skidmore. They've got one kid at Syracuse and two more at home. She doesn't work. She claimed she was at her house, alone, all afternoon until her daughter got home from the middle school. She dropped the kid off for a piano lesson and then went to the Van Alstynes'." He stumbled for a moment, breaking the smooth recital of facts. "She said she didn't see anyone except the cat."

"The cat? We don't have a cat."

"The Tracey woman said Mrs. Van Alstyne adopted it a week ago." He looked at MacAuley. "Uh, found the cat behind the barn. We took it to the county SPCA."

Mark looked toward the wall. He didn't want to watch the chief deal with the fact that he hadn't even known his wife got a cat.

Eric bent his head to his notes and went on. "She says she's very close to the victim and was worried because she hadn't heard anything from her since Saturday afternoon."

The silence in the squad room was absolute. Eric realized what he said. "Shit! I meant Mrs. Van Alstyne. I'm sorry, chief."

The chief shifted on his table. "Okay, guys." He sounded very, very tired. "This is a homicide investigation. We're not going to get anywhere if you have to apologize every time you say 'victim' or 'murder.' Let's stop worrying about my feelings and focus on breaking the case." He waved toward McCrea. "Go on, Eric."

"Um . . . that's about it. Mrs. Tracey didn't know of anyone who might have posed a threat to . . . the victim. She said the only person Mrs. Van Alstyne had been having trouble with lately—" McCrea broke off, swallowing.

"Was her husband," the chief finished.

McCrea nodded.

"Let's get that out in the open, then." The chief took off his glasses and pinched the bridge of his nose. "I think everybody here is aware I've been staying at my mom's house since the Friday before last. Lyle?" He pointed to the whiteboard, and Lyle wrote down *JAN 8.* "Except for one counseling session, I haven't seen Linda since then."

Mark wondered if he was aware he was speaking of his wife in the present.

"I don't know what rumors or stories have been making the rounds. The fact is, every marriage has its ups and downs. Linda and I started talking seriously about some issues in the middle of November. We decided we needed some perspective, so we started seeing a marriage counselor in December. Then Linda needed a break from having me around, so we agreed I'd move into my mom's temporarily. Any questions?"

Mark held his breath, waiting to see if anyone was foolhardy enough to ask the chief about the rumors of his affair.

"Okay," the chief said. "Lyle?"

MacAuley crossed his arms over his chest and stared into the middle distance. He wasn't going to hide behind his notes like McCrea, but he wasn't going to look at the chief, either. "Preliminary examination at the scene indicates the decedent was killed with a large knife. The ME won't be able to tell exactly what we're looking for until the autopsy, but it appeared to him that the fatal thrust was through the throat, which suggests the killer has at least some knowledge of professional knife-fighting techniques. There were no defensive wounds—suggesting the perp was someone either known to the decedent or someone unthreatening. There were—" Here he faltered and resorted to reading from his notebook. "Dr. Dvorak speculated that the significant postmortem wounds displayed the killer's rage."

Mark thought the chief might lose it. "What . . ." he said harshly, "what postmortem wounds?"

Eric McCrea had covered his face with one hand. He had been inside the house, Mark remembered. He had seen her. Of course, sooner or later they were all going to see her, in neatly labeled evidence photos. First the rest of the officers, then the men and women at the district attorney's office, and then, if they did their job right, a judge and a jury and a whole courtroom of spectators.

"Her face was slashed. Repeatedly." MacAuley's face puckered, as if he had something nasty in his mouth.

The chief's jaw was locked tight. He nodded once, a jerk of the head.

"I'd like to propose a working theory," Lyle said. Mark could feel the whole room's relief as the deputy chief changed the topic. "The chief hasn't checked the house yet, but it appears at this time that this wasn't a home invasion gone bad. Mrs. Van Alstyne had no obvious enemies. Chief, does anyone gain financially from her death?"

The chief's mouth worked for a moment. He shook his head. "There's her sister, Debbie. In Florida. My mom called to let her know last night. She has two grown sons. They get something. I think. We don't have a whole lot. It's mostly the house and the land, and that's in both our names."

"Insurance?"

"Just . . . just . . ." He seemed unable to find the words. His hands shaped a small rectangle.

"Burial expenses?" Kevin Flynn's voice was so tentative, for a second Mark wasn't sure he had really heard the younger man. The chief nodded.

"No financial gain," Lyle said, writing the words on the whiteboard. "But"— he wrote *RUSS VAN ALSTYNE* on the board—"the victim was married to a cop." Next to the chief's name he wrote *20+*. "A cop who's headed up our department for almost seven years. And who was an MP for twenty years before that."

"Twenty-two," the chief said automatically.

"Fact," MacAuley said. "The perp either knew Mrs. Van Alstyne would be home alone or didn't know the chief was away and expected to find him at home on Sunday."

Mark could see the others nodding in agreement.

"Fact. Of the two Van Alstynes, a lot more bad guys have a hate-on for the chief than for his wife."

"After thirty years of putting them away? Sure," McCrea said.

"Theory. Linda Van Alstyne wasn't the target of this murder. She was just the stand-in, either accidentally or incidentally, for her husband." MacAuley slashed two heavy black lines beneath the chief's name. "In other words, the intended victim isn't Linda. It's the chief."

NINE

Russ Van Alstyne loved his house. After a lifetime of living in base housing or rental apartments, he had embraced the pleasures and pains of home ownership like an ecstatic embracing a demanding god. He restored the kitchen woodwork to its origins in the Second World War. He converted the cavernous walk-in attic into an all-modern-conveniences workspace. He reinforced the sagging barn floor so it could be used as a garage. He repainted it, clapboard, trim, and shutters, one side every summer.

Now he sat in his truck, in his driveway, looking at his house. Afraid to get out. Afraid he might throw up the moment he crossed the threshold.

"A cleaning crew's already been in." Lyle sat in the driver's seat, waiting for him to get his act together. He had seen Russ in the station parking lot, fumbling with his keys, and roughly bumped him out of the way. "Shove it over," he had said. "You're not in any condition to drive." Now he continued, "After the CS techs finished last night. The kitchen was cleaned."

"That was fast." There was a service in Albany that provided crime scene and biohazard cleanup, but it usually took a couple of days for them to make it to a job.

"I called in a few chips."

"Oh."

There was a silence.

"Russ, you have to go in sooner or later. And if you want the investigation to go forward, it'd better be sooner."

"I know. It's just—"

"I know." Lyle nodded. "Look, how about we go in the front door?"

Except in the summertime, when they opened it to circulate air through the house, the formal front door was never used. In the winter, Russ didn't bother to shovel it out, and he and Lyle would have to wade through several weeks' worth of accumulated snow to reach it. But it was at the other end of the house from the kitchen. In fact, if he went in the front door, he might never have to set foot in the kitchen. He didn't worry about later. He was living minute by minute now.

"Okay. Let's."

Lyle grabbed one of the guys and asked him to unlatch the double doors from the inside. The snow was as bad as Russ had feared, but the challenge of breaking a trail through knee-deep crust and powder distracted him sufficiently so that it wasn't until he whacked his boot against the first granite step that he realized he was there.

He stomped up the steps—two, then a rectangular slab, then another two— shedding snow as he went. He pulled open the doors—tug, sweep, a kick of the boots against the jamb—and he was in.

Inside.

"You okay?" Lyle was crowding in behind him, forcing him to move forward in order to shut the doors behind them.

"Yeah." And, in some way, he was. The awful blankness of the kitchen awaited him, but in the tiny hallway, with the stairs he climbed to bed every night in front of him, he was okay. Not great, but he wasn't going to get sick all over the oriental carpet.

"What do you want to do first?"

He had decided on the way over that he would have to be methodical to get through this task. Take it one step at a time. "The workroom," he said. "End of the hall at the top of the stairs." Farthest from the kitchen. Although it was Linda's space, it was also the most impersonal as far as Russ was concerned. She designed and cut and sewed for her custom drapery business there; a workplace and nothing more. When he flicked on the lights he saw what he expected to see, the worktables clear, the racks and shelves of fabrics and hardware neat and organized.

Lyle hovered in the doorway while Russ walked around. "Everything look good?" he asked.

"I gotta be honest with you," Russ said. "Unless the place was tossed, I wouldn't be able to tell. Once I finished the renovation, I didn't come in here except to ask her if she was coming to bed." Regret squatted like a heavy toad on his breastbone. All the time and energy she had spent on her business, and the extent of his interest had been to find out when she was getting home from her fabric-buying jaunts. Why hadn't he put more effort into appreciating what she was doing? He turned toward Lyle. "Let's check the guest rooms," he said.

The two extra bedrooms were just as they always were, lavishly decorated and sterile. Once in a while they entertained couples from their army days, but most of the year they were alone. His closest relationships had always been among the people he worked with—relationships that closed Linda out without meaning to. Work had defined him and owned him. No wonder her friends were *hers,* and not *theirs.*

"Anything?" Lyle asked.

He shook his head. Stepped across the hall. Paused.

"This is your bedroom, right?"

He nodded.

"You ready to go in?"

"Hell, no." That earned him a half-smile from his deputy chief. Christ, Lyle was looking almost as cut up as Russ felt. He had always liked Linda, had been one of the few guys on the force she could talk and laugh with. Russ wasn't the only one who had suffered a loss. Not by a long shot.

Their bedroom was heartbreakingly normal. The bed neatly made. Several empty dry cleaner's bags tossed on Linda's side—she never used wire hangers. Her closet door open, a pair of high heels tumbled in front of the full-length mirror. He could see her, standing there, scrutinizing herself. Frowning, shaking her head, kicking them off. "Not these," she would have said.

"Russ?"

Lyle's voice shook him from his reverie. He forced himself to cross the plush carpeting to Linda's vanity, where she kept her jewelry in a drawer.

The first thing he noticed was her wedding ring, sitting next to her engagement diamond and the diamond and sapphire eternity band he had gotten her on their twentieth anniversary. When had she taken them off? She had been wearing them at the therapist's office.

The rest of the contents of the drawer were intact, a fact he could have told without further search. No one after easily shopped swag would have passed up those rings. He paused for a moment, trying to exorcise the ghost sitting at the vanity, examining her skin, dipping her fingers into the expensive little pots littering the mahogany surface. What else would thieves possibly take?

His gun safe was usually in his closet, but he had taken it to his mother's when he left. Linda's passport? No, it was still in her bedside drawer—always within reach for a quick getaway, she used to joke.

Lyle came out of the connecting bathroom. "It doesn't look like anything's been touched in here," he said. "Did she have any prescriptions that might have tempted somebody?"

"Not unless estrogen's suddenly become a black-market commodity."

Lyle's mouth quirked upward, and Russ found himself half-smiling, thinking of Linda cracking jokes about hot flashes, and in the next instant his eyes filled with a rush of tears and he had to turn away, fumbling for the doorknob. "Better get to the rest of the house," he said, when he could make his throat work again.

He knew before they went downstairs that nothing would be missing, and he was right. The stereo, the DVD player, the silver collection she had amassed over the years—all of it was there. He and Lyle were headed for the small office off the parlor, where Linda paid the bills and managed her paperwork, when Kevin Flynn poked his head in from the living room. "Chief?" he said tentatively. "I'm sorry to disturb you . . ."

"What is it, Kevin?"

"It's just—where did Mrs. Van Alstyne keep her purse?"

"Her purse?"

"I was going over the barn, and looking into her station wagon, and it made me think about my mom, who likes to keep her keys in the ignition in her car, so when I came back into the house I was sort of looking to see if you had some of those hooks for keys like folks sometimes have, you know, in the kitchen or the mudroom, except you don't, so then I got to thinking where do ladies keep their keys if they aren't in the car or on a hook and I figured their purses. Right?"

Russ didn't want to contemplate the amount of lung power it took for Flynn to get that sentence out. One of the advantages of being twenty-three. "Mrs. Van Alstyne hangs her purse on one of the coat hooks on the mudroom wall, Kevin. It probably has a coat tossed over it."

"No, sir, I thought of that. There aren't any purses on those hooks. I checked."

Russ was through the living room, across the kitchen, and in the mudroom before he remembered to be afraid of the room in which Linda had died. He tossed the barn coats and parkas and rain slickers on the floor, one after another, until they blocked the door to the summer kitchen and the old-fashioned iron hooks gleamed dully in the morning sun streaming through the diamond-shaped window in the mudroom door.

There was no purse.

He swung toward Lyle. "AllBanc," he said.

"I'm on it," Lyle said, fishing in his jacket for his cell phone.

Russ headed back through the kitchen, all his dread evaporated in the heat of a possible lead. "I'll get you the account numbers," he shouted over his shoulder.

"You think the perp might have taken her bag?"

Kevin's voice surprised him. He hadn't noticed the kid tagging along in his wake.

"Yeah," he said. He wanted to scream, *Why didn't you notice this last night, you idiots?!* but he knew recriminations wouldn't get him results. He opened the door leading from the kitchen into Linda's office. Two file towers flanked her desk, one for home and one for her business. He yanked open the top drawer of the home file. He might as well use this as a lesson for Flynn. "The perp leaves behind fenceables but takes the purse. What does that tell you?"

"He's an amateur," Kevin said promptly. "An opportunist. He doesn't know anyone he can palm stolen goods off on, but he can use debit and credit cards."

"Good." Russ opened a folder marked BANK STATEMENTS/CHECKS. It was empty. He bit back a curse. She was so organized, she had already moved last year's statements to the next drawer down. He slid it open. And there they were, along with folders marked VISA and MASTERCARD and oh, shit, he had to look in her business drawers, too, because she had a corporate American Express and MasterCard and checking account.

"Here, hold these," he said, thrusting the folders into Flynn's hands. He tore open the other drawers, rifling through tabs marked OROCO FABRICS and SOCIAL SECURITY and ACCOUNTS PAYABLE — SEAMSTRESSES until he found the financial materials, which he pulled without examining and laid in Kevin's arms. He was consumed with a sense of urgency. Linda's murderer had already had nearly twenty-four hours. What if he had already emptied their accounts and vanished?

"Take those to Lyle," he said.

Kevin sprinted out of the tiny office, leaving Russ alone with the paper trails of his life together with Linda: mortgage payments and electrical bills, credit card statements and snowplowing receipts. It struck him how oddly impersonal their house was without her actual presence, the office organized but not personalized, the rooms decorated but not inhabited. His mind flashed on the St. Alban's rectory on Elm Street—tabletops cluttered with photographs, books, and mementos spilling off the shelves to sit heaped by squishy armchairs. A note of longing hummed through him, the urge to go to that house and drop into one of those chairs and lay his sorrow before the woman who lived there . . .

He jerked upright. God, what sort of a monster was he? His wife was on the medical examiner's slab, and he was comparing her to another woman? He scrubbed at his face as if he could wash his guilt away, knocking his glasses askew. He steadied them, looking more intently at the files. He pulled open the desk drawers. There must be something personal here. Something connecting him to his wife and the two of them to the world at large.

Her computer. He pushed the on button, riffling through more files while it booted up. He never used the thing—he preferred taking phone calls at the station and being left alone at home—but Linda e-mailed friends, her sister, everybody.

The screen, which used to feature a slide show of fabric designs, now came up with a mostly naked guy who had more than the usual number of muscles. O-kay. Maybe that was part of the process her therapist wanted her to go through. Getting in touch with who she was in addition to being a wife. His mouth twitched upward. He'd wanted to find something personal. Well, here it was.

He sat in the rolling desk chair and clicked on the e-mail icon. A sign beneath the window informed him he was downloading mail, and a pulsing bar flashed on and off for almost a minute. When it finished, multiple windows popped up, one laid over the other. One said DEBBIE—her sister. One said SEAM-STRESSES, one IN, one MEG, one eSBW—he clicked on that; it seemed to be a mailing list for the Small Business Women's Association she belonged to.

Suddenly, he understood. Organized in cyberspace as well as in the real world, Linda had her e-mail filtering into multiple mailboxes. He clicked on DEBBIE. It looked as if she and Linda had been e-mailing several times a day since November. The most recent one—the one she would never read—was titled "You go, girl!"

There were a number of e-mails going back and forth that he guessed concerned him; they had subject lines like "That dickweed!!!" and "Men are bastards." He sagged against the back of the chair. What the hell did he think he was going to find in here? He had told his wife of twenty-five years that he was in love with another woman. What did he think she would be saying to her sister and girlfriends? What a swell guy he was?

With a masochistic sense of deserving whatever abuse he got, he clicked on the last e-mail from Linda to her sister. The subject, which appeared on a whole slew of e-mails, read "Mr. Sandman."

> D-
> I'm going to do it. 1. Don't care 2. Don't care 3. Don't care. Give me
> a call!
> Love, L

A few messages down, there was one from her sister to her.

> Hi, Lin,
> You need to ask yourself this: 1. Am I doing this just to get back at Russ? 2.
> Am I ready to be considered a bitch when I slap down Mr. S's pass? (yes, he
> will, and yes, you will) 3. Is having some man validate my attractiveness really
> going to help me figure out what I want?
> You've been down this road before, cupcake. Be careful!!
> Love, Deb

Who the hell was Mr. S, and what was he doing making passes at Russ's wife? He found the next previous e-mail from Linda.

D-

Mr. S knows all about what's going on with me and R. (In fact, he knows and respects R, which helps.) He's not going to cross any lines. Meg says I should go for it—escaping from my problems with the help of a handsome man ;) should be good for what ails me.

Love, L

Russ sat back in the chair. Someone who knew him. Who knew and respected him. He double-checked the date of the correspondence. The e-mails had all been written during the middle of last week.

Hi, Lin,

I think it's too soon to be dating, if that's what you mean. Yesterday you were bawling about what you need to do to get your idiot husband's attention back. Mr. S is looking for love in all the wrong places and he's pegged you as ND and D (Newly Divorced and Desperate). Except you aren't divorced and don't think you want to be. I know you want to give Russ a kick in the teeth but this isn't the way to do it.

Love, Deb

The part of him that was a husband was trying to fit the words "Linda" and "date" together. Even tossing aside their therapist-mandated separation agreement—how the hell could she be thinking about dating? The last time either of them had been out on a date, the Village People had been at the top of the charts and Tug McGraw was telling the Mets "You gotta believe."

D-

Remember the guy I told you about? He's making me an offer. The kind that's too good to be true. What do you think?

Love, L

The part of him that was a cop was envisioning a scenario that blew MacAuley's the-chief-was-the-target theory out of the water. "Hey, Lyle," he yelled. He heard a thwap of files hitting the kitchen table, and then Lyle strolled through the door.

"AllBanc says no activity on the checking account or the credit cards."

Russ waved the information away. "Take a look at these e-mails." He stood, gesturing for Lyle to take his place. "Linda and her sister, writing to each other."

Lyle brought out his reading glasses and leaned toward the monitor.

"Try this on. There's an evening or an afternoon out. This guy brings Linda home. Maybe he was tight, or stoned, or maybe he was just the type who liked hurting women."

Lyle, engrossed in the screen, made a *go ahead* noise.

"He pushed himself onto her. Linda said no. Probably—and I can just imagine her doing this—she handed him his head on a platter. And then the bastard pulled out his knife and—"

Where did he get a knife? If they had been on a date? Not that it was a date, of course. Just that the guy, Mr. S, had thought so. But Russ knew Linda, and she wouldn't have stepped out the door with Mel Gibson himself if he wasn't dressed right.

"We don't have the knife, do we?" he asked Lyle, who had finished with the e-mails Russ had highlighted and was scrolling down the other entries in the mailbox.

Lyle shook his head.

Oh, Christ, Russ thought. *Oh, Christ, let it not be—* "Kevin," he yelled.

The kid appeared in the doorway too fast not to have been listening to every word.

"I've got a gun locker in the barn. It's where I keep my hunting stuff, in the old tack room—"

Flynn nodded, his red soul patch bobbing up and down hypnotically. "I looked at it, Chief. There are two rifles and a shotgun. All locked down. I thought that was the right count."

"It is. What about my knife?"

"Your knife?"

"It's an old military issue K-Bar." Russ gestured, approximating the size. "I use it for field dressing. It should be wrapped in a flannel cloth, lying on the little shelf next to where I keep my recycled shell casings."

Kevin paused. Russ was so used to the young man blurting out whatever was on his mind that it took him a moment to realize Kevin was weighing his words.

"I saw the shell bucket," he said carefully. "You can go take a look yourself, but Chief, there's no knife there."

TEN

Mark hung up the phone and rubbed his eyes. They felt dry, gritty, despite the four hours of sleep he had grabbed at home. Before leaving for her shift at the hospital, Rachel had pointed out very clearly that if he was in the state police, he wouldn't have to work twenty hours out of twenty-four.

Harlene poked her head into the squad room. "Anything?"

He grunted. "Plenty." He tapped his pen against the pad he had been filling up with names, dates, and addresses. "The trick is going to be following up. Most of these guys were released from Fort Leavenworth. Where they've wound up is anyone's guess."

The chief, before leaving for the crime scene this morning, had tried to come up with a few likely names. Guys he had put away over the years who might come gunning for him. He had failed miserably. Of course, the shape he was in, it was a miracle he could remember his own name, let alone some long-gone bad guy. Harlene had come to the rescue, dragging out an ancient paper copy of the chief's service record, listing posting after posting after posting. A bunch of commendations and medals, too, which the chief had never mentioned. Typical.

Now Mark was on the trail, convincing records clerks to track down old cases, making notes of their dispositions. "Y'know, Eric McCrea really ought to be doing this," he told Harlene. "He's in the National Guard. He knows how to talk to these people."

Harlene snorted. "Yeah, like you're some sort of long-haired hippie who can't relate. You're more spit-'n'-polished than anyone in this force, Eric McCrea included."

Mark ran his hand over his high-and-tight self-consciously. "Ya think?" He took pride in his appearance. In the discipline of small things.

Harlene nudged him. "Don't worry on it. You're doing good." She tapped the bone-dry mug sitting next to his pad of paper. "I don't usually offer, but you look like you could use some coffee."

"Thanks, yeah."

There was a small noise in the doorway. Mark and Harlene both turned. "Is . . . do you know where Chief Van Alstyne is?"

Over the past two years, Mark had seen Reverend Clare Fergusson a lot of times, and in a lot of situations you wouldn't expect to find a priest. He'd seen her late nights at the hospital, soaking wet from the river, splattered with mud and blood and grimy with smoke. But he'd never seen her looking . . . lost. Her dark blond hair was drawn back in a raggedy twist and her skin was taut over her bones, giving her a more pointed expression than usual.

Harlene, who had—as the chief liked to say—a heart as big as her mouth, crossed the room, opened her arms, and enfolded the taller woman, parka and all. "You heard, did you?"

The reverend nodded. "I just got back from a week's retreat this morning. I was in a meeting when my friend Dr. Anne told me."

Harlene stepped back but still kept her hands tight over Clare's arms. "I expect it's all over the Washington County and Glens Falls hospitals by now. If doctors and nurses could work as fast as they can gossip, there wouldn't be anybody left sick in this world."

"What . . . what happened?"

Harlene sucked in a breath to tell the priest everything when Mark interrupted. "She was killed sometime this weekend. Maybe Monday. That's all we really know right now."

The reverend's eyes were huge in her narrow face. "It couldn't have been an accident?"

Mark shook his head. She looked down at the floor. "I didn't think so," she said. "I just hoped . . ." She raised her head, focusing on Harlene. "I don't even know if it's a good idea for me to contact Russ or not. But I had to do something. How is he?"

Mark leaped in before Harlene could speak again. "I guess you'd have to compare him to how he was. When did you see him last?"

"Um." She hesitated. "This is Tuesday. About two weeks ago, then."

Harlene was looking at Mark curiously. He ignored her. "Didn't you two usually have lunch together Wednesdays? At the Kreemy Kakes Diner?"

"Not since . . ." She blinked at Harlene, then at him. Her cheeks were warming to a bright rose color. "I'm not sure if you know, but he was having some . . . difficulties at home . . ."

"His wife kicked him out, and he went to stay with Margy Van Alstyne. Ayeah. We know all about it," Harlene said.

"Oh. Well, we haven't—the last time I had lunch with him was right before that."

"And of course, you were away for this retreat all last week," Mark said. "Where was that? Does St. Alban's have some sort of place where you guys can escape to?"

Her greenish-brown eyes sharpened. "Officer Durkee, if you want to know something, I'd appreciate it if you didn't hide behind the veneer of conversation."

He held up his hands. "Not meaning any disrespect, Reverend. But you are friends with the chief. And you knew Mrs. Van Alstyne."

"We had met. I wouldn't say that I knew her."

He chose his next words carefully. "Ma'am, one of the theories we're working off of is that whoever killed Mrs. Van Alstyne was trying to hurt the chief. Either they were going after him and didn't find him there, or they went after Mrs. Van Alstyne deliberately, to, you know, punish the chief. So I'd like to know where you were and if you noticed anything odd while you were there."

She paled, throwing her high cheekbones and sharp nose into stark relief. "I stayed at a cabin up by Abenaki Lake. It's owned by one of my parishioners, Leland Fitzgerald. It's remote—three roads off of Route 77. I certainly didn't see anything unusual while I was there."

"No visitors?"

She looked at him, her eyes clear and steady. "Deacon Willard Aberforth came up to see me the day before I left. To let me know the diocese was assigning St. Alban's a new deacon to help out."

He wasn't going to get anything else out of her. Her back was up. "Thanks, Reverend," he said. "Every piece of information, even if it's in the negative, helps us get a little bit closer."

She twitched in acknowledgment. "Harlene," she said, "do you think I could leave a note for . . . for the chief?"

Harlene nodded. "Of course. You come right into his office." Mark could hear the dispatcher as she led Reverend Fergusson across the way. "And you know who could probably use a visit? The chief's mother . . ." Her voice faded to a muffled sound behind the office door.

In a moment she was back, hands on her formidable hips, springy gray curls quivering with indignation. "What was the meaning of *that*?" she hissed at him.

"What?"

"Sssh. Keep your voice down. You know what. Cross-examining Reverend Clare like that."

He shrugged. "Just keeping track of the players, that's all."

"In a pig's eye. I've been working dispatch since your mama had you in Pampers. Don't think I don't know when someone's being considered a suspect."

"Harlene." He leaned forward, dropping his voice. "Think about it. She's the reason the chief and his wife separated."

"What are you, their marriage counselor? You don't know that."

"They've got something going on. Half the town knows it. She's an army vet, she's got training in survival skills, hell, she probably knows how to kill somebody with a rock and a pointed stick."

Harlene frowned furiously at him but let him continue.

"Now she's out of town, all alone, no alibi for a week. During which time Mrs. Van Alstyne, her rival"—he held up one hand to forestall Harlene's explosion—"is knifed to death. And right afterward, she conveniently returns home to find out what's happened."

Harlene's eyes bulged. "She's a priest, for God's sake!"

"Oh, that's right," he said. "I forgot. Priests never do anything wrong. Hello? Catholic choirboys?"

"You can't seriously think she did it."

He shrugged. "She's always seemed nice enough, sure. But hell, Harlene, even nice people can do some pretty bad things when push comes to shove. I'll tell you this"—he nodded toward where the squad room door stood ajar—"I don't think she's telling us the truth, the whole truth, and nothing but the truth."

ELEVEN

"You shouldn't be doing this." Lyle glanced away from the road for a second. "You're not in any condition to ask coherent questions."

Sunk in the passenger seat, Russ didn't respond.

"I mean it, man. You need to be at home, working this through. Getting support from your family."

The Dixie Chicks were in the CD player, clean bright music from a whole different planet than the one he was living on.

"Let me run you on over to your mom's house. Isn't your sister-in-law getting here soon?"

"Goddammit, I don't need to run back to my mother! I need to find out who the hell Linda was making a date with. I'll tell you how I'm going to 'work this through.' By finding her killer and putting him in the fucking ground."

Lyle looked at him sidelong again. "Make sure you mention that to Meg Tracey. I'm sure that will put her at ease and help us get a whole load of information out of her."

"I'm not an idiot. I'm not going to scare her."

"Chief, you're scaring *me*."

Russ closed his eyes and leaned against the headrest. He wasn't going to get into it with his second-in-command. This wasn't some *Star Trek* episode where Lyle got to throw him in the brig because he was acting crazy. The Chicks were singing *If I fall, you're going down with me*, a song that irresistibly reminded him of Clare, and his throat closed up again with self-loathing; his wife was dead and he still thought of, grieved for, wanted another woman. His weakness hardened his resolve. If he couldn't give Linda the undivided mourning she deserved, he could do the next best thing. He could lay her murderer out at her feet.

"This it?"

Russ opened his eyes. Lyle had pulled the pickup over to the side of the road. He gestured toward the house across the way.

"Yeah," Russ said. "This is it."

The Traceys' house was maybe a hundred years old, originally built for a grown son or daughter from the larger farmhouse next door. The farmlands had been sold off in sections years ago, and the road was strung with suburban-style tract homes, double-wides, and do-it-yourself log cabins—whatever the individual lot buyers had been able to afford.

Russ and Lyle mounted the porch steps and rang the bell. A terrific barking ensued. After a moment, the curtain at the window twitched. The door cracked open. Meg Tracey, eyes red-rimmed, thin body wrapped in an oversized sweater-jacket, blocked the narrow entrance. She stared at Russ. "What are you doing here?"

Lyle reached into his coat pocket and produced his badge. "We're here on official business, Mrs. Tracey. Can we come in?" He had to pitch his voice over the dogs barking.

She noticed the badge, but her gaze went immediately back to Russ. She looked, he realized, afraid. Of him. Suddenly, Lyle's offer to take him home took on a whole different cast. MacAuley hadn't just been trying to protect Russ's feelings. He had realized, where Russ had not, that there were going to be people they spoke to in the course of the investigation who believed Russ was responsible.

For Linda's murder.

"I already gave a statement last night. To Officer McCrea."

"I know." Lyle's voice was warm and grateful. "Thank you. But you didn't just find Mrs. Van Alstyne's body. You were her best friend. We're hoping that, as her friend, you'll be able to fill in some of the missing pieces. To give us a clearer picture of her last few days."

Her eyes flickered warily, but she stood back from the door. Immediately, two knee-high white Eskies exploded onto the porch, their thick fur giving them the appearance of hairy, short-legged marshmallows. They danced around Russ and Lyle, barking furiously. "Don't mind them," Meg said over the racket. "Snowball! Fluff! Down!" The dogs ignored her, bumping and winding through Russ's and Lyle's legs as they crossed the threshold into a well-used family room.

"Treat! Treat!" Meg said, patting her thigh, and the dogs bounded after her, around the corner into the kitchen. There was the rattle of something hard hitting the dog bowl, and then Meg returned, closing the door behind her. "Okay, that'll keep them happy." She gestured toward the sectional sofa. "Please."

Russ sat down. It was more comfortable than it looked. The sofa and the matching armchairs were upholstered in denim, which went well with the rest of the room's décor—early American teenager.

Meg must have been reading his mind, because she said, "This is the kids' room." She rapped on the blocky coffee table. "Everything's meant to be indestructible."

"Except that." Lyle nodded toward the wall, where a plasma-screen TV hung in all its pricy glory.

"I want my house to be the place where all the kids hang out," she said. "If they're in here, scarfing down pizza and watching satellite TV, I know they're safe." She paused, and Russ could see the exact moment she remembered why they were there. How safe could she claim her kids were when Linda had been murdered in her own kitchen? "Do you . . . do you have any idea who might have . . ."

Lyle shook his head. "Not yet. We have some theories, and that's why we needed to talk with you." He leaned forward. "Did Mrs. Van Alstyne talk to you about a possible, uh, rendezvous this weekend?"

Russ watched the blush turn her face red. Meg folded her hands over her cheeks and closed her eyes. When she opened them, she was looking, again, at Russ. "Yes," she said, her voice barely audible.

"Pardon?"

"Yes." She was louder this time. "Not in so many words, you understand. Just that there was something special going on and a man was involved. I told her to go for it." She switched her attention from Russ to Lyle, sitting up straighter. "I told her what's good for the gander is good for the goose."

What Russ wanted to do was stand up and snarl, *You idiot, know-nothing busybody!* What he did instead was look out the window, as if the station wagon and pickup alongside the house were the most fascinating things he had ever seen.

"Who was Mrs. Van Alstyne thinking about seeing?"

"I don't know his name. She was very discreet. She wasn't the sort to flaunt it all over town."

The pickup was rigged for plowing. One of the Tracey boys liked working outdoors—plowed in the winter and did landscaping in the summer. He and Linda had hired him a few times, but damned if Russ could remember the kid's name.

"Do you know anything about him? Do you have any idea how she met this man?" Lyle's voice was smooth as maple syrup. He was good at this.

"Through her work, I think."

"Was he a customer?"

"I don't know. He could have been. Or maybe someone she met on one of her fabric-buying trips. She didn't share what she thought were the unimportant details with me. To Linda, what mattered, what she wanted to talk about, was the way he made her feel. Valued. Appreciated. Wanted."

The kid's name. The kid's name. Maybe he should ask Meg. Maybe he should remind her that he wasn't a scum-sucking bottom dweller when he hired her kid. Maybe he should—

"Did Mrs. Van Alstyne agree to go on a date with this man?"

"I don't know what she decided! She asked me my opinion and I gave it to her. For chrissake, what does this have to do with finding who killed her?"

Eyeballing trucks and contemplating kids' names wasn't going to do it for Russ anymore. "I'm not being some sort of jealous asshole, Meg." He was too loud. She flinched. "This guy who was promising her 'something special' may have been the one who killed her. That's why we want to find him."

Meg stood abruptly and walked to one of the windows. She yanked it open, pushed the storm window up a few inches, and dug a package of cigarettes out of her sweater pocket. She patted the other pocket. "Crap. Forgot my matches." She looked at the cellophane-wrapped box. "I've been trying to quit."

Russ heaved himself off of the sofa and pulled his Zippo out of his jeans. He tossed it to her. "Here."

"Thanks." Her hand shook as she lit the cigarette.

"I'm not the enemy here, Meg." He dropped his voice. "I loved Linda. I may have done a half-assed job of it, but I loved her."

She nodded. "She knew him before you two started having troubles. She told me that. I honestly don't think she was all that interested in him as a man. He was more—when she talked about him, it was always with a reference to you. Comparing him to you, or how it would piss you off, or how you wouldn't believe someone else would find her attractive."

He shut his eyes. Linda had always been the most physically perfect woman he knew. Every man found her attractive. They would go out to dinner and bus-boys would trip over themselves passing their table. How could she not have known?

"She never told me his name or anything. However, I got the impression from some of the things she said"—she took a long drag on her cigarette—"that she had something going with him years ago."

What? Russ squinted at her, as if he could make what she said come into focus. *What?*

"What do you mean, Mrs. Tracey?"

She had almost finished off the first cigarette. She flicked it through the window into a snowbank and tapped out another. "I mean I think she had a relationship with this guy several years ago. Not long after she moved to Millers Kill. She . . ." Meg lit her second cigarette with a much steadier hand. "She never came right out and said it was the same guy. But I—" She looked at Russ, finally meeting his eyes through a veil of smoke. "Oh, God, I'm sorry, Russ. I may be wrong about this. I may have been misreading what she said entirely."

"You think . . . she implied she had had an affair?" He sounded as if he were the one who had been smoking. "Linda?"

Meg and Lyle both looked away.

"I gotta—" He could not have said what he had to do. His feet moved, and he was walking, and the next thing he knew he was standing outside, leaning against the bed of his Dodge Ram pickup, losing his breakfast.

He was scrubbing his mouth out with snow when Lyle caught up with him. "Chief?" He glanced down. "Oh, Christ almighty."

Russ spat out some icy water and scooped up another handful. He stuffed his glasses in his coat pocket and washed his face with snow.

"This is all news to you." Lyle pitched his sentence halfway between a question and a declaration.

Russ kicked snow over the mess he had made. "Yeah." He replaced his glasses. The stinging cold over his skin felt good. He wanted to scour the inside of his head the same way, turn it cold and clean.

Lyle held out the Zippo. "I got your lighter back."

Russ cradled it in one wet hand. "It was my dad's." He flipped it over. Ran his thumb across his father's initials. "Y'know, I always thought he and my mom had a perfect marriage. It wasn't until he was gone that I realized how much his drinking hurt her."

Lyle's wary look almost made him smile. "Don't worry, I'm not about to start hitting the bottle again." The doctors who said alcoholism was partly genetic got his vote. Like his father before him, he had been a drunk. The difference was, he had managed to stop before it killed him. Thanks, in large part, to Linda.

"Good." Lyle opened the passenger door for him. "I've never seen you boozing, and I for sure don't want to start now."

Russ climbed in obediently and let his deputy shut the door behind him. God, he felt wiped out. And it wasn't even noon yet.

Lyle took the driver's seat and started the truck. "I'm not going to say I told you so. You know that. But goddammit, Russ, if this doesn't show you why you ought to sit this one out, I don't know what will."

"You're right."

Lyle stared.

"Didn't expect me to agree with you, did you?"

"No, frankly."

"I'm not taking myself off the case. But you were right. I was nothing but a liability in there. I think maybe I need to leave the boots-on-the-ground work to you and stick to analyzing what you and the other guys bring in." He pressed his lips together. The next thing he had to say was hard. "If we can, I'd like to limit the number of guys we have directly investigating this lead. If it turns out there's something to all this . . . stuff that Meg Tracey says. I just—I don't want to—"

"I understand."

Russ relaxed against the seat. "Thanks." He stared out the window. House, house, farm, house. Featureless fields, corn stubble and hay roots buried beneath December's snows. "Where are we headed?"

"Back to the station. Look, as long as I've got you in a temporarily agreeable state, how 'bout you take my advice and go home for a while? You've had a hell of a morning."

Funny how his mother's place had become "home." He wondered if he would ever be able to live in his own house again. "The autopsy report's coming in," he said.

"Dr. Dvorak won't have anything until this afternoon at the earliest. You want to see it, right?"

There was nothing he had ever wanted to see less. "Yeah."

"Then give yourself a break. Rest up, eat a meal, let your mom take care of you. You don't want to be losing your cookies in front of the ME 'cause you're overstressed."

Russ grunted. It was as close as he could get to acknowledging Lyle was right.

"If I drop myself at the station, will you be able to drive home?" Lyle asked.

"Yes." Jesus, he needed to get a grip, before his men slung him in a wheelchair and started spoon-feeding him farina.

"Okay, then."

The way from the Traceys' brought them into town on Route 117, up the hill along the river, curving by the gazebo to where Elm and 117 converged onto Church Street.

Through the snowy silver maple trees, he could see the gray stone stronghold of St. Alban's. She was in there, behind one of the diamond-paned windows, a block away and as far out of reach as the moon.

On his CD player, Natalie Maines of the Dixie Chicks was crooning, *Without you, I'm not okay, and without you, I've lost my way . . .*

If he lived through this mess, he was never listening to country music again.

TWELVE

Clare Fergusson looked at the glossy pine-green door and wondered why it was that a closed door was the most frightening thing in the world. In her day, she had hauled soldiers into the open bay of her helicopter with enemy fire splattering the sands around them. She had been held at gunpoint by an angry, terrified woman. She had crawled through snake-infested swamps to prove to her survival instructor that she was as tough as any man in his course.

Those things had never scared her like a closed door. The door to her sister Grace's hospital room, the first time she had to enter, knowing there was no hope. The door to her colonel's office, the day she told him she was resigning her commission to enter the seminary. The door between the sacristy and the nave, stepping through to celebrate her first Eucharist as St. Alban's rector.

The door to Margy Van Alstyne's house.

Okay. She would give Margy her condolences and see if there was anything she could do. That was, if Margy didn't slam the door in her face. She took a deep breath. The cold air burned her lungs, and she coughed.

The door opened. "You gonna come in, or are you gonna stand out there until your feet freeze?"

Well, when you put it like that . . . Clare stomped up the low granite steps and kicked her boots against the doorjamb. Margy held the door wide to allow her to pass. The small kitchen was steamy, and Clare could hear the sloshing of the washing machine in the corner.

"Take off your coat before you parboil," Margy said. Clare shucked her parka and barely had time to drape it over one of the ladder-back chairs before she was caught in a fierce hug. "I'm glad you're here, and that's a fact," Margy said. "Want some coffee? It's shade-grown, fair-trade."

Clare almost laughed at the normalcy of it all. "That sounds good," she said.

"Help yourself to some of the coffee cake." Margy waved at the table, where cellophane- and tinfoil-wrapped platters crowded against stacks of antiwar tracts. "The food started arriving this morning and hasn't let up yet."

Clare's grandmother Fergusson reared up out of her head. *I can't believe you made a condolence call without so much as a store-bought pie!* "Uh," she said, "I should've—"

Margy finished scooping coffee into the machine and shook her head as she poured the water in. "Don't worry. If I get any more casseroles, I'll have to store 'em outside in a snowbank."

She took two mugs out of the dish drainer and gestured for Clare to take a seat. "I didn't know if I'd get to see you," she said, at the same moment Clare blurted, "I didn't know if you'd want to see me."

They smiled uncertainly at each other.

"I'm sorry, Margy. I'm so very sorry."

The older woman laid a cracked and mended sugar bowl on the table. Inside were brown crystals the size of fine gravel. "You may need to get a bit more specific with that."

"I'm sorry about Linda's death. I'm sorry I . . . came between her and your son. I'm sorry—" Clare's voice broke, and she tried to stop the tears rushing into her eyes. "I'm sorry I made her last days unhappy." She covered her mouth, but she couldn't silence her crying. Margy rested her hands on Clare's shoulders and rubbed her back. "I'm sorry . . ." Clare hiccupped. "I came here to comfort you. Not to . . ." A noisy sob cut her off.

"Seems like you're sorry for an awful lot."

Clare, wet-faced and choking, nodded.

"You let it all out." Margy continued to rub her back. "Best thing for a body, to cry it all out."

So Clare blubbered and wept at Margy Van Alstyne's kitchen table until her sobs settled to shuddering breaths and her tears dried up.

Margy tipped her chin up. "That's better, in't it?"

"I deed to blow my dose," Clare said.

Margy went to a basket next to the dryer and plucked a handkerchief from the mound of clean laundry. "You're in luck," she said, handing it to Clare. Clare blew lustily while Margy ran one of her dishcloths under the faucet. Then she mopped Clare's face with cold water.

"I feel like a seven-year-old."

"Everybody needs a little mothering now and again." Margy poured two mugs of coffee and sat down kitty-corner from Clare. "I suppose you'd like to know how Russell is doing."

Clare nodded. "Yes, ma'am."

"He's taking it hard, like you'd think. Of course, in his case, he's trying to keep it all bottled up. I wish he'd sit down and have a good cry like you just did." She spooned sugar into her coffee. "He's at work now. Can you believe it? He thinks finding whoever's responsible is going to make him feel better. My poor boy."

"Is there anything I can do?"

Margy looked at her shrewdly. "I dunno. Is there?"

Clare examined the surface of her coffee. "I mean, any way I can help you out."

"I guess I've got things well enough in hand. We can't make any arrangements until her sister gets here—poor woman, if she didn't take it some hard when I broke the news. She and Linda's all that's left of their family."

"Who are you going to have do the service?"

"Well, Linda was a Catholic when she was young, but she never attended any church as long as I knew her. I figured I'd ask Dr. Tobin. He's my pastor over to Center Street Methodist in Fort Henry. Of course"—and she suddenly sounded every one of her seventy-five years—"everything's on hold until the medical examiner finishes up whatever he has to do. I told that to her sister, but she would fly up here. Janet's husband's gone to Albany to pick her up."

Clare smiled a little. "Sounds like you have things well in hand." She examined the kitchen. Hand-hooked hot pads shared space with flyers exhorting citizens to STOP THE DREDGING. On the round-shouldered refrigerator, magnets held up grandchildren's drawings and clippings about acid rain. It was nothing like her grandmother Fergusson's kitchen in North Carolina, but it had the same feeling. Like you had rounded all the bases and come home safe.

"I should go," she said, making no effort to rise.

Margy dropped her hand over Clare's. Her knuckles were swollen. Arthritic. Clare had never noticed before. "There is something I need to talk to someone about."

Clare looked at her.

"You prob'ly know Russell moved in with me about ten days ago. He seemed to be doing okay. He went to this marriage-counseling thing they were doing and came back and was on a pretty even keel."

Clare nodded.

"But then Sunday, he took off. Didn't say where he was going. Didn't say he wa'nt spending the night here, but I didn't see him again till Monday noontime. He was . . . it put me in mind of when he came home from Vietnam. Like his body was here, but all the rest of him was gone. And wherever he was gone to was no good place. He just went upstairs and took a nap, right in the middle of the afternoon. That's not like him."

Margy pressed her lips together tightly. "The thing is, this was before we all heard about Linda. I'm . . . it seems a terrible thing to say, but I'm so worried about him. I'm worried that something might have—"

Clare opened her mouth to cut off whatever Margy was going to say, to stop her before she said something neither of them wanted to hear, but she didn't get the chance. The kitchen door swung in, and with a snow-shedding stomp, Russ was inside.

Margy's hand clutched hers. "Sweetie," she said.

Russ froze, the door still open, his tartan scarf half unwound from his neck.

"Reverend Clare called on me to offer her condolences."

Russ's glasses steamed opaque in the moist, warm air. He took them off and tucked them into his shirt pocket. Nothing else moved.

Margy sighed. "Shut the door, Russell."

"Yes, ma'am," he said. His mother's command seemed to break the spell, and he turned away from them, closing the door and shrugging out of his parka, which he hung from a hook on the back of the door.

He tossed his scarf on top of the washing machine and bent to take off his boots. When he stood, he stared straight at Clare, and she felt his regard as an actual pain down her breastbone. With his sandy brown hair and the sun and smile lines around his eyes, he had always reminded her of summer, but his face now was winter-ravaged, his eyes revealing an inner cold so deep and ab-solute that he might shatter at a touch.

Margy stood. "I need to take these clean clothes upstairs," she said, directing her remark toward an invisible person halfway between Russ and Clare. She lifted the plastic laundry basket and whisked out of the room, abandoning both of them without a backward glance.

Clare wanted to flee, through the door, into her car, down into town. She wanted to wrap Russ in her arms and make his naked hurt go away. The first impulse was unworthy. As for the second—she didn't have the right or the power to ease his pain.

Instead, she stood. Slowly. "I am sorry, more sorry than I can say, for your loss." She bit her lower lip and thanked God she had spilled her tears with Margy instead of right now. "I know you . . . you loved her very much."

"I killed her." His voice low.

"What?" For a moment, a second only, she flashed on what his mother had been saying. *It seems a terrible thing to say, but I'm so worried about him.* He couldn't have . . . he didn't . . .

Too late, she realized he was reading her thoughts off her face. He had always been scary-good at that. Or she had always given away too much around him.

"Jesus, not like that." He sounded disgusted. At himself? At her? "How could you think—"

"No," she started, but he cut her off.

"I meant I killed her when I told her about us. When I couldn't cut you out of my life and focus on my marriage. I killed her when she told me we had to separate and I didn't fight tooth and nail to stay together. I was supposed to take care of her. I was supposed to be there for her. And I wasn't."

"You can't blame yourself." It was an inane thing to say, and she knew it.

He gave her a scathing glance. Their relationship—whatever it was, or had been—didn't allow for comforting tripe.

"All right," she said, "tell yourself you would have been at home twenty-four hours a day. That you would have stayed by her side no matter what. That nothing bad would ever happen to her because you, Russ Van Alstyne, have the power to stop all evil things." She ventured a half step toward him. "Does that sound like how Linda wanted to live her life? From everything you've ever told me about her, she was a woman who loved traveling and her business and having fun. You couldn't have wrapped her in a cocoon even if you wanted to."

His face contorted. "You don't understand. I made promises to her, and I broke them. She was angry and unhappy and confused these past eight weeks, and now it turns out that's all the time she had." His voice cracked. He turned his head away.

She winced. This was too close to her own gnawing guilt. But this wasn't about her. It was about him. "Do you remember what you said to me? The night you decided you were going to tell her about . . . us? You said the two of you had walked so far away from each other you couldn't find one another with a map. And that coming clean would be a start. To walking toward each other for a change."

"And wasn't that a high-minded load of crap? Yeah, yeah, I wanted to come clean. But you know who it was mostly for? Me. So I wouldn't have to live with the guilt." He stepped closer to her. "Sure, I wanted to patch up my marriage. But you know, underneath, there was this tiny little idea that maybe I could get permission. That she might say, 'Okay, honey, whatever makes you happy.' That somehow, some way, I could have both of you."

She blanched.

"Yeah, it's not so pretty when I put it like that, is it?" He stepped closer, crowding her against the table, looming over her in a way designed to make her feel trapped and threatened. "I wanted both of you, wanted to keep my happy wife and happy home, and I wanted you, not just meeting you for lunch at the goddamn diner, I wanted you, Clare, in my bed, underneath me. I wanted everything." His voice fell to a hoarse whisper. "And now I have nothing."

The anger and grief and self-loathing rolled off him in waves. She knew he was trying to punish her, trying to make her hate him as much as he hated himself at this moment.

"No," she said, her voice shaking.

"No?" he said. "No?" He smacked himself on the forehead. "Of course, everything's changed now, hasn't it? What was I thinking? I can have you now, right? Now there's no inconvenient marriage in the way." His hand closed over her wrist in a brutally tight grasp. "C'mon, the bedroom's this way." He yanked her arm, dragging her toward the archway. She stumbled.

"Stop it!" she shrieked. She twisted out of his grasp. "What do you want from me?" She whacked him as hard as she could on his chest. "What do you want from me?" She hit him again, and again, until he batted her fists away and wrapped his arms around her, pinning her tight against him.

"God damn you," she said, and burst into tears.

"Aw, Clare," he said, his voice unrecognizable in her ear. "Clare, no. Jesus, I'm sorry. I'm so sorry."

She was shaking, and he was shaking, and over her own gasps and tears she heard a terrible wrenching noise come out of Russ's chest. His first sob was like the ricochet report of ice cracking in the spring, and then they were both crumbling, sinking to the floor, knees tangling, ribs heaving, faces wet.

She clawed her hands free and dug them into his back, hanging on as his body spasmed with grief and his pain tore free in wracking, sloppy sobs. The sounds choking from the back of his throat were so deafening that at first she thought she imagined the ringing sound. But it went on and on, clearly audible during the lulls when he gulped air and rocked against her. She blinked away the water in her own eyes in time to see Margy Van Alstyne snatch the phone and retreat with it into the living room.

A little while later, Margy returned. She hung up the phone and came toward them, kneeling beside her son, one arm around Clare and the other stroking the hair away from his forehead. Clare could feel him shake and relax, shake and relax, and she realized he was trying to calm himself down.

"Sweetie," his mother said after a minute or two, "that was Lyle MacAuley. There's been some news." Russ shifted away from Clare, purposefully this time, and she let him go. "Do you want to hear it, or do you need more time?" He sat back on his heels, wiping his face with one flannel-sleeved arm. He nodded to Margy.

"Lyle said one of the boys at the high school came into the principal's office and asked to speak to you. He claims he saw a strange car in your driveway on Sunday. Lyle wants to know if you want to go there and talk to the witness, or if he should bring the boy in for questioning."

"Yes," he said. His voice was clotted. He coughed and tried again. "Yes. I'll talk with him."

THIRTEEN

---

lare figured there might be places she felt more awkward. Fully robed
in her vestments in the middle of a snake-handling-and-speaking-in-
tongues revival, for instance. Wearing shorts and a sports bra in downtown Kandahar, maybe. But sitting in the Millers Kill High School principal's
office ranked right up there at the moment.

After Russ's mother had delivered the message about a possible break in
Linda Van Alstyne's murder case, Russ had staggered up from the kitchen floor
like a bull suffering from one too many cuts in the ring. "I'm going," he said.

"Not like that, you're not," Margy said.

"What?"

"Russell Howard, you're in no shape to be driving anywhere."

From the depths of the last few minutes, Clare felt a bubble of humor rise.
So that was his middle name. It sounded like a 1930s movie star.

"Mom—"

"Listen to me, sweetie. Losing a loved one and having a baby are two times
when you can't trust your own head. I remember one time right after your father passed. I nearly plowed into a tree. I just lost track of where I was and what
I was doing. Let me take you back to town."

"You have to be here when Debbie arrives."

"I'll take him, Margy." The offer was out of Clare's mouth before she had a
chance to think about it.

Russ looked at her.

"I have to head back anyway. I left my new deacon in the lurch." She looked at Margy instead of Russ. "I'll carry him on over to the high school, and when he's done, I'll drop him off at the station. I'm sure he can get a ride home with one of the officers."

"Okay." Russ's voice, tired and acquiescent, surrendering.

"Oh." She sounded stupid. "Really?"

He nodded. "I guess I ought to listen to Mom." He turned to retrieve his tartan scarf from the top of the washing machine. "I picked up too many guys who thought they were fine after drinking a few beers. Sometimes, you're not the best judge of whether you're good to go or not."

Margy unhooked his coat and handed it to him. "Will you be home in time for supper?"

"I'm not hungry."

Margy opened her mouth; Russ seemed to realize this was an unacceptable answer. "I'll call you if I'll be late," he amended.

She nodded and contented herself with a fast, fierce hug, one for him and one for Clare. Margy didn't say anything more, but the look she gave Clare as she followed Russ through the kitchen door didn't need any words. *Take care of my son.*

He didn't say a thing to her during the drive down to the center of town. Which was okay by her. She didn't know what he needed from her, and she sure as hell didn't know what she ought to be giving him. She pulled into the buses-only zone to let him off by the door. "I'll be waiting for you in the parking lot," she said.

"Would you come in with me?"

"What?"

"It shouldn't take long."

"I don't think that's appropriate. I don't have anything to do with this investigation."

He snorted. "Never stopped you before."

"Russ. Doesn't the phrase 'people talk' mean anything to you? We agreed—"

"Please." He laid his hand over her coat sleeve. "I feel . . . I could use a little support."

He sounded embarrassed. He was never going to be a man who was comfortable asking for help. It wouldn't make it any better if she told him his reaction was common in the recently bereaved. It was almost impossible, in the face of loss, not to cling to those around you. A good pastor—

Oh, who was she kidding. She didn't feel pastoral about any of this. She was just too stupid to say no to him.

She opened the door and stepped out. The sky overhead was the clear winter blue that looked as if it went all the way up to the edge of space, but northward she could see a solid line of gray massing over the mountains. The next storm.

The high school was long-and-low, an ugly, early seventies assemblage of unnaturally even bricks and orange panels. It had been built end-on against the old high school, a narrow three-story building with high windows and undoubtedly even higher heating bills.

"That's where the admin offices are now," Russ said, pointing toward the old school. As they crossed the parking lot, Clare could see the two schools didn't actually touch but were instead connected by a paved and low-walled walkway.

"Mine was one of the last classes to graduate from the old school." Russ opened one of the wide central doors for her, and Clare walked beneath the initials *M.K.H.S.* chiseled in Gothic lettering on the lintel.

"Nice," she said, and she could see it must have been, despite the file cabinets and spare chairs now lining the halls.

"Classrooms were great," he said. "The gym was in the basement, though. No windows, and when you went up for a dunk shot you nearly brained yourself on the ceiling. Here's the principal's office."

It wasn't, exactly—it was the secretary's office and waiting area, a former classroom that still had a blackboard running along one wall. Mottoes, quotes, and aphorisms had been scribbled all over it in different colored chalks. Clare wondered if the sayings were the work of students or teachers.

Russ zeroed in on the round-cheeked woman behind the desk. "I'm—" he began, but she jumped up and said, "Russ Van Alstyne!" before he got any further. "I'm Barb Berube," she added, bright-eyed and breathless. "Or I am now. I was Barbara McDonald back when we were in high school."

"Barbara—Barbie McDonald?"

She nodded, sending kinky red curls flying everywhere.

"I wouldn't have recognized you. You look great."

"Well, I stopped ironing my hair. That helped." The smile that started across her wide face stalled. "I am so, so sorry to hear about your wife," she said in an entirely different tone. "If I can do anything at all, or if you need someone to talk with, please give me a call. I know what it's like to lose a spouse."

Russ had stiffened as the secretary spoke; now he stood taut as a wire, his face a blend of pain and alarm. It hadn't occurred to him, Clare saw, that his private grief was going to be the subject of public comment.

"Are you a widow?" Clare asked, stepping into the lengthening silence.

"No, I'm divorced," Barb Berube said. She seemed not to have noticed Clare up to that point. "And you are . . . ?"

Clare unzipped her parka, revealing her clerical blouse and collar. "Clare Fergusson, from St. Alban's."

Barb eyed Russ once more. He was still imitating a pillar of salt. She rallied, smiled at Clare, and said, "I'll just let the principal know you're here, shall I?"

As soon as she had disappeared through the door into the adjoining office, Russ rounded on Clare. "What was that?"

"What?"

"That . . . call me to talk thing? If I've seen her more'n a half dozen times at the IGA since we graduated, I'd be surprised."

Clare sighed. "You're a widower now, Russ."

He winced.

"You don't know it, and you're not ready for it, but you've just become a hot commodity to unmarried women of a certain age."

His look of horror would have made her laugh if it hadn't been so heartbreaking.

"Russ? And, um, Pastor? Mrs. Rayburn will see you now." Barb Berube smiled sympathetically at them. Russ gave her a wide berth on his way through the door.

Jean Ann Rayburn, the Millers Kill principal, was rising from her desk to greet them. She was an angular woman, whose flyaway gray hair and fuzzy cardigan fought against a stock-necked silk blouse and straight skirt.

"Russ Van Alstyne," she said.

"Mrs. Rayburn."

She shook his hand. "I'm so sorry for your loss. I met your wife a few times over the years since you came home. She was a lovely woman."

Russ nodded. He cleared his throat.

"I'm Clare Fergusson." Clare offered her hand, and the principal took it. "I'm the priest at St. Alban's."

Jean Ann Rayburn's eyes glinted with recognition, and Clare wondered what she had heard from the Millers Kill grapevine. But all the older woman said was, "I'm pleased to meet you, Ms. Fergusson."

The principal released Clare and clasped her hands in front of her, the sort of habitual gesture that she once must have used to draw the attention of a roomful of high schoolers. "I'm grateful you could come here instead of making the boy go to the police station. He was quite distraught when he spoke to me. He's very concerned that his parents not find out."

"I can't guarantee that," Russ said. "Who is the boy?"

"Quinn Tracey."

"Meg Tracey's son?" Russ was genuinely surprised. "Huh. I guess that makes sense. We've hired him to plow out our drive a couple times this winter. I can't think of why he'd be worried about his parents knowing he saw any-thing. His mother was the one who found—who called in the crime."

"Let me take you to him, and you can ask him yourself." Mrs. Rayburn es-corted them out of her office. "We'll be in Mrs. Ovitt's room," she said to her secretary, who—Clare looked twice to make sure—had put on a fresh coat of lipstick while they were meeting the principal.

"Suzanne Ovitt is one of our guidance counselors. Wonderful woman. She has a great rapport with teens." Mrs. Rayburn knocked and opened a door al-most hidden between two aging file cabinets. "Mrs. Ovitt? Russ"—she smiled apologetically at him—"I mean, Chief Van Alstyne is here. And Reverend Fer-gusson, from the Traceys' church."

Ugh. Clare decided not to correct her. The guidance counselor's office was bright and cheerful, decorated with the sort of inspirational posters often found in corporate cafeterias. A row of all-in-one desks lined one end of the room, and the other had been converted into a conversational grouping, with an oversized sofa and several squishy chairs. Like her furniture, the fifty-something Mrs. Ovitt had a look of sturdy service about her, as if she could wipe noses, serve snacks, correct misdeeds, and drill multiplication tables si-multaneously, without raising her voice or losing her cool.

She shook their hands and murmured hellos and condolences. Clare stepped to one side to get a better look at the boy huddled on the sofa.

He looked like any other sixteen- or seventeen-year-old she might have seen hanging out at All TechTronik or the Aviation Mall. Jeans that were easily two sizes too large, a long-sleeved tee emblazoned with a picture of rapper Fifty Cent, and a middling case of acne that couldn't hide the fact that he'd be a handsome man once he grew into his nose and ears. But the expression on his face was singular—and disturbing. He was staring at Russ, and he was scared.

"Quinn, this is Chief Van Alstyne," Mrs. Ovitt said, indicating they should take the chairs. "And you know Reverend Fergusson." Clare tensed, but the kid barely gave her a twitch as they sat down.

"I know Quinn," Russ said. He didn't sound great, exactly, but he did sound warm and nonthreatening. "He's been doing a good job plowing our drive this winter." Russ perched on the edge of the chair so he could lean forward. "Quinn, why don't you tell me what you saw?"

The boy looked down to where he was linking and knotting his knuckles together. "It was a car," he said.

"In my driveway?"

The boy nodded, still not looking at Russ.

"When was this?"

"Sunday afternoon."

Clare glanced at Russ. *Was that when . . . ?* He shrugged. "What kind of car was it, Quinn?"

"A 1992 Honda Civic. New York State plates. 6779LF."

"I'm impressed. Most people don't remember vehicles with that much precision."

For the first time, the boy looked up at Russ. "It's kinda a habit. When I started the plowing job, Dad told me I'd better keep track of any cars in any of the driveways I did, in case somebody made a claim for damage later on. He pays half of my insurance, so he's, like, always thinking about my liability."

Russ nodded. "What made you notice this car? Were you out there plowing?"

Which would have been odd, Clare thought, since the last significant snow had been well over a week ago.

"Naw, I do all my plowing right after it snows. Nobody wants to wait."

"So what were you doing out on Peekskill Road?"

Quinn seemed very unhappy with this question. He twisted his hands and stayed silent.

"Quinn?"

The boy looked at Mrs. Ovitt, who had been sitting quietly, near but not too close. She nodded encouragingly. "I was hanging out with a friend." Russ opened his mouth, but the boy cut him off. "I don't want to get him involved, okay?" He dropped his head again. "My parents don't want me hanging around with him."

The boy's reluctance, his fear, all fell into place. Clare didn't know whether to be amused or appalled. A woman was dead, and in Quinn's mind, his biggest worry was getting grounded.

"Quinn, I can't promise you this will never get out to your parents, but I can promise you I won't bring it up unless absolutely necessary. I'm not here to enforce your mom and dad's rules—although I will point out that when your folks ask you to stay away from someone, they usually have a pretty good reason for doing so."

Quinn somehow managed to roll his eyes without actually moving any part of his body.

"What's your friend's name?"

"Are you gonna, you know, ask him questions?"

"Not if I don't have to."

Quinn blew out a breath. "It's Aaron. Aaron MacEntyre."

"Was he in your truck with you?"

The boy nodded.

"Did you notice anyone going in or out of the house when you saw the car?"

He shook his head.

"Can you remember what time it was?"

Quinn frowned. He scrunched up his face. "Around four o'clock."

"So it was getting dark? How did you see the license plates? Was the outside light on?"

"No. I mean, I guess it was before dark. But at the end of the afternoon. Maybe it was closer to three."

Russ sat silent for a moment. Then for another. He regarded Quinn alertly. He gave no signs of speaking again.

Finally, the boy burst out, "Is that it? Is that all?"

"I don't know," Russ said. "Is there anything else you'd like to tell me?"

Quinn's eyes grew large. He bit his lip. He shook his head no.

"You sure?"

He nodded.

Russ stood up. "Then we're done. Thank you for coming forward and telling

Mrs. Ovitt and Mrs. Rayburn what you saw. I know it was hard for you. I'm grateful."

The rest of the adults stood when Russ did. Quinn scrambled to his feet. Standing, his jeans hung low enough around his hips to give everyone a clear view of his boxers. The principal pointed, and he yanked the waistband up. A temporary state of affairs, Clare guessed.

"Quinn, you can join the tail end of your seventh-period class," Mrs. Rayburn said. "I believe Mrs. Ovitt has a note for your teacher." The guidance counselor nodded and retrieved a pale yellow slip from the top of her desk. The boy accepted it, stuffing it into one pocket and reexposing his underwear in the process. Before Mrs. Rayburn had another chance to bring him into compliance with the dress code, he mumbled a farewell and vanished through the door.

"He's a good kid," Mrs. Ovitt commented. "Once he reconciles himself to the fact he's a small-town white boy instead of an urban black gangbanger, he'll be fine."

"Who's Aaron MacEntyre?" Russ asked. "I recognize the last name, but there are several MacEntyre families in the area."

"His parents are Craig and Vicki MacEntyre," Mrs. Rayburn said. "They have a farm in the valley, off Old Route 100."

"Has Aaron been in trouble?" Clare blurted the question out before she remembered she was going to keep a low profile. "I mean . . . why would the Traceys forbid their son to see him?"

Mrs. Rayburn looked at Mrs. Ovitt. "As far as I know, Aaron's never been involved in anything questionable. Have you heard anything, Suzanne?"

The guidance counselor shook her head. "To the contrary. He's a fairly popular boy. Very self-confident."

"He's not a scholar, though," Mrs. Rayburn said. "He's bright, but he doesn't see the use in applying himself. Perhaps the Traceys think that sets a bad example for Quinn."

"And Aaron is very gung ho about joining the military. His parents and I had to talk him out of dropping out to enlist when he turned eighteen last month." Mrs. Ovitt and the principal looked at each other with a melancholy understanding. "Not a thing that would endear him to the Traceys."

"Yes, well . . . with this war on . . ." Mrs. Rayburn clasped her hands. "I can't blame any of our parents for wanting to keep their children away from the recruiting office." She looked up at Russ. "I hope at least some of this will be helpful, Chief Van Alstyne."

Clare read one of the posters. Beneath a perfectly lit swimmer powering through the butterfly stroke, it said: IF YOU HAVE A PURPOSE IN WHICH YOU CAN BELIEVE, THERE IS NO END TO THE AMOUNT OF THINGS YOU CAN ACCOMPLISH. Fortune-cookie philosophy. She wondered how it held up in the real world.

Russ nodded. "I hope it will be, too."

FOURTEEN

W hat did you think of Quinn Tracey?"

Clare looked away from the road for a moment. "Of him as a person? Or of what he said?"

"Either. Both."

She returned her attention to driving. He watched her profile: Roman nose, sharp chin, her hair, by early afternoon, already falling out of its knot. His feelings, about her and for her, were too tangled and painful to contemplate, and he was pathetically grateful to have a mutual puzzle to fall back on. One of the first things that had caught him had been her mind, her easy questions and considered answers.

"I think he was hiding something."

"More than hanging out with an unapproved friend, you mean?"

"Mm-hmm."

"Good. That's what I thought, but I wasn't sure if I could trust my instincts."

"What are you going to do about it?"

"I'm thinking calling him at home would be good. Let him know that one of us will be coming around to talk with him in a day or two. I'm betting his fear of Mom and Dad finding out is greater than his fear of spilling the beans."

"Do you think he saw more than he admitted to?"

Russ sighed. "No. Chances are the deep dark secret he's hiding is a six-pack and a fake ID. It's just . . . I want it to be more." He touched his coat pocket, where he kept his small notebook. "I want this license plate and description to lead me straight to a car with the murder weapon in the trunk. That's what I meant when I said I couldn't trust my instincts."

She flicked on her turn signal and swung her car onto Route 57. "Do you have a working theory? About . . . the crime?"

"Lyle thinks it was someone lashing out at me. That my wife was just an incidental target."

"Does that mean you might be in danger?"

"I wish. Just let the son of a bitch get within fifty yards of me."

"Don't joke about stuff like that."

"Who's joking?" He saw her expression and relented. "It's just a working theory, anyway. A way to organize the investigation. It could be complete bullshit, for all we know."

"Do you have any other possibilities?"

"You know what I really regret?" It had nothing to do with her question, but he suddenly had to unburden himself. "All those times I discussed cases, like this, without ever really giving a crap. I mean, beyond wanting to catch the bad guys. All those times I talked about the victim as an object. Like a mechanic talks about a broken-down carburetor. For me, the murder or the overdose or the car accident was a piece of the workday. But for somebody else, it was the end of the world."

"Russ, you've just lost your wife. Most people in your circumstances are still popping Prozac and crying their way through a box of Kleenex." She sounded faintly exasperated, which had the odd effect of cheering him. It was a dose of normal in a world gone strange.

"I just could have been—"

"You're plenty sympathetic to families and victims. I've seen you in action. Don't start making yourself feel inadequate for no reason."

He hiccupped a laugh. "Don't beat yourself up, honey. That's my job." He smiled. "Linda used to say that to me." Suddenly, a black bubble of grief rose up out of his chest and he let out a barking sob. Clare took one hand off the wheel and held it out to him. He clutched it in a bone-cracking grip, his chest heaving as he fought to regain some control.

"Jesus," he said, when he could speak again. "Jesus Christ. I'm losing my mind."

Clare shook her head. Her eyes were wet, too, although from sympathy or from the pain where he was grinding her knuckles together, he couldn't tell. He released her hand.

"You're not losing your mind. Grief makes us all crazy at times. You read those Kübler-Ross theories and you think grief has all these recognizable levels, like going through school. Once you pass all the tests, you get to leave. But day to day, moment to moment, grief is more like . . ."

"Losing your mind?"

"Yeah."

He leaned back against the headrest and closed his eyes. She drove on in silence. He could feel when her car climbed the hill running into town from alongside the river. Could feel the tug of gravity as they swung around the circle and came to a stop. Must be a red light on Main Street. He opened his eyes and twisted in his seat to look through the rear window. Past the circular city park, where the abandoned pavilion lay half buried in drifts like a forgotten dream of summer, the square central tower of St. Alban's rose to the ice-pale sky.

"You don't have to go out of your way," he said. "I can walk from here."

She snorted. The light changed, and she accelerated down Main.

"When are you going to give me the talk about God?" he asked.

"Which one?"

"You're a priest. Aren't you supposed to be comforting me? Telling me about heaven and all that?"

"What do you think heaven is?"

"I don't believe in it." Christ, he sounded like a five-year-old. A five-year-old who needed a nap.

"Then don't worry about it. Whatever happens, happens. It's the one thing we're all going to get to learn firsthand, eventually."

"But . . . doesn't it all seem like such a waste?"

She turned toward the police station, thumping over the depression in the sidewalk into the lot. She put the car in park and turned toward him.

"Nothing is a waste. You don't have to believe in heaven to believe that." She took his hand again. "All the good things Linda did in her life, all the people she touched, all the work she did, all that lives on. Her life had value. It had weight and meaning. She affected the world around her in ways you will never, ever even know about."

He sat with that for a moment. "Okay," he said. "Okay. I can believe in that."

She smiled, a little. "Humanist." She leaned back and unlocked the doors.

"I'll assume you have a ride with one of the guys, but if you need me, give me a call."

He nodded. Opened the door.

"Russ?"

"Yeah?"

"I'm praying for you. Day and night."

He nodded again. "Thanks." He watched her reverse, then pull into the light Tuesday afternoon traffic.

When he turned toward the entrance, Lyle and Mark were waiting for him in their shirtsleeves. He raised his eyebrows. "Mighty cold to be hanging around outside without a coat on."

"Then let's get inside," Lyle snapped.

Russ let the two of them precede him through the old bronze doors and up the marble steps. Decades ago, when the force had been twice the size it was now, there had been a sergeant's desk here at the top of the stairs, with room for a half-dozen chairs against the wall. Now it was just a bare stretch of marble you had to cross on your way down the hall, furnished with nothing except two flagpoles, one for the American flag and the other bearing the state flag.

Lyle stopped him with a hand to his chest right in front of the Great Seal of New York. Mark sidled farther down the hall and stopped, clearly listening for anyone who might come their way.

"What is this?" Even the comparatively chilly entranceway was warm enough to make Russ's glasses cloud over. He took them off. "You guys hitting me up for my lunch money?"

"Russ." Lyle sounded dead serious. "I'm not telling you this as your second in command. I'm telling you this as a friend. You're going to wind up in a boat-load of trouble if you're seen driving around town with Clare Fergusson."

"She gave me a ride back into town after paying a condolence call on my mother. For chrissakes, what do you think is going on? My wife just died!"

Lyle thumped him in the chest. "That's right. Your wife just died. And half the town has heard one sort of rumor or another about you and Reverend Fergusson." Russ opened his mouth, outraged, but Lyle cut him off. "I don't want to hear about how innocent it all is! If you don't have any sense of self-preservation, at least you could think about the lady. What're the folks who go to her church going to think of her if they see you holding hands and whispering sweet nothings before Linda's even in the ground?"

Russ reared back. His hands clenched involuntarily. "You're damn lucky you're in uniform, MacAuley, because if we were on our own time, I'd be kicking your ass right now."

"And I'm trying to save yours. What the hell took you so long? Your mom called, and I expected you a half hour ago."

Through his anger, he felt a twinge of guilt. His men shouldn't have to rely on his mother to tell them his whereabouts. "I went straight to the high school."

"Alone?"

He paused.

"Oh, for— Don't tell me Reverend Fergusson went with you."

"I got the description and license number of a car that was sitting in my drive Sunday afternoon. No sign of anybody, but the kid who reported it may know more than he's telling."

"Did it even occur to you that sharing details about this case with her might not be a good idea?"

That stopped him. The hand-holding jibe pissed him off, but this was just bewildering. "Why not?"

"Because Clare Fergusson falls within the circle of possible suspects."

"Clare?" He couldn't help it, he laughed out loud. Replacing his glasses, he looked at Lyle. In focus, his deputy chief appeared even more upset. "I'm sorry," Russ said. "You're right. I can see where people might get the wrong idea seeing me and Clare together. Trust me, it won't happen again anytime soon." And God, wasn't that a depressing thought? "You don't need to worry about the case, either. We didn't really discuss it. Just talked about our impressions of Quinn Tracey—he's the kid who saw the car—and your theory of the case. Mostly it was, you know, grief stuff." Lyle still looked skeptical. "She is a priest, you know."

"I know, Chief. I know."

From his post, Mark coughed and clomped around in an unsubtle way. Lyle gestured, and they both crossed to the hallway. Harlene was hustling toward them, her unhooked headpiece trailing wires behind her.

"There you are," she said. She looked at the three of them skeptically. "You all right?" She flapped her hands. "Never mind. Dr. Dvorak just called. He has the preliminary autopsy results."

An icy boulder rolled down Russ's gullet and lodged there. "Okay," he said. He nodded at Lyle. "Let's go."

Harlene goggled at him. "You some sort of masochist, or what?"

"Harlene—" Lyle warned.

Russ shook his head. He looked into Harlene's round eyes and felt a surge of gratitude for all the people who cared for him. None of whom, of course, had the least bit of tact. "I need to do this," he told her. "Whatever it takes to find her killer, I need to do it."

"Damn fool," she said under her breath.

"But I do think we ought to bring Mark," he said to Lyle.

"Me?" Mark snapped to attention like a Labrador sighting a duck. He had never attended a briefing at the ME's office.

"You. I gotta be realistic. I may not absorb everything, so an extra pair of ears will be helpful. Plus"—Russ shrugged—"you're detective material. We got to get you out there, exposed to this stuff."

"I'll go get our coats," Mark said, and bolted down the hall toward the squad room.

Lyle looked at him assessingly. "I guess you're not completely lost to reason."

Russ ran one hand through his hair. God, he felt old, old, old. "Don't count on it," he said.

FIFTEEN

Mark Durkee had met the Washington County medical examiner before. He wasn't sure what made him uneasy in the man's presence—the fact he spent his days elbow-deep in dead bodies, or the mad-scientist look he had perfected, thanks to an assault two summers before, which had left him with a white scar that twisted out of his short gray hair to bisect one eyebrow. He also had a permanent limp he treated with a silver-topped cane. Thumping his way down the mortuary hall toward them, his white coat flapping behind him, Dr. Dvorak looked like a figure straight out of one of the Stephen King novels Mark had devoured in his teens.

Dvorak raised his eyebrows when he saw the chief. Or rather, he raised the one that was still mobile, giving his face a satanically lopsided look. "Good lord. Are you completely lacking in good sense?" he said. "Are you sure you want to be part of this?"

The chief nodded.

"Idiot. *I* wouldn't be here if I didn't have to." Dvorak pivoted on his cane and limped back up the way he had come. The chief and the dep followed, so Mark went along, too, wondering as they moved slowly up the institutional, lino-and-fluorescent hall if they were going through the battered metal doors at its end. He wasn't sure what was behind there, past the public rooms of the mortuary, and he desperately didn't want to find out. Which, he knew, didn't make any sense for a career cop. He had seen dead bodies before. Three. But the sight was endurable in the crime scene, with the blood and the violence attending. Maybe because the bodies didn't seem like dead people there. They were evidence.

But laid out on a steel slab, with blue lips and black thread suturing up their cold skin . . . He shivered.

"Durkee?"

Mark snapped to. MacAuley was standing by one of the doorways, waiting for him. "You okay?" the deputy chief asked.

"Yes, sir," Mark said, and he was, because he saw through the door that there was nothing in the room except the same sort of 1960s government-issue office furniture they had in the MKPD.

There were only two chairs facing Dr. Dvorak's obsessively neat desk, so Mark took up a stance next to the door while the chief and MacAuley made themselves as comfortable as they could.

Dvorak sat. He picked up a manila file folder and squared it on the green baize blotter in front of him. "First thing," he said. "I am not going to show you any pictures."

The chief nodded.

"Second thing," the pathologist said. "As is my custom in the case of a homicide, I moved directly from the recorded autopsy to the preliminary report. Therefore, I won't be ready to release the body until tomorrow at the earliest."

He meant, Mark realized, that he had to finish putting the pieces that had been Mrs. Van Alstyne back together.

The ME splayed his fingers across his scarred forehead. His nails were very clean and very blunt. "I have to tell you," he said, "this has been the most disturbing autopsy I've done since I started in this position." He lowered his hand and looked at the chief. "The bulk of my work is as a pathologist. If I have more than two suspicious deaths a year, it's a banner event. That's what I wanted when I came here. Peaceful work in a quiet county. I never really stopped to think that sooner or later I'd be autopsing," his voice broke sharply, "someone I know." He looked at the chief. His pale eyes were wet.

The chief reached across Dvorak's immaculate desk and squeezed the doctor's forearm. "Thank you, Emil."

The ME cleared his throat and dropped his gaze to the folder in front of him. He flipped it open. "The subject was a healthy, well-nourished, and physically fit Caucasian, reported age fifty-one." He traced the edge of the paper. "She had wonderful skin elasticity. She easily could have been a decade younger."

The chief nodded. "Yeah. She . . ."

They all waited for a few seconds, but nothing else came out.

Dr. Dvorak cleared his throat again. "Since we know the identity of the victim, why don't I just skip over to the forensically critical parts."

"Why don't you," MacAuley said.

"The victim was not sexually assaulted in any way," the doctor began, and the chief, who had been sitting at attention, sagged in his chair. The ME went on. "The fatal assault seems to have been swift and unexpected. There were, as you noted at the crime scene, Deputy Chief MacAuley, no defensive wounds. Nor was there any bruising which might indicate a struggle or the confinement of the victim. Death was the result of a well-placed knife thrust to the throat, severing the esophagus, the airway, and the larynx simultaneously. Then the knife was withdrawn at a slight angle, severing the jugular vein. I suspect the assailant struck from behind, in what might be deemed the classic 'sneak attack' position, pulling the victim's head back to expose the neck and striking before the victim has organized a response. There would have been an almost instant loss of consciousness as the blood pressure to the brain crashed. Clinical death followed within minutes." He spread one hand over the papers in the folder and paused for a long moment. "It may be a commonplace, Russ, but from a medical viewpoint, I can assure you that she felt, at the most, a moment of surprise. She did not suffer."

The chief nodded. "Thank you," he said. His voice was hoarse.

"You said a well-placed knife thrust," MacAuley said. "Was the perp someone who knew what he was doing? Who had training?"

Dr. Dvorak pressed his already thin lips into an invisible line. "Someone who knew what he or she was doing, yes, I would say that. As to how that experience was gained . . ." He shrugged. "Military training, some forms of martial arts or self-defense, an experienced hunter. That's your call."

"He or she?" Mark said. The chief and the dep turned to look at him. He felt himself flushing, but he pressed on. "I mean, can you tell if we're looking for a man or a woman?"

The doctor shook his head. "No. As I said, I believe Mrs. Van Alstyne—the victim was surprised from behind. Since she was a somewhat petite woman, the angle of the blow would easily be within the reach of any assailant between the heights of, say, five and six feet."

Mark nodded. Let the dep chase after his bad-guy-coming-after-the-chief scenario. He knew that most murders were committed by someone close to the victim. Someone involved in the victim's life. He had his own scenario.

"Fixing time of death was difficult. The house was cool to begin with, and according to Officer McCrea, the mudroom door was open from the time the body was discovered until I got there. Lividity was less useful than usual because of the significant blood loss. I can narrow it down to a twenty-four-hour window between roughly Sunday afternoon and Monday afternoon, but I can't be more precise than that."

"What about the . . ." MacAuley waved his hand over his face.

The ME's wince was faint, but noticible. "The postmortem facial wounds? They are numerous, all delivered within, I estimate, a half hour of death. Some were quite shallow. Tentative, one might say. Others were deep and decisive. The victim's body was also pierced in several places, a fact not readily apparent from the initial evaluation at the crime scene. These postmortem wounds to the torso were stabbing rather than slashing wounds, and were themselves almost completely bloodless. Again, not readily apparent until the victim's blood-soaked clothing had been removed."

"So . . . what sort of assailant are we talking about here?" MacAuley asked. "Someone who hated Mrs. Van Alstyne personally? Someone who saw her as a stand-in for something else they hated?"

"I'm a pathologist, not one of these so-called profilers," Dr. Dvorak said. "And I'm not all that convinced you can tell what's going on in someone's mind based on the pattern of assault. The body moves and reacts in ways the mind cannot control. However, having said that, in my opinion, we have here an assailant who was technically adept enough to kill with one stroke, but who was inexperienced with death itself."

"What does that mean?" MacAuley asked.

"If I may continue," the doctor said, giving the deputy chief a measured look. "The postmortem injuries strike me as a sort of experimentation, rather than deliberate mutilation. Seeing what happened when flesh was sliced or stabbed."

The chief shuddered. Dr. Dvorak kept his eyes on him. "Often in cases where the killer enjoys having control over a body, he will treat it as a child treats a doll, moving it about, removing clothing, inserting objects into it, marking it."

It was a gruesome image, but Mark could picture exactly what the pathologist was getting at. He had seen Maddy play with her Barbies and baby dolls in precisely that way, right down to coloring them with Magic Markers.

"In this case," Dvorak continued, "the best analogy might be . . . a boy poking at a dead bird."

MacAuley nodded. "So . . . someone familiar with knife fighting but not with actually killing someone."

"In my opinion. Which may or may not be worth the paper it's written on." Dvorak looked at the folder lying in front of him with distaste. "The one other solid thing I can contribute is the murder weapon."

The chief sat up straighter. "From knife cuts? It usually takes at least a week for the state crime lab to get back on weapons."

"That's right. Which is why I bypassed the state lab. I e-mailed the photos to a friend in Virginia and let him know how important it was to me. He got back to me right before I called you." The doctor removed a sheet of paper from the folder and slid it across the desk. It was a printed version of a Web-page photo, showing a nonreflective, efficiently lethal knife.

"I'm sorry about the poor quality of the print. As you can see, it's a K-Bar, and according to my friend, it's mostly found on the secondhand or military surplus market, because—"

"This is my knife," the chief said.

"It—what?" Dr. Dvorak stared at him. Then his face softened. "It's not an uncommon style, Russ."

"I know it's not," the chief said impatiently. "It used to be marine issue, and everybody in the army bought 'em because they were so much better than the crap knives we were issued. I kept mine when I retired. This is the same knife that's missing from my barn."

"Russ," MacAuley said, "the doc's right. I mean, my hunting knife's from the army-navy surplus, and it looks a lot like this—"

"I'm not having guilt-induced hallucinations, Lyle. Think. The murder weapon was a K-Bar. My K-Bar is missing. The last time I can positively place it on my workbench would be a few days after hunting season ended. Someone could have gotten into the barn easy and taken it." He leaned forward. "Maybe someone in that car the Tracey kid saw in the driveway Sunday."

"If the perp broke into your barn to get a weapon, why the hell didn't he take your Weatherby or your shotgun?"

"Because it's a lot harder to sneak up on someone with a rifle," Mark said.

The chief nodded at him. "Exactly."

"Okay," MacAuley said. "I'm willing to go with it. I just want to point out that whether it's the chief's knife or not, it's probably at the bottom of the Kill right now."

Mark grimaced. A lot of things could disappear beneath the ice-crusted waters of the river.

"Mark, let's have you get back on that list of released cons the chief dealt with." The dep was standing, settling his hat on his head. "Thanks, Doc."

Dr. Dvorak reached over the desk and shook MacAuley's hand. The deputy chief clasped Mark on the shoulder and steered him out the office door. "Let's give them a sec," he said, once they were a few steps down the hall.

"Look," Mark said, "about the released-con theory—"

"Track down their parole officers or their wardens. We're looking for someone who had knife training while in the army, or who got in trouble for knife fighting inside. That shift switch you wanted? You got it. You're on days starting now. Investigating, not patrol."

The bump up in status that Mark had wanted so long flashed by, an irritating detail he had to hear before he got to what really mattered. "I want to spend some time looking into Reverend Fergusson," he blurted out.

"What?" MacAuley held him at arm's length. "What are you talking about?"

"Clare Fergusson. You told the chief yourself. She's in the circle of suspects."

"You mean back at the station? I was trying to crowbar some sense of discretion into the chief, for God's sake. I don't really think she's a credible suspect."

"Why not?"

MacAuley threw up his hands. "I don't know. Because I know her, I guess. I just can't picture it. I mean, okay, maybe she could possibly maybe get mad enough to lose it in a fit of temporary insanity. But cover it up? No way. She'd be signing a confession before you could finish Mirandizing her."

"But think about it. She's got the means—she did some sort of fancy survival training for helicopter pilots. She's got the motive"—MacAuley shook his head, but Mark surged on—"she does, you know she does. You think the chief was ever going to divorce his wife?"

The deputy chief paused. "No."

"Motive. And she had the opportunity—she was up in the mountains all alone for a week, including Sunday and Monday. She could have come down to the chief's house, done the deed, and split before anyone saw her."

"Durkee," the deputy chief said, "I appreciate the level of thought you've put into this. That's one of the things that tells me you're going to have a great future as a cop. But the reverend is not a suspect. Put it aside. You'll have more than enough to do compiling this list. Understand?"

"Yessir." Mark tried to conceal his seething frustration. If the deputy chief spiked the investigation, that was it. No way was anyone going to look at the most likely suspect. Unless . . .

He thought of the now-crumpled letter from the state police waiting at home on his dresser. Unless he could find someone with the authority to take the case from MacAuley. Someone who wouldn't be swayed by the chief's friendship with the priest.

SIXTEEN

I t is a cliché that there are no secrets in a small town. It is also false. In Millers Kill, it is unlikely anyone will ever know that Geraldine Bain, who has worked in the post office for thirty years and who is famous in the First Baptist Church for her deep-dish crumble-crust pie, nearly died from an illegal abortion in New York City in 1950.

The fact that Wayne Stoner, a hardworking dairy farmer and father of two, stays up after everyone has gone to bed to read his wife's romance novels has never come out, even after he spilled coffee on Suzanne Brockmann's *The Defiant Hero* and had to blame his thirteen-year-old, Hannah.

Laura Rayfield, the nurse-practitioner heading up the local free clinic, certainly hopes that no one ever discovers that during her youth in Tennessee (she followed a boyfriend to New York and discovered she loved the Adirondacks much more than the man) she was the statewide fire-baton twirling queen.

Tim Garrettson, who has been in marriage counseling with Reverend Fergusson for over a year, doubts that his wife, Liz, will ever find out that he has been unfaithful to her three separate times while attending insurance industry conferences. Unless he's foolish enough to spill the beans himself.

But something like the violent death of the police chief's wife will not stay secret, or low-key, or undiscussed. Especially when rumors had already been circulating that his recent relocation to his mother's house was because his wife caught him out in an affair. The first story of the murder would appear

Wednesday morning, in the *Glens Falls Post-Star.* It had almost no details from the Millers Kill Police Department, and only a single quote from the victim's friend Meg Tracey. The reporter, Ben Beagle, was unable to obtain a statement from the widower. That did not stop the residents of Millers Kill from filling in the blanks themselves.

Dr. Emil Dvorak, in addition to his duties as the county medical examiner, also served as the Washington County Hospital's pathologist, and he had been sitting a consult with Drs. Phillip Stillman and Molly Cline Monday evening when his pager went off. He had excused himself, grabbed Dr. Stillman's phone, and called in. Stillman and Cline, who still found it vaguely amusing that someone who worked exclusively with dead people could have emergency calls, ignored what was going on across Dvorak's desk, until he gasped out, "Oh, my God, no," and buried his face in one hand.

When he hung up, Dr. Cline tentatively said, "Bad news?"

And Emil Dvorak, the soul of professional discretion, lifted his head and blurted out, "Russ Van Alstyne's wife has been murdered."

He terminated the consult and was on his way to the crime scene before the two other physicians could cobble together something appropriate to say.

Dr. Stillman, who had met both the Van Alstynes when he treated the police chief's fractured tibia less than a year ago, used the extra time from the now-canceled consult to check in on one of his orthopedic surgical cases. On his way out, he bumped into the emergency department charge nurse.

"You know the police chief, right, Alta?"

"I ought to, the number of times he's been in the ER picking up drunk drivers or talking with kids who got in trouble."

"I just heard his wife's been killed."

"Jesus, Mary, and Joseph!"

By the start of the swing shift, the entire on-duty staff had heard the news.

Tuesday morning, an internist named Dr. Palil Ghupta drove from the hospital to the Millers Kill Free Clinic for his monthly supervisory meeting with Laura Rayfield, NP. He regaled her with the story and, because he was a fan of police shows, buffed it up a bit with the phrase "She was blown away."

Laura was suitably shocked and impressed, and when at lunchtime she bumped into Roxanne Lunt, the director of the historical society next door, she passed the news on.

"A shotgun blast took her out," Laura said, maneuvering past a slick spot of ice and packed snow. The sidewalks were in bad shape, but it was still easier to walk to Silvio's Italian Bakery than to try to find parking spaces on the snow-lined street.

"Good heavens." Roxanne pulled her fur collar closer, as if the icy winds of mortality were blowing around her neck. "I wonder if Clare Fergusson knows yet."

"Reverend Fergusson? The minister?"

"Mm-hmm. She's evidently a particular friend of Chief Van Alstyne's." She tugged open the door to Silvio's. A swirl of yeasty steam swallowed them. "What's really scary is the thought that whoever did it is still out there. I mean, if the police chief's wife can be murdered in her own home, what chance do the rest of us have?"

"Most murders in the North Country result from domestic violence," Laura said, unwinding her scarf. "If you aren't married to or involved with the man who kills you, chances are, you're safe. Just how good a friend is Reverend Fergusson?"

"Omigod! You can't think the chief—"

"I'm just saying."

Roxanne poked distractedly at her perfectly blown-out coif. "I'd better call her as soon as I get back to the historical society."

Waiting for his hot meatball sub to go, Dan Hunter, vice president for finance at AllBanc, listened to their conversation. Back at the bank, he stuck his head in Terrance McKellan's office. "Hey, Terry," he said. "Isn't Clare Fergusson the minister at your church?"

"Priest," Terry mumbled around a tuna pita pocket. His wife had lately put him on a diet, and he wasn't happy with it.

"Whatever. Is she involved in some way with the chief of police?"

Terry McKellan brushed a stray whole-wheat crumb from his luxurious brown mustache and looked at his colleague suspiciously. "Why?"

"Evidently somebody gunned his wife down in their home, and he's a suspect."

Terry dropped the pita on his desk. "You're kidding me."

"I swear. They were talking about it at Silvio's."

"Good God." He stared at his desk calendar. "Thanks for letting me know. I've got some people I'd better call." He was dialing Robert Fowler, the senior warden of St. Alban's, before Dan had vacated his doorway. Fowler, the owner of a small construction and development firm, was out to lunch, according to his secretary. Terry left him a brief message in his voicemail. Geoff Burns, junior warden, was in a meeting with a client at his law offices. Voicemail message.

McKellan flipped through his Rolodex and started in on his fellow vestry members. Sterling Sumner, ostensibly retired, was teaching an architecture class at Skidmore. He was also the last man in America to employ a live, human answering service. Terry left as long a message as he dared with the terse woman who, unfortunately, sounded nothing like Judy Holliday.

Mrs. Henry Marshall was at home, getting ready for her Tuesday afternoon bridge group. "Terry McKellan, I can't believe you of all people would be spreading gossip," she scolded, after he had told her the news. "You can't seriously think that nice Russ Van Alstyne had anything to do with his wife's death. Poor thing!"

"It's not that," he said. "Sooner or later, something like this is going to have the press all over it. And when that happens, they're going to be digging into Reverend Clare's relationship with the man."

"What relationship?" Mrs. Marshall was nothing if not stouthearted in defense of people she liked.

"Lacey . . ." He had known Mrs. Marshall for over a quarter century and had recently begun calling her by her first name.

"The best way to handle gossip is to ignore it," Mrs. Marshall said. "If there's no wind, the fire will die away."

She soothed him a little more, assured him that no, there was no reason they should have a special meeting to discuss the problem, and got him off the line just as her doorbell rang with the first three members of the bridge group. She probably wouldn't have thought much more of it if, during a lull after bidding out her hand, she hadn't overheard Yvonne Story telling the rest of the north table that Reverend Clare Fergusson had demanded a resolution to her affair with Chief Russ Van Alstyne, which is why he had shot his wife after she refused to divorce him.

"Yvonne Story! Where on earth did you hear such nonsense?"

The retired librarian had a homemade-dumpling face, imperfectly round and pastry-pale, and a lifelong, passionate love affair with the sound of her own voice. "Oh! Lacey! It slipped my mind, but she's your pastor, isn't she? I'm so sorry. Isn't it awful the things that men and women of God get up to these days? That's why I stopped going to church years ago. I follow this wonderful minister on the television, Dr. Peter Panagore. He's a lovely, lovely man. And it's so convenient, not having to get my stockings on of a Sunday morning."

"Yvonne," Mrs. Marshall cut in, "there's not an ounce of truth to that story you were telling about Reverend Fergusson and Chief Van Alstyne."

"Oh, but there is! I volunteer at the Infirmary, you know, reading to the old folks and keeping them company, and the director, Paul Foubert—you know Paul, don't you? He's a lovely, lovely man, and so well spoken, although, you know, most of that sort of men are—"

"Yvonne. Are you telling me the director of the Infirmary told you Chief Van Alstyne shot his wife? I don't believe it."

"Well, I did happen to overhear him saying that Mrs. Van Alstyne—the younger Mrs. Van Alstyne, not the older—had been killed, and that his, you know, special friend, the medical examiner, was on the case because it was foul play." She let the last words echo dramatically, a refinement Mrs. Marshall had thought her incapable of. Most of Yvonne Story's conversational efforts went into quantity, not quality. The women at her table, who had been looking either annoyed or shell-shocked at the flow of words, were perking up at the interesting revelations.

"I understand the chief's wife was found dead. That doesn't mean that he had anything to do with it."

"Geraldine Bain at the post office told me right before I came over here. She said the chief's wife kicked him out of their house because he was having an affair."

"That doesn't mean—" Mrs. Marshall stopped herself from defending Russ Van Alstyne. Wind to fan the fire. "Geraldine Bain is one of the worst gossips in Millers Kill."

"But she's cousin to the Dandridge Bains, who live in Cossayuharie. Their daughter is married to a police officer."

"It's always the husband in cases like this," Yvonne's West hand said authoritatively.

South hand nodded. "I only met Linda Van Alstyne once or twice, but she seemed like a delightful woman. She hired a lot of local women for her business, you know. Women who needed the work."

"It'll be a shame if nothing ever comes of it." Mrs. Marshall's own North hand spoke up, loud enough for everyone to hear. "I figure the police department will take care of their own. Mark my words, there'll be a cover-up."

"There's nothing to cover up," Mrs. Marshall protested, but she was drowned out in a sea of voices, as everyone began speculating how and why the chief of police had killed his wife.

She had been wrong. Someone had to speak to Reverend Fergusson about this. The sooner, the better.

SEVENTEEN

The rector of St. Alban's had spent the rest of the afternoon avoiding her new deacon and her personal miseries. Wrung out from the morning's revelations and jittery after spotting Russ's deputy chief and one of his officers eyeing her as she left the station parking lot, she had—*sneaked* was such an ugly word; she preferred *entered with stealth*—at any rate, she made it into the church without being seen. A quick reconnoiter outside the hall confirmed that neither Lois nor Elizabeth de Groot was around. Clare dashed into her office and grabbed her appointment book and while-you-were-out memos. From the sacristy, she took her traveling kit: a plain leather box containing wafers, wine, clean linen, and the silver pieces used in celebrating the Eucharist. God-in-a-box, as she sometimes thought of it.

Suitably prepped, she set out to lose herself in the halls of the Washington County Hospital and the Infirmary. Father Lawrence had covered her duties as celebrant during the time she was off, but the hospital and old-age-home visits were a week overdue. In her car, she put in a quick call to the secretary, which she knew would be answered by the parish office's machine. "Lois, it's Clare. I'm going to be out for the afternoon"—she kept it vague, in case de Groot got the idea to tag along after her—"but you can reach me on my cell if it's an emergency. Please apologize to Deacon de Groot, and you can ask her to . . . to . . . help collate this month's newsletter." Then she felt guilty and added, "Show her the January and February schedules and see if she can sit in on some of the committee meetings. We want everyone to get the chance to know her."

Over the next few hours, visiting the sick and elderly in her care, she managed to forget, from time to time, the bishop's judgment hanging over her, her new watchdog-deacon, and her unease about being seen in Russ's company today of all days. It was impossible to think of herself when confronted with others' overwhelming needs. Gillian Gordounston, who had just moved from Albany to Millers Kill with her husband because she thought it would be a good place to raise children, only to wind up on bed rest with triplets, not knowing a soul except her doctor and the rector of the church they had attended exactly two times. Twelve-year-old Joseph van Eyk, whose kidneys had failed last year, hospitalized the third time for a post-transplant infection. Liz Garrettson's elderly mother, who went in and out of the emergency room while her daughter and son-in-law remained locked in battle over whether she should be moved to their house or institutionalized. Today she was weepy and confused, convinced that men were breaking into her home to kill her cats. Mrs. Oliver, her wit still Dorothy Parker–sharp at ninety, trapped in a body that could no longer stand or walk or even lift a cup to her lips without aid. Oh, yes. Always, in serving, Clare could forget herself.

But she could not forget Russ's pain, his poor murdered wife, or the guilt—equal parts sin and complicity—that clung to her like a wet dress. In the quiet moments, walking down institutional hallways where her own footsteps seemed to dog her, she prayed, comforting rote prayers she had always known by heart. Ave Maria and St. John Chrysostom's. The Magnificat and the prayer of St. Jerome. *Lord, thou hast sought me out and known me.*

Returning to the rectory at the end of the day, she drove through a darkness punctuated by still-shining Christmas lights and glowing windows framing families gathering around the dinner table. The pretty displays made her heart ache. They were like visions of a lost paradise to all the souls for whom there was no home, no welcoming arms, no happy endings. She was in a thoroughly melancholy mood when she pulled into the miniature parking space behind the church and saw that all the lights were still on.

She checked her watch. Six thirty. The Tuesday night AA meeting that took place in the parish hall didn't begin until seven thirty, and they never set up before seven. She got out of her Subaru, dread on one shoulder and curiosity on the other, and let herself in the kitchen door. She threaded her way through the shadowy undercroft and climbed the stairs. She heard a buzz of conversation from down the hall. She replaced her traveling kit in the sacristy and started toward the noise, which seemed to originate from the meeting room.

"There you are."

She whirled around. Geoffrey Burns, the junior warden, stalked down the hall toward her, a tall cardboard coffee cup in one hand. "We've been waiting for you to get back."

"We?"

He shrugged toward the chapter room, where committee meetings were held. "Terry McKellan called me. Told me about the situation. I suggested we get your input before we decide how to respond."

"Respond?" She knew she sounded like a feeble-minded parrot, but she couldn't get her head around which *situation* Geoff or Terry thought they needed to *respond* to.

"Linda Van Alstyne's death. Look, come on inside and sit down. You look like crap warmed over." Burns, a short, darkly intense man, wasn't exactly known for his charm, but Clare allowed him to usher her into the chapter room. Normally, the graceful space with its oak paneling and leaded windows soothed her. Normally, she didn't walk in there to be ambushed by Terry McKellan sitting at the large mahogany table with Mrs. Henry Marshall *and* Elizabeth de Groot. The new deacon looked at her reproachfully, as if she were a dog Clare had left alone too long.

"Elizabeth." Clare tried to keep her lack of enthusiasm from showing in her voice. "I didn't expect to see you this late. You must have a long ride home."

"I do," Elizabeth said, a touch of gentle censure in her tone. "But I hoped we'd have the chance to finish our talk. I was waiting in the church when Mrs. Marshall let herself in."

"Clare, you didn't tell us the bishop was sending us a deacon." Mrs. Marshall shook her head.

"I only just found out yesterday." She glanced from the elderly lady in toucan-pink lipstick and matching sweater to Terry McKellan, whose glossy brown mustache and habitual brown tweed jacket made him look like an overweight seal. "I wish you had called me if you were planning a meeting."

"I spoke with Lacey earlier today, but she decided to come over on her own," Terry said, rising from his seat as Clare sat down. "Glad we got here in time to meet Ms. de Groot, though."

"Please. Elizabeth."

Clare had the sensation of being a character in a bad Pirandello play. "What's going on?"

There was a sudden silence. The three vestry members looked at their new deacon. She met their gazes, smiling, until the penny dropped. "Ah," de Groot said. "Clare, I'll wait for you in your office." She rose smoothly from her chair and glided through the chapter room door.

"Nice woman," Terry McKellan said. "Seems very sensible." Although she was almost certain he didn't mean it as a jab, Clare found herself flushing.

"I'll ask again. What's with the surprise inspection?"

Geoff Burns plopped into the chair next to her. "Don't get your back up, Clare. All of us have heard the stories flying around town today about Linda Van Alstyne's death. Most of 'em revolve around why her husband shot her. And most of 'em cite you as a proximate cause."

"*Me?*" Then the rest of his statement caught up with her. "Russ? Killing his wife? That's . . ." Words failed the wrongness of the idea. "Ludicrous," she settled. Mrs. Marshall bobbed her head in agreement. Geoff Burns shrugged. "Geoff, he couldn't have done it. He wouldn't have. Not ever. Not for any reason."

"Clare, I do a lot of criminal work these days. My clients have one thing in common. They're all innocent." He sounded as if he were drinking cynicism instead of coffee.

Clare shoved against the table. "You better have a *situation* besides ignorant gossip, or I'm out of here."

"Please, dear." Mrs. Marshall rested one hand on Clare's arm. "I know this is hard for you. It doesn't seem like it, but we're here to help." Her face, every edge softened by seventy-seven winters, radiated concern.

"None of us like the gossip any more than you do," Terry McKellan said. "But it's already loose in the town. The issue is, what can we do to stop it and minimize the damage to your reputation."

"And to the church's." Clare didn't know why the words were bitter on her teeth. Since the November day two years ago when she had first passed through the great double doors of St. Alban's as its first female pastor, she had known that she was the public face of the church. Had known that she would always be under scrutiny, by those seeking a pattern for Christianity and by those wondering when she would screw up. She had tried to live up to her office. She had tried for two years of loneliness and isolation, with no one knowing who she really was except God and Russ Van Alstyne.

"I was thinking." Terry McKellan stroked his mustache. "There's that fellow you've been seeing down in New York."

"Hugh Parteger?"

"How serious are you two?"

Clare spread her hands. "We enjoy each other's company. I've been down to the city to visit him a few times, and he's come up here a few weekends."

"Nothing in the offing?"

"He's climbing the ladder at an international capitalizing firm. I'm making twenty thousand dollars a year in a dinky rural parish. There's a gap there."

"Oh." Terry's shoulder's sagged. "So . . . do you think he'd be willing to pretend to get engaged to you?"

All three of them stared at him.

"You want me to ask Hugh Parteger to be my beard?" Clare's voice cracked with incredulity.

"Terry, you sound as if you've been reading one of my Regency romances." Mrs. Marshall shook her head. "False engagement, indeed."

Geoffrey Burns was, for once, speechless.

"Well . . ." Terry's round cheeks reddened. "It may sound silly to you, but I bet it would work. What else are we going to do?"

"Ignore it," Clare said.

"A word into the right ear can work wonders." Mrs. Marshall deliberately touched her eye-scorchingly lipsticked mouth. "Pretty soon, everyone who's anyone knows the truth."

Geoff shook his head. "The story is a lot better than the truth. People want to hear about illicit sex and murder. No, I think we'll have to be ready with a credible threat of a defamation of character suit. This is a classic case of slander. Van Alstyne may have killed his wife, but he sure as hell didn't have an affair with our priest."

Clare didn't know whether to laugh or cry. Her defenders. "There is no illicit sex. There is no murder. There is no story." She got to her feet. "I'm not a dreamy-eyed girl in the throes of her first love. I knew I couldn't have Russ Van Alstyne. I made a choice. I chose my congregation and my position as your pastor. If you can't appreciate that and support me now when I need you, then to hell with you."

The meeting broke up very shortly afterward.

When Clare went out the open door of the chapter room and in the open door of her office, she discovered Elizabeth de Groot, sitting wide-eyed and well within earshot, waiting for her.

"I couldn't help but overhear—" de Groot began.

"Go home, Elizabeth." Clare sounded rude and didn't care. "I'm talked out for the night. Go home to whoever it is that loves you and thank God for your blessings. I'll see you tomorrow."

EIGHTEEN

Wednesday, January 16

Russ's third day as a widower started at bad and went to worse. He dragged himself down his mother's stairs—after taking twenty minutes to dress, stupidly holding up pieces of his uniform, trying to remember how they went—to find his mom and sister whispering furtively across the kitchen table. They both jumped up to hug and squeeze him, to rub his back and inquire how he was and how he had slept, and while he appreciated their heartfelt concern, he also knew they were trying to shield him from something.

"What's going on?" he asked.

His mother and Janet looked at each other.

"Mom?"

She turned to the coffeemaker on the counter. "Linda's sister's plane was delayed last night. Mike was in Albany for nine hours, waiting to pick her up."

Considering how reluctant his brother-in-law was to leave his dairy herd's milking to anyone else, this was a true sacrifice. Then the import of it struck him. The silence. The lack of we-have-a-guest bustle. "She didn't come here after I conked out, did she?"

His mother, dumping spoonfuls of sugar into his mug, shook her head.

"Is she at your place?" he asked Janet. "Oh, Christ, she didn't go to the house, did she?"

"No, no, no." Janet let out a breath, half sigh, half exasperation. "She's at the Queensbury Hotel in Glens Falls. She refused to stay with either of us. In fact, she wouldn't even let Mike take her to the hotel. She rented a car and drove herself."

"She drove herself? That's nuts. She's lived in Florida all her life. She can't drive for shit in the snow."

"Russell!" his mother warned.

"'Scuse my french, Mom. But Debbie shouldn't be on the roads up here in January." He turned back to Janet. "When did she decide not to stay with Mom?"

Janet's mouth twisted. "She had reservations when she got off the plane."

His mother snorted. "Too bad she didn't mention that before Mike wasted a day at the airport." She handed Russ his coffee. "Never mind. She's heartbroke and angry, and folks do foolish things when they're in that state." She tilted her head back to meet her son's eyes. "You remember that, Russell."

That was the bad. The worse was waiting for him when he arrived at the station. He hadn't even made it to his office when Harlene stopped him. "I got a message for you from the mayor. He wants to see you to meet with him and a few of the aldermen as soon as you set foot in the door."

Russ checked the clock. "I got the morning briefing in twenty minutes."

"I think you better do as he said, Chief." Harlene, who had been known to claim she could replace all seven members of the governing board and still do a better job, looked worried. "He sounded pretty urgent."

Russ turned around and stomped out of the station. He didn't have far to go; the Millers Kill town offices were just down the block. The original building, an overelaborate Italianate built during the boom times of the 1870s, had been torn down in an early-fifties improvement fit, when all things Victorian were anathema. It had been replaced with a then-cutting-edge cube faced with painted aluminum panels that had not worn well over a half century of harsh Adirondack weather. Every year it looked more and more like a giant child's building block that had been kicked around too much and left out in the rain.

Russ took the concrete steps two at a time. Inside, the furnace blast of heat steamed up his glasses and forced him to remove his coat and scarf. He went up the blurry stairs and into the secretary's empty office, where he wiped the condensation off his glasses with the tail of his shirt, retucked it, and strode into the mayor's room.

Jim Cameron was seated not at his modest desk but at the rectangular table that took up much of the room's space. With him were three of the six aldermen who ran the town board and a thirty-something woman Russ had never seen before. He had time to wonder if they had replaced the town's attorney before Jim rose, clasped his hand, and said, "Russ."

He sounded like he was speaking in a sepulchre. "I can't tell you how sorry I am to hear about your wife. I just can't imagine what you're going through. I know if I lost Lena, I'd just . . ." The whole time he spoke, Jim continued to pump Russ's hand up and down. "Anyway. I'm so sorry."

"Thanks," Russ ground out.

Jim released him. "You know Garry Greuling." The retired teacher, his scalp tanned from his annual trip to Florida, rose and shook Russ's hand with a brief condolence. "And Ron Tucker." Ron ran the best garage in town, and when he leaned across the table to shake hands a faint smell of oil and gasoline followed him. "This is Emiley Jensen." The unfamiliar woman nodded to him. "And you know Bob Miles." Miles, a public works engineer for the county, was the only one in the room, besides the strange woman, wearing a suit. Their tastes were very different, though. Bob's ran to expensive and conservative. Her pink tweed jacket was trendy but cheap. The sort of thing Linda used to call—

He sat down.

Jim Cameron took the seat at the head of the table. "Russ, we wanted to talk with you this morning because we're concerned about you investigating Linda's death." He spread his hands on the table, revealing hairy forearms. The mayor habitually worked with his shirtsleeves rolled up, as if he were about to wrestle the problems of government to the ground at any moment. "It's a hell of a time for you personally. You ought to be at home with your family, processing your loss and dealing with your grief."

"I appreciate your concern. But right now, the only thing I want to process is the perpetrator's county lock-up papers."

Cameron glanced toward Garry Greuling. Russ remembered him from high school, when he had been the super-cool science teacher who grew sideburns down to his jaw and assigned *Star Trek* as homework. "Russ," he said, "as I recall, the department regulations say any officer who's undergone a traumatic experience gets a minimum one-week suspension with pay."

"They're supposed to seek counseling, too," Bob Miles added.

"That's for an on-the-job event, like a shooting," Russ said.

"Shooting a criminal is more traumatic than having your wife killed?" Miles sounded incredulous.

"Dammit, can we not tippy-toe around why we're here?" Ron Tucker had a surprisingly soft voice for a man of his size. "Russ, everybody in town's flapping their gums over this thing, and half of them are sayin' you had a hand in it."

"What?" He had once taken a bullet to the chest. The body armor he had been wearing saved his life, but the force of the impact, smashing the air out of his lungs, hammering him to the ground, had convinced him he was dying. That was how he felt now.

"Easy on," Tucker said. "We all know it's a load of horsepuckies. But it sure in't gonna help your investigation any. We gotta deal with this"—he looked for the first time at the woman, who had been sitting calmly throughout the discussion—"conflict of interest."

"Is she a lawyer?" Russ was surprised to find he still had a voice. "Does this have something to do with the town's liability? You're worried someone's going to sue you if I'm not shunted off to the sidelines?"

"Slow down, Russ." The mayor spoke quietly. "This is *Investigator* Jensen from the state Bureau of Criminal Investigation." She tilted her head in acknowledgement. "I spoke with Captain Ireland of Troop F last night, and he told me Investigator Jensen was the woman we wanted."

Russ looked at him, incredulous. "Wanted for what?" He glanced at Jensen. "No offense, detective, but I was working homicides while you were still learning to tie your shoes. I was born and bred here, I've headed up this department for seven years, and I know half of Millers Kill by name and the other half by reputation. What can you possibly bring to this investigation?"

She held up one manicured finger. "Objectivity." A second. "The ability to function, not as your coworker or friend, but as an impartial observer." A third finger. "Another trained investigator for an eight-man department that must be strained to the breaking point by this crime."

"We can handle a murder investigation."

"I didn't mean strained to the breaking point because of the demands of the case. I meant psychologically. Emotionally." She leaned forward, spidering her hands on the table. "Chief Van Alstyne, I guarantee you, every officer in your department is walking around with the same nasty thought in the back of his head: Could it happen to me? Is someone I love going to die next?"

He cleared his throat. "There's no evidence we're dealing with some sort of pattern."

She shook her head. "Doesn't matter. It's what's here"—she tapped her heart—"and not here." She tapped her head.

"Russ, the decision's been made." Jim Cameron didn't look happy, but Russ knew that wouldn't stop him from doing what he thought was right. "You and the department need the support, and the public needs to know that there's someone on the case who isn't involved personally. I want you to take Investigator Jensen back to the station and put her experience to good use." He stood up. The rest of them followed suit. "We all want the same thing. We want the person responsible for this atrocity behind bars."

"Or strapped to the gurney in Clinton," Eddie Palmer mumbled.

Russ stood to one side. "Get your coat and your things," he said to Jensen. "I'll walk you over to the station."

She tripped past him in high heels. He hoped she'd brought something more sensible, or her feet'd be frostbit by nightfall. The aldermen trailed her through the door. The mayor would have followed, but Russ stopped him with a hand on his arm.

"I just want to get one thing straight. Was it the gossip that decided you to call Captain Ireland at Troop F? Or did the board put you up to it?"

Cameron looked surprised. "I didn't call Ireland," he said. "He called me."

NINETEEN

S
he did have boots. In the time it took for Russ to get the mayor's two-by-four between the eyes—*I didn't call Ireland. He called me*—she had changed into mukluks and was zipping up a midsized duffle. "This way," he said, jerking his head. He didn't register leaving the town hall and walking to the station. All his attention was inward, trying to construct some Rube Goldberg logic machine that would enable him to believe the staties hadn't been tipped off by someone in the Millers Kill Police Department.

He couldn't do it.

They had been keeping a near-blackout in the press. The *Post-Star* reported the MKPD was investigating "a suspicious death," a semifiction they carried off because the department, with MacAuley as its affable spokesman, was usually transparent to the local media. It might have become an item of gossip around town, but what civilian would know to call the state police and get them involved? One of the aldermen? But no, Jim Cameron would have said something.

It had to have been one of his own.

"Hey, you're back."

Russ blinked. He was startled to find himself standing in front of Harlene, who was staring at Jensen with open curiosity.

"Uh," he said. "Harlene, this is Investigator Jensen. She's here from the Troop F BCI to help us with the investigation. This is our dispatcher, Harlene Lendrum." He didn't quite turn toward Jensen.

"Chief? That you?" Mark Durkee strode into the dispatch area, his hands full of manila files.

"What are you doing here?" Russ asked.

Mark stared at Jensen stripping off her wool coat, then at Russ. "I got put— I'm on day duty now, remember?"

He didn't, but that was fine. Mark was the perfect person to unload his unwelcome guest on. "This is Investigator Jensen of the New York State BCI," he said. "She's going to be joining us for the investigation." Durkee's eyes widened. "Show her the file and get her up to date on everything." He spun on his heel and disappeared behind his closed office door before either of them could reply.

He needed more information. Who could he call? He leaned against one of the window frames, watching the traffic crawl down Main Street. The plows had shoved the remains of Sunday's storm off the road, but the parking spots on either side were still clotted with snow. Trucks and SUVs that forced their way into the compacted mess stuck out into the roadway, narrowing the thoroughfare into a single lane at spots. He would have to call in Duane and Tim, the part-time officers, to hand out a few tickets and get the TEMPORARILY CLOSED TO PARKING signs up.

Nathan Bougeron. Of course. He had been a talented young officer when Russ took over the MKPD seven years ago. Too talented—within two years he had been wooed away by the staties. He was in Lafayette now, in plainclothes. Russ dropped into his chair and riffled through his Rolodex. He punched the number in.

"Investigator Bougeron."

"Nathan, it's Russ Van Alstyne."

"Hey, Chief! Good to hear from you. How's it going?"

The commonplace nicety threatened to swallow Russ whole.

"Chief?"

He decided to skip over the end of his life as he knew it. "I've got a situation here, and I was hoping you could give me some information."

"If I can. What's up?"

"We've been assigned an investigator from the Troop F BCI. Name's Jensen. She's young, about your age—"

Bougeron snorted in amusement. "I'm thirty-two, Chief. I don't know if that qualifies as young."

"Trust me, when you're fifty, it does. Anyway, do you know anything about her?"

"She doesn't sound familiar. What's her first name?"

"Uh . . . I don't know. We haven't gotten that informal yet."

"Doesn't matter. There can't be too many Jensens working out of Middletown. Let me make a few calls, and I'll get back to you."

Russ thanked his former officer and hung up. As soon as his line was free, Harlene buzzed him. "Are you gonna give the morning briefing now?"

"No," he said. "I'm waiting for a callback. I'll round up everybody as soon as I'm finished."

"Sure thing, Chief. I'll let the guys know not to disturb you."

He hated the way people talked to him now. Four days ago, if he had told Harlene he was postponing the morning briefing, she would have made a crack about him getting lazy in his old age. It was if he had found himself in a foreign country, surrounded by natives who spoke at him very . . . slowly . . . and . . . clearly so he might understand.

"Wait," he said. "Is Lyle here yet?"

"Yeah."

"Will you ask him to come in?"

"Sure thing."

The door opened within seconds, leading Russ to guess that not only had Lyle been in the building, he had been standing next to Harlene asking her about the morning's events. The deputy chief strolled in and took one of the chairs, relocating a few file folders onto the floor. He tipped back on the rear legs, balancing himself on the toes of his boots.

"You meet this investigator from the BCI yet?"

If Lyle was surprised at Russ's brusqueness, he didn't show it. "Yep. Mark introduced us. She's in the squad room right now, going over the initial reports and the autopsy."

"Did you call the BCI in on the case?"

"What?" Lyle lurched forward as the chair crashed onto all four legs. "Hell, no! I've been trying to keep the lid on this thing since it happened. Why the hell would I invite the staties in?"

Russ pinched the bridge of his nose. "You've been encouraging me to stay home and back off of the investigation. I thought maybe—"

"You thought wrong, as the saying goes."

"Sorry." Russ sighed. "But the only thing I can figure is that one of us blew the whistle. I mean, I'm not being irrational, right? I ought to welcome any and all help to bring in this guy, I know that, but Jesus Christ, the thought of one of my own guys calling down the staties . . ."

The phone rang. Russ snatched it up. "Van Alstyne here," he said, motioning Lyle to sit back down in his chair.

"Hey, chief, it's Nathan Bougeron."

"That was fast. Whattaya got for me?"

"It was fast because your girl has made herself well known. Her name's Emiley, Emiley-with-an-extra-*e*, by the way."

"An extra *e*?"

"I think it stands for energetic. She's been with the force for ten years now, at BCI for six. The guy I spoke to said she's poised to become a senior investigator, if she wants the job."

"Senior investigator? After six years? That's unbelievable. Why wouldn't she want it?"

Across the desk from him, Lyle was raising his bushy gray eyebrows.

"My guy says she's got her eye on politics. She has a master's in psych, and she's working on a law degree. The word is, when she finishes, she'll jump ship to some district attorney's office downstate."

"Huh. Well, she wouldn't be the first to use the DA's office as a launching pad. Does this mean that I can expect her to spend all of her time with her nose in a law book?"

"Nunh-unh. She's a tough cookie, according to my guy. Very, very focused. Here's the kicker: She put in a couple of years in Violent Crimes, and then moved to Homicide for a couple more, but last year she was reassigned—my guy didn't know, but he thinks she asked for the job—to the Ex squad."

"The what?"

"Oh, sorry. That's our nickname for it. The External Law Enforcement Investigation squad. The guys who work with DAs and county prosecutors to take down dirty cops in departments where they don't have an internal affairs division."

Or where the IA department was corrupt as well. "Okay," he said. "Yeah. I just never heard the nickname." The Ex squad. Christ on a bicycle. What had the mayor said? *You and the department need support.* Yeah.

"So I'm wondering, what's going on up there? I can't believe you've got a rotten officer."

Russ cleared his throat. "She's helping us with a homicide."

"Really? Huh. Maybe my guy got his info messed up."

No. He didn't.

"Thanks for taking a look for me, Nathan. I appreciate it."

"Anytime, Chief. You let me know if I can do anything else for you. And say hi to all the guys."

"I will. Thanks." After he hung up he said, "Nathan says hi."

"Talk's cheap. Let him drive over here and buy me a drink." Lyle leaned forward onto Russ's desk, propping his elbows on a broadsheet from the department's HMO and a smear of opened envelopes. "What about Jensen?"

"She's bright, ambitious, and evidently on her way to becoming the first female governor of New York, after a brilliant career in law enforcement and a successful stint as an ADA."

"Yeah? Then what's she doing sitting in our squad room, drinking Harlene's day-old coffee?"

"Since she made investigator six years ago, she's worked VCAP, Homicide, and the External Law Enforcement Investigation squad."

Lyle grew very still. Then he shook his head. "That doesn't make sense. If she's all smoked to work for the DA's office, she's going to need to stay in tight with the rest of us out here humping our tails to catch the bad guys."

"Unless she wants to be able to tell the good people of New York how she brought down a crooked chief of police and the department he had in his back pocket." He rolled his chair back. "Somebody in our department thinks I murdered my wife."

Lyle shook his head again. "No."

"You were the one who pointed out that I was a logical suspect."

"Yeah, but I was just trying to get you to see—"

"Doesn't matter. Jensen is going to tap me as a suspect." He got up and paced across the floor. "It's what I'd do if I were walking into this investigation. Hell, Lyle, it's what you'd do if you and I weren't friends." He looked out the window. Same snow, same shoppers, same SUVs. "Let's say you're Jensen. Your boss at BCI has sent you out here because he believes I've killed my wife and I'm using the department to cover it up. You go over the records of the evidence so far. Do you find anything to rule that theory out?"

"No."

"Hell, no. I've got no alibi for the time when the murder occurred. In fact, time of death was muddled because Meg Tracey left the door open and you guys never closed it."

Lyle dropped his gaze and mumbled something.

"I'm not blaming you, Lyle. Linda was your friend, too. Everybody was shook up that evening. But to Jensen, it's going to look like collusion. Now, add in the fact that my missing knife could be the murder weapon and e-mails on my wife's computer suggest that she was seeing someone else when she died. You're Jensen, with the mayor and the aldermen and the power of the BCI behind you. What are you going to do?"

"Put you on leave. Immediately, if I can."

"She can. You should have heard the aldermen at the surprise meeting this morning. They were dropping fifty-pound hints that I take a week off."

"It's times like these that being an elected sheriff would come in handy. No town board waiting in the wings to hand you a pink slip."

"Huh. So you boot the chief. But you're also worried about the deputy chief, because he's your suspect's right-hand man. You can't suspend him, though, because you need someone who can run the police department while you're working the homicide."

Lyle's mouth twisted in a sort of smile. "If she knew anything, she'd put Harlene in charge."

"You can bet Jensen thinks Harlene's a gossipy old broad who should have been retired years ago. What do you do?"

Lyle sighed. "I isolate him. Take him off the case and route all the investigation reports directly through me."

"Okay. So you and I can figure out which direction she's going to take the investigation in. Here's the tricky part: What's she going to do in the next hour? And what does she think I'm going to do?"

"What are you going to do?"

"I don't know yet. I figure I have three options. I could go back to my mom's place, crawl into bed, and not come out again until spring or an indictment, whichever comes first. Or I could figure out some way to sidestep her, so that I can keep on with the investigation. I'm worried that if she likes me as the perp, she won't pay enough attention to the other evidence lying around." He paused. The light was changing outside. A little more white, a little less bright. As if ice were sheeting over the sky. More snow coming.

"What's the third option?"

"I could eat my gun."

"Don't joke about that." Lyle's mobile face was dead serious.

Russ flipped his hand to show it was open. "Sorry."

"I think she'll assume you're going to go head to head with her," Lyle said, dragging the conversation back to Russ's question. "Once she pegs you as the prime suspect, she's got to assume you're going to be busy covering your ass with both hands. Maybe by hauling her back out to the mayor's office for a showdown while the rest of us trash the files. Or manufacture some new evidence implicating somebody else."

Russ thought for a few seconds, then pushed away from the window frame. "I want you to do two things for me."

"Okay . . ." Lyle's voice was tentative. "What?"

"I want you to get me the registration info for the license number of the car the Tracey kid saw at my house. But before that, I want you to have an accident in the squad room."

"A what?"

"Carry in some coffee or one of Harlene's strudels and drop it all over the floor. Make it big and messy and make sure everybody's paying attention to you."

"And in the meantime, you will be doing what, exactly?"

"Getting out of Dodge." He could see the question taking shape in his deputy chief's mind. "It'll be better if you don't know anything else. Plausible deniability and all that. When you've got the car owner's info, leave me a message on my cell phone."

"Leave you a message."

"I'm getting on in years. I may forget to turn it on."

"Uh-huh." Lyle levered himself out of his chair. "We got fifty-odd years of law enforcement experience between us, and here we are, plotting like a couple of junior-grade James Bond wannabes." He grinned up one side of his mouth. "I like that." He stuck out his hand. "Good luck, Russ."

He left his office door open after Lyle left and listened as his deputy chief loudly asked Harlene if there was "anything good" in the kitchen. Of course there would be, since Harlene baked compulsively during the winter months and brought the resulting sugar bombs in to work so that her husband, Harold, fighting the onset of Type II diabetes, wouldn't fall to temptation.

Russ put his coat on and wrapped his old tartan scarf around his throat.

He heard Harlene asking, "You want me to help you with any of that?" and Lyle refusing.

Russ shoved his gloves into his coat pocket. Looked around the office. Was there anything he had to take with him?

The clatter and clash from the squad room startled even him. He heard Harlene's chair squeak, roll, and thud into her file cabinet. He glanced through his doorway in time to see her disappearing in the direction of the noise, which now consisted of loud swearing, shouts from someone whose uniform had been wrecked, and Kevin Flynn laughing hysterically.

He stepped out into the dispatch room, closed his door behind him, and, unnoticed and unheard, left the building.

TWENTY

Driving away from the station house in his red pickup, Russ could have felt guilt, or anger, or panic. He guessed any of those would have been more appropriate than the almost giddy sense of escape that filled him. Maybe, after all those years of the straight and narrow, walking on the wrong side of the law had a certain wild appeal. That would explain a lot about his relationship with Clare.

Thinking of her dampened his spirits, and the first left that led him out of town and toward his house extinguished them. His house. The thought of going back there yet another time nauseated him. He was going to have to sell it. Or better yet, burn it. Make it a pyre for his marriage. Slain jointly by a stranger's knife and his own infidelity.

He drove through the outskirts of town, into the farmland that rolled higher and higher out of the east, until it crashed against the mountains in the west. The sky was thicker now, the ice-pale cloud cover turning leaden. He realized he hadn't listened to the news or caught a weather report in three days. He switched on the talk-radio station in time to catch the 9:00 A.M. highlights. War, a helicopter crash in Afghanistan, terrorist cells in the U.S., and a record-breaking deficit. New England was celebrating the Patriots making it to the Super Bowl. The North Country could expect a slowly developing storm to drop another four to six inches of snow within the next twenty-four hours.

The rousing music of the Dr. Adele show swelled behind the psychologist's voice, telling him today's show was for all those women who couldn't enjoy sex because they were self-conscious about their bodies.

Christ. He snapped the radio off. If he hadn't been depressed before, that would have done it for him.

The Peekskill Road was empty of traffic. Empty of all signs of life around the widely spaced farmhouses, save for the threads of smoke rising from every chimney except his. And the folks who lived to his left, the Andersons. He frowned. Had something happened to the elderly—no. It was all right. They were away in Arizona.

Good enough. He didn't want any witnesses if Investigator Jensen came around asking questions.

He powered up his driveway and parked in front of the barn door. He got out, hauled it wide open, and, getting back behind the wheel, inched his truck into its space next to Linda's wagon.

He grabbed his soft-sided CD holder and squeezed out the driver's side, reflexively careful not to scratch the Volvo, and rumbled the big door shut along its track. He paused at the hard-packed walk to the kitchen and went instead to the front of the house. Wading through more snow was a small price to pay not to have to step into the room where his wife had—

He forced his attention to unlocking the door. Inside, the air was so cold he could see his breath. Either one of the responders had turned the thermostat off, or they had run out of oil. There was a pronounced smell of cat, and he remembered Eric McCrea telling him about his wife's new pet, and how it had been stuck inside after she had been—

He realized the damn cat was probably a witness to the murder. Not that that was going to do him any good.

He strode toward Linda's tiny office, looking as little as possible to the left or right. He dropped into the desk chair and pushed the computer's on button, hoping that the cold wouldn't affect the machine. It slowly blinked into readiness, and he turned to a stack of blank CDs she kept at hand. He loaded one into the disk drive, opened the hard-drive menu, and started copying.

E-mail, Word documents, spreadsheets, photos. Not knowing what might yield something useful, he copied it all. Browser, Web sites, fax program, music player. He went through three CDs, then four. While the computer burned data, he riffled through Linda's paperwork again, looking for anything out of the ordinary, anything that would point to one direction or another.

A notice popped up on the screen. DISK FULL. PLEASE INSERT AN-OTHER DISK AND PRESS CONTINUE. He released the CD drive, scooped out the disk, and replaced it with an empty one.

The phone rang.

He froze. In the silence between rings, the disk drive clicked smoothly into place.

CONTINUE COPYING? The computer asked him.

He fished his cell phone out of his pocket and thumbed it on. The house line rang again. His cell displayed its service logo. The house line rang again. The cell's signal and battery indicators ramped up. The house phone rang again. The cell phone beeped loudly. Its screen read 2 MISSED CALLS. He thumbed the selection button. The screen displayed the numbers he had missed. Both were from the station.

The answering machine picked up, and he heard his own voice asking the caller to leave a name and number.

"This is Investigator Jensen of the BCI, looking for Russ Van Alstyne. Chief Van Alstyne, if you get this message, it's very important that you contact me. I need to meet with you as soon as possible to discuss the direction of the case. Please call me at the station or on my cell phone at 518-555-1493."

He released a breath he hadn't realized he was holding. She worked fast.

He pressed the CONTINUE button on the screen. One more disk, and then he was gone. If he were Jensen, he'd be sending out squad cars to try to pick him up at the most likely locations. His house, Mom's house, Janet's farm. All addresses readily available from his personnel file.

Unzipping the CD holder, he considered his options. He could blow town completely, find an Internet café in Saratoga and go over the files. Of course, if she put an APB out on him, that might not work so well. A public place was risky. He needed somewhere where he couldn't be brought in or disturbed un-til after he'd had a chance to sift though the megabytes of information he'd taken from Linda's computer. He needed a sanctuary.

DISK FULL. PLEASE INSERT ANOTHER DISK AND PRESS CON-TINUE.

No time to download any more. He would have to hope he had gotten what he needed. He removed the disk, hit the CANCEL button, and directed the computer to shut itself off.

Sanctuary. What better place than a church?

TWENTY-ONE

Clare knew she was in trouble when attendance at the 7:30 A.M. Wednesday Eucharist doubled. Admittedly, only fourteen people showed up, but that was seven more than the usual group: one businessman on his way to work in Saratoga, one young mother who couldn't make it on Sundays, and five retirees who had never warmed up to the modernized 1979 version of the Book of Common Prayer.

Clare didn't even recognize some of the people in the pews. That worried her. On the other hand, Elizabeth de Groot wasn't among them. Praise God.

Nathan Andernach, who was assisting her, finished the intercessions and glanced at her. She stepped forward. "Ye who do earnestly repent you of your sins," she said, "and are in love and charity with your neighbors, and intend to lead a new life, following the commandments of God, and walking henceforth in His holy ways; Draw near with faith, and take this holy Sacrament to your comfort; and make your humble confession to Almighty God, devoutly kneeling."

The three people she didn't know remained awkwardly standing for an extra beat as everyone else knelt. Clare waited for a moment to begin the General Confession.

"Almighty God," she said, and the others' voices chimed in, "Father of our Lord Jesus Christ, Maker of all things, Judge of all men; We acknowledge and bewail our manifold sins and wickedness . . ." For all that Clare preferred the simpler constructions and the more gender-neutral language of the modern

Eucharist, she had always thought the Confession fell flat. "We are truly sorry and we humbly repent" sounded like an apology to a meter maid. The old Confession was written by men who knew what it felt like to have done bad things: "We do earnestly repent, and are heartily sorry for these our misdoings; The remembrance of them is grievous unto us; The burden of them is intolerable."

Indeed.

She pronounced absolution, focusing hard on the words to block out the voice in the back of her head that suggested she was hardly fit to be forgiving anyone's sins. She gratefully lost herself in the ritual of the holy Eucharist: washing her hands and girding herself with a blessing; the white linen and the red book. Here, she never felt the sting of unworthiness. This was God's miracle, not hers.

Andernach, whose thin chest concealed a bell-like baritone, led them in their communion hymn. It was low-pitched and easy to sing, the tune a melancholy French carol from the seventeenth century. Clare, at the altar, did not sing but stood, head bowed, and listened to the grimly mystical text.

"Let all mortal flesh keep silence,
And with fear and trembling stand;
Ponder nothing earthly-minded,
For with blessing in his hand
Christ our God to earth descendeth,
Our full homage to demand."

Ten people came up to receive communion. Three did not. She and Nathan wrapped the service up quickly. She hadn't told him yet that Elizabeth de Groot expected to take over his liturgical functions. Nathan had the fussy precision of a lifelong bachelor, but he was dedicated to his work at St. Alban's, and she suspected it was one of the anchors of his life.

She greeted people beside the narthex door, sheltered somewhat from the cold that billowed in whenever the great outer doors were opened. Her young mother and businessman dashed by with a hurried hello as always, but the retirees clustered around her, eyes shining with interest, to ask how she was. The new people hung at the edges, clearly dying to hear some juicy revelation but too bashful or well-mannered to come right out and ask her if her affair with the chief of police caused him to shoot his wife. Clare stuck resolutely to the weather and the upcoming spaghetti dinner fund-raiser, which, she realized, was probably going to be very well attended this month.

Eventually, the retirees and the curiosity-seekers trickled out. A man about her own age had been dawdling along the south aisle, looking at the stained glass windows. He wore a heavy-duty parka over a coat and brightly striped shirt, and his loosely knotted tie had a picture of Snoopy on it. Not a lawyer, that was for sure.

"Great place you have here," he said.

"Thanks."

"When was it built?"

"Right around the Civil War. You'll notice that the dedication names on that window you're looking at have several death dates in the 1860s."

"Who's the Roman soldier with the halo?"

"That's St. Alban, our patron. He was a centurion stationed in Britannia when he became a Christian. Legend has it, when the priest who converted him was sentenced to death, Alban switched clothes with him and died in his place."

"So. A soldier disguised as a priest." He looked at her. "I hear that describes you."

"Ex-soldier. I used to fly helicopters, but that was a long time ago." She smiled easily. "You doing a story on the church?"

He grinned. "Am I that obvious?" He held out his hand. "Ben Beagle, from the *Post-Star.*"

"Well, you have this slightly rumpled, *Front Page* kind of look going on." She shook his hand, all the while thinking, *Crap! What do I say? What do I do?* She didn't think that a word in the right ear, as Mrs. Marshall suggested, was going to do much good. On the other hand, looking at the reporter's cheerful, intelligent face, she knew she couldn't threaten him with a suit for slander. Or libel. Whatever.

Then his name registered. There couldn't be more than one Ben Beagle. "You do investigative stuff for the *Post-Star,* right? Didn't you win an award?"

He nodded, his cheeks pinkening. "Believe me, most of the day-to-day stuff is much less sexy. A few weeks ago the biggest story I had was a part-time farmer who lost a pig to somebody who decided to help himself to a Christmas ham right there in the sty."

She blinked. Every once in a while, she got a visceral reminder of exactly how rural her parish was. "I see your point. I guess Woodward and Bernstein didn't get to investigate many hog butcherings."

He laughed. "No." He pulled a small notebook out of his pocket and flipped it open. "I'm working on something much more significant this week. The death of Linda Van Alstyne. You've heard that she was killed." It was not a question.

"A terrible tragedy." How had he known? She didn't think the murder victim's identity had been released to the press yet.

Beagle was evidently a mind reader, because he tilted his head toward the other side of the church, where a woman sat hard against the stone of the north wall. "I was contacted by Debbie Wolecski, Mrs. Van Alstyne's sister."

Clare had crashed a helo once. She had walked away from it—barely—but she had never forgotten the anxious accumulation of problems, blossoming into the realization that she was screwed. She had that same feeling now.

"I don't know if I can help you," she said. "I only met Mrs. Van Alstyne a couple of times."

"But you do know her husband."

She decided to brazen it out. "Of course. Russ and I are good friends. We have lunch together almost every Wednesday at the Kreemy Kakes Diner, barring urgent police business or pastoral emergencies."

"According to Mrs. Van Alstyne's sister, you two were more than just good friends."

Clare forced a small smile. "We live in a small town, and there are always people who are going to find it impossible to believe a man and a woman can be friends." Lacking pockets in her alb, she slid her hands inside her sleeves and clenched her forearms. Her flesh was icy. "The chief of police and I have a lot of professional interests in common. We're both trying to serve the well-being of the people of Millers Kill."

"So . . . does the chief also have regular meetings with the Presbyterian and Baptist ministers?"

"Uh . . . I really don't know," she answered truthfully.

"You know that two weeks before she died, Linda Van Alstyne asked her husband to leave their marital home."

Clare nodded.

"According to Debbie Wolecski, that was because Russ Van Alstyne told his wife that he was having an affair with you."

Clare closed her eyes for a moment. "Mr. Beagle—"

"Call me Ben," he said cheerfully.

"Ben. I don't know exactly what the chief said to his wife before or after their decision to separate, but I'm dead sure it wasn't that we were having an affair. May I suggest that thirdhand quotes from a grief-stricken family member who was speaking to a woman struggling through a crisis point in her twenty-year marriage might not be the most reliable information in the world?"

"So, you're saying you and Russ Van Alstyne weren't involved in a relationship?"

God, she hated this. If she told the truth, she'd be throwing Russ to the wolves, and if she sidled around it, she'd be painting Linda Van Alstyne as a jealous, paranoid woman.

That was it. She could tell the truth about not being able to tell the truth.

"Anything I say at this point is going to reflect badly on Mrs. Van Alstyne and probably cause pain to her sister. I'm not going to do that."

He nodded. "How long have you been here at St. Alban's?"

"Uh." She thought he'd keep pressing her about Russ. His switch to another topic threw her. "A little over two years."

"Where were you before this?"

She snorted. "At seminary. And before that, in the army."

He grinned. "Interesting career choice."

"It kind of chose me."

"Hah. Right. Well, thanks for talking with me." From the depths of his parka, a cell phone began to ring. "If I have any other questions, I'll call you."

I'll make sure I'm out, she thought. Beagle checked the number and half-turned away from her to take the call.

She headed up the aisle toward the sacristy, eager to shed her alb and stole and get into her office, where there was at least an occasional wheeze of hot air from the vent. Something tickled in the back of her mind, something off, but it wasn't until she was stripping the alb over her head that she realized: The woman who had been sitting near the north wall had disappeared. There was no way she could have gotten past Clare at the main entrance, which meant that she had to be back in the offices or in the parish hall.

Maybe Linda Van Alstyne's sister had to use the ladies' room before leaving.

Maybe the archbishop of Canterbury was going to come through the door to congratulate her on a job well done. Clare hung up the long white robe, checked herself in the sacristy mirror—hair still up in its usual knot, blouse buttons done up around her clerical collar, no obvious lint clinging to her long black skirt—and strode down the hall toward her office.

She didn't make it very far. Debbie Wolecski stood in the doorway, arms crossed, glaring at Clare. Linda Van Alstyne had been a beautiful woman, and her sister had traces of her looks in her large blue eyes and her delicate bone structure. But Debbie Wolecski's features had been dried to hardtack by a life-time of Florida sun, and the roundness that had softened her sister had been ruthlessly banished. Clare could see Wolecski's collarbones slicing across the neckline of her skimpy sweater.

"I want to talk to you," the woman said.

"All right." Clare gestured toward the door. "Do you want to come into—"

"My sister would be alive right now if it weren't for you."

Clare gaped.

"You ran around with her husband, and filled his head with lies about Linda, and then when push came to shove you gave him an ultimatum, didn't you? You told him it was you or her."

Clare meant her response to be a measured *I'm so sorry about your loss.* Instead, she blurted out, "That's not true!"

"You must have brass balls to get up in front of a church and pretend to be all holy. You're nothing but a cheap tramp home wrecker. You wanted my dear brother-in-law? Well, now you got him. Did you know he was a boozer? He used to drink himself into a stupor every night. And when he wasn't drinking, he was off on deployment or on a case. Did he tell you that my sister had three miscarriages and he wasn't there for a one of them?"

Clare went pale.

"Didn't get into that during your romantic interludes, did he? Bet he didn't tell you he left the army because he had a fucking breakdown and nearly got his whole platoon blown up, did he? Or that he dragged my sister back to this god-forsaken hole because he was such a mama's boy he couldn't cut a real job in Phoenix?"

It was like being battered by a howling wind, her breath snatched away, her eyes tearing.

"What did you get? Flowers? Fancy dinners? Dirty weekends at expensive hotels? You know who bought that? My sister! Every penny he has comes from her, her work, what she got from our parents. I'll see you in hell before I let ei-ther one of you touch it. In fact"—she stepped forward, jabbing a shiny acrylic nail at Clare's chest—"I'm going to see to it that everyone knows what a slut you are. We'll see who wants to come to your church once they hear—"

"Shut up, Debbie."

Clare blinked. Russ stood in the doorway to the parish hall, his hands jammed so tightly into his parka pockets that she could see the outline of every knuckle.

His sister-in-law sucked in her breath. "My God, it is true," she said. "Linda isn't even in the ground yet and you can't keep away from your girlfriend."

Russ's boots sounded heavy as he walked up the hallway. "You don't know what the hell you're talking about." He opened his mouth, then closed it again. "I'm going to cut you some slack because you're angry and upset."

"Angry? Upset?" Debbie stared at him, loathing written across her heavily made-up features. "You bastard. I'm going to see you strung up by the nuts for what you did to my sister."

"You can do what you want after I've caught whoever killed her. I don't care." Russ stepped toward her. In the narrow confines of the hall, he seemed to loom even larger than usual. "You got that? I don't care." His glance flickered toward Clare, so briefly she wasn't sure she hadn't imagined it. "I've already lost everything. You want to hang me up by the balls? Fine. I'll hand you the rope. But first, tell me who Mr. Sandman is."

What the hell?

"How did you know about that?" Debbie asked. "That's private! Have you been reading her private mail?"

"This is a goddam murder case, Debbie. There isn't a single detail of Linda's life that's going to remain private by the time this thing is through. Who was she seeing? Tell me!"

Clare was utterly lost.

"I don't know!" For the first time, Debbie sounded more defensive than angry.

"Was it the same guy she was seeing after we moved back to Millers Kill?"

Clare should have enjoyed the about-face as Debbie gasped and went pale beneath her tan, but she just felt sick. Sick for Russ, and for Linda's sister, and for everyone who was going to be hurt by the corrosive secrets splashing out into the open.

"Hey, guys." There was a faint creak as the door to the church swung open. "What's going on?" Ben Beagle ambled down the hall, his eyes bright. "Chief Van Alstyne?"

"Who's he?" Russ growled.

Clare resisted clamping a hand over her eyes. This was getting to be like a bad French farce. "Ben Beagle," she said. "*Post-Star.*"

"I'm very sorry about your loss, Chief." Beagle fished his notepad out of his pocket. "If you have a moment, I'd like to ask you a few questions."

"No."

Russ's expression would have sent most people scurrying for cover. Beagle smiled gently. "What brings you to St. Alban's this morning?"

There was a pause. Russ's gaze darted between Clare and his sister-in-law. "I was looking for Debbie," he said.

Beagle's sandy brows went up. "You knew she was here?"

"I'm here as part of an ongoing murder investigation," Russ said. He sounded as if he were chewing on rocks and spitting out gravel. "I'm not making a statement to the press."

"Ben." Debbie's voice was thin. "Please. Will you excuse us for just a moment?"

"You know, if I'm going to tell your sister's story, I'm going to need to talk with Chief Van Alstyne."

"This doesn't have anything to do with that. Please, Ben."

For the first time since Debbie lit into her, Clare felt sorry for the woman. Her voice shook, and Clare realized that beneath the vitriol and bravado, Linda's sister was a hairsbreadth away from completely losing it.

"O-kay. If that's the way you want it." The reporter snapped his notebook shut. "I'll wait for you out by the cars."

Debbie nodded. The three of them watched in silence while Ben Beagle disappeared back through the church door. As soon as it swung shut behind him, Debbie turned to Russ. "You have to understand, it didn't mean anything." Her voice was low, urgent.

"Oh, for Christ's sake."

"Look," Clare said desperately, "I should go."

Russ caught her sleeve. "Stay. Please."

"You dragged her here where she didn't know a soul and then left her alone in that moldy old farmhouse while you worked twelve hours a day. She got lonely!" Debbie shot a poisonous glance toward Clare. "At least she didn't come yapping to you about true love. She kept it to herself and she got over it. She never forgot where her loyalties lay."

"Who was it?"

"Some guy named Lyle. I don't know his last name."

Clare stared at Russ. *Oh, God,* she thought. *Not this. Please, not this.*

Russ swallowed. "Lyle," he said. "From Millers Kill?"

Debbie nodded. "She met him at the mayor's Christmas party, the first year that you guys moved here." She peered more closely at Russ. "You know him?"

Russ nodded.

Clare wanted to close her eyes. How many times could your heart break for someone?

"I don't know if he was the same guy she was e-mailing me about for the past few weeks. The Mr. Sandman guy. She was always pretty private, but she got extra quiet about what was going on after you dropped your love bomb on her. Probably worried about leaving a paper trail for the divorce lawyers."

"There wasn't going to be any divorce," Russ said from very far away.

Debbie shot him a look. "The only thing I can tell you is that he was making big time after your announcement. And that she knew him from work."

"Work," Russ said. "She didn't say *her* work, did she?"

"I . . . I guess not." Debbie's face wavered between pain and hopefulness. "Do you think he might be a suspect? This Lyle guy?"

Russ didn't say anything for a long moment. Clare wrapped her hand around his arm and squeezed hard. To hell with what Debbie thought.

"I don't know," Russ whispered. "I don't know anything anymore."

TWENTY-TWO

Clare showed Debbie Wolecski the way out. Or, to be more precise, the two of them stalked to the church door like cats refusing to yield territory, rigidly apart, unhappily together.

"This isn't over," Debbie said at the door.

"I didn't think it was." Clare had plumbed the depths of her priestly goodwill and discovered the bottom of it. She sounded like a bitch, and she didn't care. She wished she could slam the narthex door on Debbie's behind instead of watching it hiss gently and hydraulically into place.

Russ. Oh, God.

He was still standing in the corridor where she had left him, like a glaciated creature given the appearance of life because the ice all around was keeping him upright. Like the five-thousand-year-old Bronze Age man, found with flowers still fresh in his pouch. He, she had read recently, had been murdered. Betrayed, then left to the cold.

She had a flash of understanding, seeing Russ frozen there. If she let herself soften, if she held him and wept and sympathized as she wanted to, he would shatter. He would shatter, and she did not have the ability to put him back together again. She didn't know if anyone did.

She swept her arm toward the door. "My office," she said.

He stared, then lurched into life. She shut the door behind them, glancing at her watch. Nine o'clock. Lois would be arriving at any minute. She pointed to the sagging love seat. "Sit." He did.

She crossed to her desk and unscrewed her Thermos of coffee. She poured him a mug and stirred in three spoonfuls of sugar from her private stash. "Why did you really come here?"

He accepted the coffee without batting an eyelash at the mug's DEATH FROM THE SKY! logo. "I . . ." He patted one-handed at his pockets. "I need someplace to look at these." He pulled out a handful of jewel cases and dropped them disinterestedly onto the sofa.

She picked one up. An unmarked CD. "What are they?"

"The contents of Linda's computer. Most of it."

"Why can't you just take these to your office?"

He shook his head. It was the first unsolicited movement he had made since Debbie's hateful revelation. "I can't. The state police have sent in an investigator to take over the case. Right now, she wants to 'talk to me.' In the best-case scenario, that'll mean pulling me off the case due to conflict of interest. In the worst-case scenario, she could detain me."

She didn't have to ask what he'd be detained for. "How can the state police just come in and take over? Isn't there something about jurisdiction?"

"They have jurisdiction. When the cops running the show are dirty."

Stupid, stupid! She held her tongue. "What can I do to help?"

He waved a hand over the CDs. "Find me a quiet place with a computer." He looked into his coffee cup. "I'm expecting a phone call from—a call about the vehicle the Tracey kid says he saw in the driveway. I'm going to try to follow up on that."

"Use my office."

He started to stand. "No, I can't—"

"Yes, you can." She pressed her hand against his shoulder and pushed him back onto the love seat. "I don't have any counseling sessions today." She swept her Day-Timer off the desk and pocketed her keys. "This room locks from the inside. The only people with keys are me and Mr. Hadley, the sexton." She lifted her coat off the rack. "I'll tell Lois I've turned off the heat and closed the door to save on oil." She made a face. "Unfortunately, that's all too believable."

"Won't somebody wonder why the door's locked?"

She shrugged. "If anyone's nosy enough to try it, they'll think I'm worried about nosy people." She felt a smile trying to tug at the side of her mouth. *"Honi soit qui mal y pense."*

"Huh?" He sat up straighter.

"Shame to him who thinks evil." The thought of what he had found out this morning wiped the incipient good humor off her face. "That's not a bad philosophy to keep in mind, Russ. People don't always know what they think they know."

Lois was just taking her coat off in the main office. "Good lord, did you see the clouds out there?" The secretary followed the Weather Channel religiously. "We're set for a big one. The National Weather Service is predicting it'll start up this afternoon. Two to four inches."

"That's not bad." No greater proof that Clare was becoming acclimatized to the Adirondacks. Two years ago, a forecast of two to four inches of snow would have paralyzed her.

"That's just to start." Lois dropped into her chair and switched on an all-talk AM station that gave detailed forecasts every twenty minutes.

Clare surprised herself by saying, "I'm going to make my home visits this morning."

"Home visits! But it's Wednesday."

"So?"

"You always work on your sermon Wednesday morning."

"I do?"

Lois gave her a look that said, *You put the less in hopeless.* "Yes, Clare. You do."

A reason. She needed a reason that wasn't *I'm clearing out so Russ Van Alstyne can use my computer while laying low from the state police.* "Well . . . I want to beat the weather." The rationality of this caused her to smile proudly. "If we *are* due for a dump, I might not be able to make it around to the shut-ins for a few days. Better get them now."

"What about your sermon?"

"Oh, I'll wing it."

"You'll *wing* it?"

Clare grinned. "Jes' joking. I'll—" The sound of footsteps in the hall jerked her around.

Elizabeth de Groot entered, in an impeccably cut red wool coat with fur collar and cuffs. "Good morning, Lois," she said. "Good morning, Reverend Fergusson." Her alert and helpful look didn't quite cover up the wariness left over from last night.

Clare stared at her as the idea dropped like the last ripe pear of the season into her palm. "I'll ask Elizabeth."

"Ask me what?"

"To deliver the sermon this Sunday."

The deacon wrinkled her brow. "Me? This Sunday? Why?"

"Can you think of a better way to introduce yourself to the congregation?"

"Well—"

"You don't have to preach on the readings, if you don't want to. Make it something personal, something that will let us all get to know you."

"That's an idea." Lois's voice was carefully neutral.

"You think so?" Elizabeth brightened. "Okay. I'll do it." She shrugged out of her coat. "Lois, do we have another computer I can use?" She turned toward Clare. "I didn't get a chance to tell you yesterday, but Lois is putting me up in the copy room." The copy room was a smudge of a space off the main office, originally intended to house the bulky files and mimeograph machine that were standard office equipment when the parish hall was modernized. The file cabinets had long since been replaced by Lois's hard drive, and the smelly mimeograph drum by a tabletop Canon.

"I'm moving the copier in here," Lois said to Clare. "It's not a lot of space, but we can fit a desk and a couple of chairs in there." She narrowed her eyes at de Groot. "You're going to need a computer." Her long, thin fingers drummed in calculation. "Maybe I can work somebody for a donation. In the meantime, why don't you use Clare's? She's going out on home visits."

"No!"

Lois and Elizabeth stared. Clare had flung one hand forward, as if she were about to forcibly prevent the new deacon from leaving. She dropped her arm. "I mean, I want Elizabeth to accompany me on the home visits. It'll give us a chance to talk."

"Really?" Elizabeth beamed. "Thank you. I'd like that."

Oh, God, she was such a dissembler. She was going straight to hell, no passing Go, no two hundred bucks. "Okay, I'll get the traveling kit from the sacristy. I'll drive, and you can get a sense of where people live. Lois, maybe you can rustle up a map and one of the parish directories—"

"I gave her one yesterday." Lois said.

Of course. "Great," Clare said. "Um, I've turned off the heat in my office and shut the door."

Lois nodded. They were so used to penny-pinching, Clare's statement was unremarkable. "See you later," the secretary said. She was already turning up the latest weather news.

Clare had to pass her closed door twice, to retrieve the traveling kit—did she hear the sound of a computer booting up?—and to leave by the back way to collect her car.

She and Elizabeth paused on the parish hall steps. The clouds piling up along the edge of the mountains looked like a fleet of battleships, menacing their small town from an arctic sea. Lois was right. Of course, Lois was usually right. Something caught at the corner of her eye—a movement behind the diamond-paned windows of her office. "We'd better get going," she said, steering Elizabeth toward the new Subaru. She was careful to keep herself between the deacon and the building. "I want to make sure we beat the snow."

"It sure looks like a storm's coming, doesn't it?"

"Oh, yes," Clare said. "It sure does."

TWENTY-THREE

The morning visits went better than Clare had hoped, considering she had trapped herself voluntarily with the bishop's watchdog. Elizabeth de Groot never asked her outright about her "I had an affair with him" statement last night, a fact that would have eased Clare more had she not been sure that de Groot would find someone else to pump for details. Terry McKellan? Geoff Burns? One of the vestry was bound to get an invitation from the new deacon to meet for lunch. A very informative lunch. Clare found herself counting votes in her head, calculating who on the parish's governing board would be for her and who against. Which is why she wasn't paying as much attention as she should when de Groot complimented her on her new car.

"So practical for the weather around here," the deacon said. "I had heard you had some sort of *sports car*."

Would Norm Madsen be in her camp? He was conservative, which argued against it. "You're thinking of my Shelby Cobra," she said. "It got blown up this past November." On the other hand, he was sweet on Mrs. Marshall. She might sway him to the pro-Fergusson side.

"It got . . . blown up?"

Oops. "In a manner of speaking."

Elizabeth looked at her strangely. "That must be a manner of speaking with which I'm unfamiliar."

Clare wrenched her attention away from vestry vote-counting and diverted the conversation by giving de Groot a complete rundown on the shut-in parishioners they would be seeing.

Elizabeth was good in people's homes, a little formal, but with a well-honed gift for asking questions about photos and mementos that encouraged conversation. Year-round, there were always a few shut-ins, but the number tripled in the winter months, when snow and ice kept many of her frailer parishioners off the sidewalks and away from the roads.

"Have you thought about volunteer transportation for some of these people?" Elizabeth asked after they had left one lively old lady's house. "It sounds like Mrs. Dewitt would come on Sundays if she had a ride."

"I've tried," Clare said. "It hasn't been too successful. You get, say, a younger couple to volunteer to pick somebody up. Then two weekends later they decide to go skiing instead of coming to church, and the arrangement tends to fall all to hell after that."

"When it comes to volunteer jobs, I've found it's not so much having a rota of names to call, as it is having one person responsible for riding herd over them. I could take on the task, if you'd like."

"Really?" Clare hadn't seriously thought of de Groot as an asset to St. Alban's. She felt a little embarrassed by her oversight. "That would be great."

"I want to be of use." Elizabeth's face was serene and serious. Clare wondered if the woman ever laughed or cracked a joke. "You've taken on an enormous job all by yourself, when you think of it."

"I don't really think of rectoring as an enormous job. And I'm certainly not alone."

"Well . . . I was under the impression you haven't made a lot of connections with your fellow ministers here in town."

"Dr. McFeely and Reverend Inman are supportive enough, I guess. It's just they're both a good twenty, twenty-five years older than I am, so we don't have a whole lot in common. We've gotten together at a few ecumenical events. They both like talking about their grandchildren. They have these little photo albums."

"There are younger priests in the area in our own church. That fellow down in Schuylerville, and Philip Ballentine at Christ Church in Ballston Spa. You haven't gotten the chance to make their acquaintance, have you?"

"I've met quite a few people at the diocesan convention. The work here in Millers Kill has kept me pretty close to home the rest of the year."

"Then that's something else I can do for you." Elizabeth sounded pleased. "Free you up to be not just St. Alban's priest but the diocese of Albany's priest as well. You must miss the collegiality you knew in the seminary."

"I guess so."

"I knew it. There's a get-together at Father Lee's house in Saratoga this Friday. Evensong at Bethesda followed by potluck. Why don't you let me cover for you that afternoon, and you can go."

"Uh . . ." The last thing Clare wanted was a social obligation with a bunch of priests she barely knew. Recent events had rubbed her raw; the only thing she wanted to do on Friday night was make soup and curl up in front of a roaring fire in her living room. Alone. *Or with one other person,* her mind mocked. *And if you're alone, what's to keep you from calling him and inviting him over?* She realized de Groot was watching her. "That would be great," she said.

"Wonderful." Elizabeth touched her fingertips together. "I appreciate your willingness to hand over some of the reins to me. I realize you must be used to a pretty independent style of leadership. Anyone who headed up a helicopter crew during Desert Storm has to be more comfortable making important decisions on her own."

"Not crew," Clare said. "I'm a—I was a pilot." Oh, what did it matter if de Groot got the names wrong? All at once, it occurred to her that the new deacon knew a great deal about her. As in, read her personnel file at the diocesan offices. What else might they have let de Groot be privy to, if she was to be Clare's Virgil, guiding her safe through the circles of disobedience and inappropriate relationships? The evaluations from her teachers at VTS? The psychological profile from her discernment process? And what about this potluck she had been so deftly manipulated into? Was it going to be stocked with a carefully vetted array of line-toeing peers? Maybe a few unmarried men thrown in, for interest?

Would there even have been a potluck if she hadn't just agreed to go?

No. No, no, no. She wasn't going to make herself paranoid. This was her diocese, after all, the same people whose monthly newsletter had at least ten typos and who had never managed to get all the box-lunch orders right at the annual convention. Besides, she was one very junior priest. She wasn't worth that much effort.

Right?

For the rest of the morning, Clare remained taciturn, listening closely to de

Groot's statements—she noticed they were framed as questions, but worded in such a way as to call forth only one reply—before speaking. By the time they got back to St. Alban's she was tense, jumpy, and more paranoid than she had been since her "capture" and "questioning" during SERE training, back in her army days.

Bless her heart, in the three hours they had been gone, Lois and Mr. Hadley had started the conversion of the copy room into de Groot's office. The promised desk and chairs were in place, along with a small bookcase and a pair of lamps Clare recognized as white-sale donations. The copier now squatted in front of Lois's desk, blockading Clare's favorite spot to park herself when she and Lois conferred. Oh, well. It was a sacrifice she was willing to make. There was, of course, still no computer, but the sexton had drilled a hole through the baseboard and run a phone line in, connecting the new deacon to the wider world.

Clare left Elizabeth expressing her gratitude and hustled down the hall toward the sacristy. Her door, she saw, was still shut. Not that that meant anything. If Russ had left, he would have closed it behind him. She stashed her traveling kit and returned to the office. On the way, she tried her door handle.

It was locked.

"Lois, I'm going to hunker down and try to catch up with the paperwork," she said, interrupting an exchange of office supplies.

Elizabeth's eyes brightened. "Anything I can help with? Or should know about?" She shifted a box of envelopes and a rubber-banded bundle of pencils to one hand, indicating her readiness to tackle anything.

"No, no," Clare waved away her suggestion. "It's routine stuff I've let pile up. The best thing you can do is to get that homily out of the way. And . . . and . . ." She needed another task, in case the frighteningly competent deacon turned out to be someone who wrote her sermons in under an hour. "And Lois can give you the stewardship and capital campaign files. You'll need those to get a clear picture of the parish."

Lois looked at her oddly. Clare could tell she was wondering why the sudden eagerness to let the new deacon into every aspect of their business.

"You said you worked successfully in both those areas at St. Stephen's, right? I'd like you to write up any recommendations you have for us to improve our ingathering during the upcoming year. I know the members of the stewardship committee will want to benefit from your experience."

"Certainly," Elizabeth said, her face reflecting a calm gratification.

Lois, on the other hand, was a study in skepticism. The stewardship committee had a hard time benefiting from each other's experience, let alone that of a woman who had been at St. Alban's for all of two days.

"You'll see that Elizabeth gets that, won't you?" Clare asked, hoping her bright tone masked her desperation.

"Mmm."

Clare chose to take that as agreement. "I'll leave you to it, then!" She escaped down the hall, fishing her keys out of her pocket as she went.

She unlocked the door quietly. It swung open easily. She stared. The lamp was lit and the computer was on, but her desk chair sat unoccupied. As did the sagging love seat and the two admiral's chairs in front of the fire. A sharp cut of emotion slashed through her, low. Disappointment.

She pressed her lips together, determined not to feel like an abandoned child, and shut the door.

And would have screamed if Russ hadn't clamped his hand over her mouth.

TWENTY-FOUR

orry," Russ whispered. "I didn't know if it was you. Or if you were alone." He released her.

"Good God." She clutched at her breastbone. "You scared the sh— sheep out of me."

The edges of his mouth curled. "Scared the sheep?"

She shot him a dirty look. "Don't start with me."

He held one finger up to his lips. "Unless you're in the habit of talking to yourself, you'd better keep it down."

She had a small cache of CDs she kept on the bookcase for office ambience, a sort of Anglican top ten, heavy on Purcell and Elgar. She dropped one of them into the small Bose player her parents had given her for Christmas. She tilted it, directing its speakers toward the door, and switched it on. The rigorously romantic music of Ralph Vaughan Williams filled the air.

"Have you found anything?" She pulled one of the admiral's chairs toward the desk.

"Yeah. There are some e-mails from a guy named Oliver Grogan. Owns some sort of fabric shop in Saratoga. Looks like they met at a trade show in New York and she's bought some stuff from him. There's a lot of flirting back and forth in the e-mails, from both of them."

"Do you think he might be the man she was seeing?" She caught herself. "Possibly seeing?"

He gave her a look of weary thanks. "I'm certainly going to check him out. The trouble is, it's all spelled out there in the file, with his name and address and everything. I find it hard to believe that if she was seriously thinking about . . . someone in a romantic way, she'd leave an electronic trail. I mean, she referred to the man by a code name, for chrissakes, like she was Agent 99 or something."

Clare chose her words with care. "That doesn't mean she was skilled at covering her tracks."

"Oh, she was skilled all right. Seven years, and I never suspected a thing. Not a damn thing."

"Do you really think . . . is it possible Lyle could be involved?"

He gestured toward a pad of paper he had covered with notes. "In the e-mails to her sister, she never reveals who Mr. Ooo, Sweep Me off My Feet is. But I've developed a time line for the dates she mentions seeing him." He looked at Clare full on, now. "It could—the times correspond to—it could be Lyle."

"You can't believe that."

"I don't know what to believe. Seven years MacAuley's been my right-hand guy. The closest thing I had to a friend until you came along. I went to the mat with the aldermen to get him promoted to deputy chief. Now I find out the bastard was nailing my wife."

"You only have Debbie's word for that. Has it occurred to you she might have told you that deliberately? To hurt you?"

"As in, she made it up to get back at me?"

"Yes."

"You heard her. She wasn't lashing out at me, she was defending her sister. Besides, I don't think she had any idea who Lyle was. Other than the guy Linda was—" He shook his head, his throat working. "I just can't believe it," he said finally. "I can't believe she had an affair and I never knew. She always seemed so"—he spread his fingers flat against the air, miming a pane of glass—"transparent to me."

Clare opened her mouth to deliver a consoling word but snapped it shut again. She imagined she could see his pain, spiky and fragile, spreading through him like frost lines along the frozen surface of a lake. *Right now, he needs clarity instead of comfort,* she reminded herself.

"Did you find anything else?"

He sat still for another moment, then gave himself a shake and turned toward the monitor.

"More e-mails to and from her sister. She was pretty mad at me."

"That can't have been a surprise."

He sighed. "It wasn't."

"Anything else?"

"Nothing that twigged me. I looked at her Internet history, the stuff she had bookmarked. Lots of fabric sites, lots of other drapery business sites. The only thing that might be related to Mr. Sandboy is a sort of regional craigslist—you know, lots of personals and help-wanted ads. Vacation housing swaps and things for sale. Pet sitting and snow shoveling."

"Did she have a profile in there?"

"Not that I could find."

"Maybe she was using it to find more seamstresses for her business."

He shook his head. "She always hired her workers locally before. By word of mouth."

"Had she taken on a job that was bigger than usual? Something that might have caused her to turn to other ways of finding seamstresses?"

"Her last big job was doing the draperies and whatnots for the Algonquin Waters resort."

"Is she replacing them in the sections they're rebuilding?"

"She will." He winced. "I mean, she would have. From what I understand, they're still doing the finish work in the parts of the hotel that were destroyed in the fire."

Clare nodded. She had been there, at the resort, the night an explosion and fire wrecked the grand ballroom and a sizable portion of the ground floor. She'd be surprised if it was ready to reopen by the spring.

"If there's anything else pertinent in her computer files, I'm not seeing it." Russ tapped the notepad again. "That leaves me with three leads to follow up on. Oliver Grogan, which is probably the weakest of the bunch. Aaron MacEntyre, the kid who was with Quinn Tracey when he allegedly drove his snowplow past my house and saw a car parked in the drive. Another one that's not likely to get me anywhere. And finally, the mystery car itself."

"What do you know about it?"

He fished his cell phone from his pocket. "You're going to tell me that." He tossed the phone to her.

"Me?"

"I got three calls from the station while you were away. One of 'em's going to be"—his lips tightened whitely around the words—"Lyle. With whatever he dug up on the car."

"You . . . don't want to hear his voice?"

He gave her a look that could only be described as dry.

"Ah." She put the pieces together. "You don't want to hear anything from the state investigator."

He tapped his nose. "Smart girl."

She hit the menu button and selected "listen to messages." The phone connected to his voicemail. "What's your PIN?" she asked.

"Eleven fourteen."

His birthday. She keyed it in. The first message was from Harlene. She was asking him to call in and report his whereabouts. She sounded odd. Far too formal and respectful. The next one—"Chief? It's Lyle," the recording said. She gestured for Russ to pass the paper and pen. "The license you gave me belongs to a 1990 Buick LeSabre registered to Audrey Keane. Her address is 840 Bainbridge Road, Cossayuharie. She's got a clean record and no priors." He paused. Clare could hear the hiss of the recording. "Things are pretty hectic here. I'm going to sit on this until you let me know what you want to do. Call me if you need anything."

Clare jotted the information down and tilted the pad toward Russ as the next message played. "Chief Van Alstyne?" It was a woman's voice, crisp and sharp as a winesap apple. "This is Emiley Jensen. I need to talk to you about the ongoing investigation as soon as possible. Please call me when you get this message."

Next was the familiar sound of Margy Van Alstyne, her usual matter-of-fact tone sharp with worry. "Russell? It's your mother. What in the Sam Hill is going on? I've had two calls from Harlene, trying to find you. That's not like you. I know you're feeling bad, sweetie, but I promise things will get better. If you don't want to deal with work, come on home and I'll bar the door and take the phone off the hook so no one can bother you. Please don't . . . do anything foolish. I love you. Call me back."

"Your mom is worried about you," Clare said, closing the voicemail.

"I'll call her." He studied the paper. "Anything else from the station?"

"Lyle's not going to tell anyone about the license of the car until you contact him."

Russ grunted.

"Is the state investigator named Jensen?"

"Emiley Jensen. Emiley-with-an-extra-*e*, my contact said. The extra *e* stands for expedite, as in, seeing this case to a quick close by pinning Linda's murder on the most expedient—there's another *e*—suspect."

"You."

"Uh-huh."

She handed him his cell phone. "What can I do?"

He looked at her a long moment, then snorted a half-smothered laugh. "You're something else, you know that? If I get hauled in and charged—which, by the way, I fully expect will happen—you'd be an accessory."

She shrugged. "I'm not if I didn't know you were wanted for questioning." An image of Willard Aberforth sprang up before her, all baggy eyes and inconveniently pointed moral questions. *Straight talking is what you need at this point.* "I take that back," she said. "I won't lie. But it's not like I'm protecting you. I'm offering to help find out who did this terrible thing."

"What if I did it?" He sounded distant, as if he were talking about someone else.

"You couldn't have."

"What if I did?"

"You're not capable—"

"Clare, if there's one thing I've learned in twenty-five years of law enforcement, it's that anyone is capable of anything if pushed hard enough. What if I did it and I'm just racing around trying to cover my ass at this point?"

"Why are you asking me this?"

He rocked forward in the chair suddenly, snapping it on its springs and leaning into her space. "I want to know what you *wouldn't* do for me."

She stared into his eyes, crackle-glazed blue. They hadn't been this close since . . . she cut off that thought. For whatever reason, this was a deadly serious question for Russ. Not what would she do for him, but what wouldn't she do?

"I wouldn't deny God for you," she said slowly. "I wouldn't betray my country for you. I wouldn't break a parishioner's trust for you." Without conscious intent, her hand started to curl over his. She yanked it back into her lap. "I wouldn't let you get away with it if I found out you were doing something wrong."

"I am doing something wrong. I'm evading questioning by a New York State Police investigator."

She made a face. "That's rule-breaking. I mean *wrong*. Sinful. Wounding others. Wounding your own soul."

He creaked back in his chair. His eyes went flat. "Too late for that."

"No," she said firmly. "It's never too late for redemption."

"I'm never going to be able to make this up to Linda. She's gone. It doesn't matter what I do, what I say, how sorry I am. She's gone."

"I don't believe that. Even if I did, even if the death of the body was the end of everything, you're still alive. And while we live, it's not too late to ask for forgiveness. To mourn the lost chances and the bad choices and to do better going forward."

"Who do I ask forgiveness from, Clare? Who? You? Linda? Your God?"

"Try asking yourself."

"Christ." He closed his eyes, shook his head. His lashes were wet. "I don't deserve it."

"Oh, Russ." She felt a stinging behind her eyes. "We none of us get what we deserve, thank God. We get what we're given. Love. Compassion. A second chance. And then a third, and a fourth."

He took off his glasses and wiped his eyes. "How the hell can you be so damn certain? How can you sit there and be so goddamn serene?"

She laughed, a sound that came out as a harsh rasp. "Serene? Me? You don't think I'm carrying around a guilt overcoat for what I did to your marriage? I can barely look at myself in the mirror."

He sat up straighter. "You? You didn't do anything. I was the one who was married. I was supposed to, I don't know, keep my guard up."

She leaned forward, resting her elbows on her knees. "Do you forgive me, then?"

"For what? Being the sort of person I couldn't help falling in love with?" His laugh didn't sound any better than hers. "Yeah. For what it's worth, I forgive you."

A kind of power filled her at his words, a moment of rare certainty that the Divine was right there, with her, in her, moving through her. She stood up. "What gives you the right to forgive me for the sins I committed against Linda?" She ducked her head close to his.

Whispered. "Love?"

She laid her hands on his head, not lightly, as if she were giving a blessing, but hard, molding his hair and skull beneath her fingers and palms. "Who here condemns you?" she quoted.

His chest moved with shallow breaths. "No one," he said, finally.

"Then Love does not condemn you, either." She was close to him, close enough for her forehead to touch his, close enough to smell the faint pine and wool scent of him. "Go, dear heart, and sin no more."

TWENTY-FIVE

H e could not have moved if his life depended on it. The pressure of her hands, her breath on his face—it should have been sexual, if it was anything, but it wasn't. It was a current, there and gone again in an instant, leaving him trembling. Except he wasn't. His hands, resting against the wooden arms of the chair, were steady. It was a blow. Or a sound. That he hadn't felt, didn't hear.

What the hell?

She released him, and he thought his head might float away. Or his heart. He cleared his throat. "I . . ." he began.

She not-quite-touched a finger to his lips. "Let's think about what you need to do. And what I can do to help."

He nodded. Yeah. That would be good.

"Maybe we could split up your leads. I could check out this Oliver guy in Saratoga, and you could follow up on the car they saw in your driveway." She glanced at her battered Seiko. "High school will be getting out in an hour and a half. Maybe we could catch Quinn Tracey's friend then."

He nodded.

She frowned. "Are you all right?"

He cleared his throat again. "Yeah," he said. And he was surprised to find, as he said it, that he was all right. Not great, not happy—he wasn't sure if he would ever be happy again—but . . . all right. "Yeah." His voice was stronger.

He stood up, his back cracking along with the old desk chair. "That's a good plan." He bent over the desk and scribbled Oliver Grogan's address and phone number on a scrap pad. "Here." He handed the paper to her. "Call me after you've checked him out. If anything seems off, if anything at all trips your wire, get out first and call me later."

She nodded. "Are you going to be okay driving around? What with being a wanted man and all?"

"I switched vehicles when I was at home. I left my truck in the barn and took the station wagon."

"Won't they be looking for that, too?"

"If whoever Jensen sent to check my house reports seeing tracks going in and out of the barn, yeah. I'm gambling it was someone inclined to cut me a break." His mouth twisted. "Gamble being the operative term. Somebody from the department complained to the staties about the investigation."

"Ah," she said. "I'm sorry."

"So'm I." He folded up his notes and stuffed them into his inside pocket. "We'd better get going."

"Where are you parked?"

"Up the street, tucked in tight in the Balfours' driveway." He flashed a grin. "They're in Florida for the season."

"That's very sneaky of you," she said. "I admire that in a man."

Coat over her arm, she poked her head out of the door first. She nodded to him. He followed her, not toward the parish hall, where he had come in that morning, but toward the church. She heaved the inner door open, and they entered the dim space of the sanctuary. She led him down one of the side aisles, all the way to the rear of the church. "Wait in the narthex for me. I'll be right back."

"The what?"

She pulled open a pair of double doors, revealing a square, towerlike space fronted by the great doors of the church, palisade-high wooden structures faced with enough ironwork to repel the Norman invasion. "The foyer. The vestibule. The narthex," she said, then disappeared back into the church.

The doors swung silently shut behind him. Four arrow-slit windows let in what light there was, through their narrow, stained glass depictions of a lion, an eagle, a man, and an ox. Cold radiated from the stone walls. He shivered. What the hell had possessed the architect of this place? Even back in the 1850s, they had known there was more effective insulation than a square foot of dressed stone. But they went ahead and erected the cutting edge of eleventh-century technology. He shuddered to think how they heated this anachronism in the decades before the radiators were installed.

The interior door opened, slowly and silently, and he backed himself against the wall. "It's me," Clare said. She had a paper sack folded beneath her arm and was holding an ancient buffalo-check coat that looked like it had been doing duty as a rug. In a garage. She had a greasy flap-eared cap to go with it. "These are our sexton's."

"For God's sake, give the man a raise so he can afford something better."

She thrust the coat at him. "These are what he wears for dirty jobs. He's off today, he won't miss them."

"No lie." Russ shrugged out of his department-issued parka and slipped on the coat. It reeked of cigarette smoke.

Clare wadded up his coat and squeezed it into the sack. "Here. Take the hat, too."

He tipped it and looked inside. "This isn't going to give me lice, is it?"

"Mr. Hadley is a very nice man."

"I'm walking a half block down the street. This isn't really necessary."

"Says the man who parked behind the snowbirds' empty garage. You're not exactly inconspicuous, you know."

He grunted but put on the disgusting hat.

Outside, the same wind that was shoving a mass of gray, snow-laden clouds across the sky pushed against their backs, giving them both good reason to bow their heads and bury their faces in their coat collars. St. Alban's walkway was well cleared, but the sidewalk running along Church Street and up Elm was icy. Russ reached out instinctively to take hold of Clare's arm and steady her, but she twitched out of his grasp. "Mr. Hadley wouldn't touch me," she said, her voice barely audible in the sighing of the wind.

He wasn't so sure anyone would mistake him for the church's janitor, even with the coat and hat. "Isn't Hadley, like, six inches shorter than I am?"

"Hunch harder," she said.

He wasn't that worried—not yet, anyway. The department didn't have enough men on this morning to lay down an effective beat presence and run an investigation, too. The moment he was in trouble was the moment Jensen decided she had enough to upgrade him from party-of-interest to suspect. He wondered how long it would take her to get an arrest warrant from Judge Ryswick. Russ had annoyed the old coot with enough middle-of-the-night and dawn hearings over the past seven years to likely make the judge quick on the draw. Once Jensen had a warrant, every cop, sheriff, and trooper between Plattsburgh and Albany would be looking for him.

They had come to the rectory drive. "I'll call you with what I find out," Clare said, handing him the bag with his parka. Her cheeks were red from the cold. "Don't forget to call your mom."

He nodded and forced himself to continue up the sidewalk instead of watching her make her way up her drive.

He retrieved the station wagon. He quite carefully named it in his thoughts, to avoid the words "Linda's car," and was grateful beyond words that she had been a meticulously neat person who never treated her vehicle like a mobile closet. There was nothing personal to haunt him, no commuter mug or discarded shoes or overdue library books to tell the story of the woman who, until a few days ago, had driven this car. Only two fifty-pound bags of kitty litter in the back—for weight and traction, not for the cat she had acquired as soon as the door had shut behind him—and the emergency kit he packed her every winter: thermal blanket and flares, collapsible shovel and gorp, battery and phone recharger.

He chucked Mr. Hadley's smelly garb in the backseat and headed out toward Cossayuharie, driving the long way round, avoiding the town and the stretches where Ed and Paul, despite his directions to vary locations, habitually camped with their radar guns.

Bainbridge Road, like all of the roads through Cossayuharie's dairy country, rose and fell across ridges and hollows, running past well-tended farms and abandoned barns alike, past brook-threaded fields marked out by modern barbed-wire and ancient stone fences, past distant, dilapidated houses more likely to produce meth than milk. He knew two families who lived on the road, the Montgomerys and the Stoners, both of them still hanging on with their herds of forty or fifty cows, following in the manure-edged boot prints of their fathers and their fathers before them. Probably the last generation to do so— the two Stoner kids and the Montgomery boys would likely have long shaken the barnyard dirt off their feet by the time their turns came.

Audrey Keane he did not know. At 840 Bainbridge Road, he found a small two-story house, with an enclosed front porch sagging away from the foundations and two cars in the dooryard of a Depression-era garage. One was a late-eighties Buick Riviera, whose half-deflated tires and crust of snow indicated it hadn't been driven in some time. The other was a 1992 Honda Civic, with New York State plate number 6779LF.

The drive was a combination of scraped-clear ruts and hard-packed snow. He eased the Volvo up behind the Civic and put on the parking brake. He pulled his service weapon out from beneath the passenger's seat and checked the clip. Leaning forward, he snapped his belt holster in place and slid his gun in, heavy and snug against the back of his hip. He shrugged into his parka and slid out of the station wagon.

He strolled slowly past the Honda, checking it out. It was the opposite of Linda's car, littered with crumpled fast-food bags and empty soda cans, glittery Mardi Gras beads hanging off the rearview mirror, a Dunkin' Donuts mug wedged between the two front seats. There was no K-Bar knife or blood-saturated clothing. At least not where Russ could see.

There was a buzzer next to the door to the enclosed porch. He pressed it, once, twice, three times. No response, either human or animal. He tried the door. It was locked. The wooden frame and the lock made it just one step up from a screen door, rickety enough that a good hard kick would open it. He pursed his lips thoughtfully and walked around the side, where the wind whipping between the house and the garage had scooped out most of the winter's snow, leaving a hard, easy-to-walk-on crust. From this sheltered position, his chin was level with the bottom sill of the house windows. Through the gauzy sheers he could glimpse what looked like an ordinary and empty living room and kitchen.

The low-slung, square window of the garage revealed the usual detritus of an unused country garage—push mower, car parts, moldering cardboard boxes, and antiquated tools hanging off the walls. He turned the corner and saw, half buried in a drift, what he expected to see: an unused kitchen door, from the days when the lady of the house needed to bring her wet washing out to the line or harvest part of dinner from her vegetable garden.

Russ waded through the snow and scraped away as much as he could from the edge of the door. The lock was a simple handle latch, $10.99 at your local Home Depot. Russ considered the situation. Audrey Keane had most likely been at his house interviewing with Linda about a seamstress job. She had no criminal record, and there was nothing overtly suspicious about her home or car. Based on what he had right now, he'd never get a warrant to search her house. One more step and he would be breaking and entering.

It took him thirty seconds to pop the lock with his Visa card.

He opened the door slowly, brushing the snow back one-handed as it collapsed into the kitchen. He kicked his boots against the door lintel and stepped in.

The kitchen looked as if it had been modernized in the 1950s and not touched since, although the coffeemaker, microwave, and wall phone were all more recent additions. He grabbed a couple of paper towels from a roll hanging next to the sink and tossed them over the snow puddles spreading across the linoleum.

The refrigerator was covered with yellowing newspaper funnies and horoscopes, held in place with the sort of cutesie cat-themed magnets Linda wouldn't have allowed into the house. He tugged open the door. Bacon and eggs. Tupperware containers and a half-full jar of spaghetti sauce. Beer and milk. He uncapped the milk and sniffed. Still fresh.

He walked quietly into the front room. Most of it he had seen from the side window—a living room suite in serviceable brown corduroy and darkly varnished pine, the sort of stuff people got from rent-to-own places. He supposed even the plasma television in the corner, with its gleaming white satellite service box, might be a rental. A scattering of family photos hung from one wall, sepia-toned wedding pictures next to early-seventies prom portraits. An old lady in a poly pantsuit smiling in front of a Sears backdrop; a good-looking blonde with teased-up hair in a misty Glamour Shots photo. It all fit with the image he was building of Audrey Keane, a single woman earning enough to get by but not much more, living remote in a house she had picked up on the cheap or inherited from her parents.

So what were three computers doing open on a table shoved against the far wall? He crossed the room and ducked down, looking beneath the table. Behind the tangle of power cords, he saw a wireless router plugged into a cable line. Straightening, he dug a tissue from his pocket, folded it over his finger so as not to leave his prints, and turned on each of the three laptops in turn.

They must have been in hibernation mode, because they came on almost instantly. Unfortunately, that was far as he got, because the three screens displayed a password log-on request. Why would a woman living alone keep her computers password protected? Why would she have a three-computer network with instant, always-on access to the Internet? If Audrey Keane was self-employed in some sort of legitimate high-tech job, why did everything about her house and car scream that she was just getting by? Was the money going in her arm or up her nose?

What the hell had she been doing at his house on Sunday?

He had seen the entire first floor. The second would be two rooms and a bath. He mounted the stairs, careful not to confuse the prints by touching the banister. He had to come up with some way to persuade Judge Ryswick to warrant a search of this place. And the computers. Mark Durkee was probably more adept with them than any other officer in his department—that went with being a twenty-eight-year-old male—but if those hard drives held any evidence, he needed someone trained in cybercrime to crack them open.

He paused near the top of the stairs. Three open doors, just as he predicted. He could make out the white gleam of the bathroom tiling. If there were any drug paraphernalia in the house, it ought to be in there. He could—

A man launched himself from one of the bedroom doors.

TWENTY-SIX

There was a blur—balding, big, dark mustache, arms braced like a linebacker. Russ clawed for his gun. The man smacked into his chest. Russ went over, crashing against the stairs, flipping ass over teakettle, his shout of "Stop! Police!" converted into an inarticulate yell that became a scream as he smashed his knee into a step and kept rolling, bouncing, thudding downstairs.

His assailant leaped over him, leaped on him, his boot driving whatever breath Russ had left out of his lungs. His glasses went flying, and the edges of his sight darkened as his chest heaved for air. He thudded to a stop at the foot of the stairs. The man wrenched the front door open, smashing it into Russ's hip, and disappeared as Russ lay there shuddering, gasping for oxygen, every part of his body in pain.

Then he heard the car engine starting up.

"Shit," he wheezed, staggering to his feet. It felt like someone had taken an ax to his kneecap. The world was a blur. He looked frantically around the living room floor. A glint of gold tipped him off, and he lunged for his glasses. His surroundings snapped into focus again. He limped onto the enclosed porch just in time to see his Volvo station wagon fishtailing out of the drive.

"Shit!" He started to run, but a sharp pain fetched him up. Christ, between landing on his gun and the blow from the door, he probably had nerve damage in his hip. He dug for his cell phone as he limped toward the Honda Civic. Had he seen keys in the ignition? No, he had not.

"Shit!" He spun around. From down the road, below the rise where the Keane house stood, he heard the screech of brakes and the rubber-stripping squeal of tire against asphalt. Then the crash.

"Shit! Shit! Shit!" He gimped down the drive as fast as possible, slipping and sliding on the rock-hard snow, trying to ignore the stabbing pain in his knee and hip. Bainbridge Road's shoulder was packed with gritty dirt- and salt-crusted snowbanks, so he took to the dry middle of the pavement, praying no one would come bombing along over the ridge.

He heard an engine starting up again. Something—a yell? A car gunned. Accelerated. Back up the ridge. Toward him.

He didn't waste time swearing at this latest shitstorm. Russ flung himself over the filthy snowbank and scrambled on fingers and toes away from the road. The crumpled front end of the Volvo, Linda's Volvo, roared past him, broken headlights spattering glass in its wake. Russ swarmed over the hard-shelled snow, back to the road, back toward the angry shouting he could hear drifting up from the base of the hill.

Limping over the ridge crest, he could see the other party to the accident, a tall young man with hair shaved so short all Russ could make out was the pink of his scalp. He was stomping back and forth in front of what must have been a fine-looking Camaro before the rear quarter had been smashed in, cussing in a way that made up in sheer filthiness what it lacked in originality.

"Hey!" Russ shouted, and the young man turned, his fists ready, his teeth bared. Russ held up his hands. "It wasn't me!" He limped closer.

The young man dropped his hands. "Chief Van Alstyne?"

Russ squinted. "Ethan? Ethan Stoner?" He hadn't seen the Stoners' oldest since about a year back, after the boy had finished up community service for a piece of trouble he had been involved in. He sure hadn't had a buzz cut and a car back then.

"Yes, sir, it's me."

Sir? Ethan wasn't a mean kid—Russ always figured his problems arose from too much leisure and not enough opportunity—but he also wasn't the sort to sir and ma'am his elders. Russ finally reached the boy and his brutalized car. "What happened?"

"Are you all right, sir?"

Russ raised an eyebrow. It hurt. "Just banged up a bit. Courtesy the same guy who just totaled your car. What happened?"

Ethan pointed toward a driveway entrance down a few yards and across the road. "I was visiting the McAlistairs." Way back through the field, some half mile from the road, the drive ended in a graceful old farmhouse. "I had just pulled out onto the road—I was going slow, Chief, really I was. I know you have to be extra careful right below the hill."

Russ nodded. "I believe you."

"Anyway, this asshole comes sailing over the top of the hill and bam! Before I could get out of the way, he nails the rear of my car." Ethan looked mournfully at the vehicle. "Man, I still got two years of payments to make on this thing."

Russ sighed. "Don't worry. The Volvo he was driving was well insured."

"If I get my hands on the jerk, he better pray he's got good medical insurance."

Russ fished his cell phone from his pocket. At least he wasn't going to have to worry about getting a warrant now. He dialed the dispatch number.

"Millers Kill Police Department."

"Harlene? It's Russ."

"Chief! Where have you been? I've been calling all over for you!" Harlene dropped her voice. "That rhymes-with-witch from the state PD has been carrying on like you escaped from custody."

"I'm on Bainbridge Road, in Cossayuharie." He glanced toward the McAlistairs' farm. Two people were hurrying down the long drive.

"We've just got an accident report from there. Hit-and-run. One Scotty McAlistair called it in. Kevin's responding."

"We'll need more people than Officer Flynn. I want a crime scene workup at 840 Bainbridge Road. That's just up the hill from the McAlistairs. And that hit-and-run? Assaulted an officer and stole his personal vehicle."

"You and yours?"

"That's right. I want an APB on him, male, Cauc, balding, black or dark brown Fu Manchu mustache. Middle-aged, medium height. He's in a 1993 dark green Volvo wagon, New York plate number RYF 3050. He's got damage to the grill and headlights."

"Are you all right? Shall I send an ambulance?"

"I'm okay." He held the phone away from his ear. "Ethan. How are you feeling? Do you need to have anybody take a look at you?"

"Nah," Ethan said. "I got smacked up worse in Parris Island."

Parris Island. So that explained the bald eagle hairdo. "We're all good here, Harlene. When you bulletin this perp, make sure you add he's wanted for questioning related to a homicide."

"He is?"

The hurrying figures reached the road. A farmer in his forties, knit hat framing a red, weather-beaten face, and a curvy little girl Ethan's age who launched herself into the boy's arms.

"I gotta go, Harlene. I'll fill you in later." Russ clicked off the phone.

"Are you all right?" the girl said, high-pitched and breathless. "Daddy called the police. I saw the whole thing. He just drove right into you! I swear, for a moment, I thought—I was terrified . . ." She buried her face in Ethan's parka and sort of quivered, which, Russ judged, must feel pretty good, even through two layers of down and Gore-Tex. Ethan's cheeks pinked up. He tried to school his gratified expression into something more concerned.

"You okay, Ethan?" The farmer ignored his daughter's theatrics in favor of an assessing look at the boy.

"Yessir. He did a number on my car, though."

"Cars can be replaced." The farmer frowned at Russ. "You the guy responsible?"

"No, sir, he didn't have nothing—anything to do with it. This is Chief Van Alstyne. Chief of police."

The farmer held out his gloved hand. "Scotty McAlistair. You're fast. I only just called nine-one-one."

"I was already here. The man who ran into Ethan was fleeing custody." He thumbed up the hill, toward McAlistair's neighbor's house. "What do you know about Audrey Keane?"

"Audrey Keane?" McAlistair looked surprised. "Not much. She moved in a couple, three years ago. The house was empty for a year after old Mrs. Williamson died."

"Does she live alone?"

"I think so—"

His daughter cut in. "Not anymore."

"This is my oldest, Christy," McAlistair said. "Christy, don't interrupt when grown-ups are talking."

"Daddy!"

Russ held up his hand. "I'd like to hear. You say Ms. Keane doesn't live alone anymore?"

She nodded, her cheek making a whispery noise against Ethan's jacket. "Since about October. There's been a man living there, too. First he was driving, like, a white Buick, then I started seeing him in her car."

"Balding guy? Mustache?"

She nodded again.

"Do you know anything else about him, Christy? Or about her?"

"Not really. We said hi a few times at the IGA. She was always nice. Not, like, pushy or anything. But nice."

Russ glanced at the father. "Do you know what she did for a living?"

McAlistair shook his head. "She was quiet. She didn't go out much, and she didn't have many folks over, as I could tell."

"Not even since October? When this man came to live with her?"

"Nope."

That cut down on the possibility that she was dealing.

"Sometimes she'd go away for days," Christy said. "Like, over a long weekend, or for a week."

He tried to fit that together with the computers. Porn? Procurement? Maybe she was just a fanatic eBayer.

"When was the last time either of you saw her?"

"Ummm," McAlistair said.

"Friday," Christy said. "I saw her drive past in her car. Her and the guy with the mustache."

"You see a lot."

She flushed. "I babysit the Montgomery boys afternoons. They *always* want to play outside. So I spend, like, a lot of time in their front yard."

A siren's shriek cut through the heavy, cold air. Christy McAlistair shivered.

"That'll be Officer Flynn, to take your report," Russ said to Ethan. "Thank you for the information," he said to the farmer.

"Welcome. Sorry I didn't have any more." He touched his daughter's shoulder. "C'mon, Christy. Let's wait inside and let Ethan finish his business with the police."

"I'll come in as soon as I'm done," Ethan promised the girl. She reluctantly released him and followed her father up the long, rutted drive.

"So," Russ said. "You signed on with the marines."

Ethan straightened. "Yessir."

"I'm surprised. Pleased, but surprised. I figured the closest you'd get to fighting was Death Match 3000 at All TechTronik."

The young man flushed. "I had sort of a wake-up call. Between Katie's death"—his high school girlfriend, killed over two years ago now—"and September 11, I realized nobody knows how long they got. And I thought, do I want to piss my life away working part-time at Stewart's and helping my dad steam-clean the milking equipment?" He ducked his head. "I can't blame you for being surprised and all. I was pretty wild for a while there."

Russ thought of himself at eighteen, two years younger than Ethan was now. Drinking and getting stoned and pulling stupid pranks. Desperate to get away. "Are they sending you over?"

Ethan glowed. "Oh, man, I hope so. I'm going for further training soon as I get back. Sniper school. That must mean I'll be seeing action, don'tcha think?"

"I'd think so, yeah." Had he really ever been that young? Yes, he had. He had been chomping at the bit to get to Vietnam. God, boys were stupid. In his day, the town's chief of police had said good-bye and wished him well. Probably wondering, like Russ was now, if he'd ever see that wild young man again. Certainly never imagining that one day Russ would be standing in his shoes, wearing his badge.

Crimson lights splashed over the top of the far hill. Kevin Flynn's squad car. Russ smiled a little. Maybe thirty-some years from now, Chief Ethan Stoner would be watching over Millers Kill. He laid a hand on the young man's shoulder. "Take care of yourself. Come back safe to us."

Ethan gave him a look of disbelief. Russ wasn't sure if it was for the idea that anything might happen to him, or the idea that he might make his way back to Millers Kill once he had escaped it. "Hey, I thought of another thing about Audrey Keane," he said. "I've seen her around a time or two since she moved out here. I didn't want to mention it in front of Christy and all, but have you seen a picture of her?"

"I don't know. I saw a bunch of pictures up in her house. Maybe."

"You'd know it if you had. She's a total babe. I mean, I know she's old and all, but she's hot. I was thinking, when Christy said about her going away and all? She might have been going with guys. If you know what I mean."

"You think she might have been working as a prostitute?" How would that fit in with three computers and a fleeing boyfriend? Internet dating? Meeting men and rolling them?

Ethan shrugged. "I dunno." He rubbed his nonexistent hair. "I'm just saying, she may be my mom's age, but she sure didn't look nothing like my mom."

TWENTY-SEVEN

Mark Durkee broke his own record, Millers Kill to Cossayuharie in under fifteen minutes—and that included stopping for a train rumbling its long, slow way into Fort Henry.

He swung wide around where Kevin was writing up the accident and gave the gas one last touch, surging up the hill and fishtailing into the rutted driveway of 840 Bainbridge Road. His was the first car there. Thank God.

He had been up and down so many times this morning it was a miracle he hadn't snapped something in the process. First, elation at finding Captain Ireland had believed him, had agreed with him enough to send a top investigator to take a look at their murder case. Mark had sweated out a sleepless night after calling the state police, worried Ireland would interpret his concerns as whining from someone rightfully passed over by his superiors.

Then, disappointment, as he realized Investigator Jensen, like Deputy Chief MacAuley, had a pet theory to account for the murder of Linda Van Alstyne and was no more amenable to Mark's suggestions they look at the priest than MacAuley had been. Only it was worse, because Jensen thought the *chief* had killed his wife.

Then a giddy glee as the chief came up missing, out of reach of Jensen's questions or orders. Sly glances and swiftly hidden grins shared with his brother officers.

Followed by the uncomfortable realization that, with nothing more than what evidence they'd already gathered, Jensen was prepared to request a warrant for the chief's arrest. And that he, or one of the others, would have no choice but to hunt the chief down, as if he were no more than some scum-sucking lowlife to be hauled in on probation violation.

The radio splash from Harlene, saying the chief had called in—up! Because he had been assaulted and his vehicle stolen—down! And that he needed a crime scene team for this house no one had ever heard of.

He got out of his car and thunked the door shut. In a matter of seconds, the chief appeared, limping across the enclosed front porch to let Mark in.

"Chief! Oh, man, am I glad to see you!" Mark glanced involuntarily over his shoulder. "Investigator Jensen is on her way. She's really pissed." He stepped onto the chilly porch and took a closer look at the man holding the door for him. A bruise was purpling down the side of his face, and his jeans were smeared with dirt.

"You look like hell," Mark said.

"Yeah, but you should see the other guy." The chief let the flimsy door drop into place and led Mark into the living room.

"What's going on?" The living room was the definition of ordinary. It could have been his mother-in-law's, albeit with fewer embroidered doohickeys lying around. And more computers. Way more computers. "Three desktops?" he said. "They got kids or something?"

The chief shook his head, then winced at the movement. "A witness places that Honda Civic"—he pointed toward the partially visible driveway—"at my house on Sunday afternoon. The day Linda was killed. The woman it's registered to has no record, but when I came here to check things out, the guy she's been living with for the past four months, according to the neighbors, jumped me. Knocked me down the stairs, stole my wife's—my station wagon, and disappeared."

Mark whistled. "You find anything here?"

"I haven't had a chance to check out the upstairs yet. I got back from the accident scene right before you arrived. I want you to bust into those computers. Find out why Audrey Keane and her steroidal boyfriend need three of 'em. Somehow, I doubt they're making their livings as Web site designers."

"Will do." Mark unzipped his parka and slung it over the back of the kitchen chair doing desk duty in front of the computer table. One computer was already running, its otherwise blank screen requiring a password to get any further. He rebooted it, starting it up in safe mode, and set about convincing the machine he was an administrator. The chief's footsteps thumped about over his head.

"Mark! Get up here!"

He shoved away from the table and sprinted up the stairs. "In here, the back bedroom," the chief said. He sounded strangely shaky.

The back bedroom was obviously used for storage. The double bed was heaped high with dresses in dry cleaner's plastic; old magazines and worn-down shoes were piled atop cardboard boxes with WINTER SWEATERS and SUMMER PANTS scrawled on the sides in black marker. The chief was standing beside a girlish dresser whose top was cluttered with bowls and boxes of cheap jewelry. The lowest drawer was open.

"I was looking for something identifying the guy who jumped me."

Mark stared. The chief had obviously rummaged through the colorful shirts and scarves stuffed in the drawer. Swaths of silky material fell from the edges, where he had pulled them away to reveal two snub-nosed Saturday night specials, a sap, and a large, wicked knife. Mark had seen the knife before. At yesterday's meeting with the medical examiner. "It's a K-Bar," he said.

"Yeah."

"You didn't touch it, did you?"

"No. I hit one of the guns with the edge of my hand. That's when I took the rest of the clothing out."

Mark felt a fierce smile fighting its way free on his face. He tried to stifle it. The chief certainly wouldn't be smiling, not staring at the weapon that killed his wife. But all Mark could envision was Investigator Jensen's face, when she saw how wrong she had been about the chief. Sure, it meant he was wrong, too, about Reverend Fergusson, but that he could live with.

Yeah, he could certainly live with that.

"We'd better leave this intact for the CS unit," the chief said. "You have the chance to develop anything on those computers?"

"C'mon downstairs," Mark said. "I'm about to get into the first one. If they're networked together, I'll be able to access them all."

Seated back at the rickety computer table, he finished reassigning himself as administrator. "I'm in," he said to the chief, who was slowly and methodically examining each of the two dozen photos hanging above the couch.

"Whaddya see?"

"I'm going to run a search function to find all the files created or modified in the past twenty-four hours."

"Can you do that for any date?"

"Sure."

"Look for any action on Sunday."

"Okay." While the search was running, Mark clicked on the Internet connection. He called up the history to see what the computer's users had been up to online.

The chief leaned over his shoulder. "Anything of interest?"

"Lots of foreign sites." Mark pointed to the entries with .de and .ch designations. "These Chinese ones might be some sort of spam harvesting or robot scraping sites."

The chief stabbed a finger toward the screen. "What about this?"

"Northcountrylist.com?"

"My wife has that bookmarked on her computer."

Mark clicked through. The Web site sprang up instantly. Whoever used these computers wasn't fooling around when it came to access speed. "Looks like a help-wanted and swap site," he said.

"I know. When I checked it out, I searched for Linda. Didn't find anything. See if you find anything for Audrey Keane."

Mark typed in her name. In seconds, it popped up. "Here she is." He followed the hyperlink. "She's advertising her services as a pet sitter. Huh?" He glanced around the living room, devoid of any sign that an animal lived in the house. "You'd think a pet sitter'd have a dog or a cat or something."

"Oh, my God," Russ said. "The cat."

As soon as he said it, Mark understood. "Mrs. Van Alstyne got a cat. After you moved out."

The chief stood up, his eyes distant, following a cloud of maybes and might-have-beens. "Linda hired the Keane woman to take care of the cat."

"Was Mrs. Van Alstyne planning on going away?"

"Not that she told her sister. Or her friend Meg. Of course, she wasn't used to clearing her schedule with them. Time was, if anyone was looking for her, I'd be able to tell them where she was." He fell silent for a moment. "Maybe she thought her date with Mr. Wonderful might really go somewhere. Or maybe she had a trade show in New York she forgot to tell me about."

"Her car was in your barn, though."

"Maybe she changed her mind. Came home unexpectedly and surprised the pet sitter and her boyfriend doing . . . what? What can you do if people give you their keys and have you come over to feed and water Fluffy and Spot?"

"What couldn't you do? Back a truck up to the front door and clean the house out while the family's on vacation."

"But the victims'd twig to that right away. First thing you'd think of when reporting a theft to the cops would be the stranger with a key. Besides, there hasn't been a rash of burglaries in this area."

Mark called up the search results.

"Hey," the chief complained as Audrey Keane's page winked out of view.

Mark opened one of the files, then another. Strings of numbers, interspersed with random letters. Clusters of letters. He counted a few. Fourteen. Ten. Fifteen. Twelve. Just about the right size, he figured, for first name, last name, and middle initial. Followed by twenty-five or forty-one or fifty-seven numbers. Some were much, much longer. None of them had fewer than nine. Nine. "What always has nine digits?" he asked the chief.

"Zip Code Plus. Bank routing codes. Social Security."

Social Security numbers. The keys to the kingdom. "Identity theft," Mark breathed.

"Say again." The chief, who had been twitching around waiting for Audrey Keane's page to reappear, leaned over Mark's shoulder.

"I think they're stealing identities. Names, dates, Social Security numbers . . ." He pointed to where a long string of numbers trailed after a cluster of letters. "I bet these are credit card numbers. Maybe even passports."

"But those aren't names."

"It's been encoded. With what looks like a cheap program. Maybe some freeware they downloaded off the Net. A good decryption program will break this in fifteen seconds." He looked up at the chief. "I'm just guessing, based on what we've found so far. But I'd lay money I'm right."

The chief nodded, his eyes alight. "It makes sense. The Keane woman hires out as a pet sitter. While she's in the house, either she or her boyfriend goes through the old credit card bills, the tax returns—"

"She could take things like birth and marriage certificates, make copies, and then put 'em back."

"The vacationing pet owners come home, everything's in order, nothing missing, Fido and Precious fat and happy—Keane takes damn good care of those animals, I'll bet." He straightened. "It fits perfectly." He glanced around the house. "The neighbors said she's lived here two or three years. If she was pulling this scam off all that time, I think she'd be living a little higher on the hog, don't you?"

Mark nodded.

"My guess is, the job started out as legit. Then her boyfriend arrives, after a year or two of her living alone. What does that suggest to you?"

"He was doing time."

"Uh-huh. I bet he's got a record for fraud as long as my arm." He stalked to the window and glared out at the road. "When the hell is that crime scene technician getting here? The sooner we lift his fingerprints, the sooner we get his name off the d-base."

As if in response to the chief's complaint, an MKPD squad car crested the ridge, followed by an unmarked and the NYSP mobile crime lab. Noble Entwhistle, in the cruiser, pulled ahead, letting the unmarked and the CS van squeeze into the last of the driveway. Noble parked his car opposite, lights on in warning.

Emiley Jensen and Lyle MacAuley emerged from the unmarked. It was a toss-up which of them looked less happy. The investigator's teeth were gritted, as if she had torn off a hunk of nasty and now was going to have to give it a good chew. The deputy chief's chin was jutting out and locked in place, as if he had something so enormous lodged in his craw he had to keep his jaws clamped to prevent it spilling out.

The chief vanished through the front door. Mark scooted the chair over to work on the next computer in line. He could hear the chief limp across the porch floor, the squeak of springs as he opened the door.

"Chief Van Alstyne!" Investigator Jensen's voice cut through wall and glass like a blowtorch through butter. "You're under arrest! Officer Entwhistle, cuff him."

TWENTY-EIGHT

R uss ignored the woman crunching up the walk toward him. Instead, he focused on the state police technician, who was pulling equipment out of the rear of the van. "Hey! Sergeant Morin! You got a computer uplink in there?"

"Sure," Morin shouted back. "Can't guarantee it'll pick up a signal out here in the middle of nowhere."

"Did you hear me?" Jensen demanded. "I'm arresting you on suspicion of murder."

Russ glanced at her. "Don't rush the gate, Investigator. There's no way you've gotten Ryswick to sign off on a warrant this soon." He turned to Morin again. "I need you to run some fingerprints for me right away. The perp who stole my car's just moved up into the prime suspect slot for our homicide." He could say "our homicide." It put a welcome distance between his heart and his brain.

"You're the prime suspect in the murder of Linda Van Alstyne," Jensen said. She barreled through the porch door, followed by Lyle, who lifted one bushy eyebrow and tilted his head in query. *What's going on?*

Russ looked away. "Come on into the living room," he said to Jensen. "I'll fill you in on what Mark and I have found out."

"Resisting arrest," Jensen said.

"I'm not resisting anything." He stood out of the way so Noble, holding up the other end of Sergeant Morin's box of tricks, could back through the door. "Just as soon as Noble here comes at me with his cuffs, I'll surrender gracefully."

Noble shot him a worried look.

"You want fingerprints?" Morin asked. "Best place is usually the bathroom."

"Upstairs." Russ caught at Morin's parka sleeve before the technician could turn. "In the second bedroom back, you'll see a dresser on the other side of the bed. There are two automatics and a K-Bar knife in the bottom drawer."

If they hadn't been paying attention to him before, they were now. "Let me bring you up to date," he said to the room, as Morin clomped up the stairs. He outlined Quinn Tracey's statement about the car and how Lyle had run the plates for him. Jensen shot MacAuley a dirty look but didn't interrupt as Russ described what he was now thinking of as the chain of crime: his breaking and entering followed by assault and grand theft auto. He conveyed the information he had gotten from the McAlistairs and told how he had uncovered the weapons. By the time Sergeant Morin thudded back down the stairs with his fingerprints and disappeared into his van, Mark was explaining his identity theft theory. Then he and Russ pieced together the possible events leading up to Linda's murder.

Noble looked impressed. Lyle, the rat bastard, was nodding.

"Your wife hadn't told anyone she was planning to be away?" Jensen asked.

"No, but that—"

"Do you have any evidence she hired this Keane woman? A check, maybe, or a record of a phone call?"

"We'll have to look at the phone records and the bank statements again, now we know what to look at."

"So you're basing the entire connection between the pet sitter and the victim on the fact that your wife got a cat?"

"Quinn Tracey positively ID'd Keane's Civic!" He expected her to treat him as a suspect. He didn't expect her to blow off credible evidence pointing to another. He took a breath.

"A minor whom you questioned without the permission or presence of his parents."

"I'm sure he'll be willing to testify again. On the record."

"I'm sure he would be. If you want him to."

Now he really was mad. "What the hell are you implying? That I'm some sort of small-town Machiavelli who can co-opt anyone I come in contact with?"

"I'm not implying anything. I'm stating outright that this investigation has been tainted from the beginning. Your men left the goddam kitchen door open for hours, dropping the temperature and hopelessly muddling the time of death. Despite the fact that you were separated from your wife and have no alibi for the hours during which she might have been killed, you've refused to submit to questioning."

"I have not—"

"You steered the investigation toward a mysterious 'released felon'"—she air-quoted with her fingers—"who killed your wife out of spite. When I showed up asking questions, you disappeared. Now you pop up again with a new theory, supported by a conveniently absent pair of scam artists who—surprise, surprise!—have a knife identical to the murder weapon in their underwear drawer."

Rage rendered him nearly inarticulate. "Are you saying I tossed a throwdown? You saying I framed this perp?"

She looked at Mark. "Officer Durkee, were you with Chief Van Alstyne at all times when he was upstairs?"

"Uh . . . mostly."

"At all times, Officer Durkee."

Mark stared at the floor miserably. "No, ma'am."

"Did anyone witness this alleged assault?"

Russ broke in. "You can't deny that. The bastard rammed right into Ethan Stoner's car trying to get away."

She stared at him, her eyes narrow. "For all I know, this unknown man fled the house after you threatened him. You have your service weapon, don't you?"

He couldn't speak. He jerked his parka to one side, revealing his holster.

"Officer Entwhistle, take custody of that sidearm."

"Oh, for the love of Mike," Lyle said.

"No!" Mark lurched forward. "The chief didn't do it. He couldn't have! For God's sake, we needed your help because nobody was looking at Reverend Fergusson as a suspect. Not because anybody suspected the chief!"

"We needed her help?" Lyle hitched his thumbs over his belt. "You were the one who called the staties down on us?"

Mark flushed red. Russ's heart sank. Oh, no. Oh, crap. He had just about convinced himself it must have been Lyle. Not his best and brightest. Not the one he thought of as his protégé.

"Chief . . ." The naked pleading on Mark's face was painful to watch. "I didn't do it because I thought you were involved. I just thought . . . Reverend Fergusson had the means and the motive and no alibi and Lyle refused to even consider questioning her . . . and I thought, maybe if someone not so close to what was happening came on board . . ."

Noble stood stock-still, walleyed, a kid witnessing his parents' marital melt-down on Christmas Eve. Lyle just shook his head, his face screwed up into an expression of disgust. "I've heard some stupid rationalizations for screwing someone over before, kid, but this takes the cake."

The hypocrisy was more than Russ could bear. "He may have finked me out to the staties, Lyle, but at least he didn't fuck my wife."

Lyle's face bleached white. Out of the corner of his eye, Russ could see Mark and Noble imitating widemouthed bass, and Investigator Jensen's perfectly plucked eyebrows crawling into her hairline. But all his attention was focused on his deputy chief. His right-hand man. His *friend*.

"Aren't you going to say something? Maybe a stupid rationalization? Let me guess. You couldn't resist. Wait, I know. It didn't mean anything. No, no, I got it. She came on to you."

"Jesus Christ," Jensen said. Her rounded, modulated voice had given way to a broad, flat central New York accent. "This is the most fucked-up department I've ever been sent to. It's like a fucking Peyton Place."

Lyle ignored her. He looked at his hands. At the ceiling. Finally, he looked at Russ. "I'm sorry."

"That's it? You're sorry? For what? Me finding out? I mean, if you were sorry about screwing my wife, you might have mentioned it some time in the last seven years, right?"

"I—"

Someone cleared his throat in the doorway. They all turned. Sergeant Morin stood there, holding an old-fashioned rolled fax flimsy in one hand, not meeting anyone's eyes. "Unh, sorry to interrupt," he said. "Not that I heard anything. I mean, I just got here."

Russ pinched the bridge of his nose. "Did you find anything?"

"Yeah." Morin thrust the flimsy toward Russ. "Got a hit on one set right off. Nothing yet on the other." He pointed toward the stairs. "I'm just going to go back up there and take my photographs, okay?"

Russ nodded. Morin bolted up the stairs. No one else moved. The flimsy curled in Russ's palm, so light a breath of air could carry it away. He closed his eyes for a moment, trying to remember his way back into being a cop. Trying to give a damn about whatever information Morin had uncovered.

"Chief?" Noble's voice was tentative. "What's it say?"

Russ breathed out. Opened his eyes. Unscrolled the flimsy. "Prints belong to Dennis Shambaugh. Why does that name sound familiar?"

"Dennie Shambaugh," Lyle said, his voice thin. "You remember him. The Check Burglar. Must have been six, seven years ago. Right after you took over from Chief Brennan."

"Oh, yeah. Didn't he go up to Plattsburgh?"

"Was he from the Czech Republic or something?" Jensen asked.

"Not that kind of Czech," Russ said. "His specialty was jimmying the locks on houses and camps and making off with extra checks and a signature sample. The victims didn't even know they'd been ripped off until they got their bank statements. Sounds a lot like the operation you described here." He held the scroll at arm's length, trying to read the tiny print containing Dennis Shambaugh's record. "He got ten years. He must have been squeaky clean to get out this early."

"He got a dime for theft by breaking?" Jensen said.

"Assault," Lyle told her. "He accidentally picked a house where the owner was home. The guy had a gun and thought he'd go all self-defense on Shambaugh. Who yanked the weapon away from the homeowner and pistol-whipped the hell out of him."

"Didn't he have a fiancée?" Russ said. "I thought the DA's office tried to get his girlfriend to roll on him."

"She claimed she didn't know anything," Lyle said. "Just thought he was a well-paid arborist."

"Arborist?" Jensen said.

"That's a tree cutter," Lyle said.

"I know what a goddam arborist is."

"Anyway, there wasn't anything that linked her to the burglaries or the money. I think she dumped him. I don't recall her even being at the trial."

"What was her name?" Russ looked at Lyle, then at Noble, who, while slow off the block when it came to original thinking, had a prodigious memory for names and dates.

He shook his head. "Sorry, Chief, I wasn't involved with that one."

"You thinking Audrey Keane may be the former fiancée?" Lyle frowned.

"She wouldn't be the first woman to forgive and forget," Russ said sourly.

"Is she working with him? Or just giving him bed and board and closing her eyes to whatever's going on?" Lyle looked at Mark.

"If they're stealing identities the way I think they are, I can't see how she couldn't know," the young officer said. "Digging up passports, checks, credit card bills—that all takes time. What does she do, walk the dog unawares while he rifles the house? She's got to be helping him."

"Dennie's previous offense certainly lines up with the scenario you two came up with," Lyle said. "Mrs. Van Alstyne comes home, catches them in the act, and Dennie . . . shuts her up."

"I think it lines up a little too conveniently," Jensen said. "We still have nothing tying Shambaugh and Keane to the Van Alstyne house. Who's to say you didn't know about Shambaugh's release, peg him as a perfect fall guy, and set the scene to mimic a home invasion?"

"I saw the autopsy report." Mark bristled to the defense of his chief. "Even if you could believe the chief could kill his wife, there's no way he could have defaced her like that."

"That makes it more likely he did it than the Check Burglar," Jensen shot back. "If you're just shutting somebody up for good, you slice their throat and be done with it. Whoever defaced Linda Van Alstyne did so out of rage and hate. Does that sound like a guy rifling people's closets for deposit slips? Or a husband whose wife refuses to fall in line?"

"Deface," Russ said.

"I think you ought to just shut up right about now," Jensen said.

"You both said 'deface.'" He had seen a movie portraying the creation of a planet once—shards and shafts of matter and light falling inward, coalescing from a vaporous cloud to a brilliant, glowing core and a hard outer shell. That was what was going on in his head right now. "Deface."

"Look, Van Alstyne—"

"Ssh," Lyle said.

"What if the woman in our kitchen was mutilated deliberately? Not by someone playing with death, but by someone who wanted to disguise her identity?" He whirled toward Lyle. "Ethan Stoner said Audrey Keane was a good-looking blonde. He said even though she was his mother's age, she had a great figure. Like Linda."

Lyle shook his head. "Aw, no, Russ. Don't start thinking—"

"What if that woman wasn't Linda at all? What if it was Audrey Keane?"

"Russ." Lyle's voice was gentle. "It was her. I saw her, there on the kitchen floor."

"What did you see, Lyle? A blonde with an unidentifiable face? How long did you look at her?"

Lyle turned his face away. "Not long. I couldn't—"

"Not that I don't appreciate the sensitive personal issues arising from the fact that her *husband* and her *lover* were responsible for investigating her murder, but Linda Van Alstyne was autopsied, for chrissake!" Jensen glared at them. "Unless you're telling me the ME was sleeping with her, too, I'm going to take his report as definitive."

"Don't you get it?" Russ demanded. He felt as if a ball of light were expanding within his rib cage. "Emil Dvorak *assumed* the woman he was autopsying was my wife. Because she'd already been positively identified as Linda Van Alstyne. Why would he check her identity against dental records or fingerprints when we already all knew who she was?" The ball of light burst, and he felt himself lifted up, so light it was amazing his boots still touched the ground. "That woman in the mortuary isn't my wife. My wife is still alive."

TWENTY-NINE

Clare knew thirty seconds after meeting Oliver Grogan that he would only have killed Linda Van Alstyne if she had ruffled a swag better than he did. The proprietor of Fringes and Furbelows was charming and flirtatious, and batted solidly for the other team.

"*J'adore* Linda Van Alstyne," he said, leading Clare between shining, spindle-legged tables piled with rolls of velvet trim and silk grosgrain. "Once you can get her away from the Little House on the Prairie look, she does some wonderful work. Have you seen the draperies and soft furnishings she designed for the Algonquin Waters? To die for. Simply to die for. At least, before it charbroiled." He pushed a stack of fabric samples off a Victorian tête-à-tête. "Sit. Can I offer you some espresso?"

"No thanks." Clare sat, narrowly missing pulling down a string of plump gold-and-green tassels hanging from one of the rafters overhead. "Look, I don't want to mislead you. I'm not here looking for trimmings for some window treatment Linda's making up for me."

"My dear Reverend, I didn't think you were. I expect most clergy persons are as poor as church mice and too busy doing good to bother about silly, self-indulgent things like interior décor."

She brushed one of the fat tassels away. It was exquisitely soft, the colors in its tail flowing like water. "I'm here with bad news, I'm afraid. I have to tell you Linda Van Alstyne is dead."

Grogan rocked back into his Louis XIV desk chair. "You've got to be joking."

"I'm sorry."

"Good God," he said. "I'm sorry, too. She was a great gal. I considered her a friend as well as a customer." He shook his head. His hair, in the soft light thrown by the shop's many chandeliers, shone like the tassel threads. His face, however, suddenly seemed much older. "What happened?"

"She was found dead in her kitchen," Clare said carefully. "The police are investigating."

"Good heavens. And how did you get roped in?"

"Her . . . family is seeking some closure. I volunteered to help."

"Well, I don't know what I can tell you about her that you wouldn't already have heard from them."

"Did she ever mention seeing someone? In a romantic way?"

Grogan arched his eyebrows. "I understood she was married."

"She and her husband recently separated."

He laced his fingers together and pressed them against his lips, thinking for a moment. "I'm sorry," he said finally. "I can't think of anyone. We talked and e-mailed back and forth, but it was mostly just gossipy stuff. The only thing I recall her being serious about was her work. I suppose if you spend your days saving souls, it seems awfully trivial to you, but she was passionate about her draperies. She was distraught when the Algonquin Waters fire ruined so many of her pieces. She went straight back to work on them, re-creating what had been lost. No, let me amend that. *Improving* on what had been lost."

"I thought the resort was closed for repairs until the end of January, early February."

"*Bien sûr.* They're going to have a Valentine's Day extravaganza to celebrate the reopening." He leaned forward and lowered his voice. "Although considering what happened the last time they had a gala event, I think they'd be better off just handing out drinks coupons to the guests. But! It's Mr. Opperman's business, not mine."

"So Linda was working on site, even though it's not technically open?"

"From what she told me, she was primarily working from home. But yes, she also worked at the resort itself occasionally. With all those muscular, sweaty carpenters around, who wouldn't?"

Clare couldn't help herself, with a straight line like that. "I'm only interested in one carpenter, myself."

Grogan smiled, delighted. "And why not? When you find someone divine, stick with him, I say."

Driving north on Route 9, she tried to get Russ on his cell phone. After three calls, and three invitations to leave him a voicemail message, she gave up and punched in the station's number instead.

Harlene's voice greeted her. "MillersKillPoliceDepartmentpleasehold."

The line went to Muzak before Clare could say anything. She took advantage of the wait by switching on her lights. Even though it was still midafternoon, the dark mass of clouds stretching from the mountains in the west to the horizon in the east cast everything into dimness. She passed an old house where Christmas lights dangled drunkenly from the roofline, like party guests who hadn't realized it was already past time to go.

"MillersKillPoliceDepartmenthowmayIhelpyou?"

"Harlene? It's Clare. What's going on? You sound rushed off your feet."

"Oh! Hang on." Clare heard a rustling noise, then Harlene was back, speaking quietly. "They brought the chief in."

"Brought him in? What do you mean? Is he under arrest?"

"Not yet. He and Mark Durkee found some computer-scamming operation out in Cossayuharie, and the chief insists it's tied to his wife's murder. Except he's also insisting it's not his wife who's dead."

"Not his wife?" Clare's heart sank. That was denial in the extreme.

"I know," Harlene said. "He's making things a lot harder for himself, but you know how he is. He wants the boys to go back to the phone records and the billing statements, and he wants this investigator woman to send a fingerprint team back out to his house to look for more prints. Oh, and he wants the medical examiner to get over to the Kilmer funeral home and take fingerprints."

Oh, God.

"Of course," Harlene continued, "this Jensen woman's not playing ball, because, let's face it, he's starting to sound like his door's come unhinged."

Clare was afraid to ask Harlene for an explanation of how computer scamming and billing statements could possibly lead to Linda Van Alstyne dead on her kitchen floor, so she snatched at the one piece of the puzzle she knew about. "Did he mention anything about the MacEntyre boy? A friend of Quinn Tracey who may have witnessed the car in his driveway on Sunday?"

"The car that belongs to the couple in Cossayuharie? No, but I think he's gone beyond looking for that kind of witness. He's gonna have to place those people inside his house, and he's not going to be able to do that if *she* won't cooperate."

No need for Harlene to elaborate who *she* was.

"What did you mean when you said he's not yet under arrest? Does it look like the state investigator is going to charge him?"

"She's suspended him from duty. Noble came in with the chief's weapon, and I swear, I never seen him as upset as he was locking the chief's gun away. She wants a formal interrogation. On tape. My bet is, she's going to give him enough rope so he can tie himself into a pretty knot and then she'll use what he said as probable cause."

"He doesn't have to speak to her if he doesn't want to."

"He does if he wants her to give the go-ahead to relook at all that evidence. Besides, he's so convinced he's right and his wife's not dead, he'll probably talk himself right into a jail cell without realizing what he's saying."

"Has he asked for a lawyer?"

"Are you kidding?"

"Okay, I'm going to get someone. He needs an attorney there. If you can think of any way to stall him from giving a statement, do it."

"I suppose I could go in there and spill coffee on everyone."

"Whatever. I'm going to follow up on this kid he wanted to talk with, since it looks like nobody else will. I'll come to the station as soon as I'm done. And Harlene?"

"Ayeah?"

"Let his mother know what's going on?"

"Will do."

As soon as Harlene was off the line, Clare called her junior warden.

"Law Offices of Burns and Burns," the receptionist said. Clare thought, not for the first time, that the name sounded like a line from a hemorrhoid commercial.

"This is Reverend Clare Fergusson. I need to speak to Geoff Burns."

"Mr. Burns is busy. May I take a message?"

"No, you may not. It's an emergency. Get him out of his meeting or the bathroom or wherever he is, but I have to speak with him now."

"Oh," the receptionist squeaked. "Okay. In that case, please hold."

The receptionist's voice was replaced by the Beatles singing "Something in the Way She Moves." The Burnses definitely had a higher class of easy listening music than the police department. Sir Paul McCartney had just reached "Something in the way she moves me" when he was cut off by an irritated Geoffrey Burns.

"Clare? What the hell's going on? Heather hauled me out of a conference call. What's the emergency?"

"The state police have taken over the Van Alstyne murder. Their investigator has Russ in custody at the police department, and she's about to question him."

"Good. Maybe he'll confess and save all us taxpayers the cost of a trial."

"Geoff. I want you to get over there and represent him."

"Him? Sheriff Matt Dillon? The guy who thinks the only things left alive after the bomb goes off will be cockroaches and lawyers? This is what I canceled a possible snowmobile personal injury case for?"

"Please, Geoff. I've never asked you to do anything before."

"Sure you have. Plenty of times."

"Church business doesn't count. I mean for me. Personally."

There was a long pause. "I'm not giving him any sort of discounted rate."

"Full freight," she guaranteed. "His mother's probably already on her way down there with a checkbook."

"Has he actually been arrested yet?"

"No. Harlene Lendrum told me Investigator Jensen wanted to get him to make his statement first."

"Typical lazy policing," Geoff said. "Trying to get the defendant to make their case for them. I'm on my way. Anything else vital for me to know?"

She hesitated. "He's convinced his wife's still alive."

"Oh, Gawd." Burns groaned. "I warn you, I charge more for crazy people."

THIRTY

F at snowflakes were spinning out of the leaden sky and splattering against her Subaru's windshield by the time Clare saw the sign she was looking for: MILLERS KILL 8 MILES, FORT HENRY 11 MILES. She turned off Route 9 onto Sacandaga Road, which wound through farmlands and woodlots and crossed the Hudson River twice before curling beneath the footprint of the mountains to enter the town at the western edge.

Her route ran past the entrance to the Algonquin Waters Spa and Resort, the narrow switchback road marked by stone pillars and a softly lit oval sign, partially covered now by a CLOSED FOR RENOVATIONS sheet. A mile or so after it was the Stuyvesant Inn, its riotous Victorian paintwork grayed into ghost colors by the falling snow.

She spotted the turnoff to Old Route 100. A battered blue and gold sign announced she was on a historic trail, but she didn't need to stop and read it to know that the road beneath her tires had been old before Henry Hudson sailed the *Half Moon* up the river that was to bear his name. The broad and easy trail led Mohawks into the mountains for autumn hunting and to the river for springtime fishing. War parties of Algonquins and Mohicans, French *soldats,* and British infantrymen widened it and rutted it with cannon tracks. When the canals and the mills brought money into the area, it became a corduroy post road, and when the Depression emptied out the coffers, it was paved by the WPA.

She knew all this, not from the sign—had she ever been anywhere that marked as many historic spots as New York?—but from a book that Russ had given her. He loved this place, loved its history and its geography, loved its weather and its seasons; even, although he wouldn't describe it as such, loved the people he tried to guard from every bad thing.

Quis custodiet ipsos custodes? A phrase from third-year Latin. She saw the MacEntyres' mailbox through the scrim of snow and flicked on her turn signal. *Who guards the guardians?*

I guess that would be me and You, Lord.

The house she turned into was similar to many along this stretch of Old Route 100, a comfortably sized prebuilt installed, in all likelihood, over the bones of the last house after the owners tallied the costs of modernizing the heating, plumbing, and electrical systems and discovered it was cheaper to knock down the old and truck in the new. Farmers could not afford sentiment. Across the road, a well-kept barn at least three times the size of the house stood like a garrison, its fields running away into snowmists behind.

She parked behind a Ford Taurus with MY CHILD IS AN HONORS STU-DENT AT CLINTON MIDDLE SCHOOL plastered on the bumper and an overmuscled, football-clutching Minuteman stickered to the rear window. It occurred to her, as she stepped out into the falling snow, that she had no idea what she was going to say to the MacEntyres. They weren't members of her parish; they weren't involved with counseling; she wasn't marrying or burying any of them. She wouldn't have to be here if the Millers Kill Police Department hadn't been hijacked by that state police investigator. It would be a miracle if the MacEntyres didn't send her packing within the first sixty seconds.

She rang the bell. *Okay, God. I hope You have something, because I don't.*

The door opened. A brown-haired woman in jeans and a sweater stood there, smiling with the reserved politeness country people greeted strangers with. "Hi," she said. "Can I help you?"

"I hope so," Clare said. "I'm Clare Fergusson, I'm from St. Alban's Church—"

The woman's smile thinned. "Thanks very much, but we belong to High Street Baptist." She started to close the door.

"Please!" Clare threw her hand against the edge of the door. "I'm not trying to raise money or convert you or get you to sign a petition. I'm here because of Linda Van Alstyne's murder."

"What?" The woman frowned, but she opened the door wider.

"Are you Aaron MacEntyre's mother?"

"I'm Vicki MacEntyre, yeah." She studied Clare for a fraction of a second, then said, "Better come on in before we let all the heat out."

Clare brushed the snow off her jacket and stepped inside onto a large square of tiling that kept incoming boots and shoes from immediately soiling the wall-to-wall carpeting rolling out through the rest of the living room.

"What did you say your name was?" Vicki MacEntyre crossed the room and snapped off the widescreen TV, cutting Oprah off midsentence.

"Clare. Clare Fergusson. I'm a friend of Russ Van Alstyne's."

"The chief of police?"

"Yeah," Clare said. She shucked off her parka and held it beneath her arm. "A friend of your son's told Russ that they saw a car parked in the Van Alstynes' driveway the day Linda Van Alstyne was killed. I was hoping your son might have noticed something."

"And you want to talk to Aaron."

"That's right."

"No offense, but if this is part of a murder investigation, how come the cops aren't here?"

"The state police have taken over the investigation. They're holding Russ as a suspect right now, so no one's pursuing any alternate theories." That wasn't precisely true—she had no doubt that every cop in the department would be looking for alternatives as soon as their hands were untied—but it was a good bet no one would get around to the MacEntyres for some time yet.

"So you're doing it?" Vicki looked her up and down, taking in Clare's loose-fitting black velour dress and white collar. "Are you a private eye or something?"

Clare reflexively ran a finger along her dog collar. "No, I'm an Episcopal priest."

"You've been watching too many episodes of *Murder, She Wrote*, haven't you? Tell you what, whyn't you take off your boots and come into the kitchen? The school bus'll be here any minute."

Clare did as she said. The big eat-in kitchen was clearly the nerve center of the MacEntyre house. Every surface, vertical or horizontal, was covered with photos, lists, magazines, school handouts, and calendars, heaped and stacked and tacked and taped one on top of the other.

"Pardon the mess," Vicki said. "I cleaned up after Christmas, and I haven't had the time to tackle anything since then. Want some cocoa? I was just going to get some ready for the kids."

"That would be lovely, thanks." Clare took up a post beside the refrigerator, out of the way but close enough to talk with her hostess. "Looks like you have a busy family."

"You got that right." Vicki slid a quart measuring cup full of water into the microwave. "My youngest's got Boy Scouts, Pee Wee football, karate, and band. My girl's junior varsity cheerleader, gymnastics, and a different band." She ripped the end off a package of instant hot cocoa and dumped the contents into a mug. "Aaron's slowed down, thank God. He's just doing karate and his guitar lessons. Which is fine by me, 'cause I want him to concentrate on getting his grades up his last year in school."

"The guidance counselor said he wants to join the military?"

The microwave dinged. Vicki paused, her hand on its door. "You talked with his guidance counselor?"

"Not about Aaron specifically, no. She was there when we spoke with Quinn Tracey."

"Ah. That explains a lot." Vicki carefully removed the hot water and poured some into the mug, stirring. "Yeah, Aaron wants to join up pretty bad. Army or marines. We nearly had to hogtie him when he turned eighteen last month. We made him promise to graduate high school." She handed the mug to Clare. "Careful, it's hot. Aaron, of course, thinks all he needs is muscles and gung ho. I keep telling him the army wants smart guys, guys they can train, nowadays."

"True," Clare said, blowing across her cocoa to cool it. She didn't add that there were still plenty of places for young men with nothing more than muscle and gung ho. There would always be a need for boys with more brawn than brain. "When I mentioned Quinn Tracey, you said that explained a lot."

Vicki poured herself a mug. "Quinn's a sweetheart, but I don't think he says boo without Aaron's help. Wanna sit down?"

Clare followed her to the table. "What do you mean?"

"The Traceys moved here in his sophomore year, which can be tough, since most of these kids have known each other since they were finger-painting in kindergarten together. Aaron kind of took him under his wing. Introduced him around to his friends, made sure he wasn't left hanging on the sidelines." She sipped her cocoa. "They've been good buds for three years now. But see, Aaron has always been one of those kids other kids like to be around. He has a lot of friends. Quinn, on the other hand, has Aaron."

"He hasn't made any other friends?"

"Not that exactly. It's more—here's an example. A bunch of the boys will all get together and hang out at Quinn's house. But once Aaron leaves, everybody leaves."

"Aaron goes over to the Traceys' house?"

"Sure. I mean, we'll have them over here in the summer, but when the weather's bad, the Traceys have way more room than we do. And Quinn's mother always has snacks and sodas and pizza for them. How she does it without breaking her budget, I don't know. I have enough trouble feeding one teenaged boy, let alone five or six of 'em."

Clare shook her head. "Quinn told us his parents didn't want him seeing Aaron."

Vicki laughed. "Well, if that's how they feel, they hid it pretty well from us."

Outside, there was a hissing and a clank, and then the sound of an engine revving up and pulling away. The garage doors rattled in their tracks, vibrating the kitchen.

"There are the kids now."

The kitchen door banged open, and Clare had a glimpse of the mudroom beyond before a young man came in, already divested of his coat and boots. Aaron MacEntyre, Clare presumed. He had the look of a natural karate student: not too tall but powerfully built. Dark hair and dark eyes, his cheeks ruddy from the cold.

"Hey, Mom," he said, glancing at Clare.

"Hey, babe. Did you have a good day?"

"Got an eighty-seven on that math test."

"Good on you!" A girl of ten or eleven sidled in through the door. She had the same Snow White–style mix of dark and fair as her brother. "Alanna, honey, how was your day?" her mother asked.

"Okay," the girl said. "Can I get on my computer?"

"Chores first," her mother said. The girl made a face, slung her backpack onto one of the kitchen chairs, and retreated back to the mudroom outside.

"Aaron, this is Clare Fergusson," Vicki said. "She's a friend of the police chief's. He's in a bit of trouble, and she's helping him out."

The boy held out his hand. "Pleased to meet you." His smile was easy and infectious, making him seem less like a polite child and more like a man who genuinely was pleased to meet her.

"Hi, Aaron." Clare couldn't help but smile back. "Like your mom said, I'm trying to follow up on a few loose ends concerning the Van Alstyne case. You've heard Mrs. Van Alstyne was murdered, right?"

He plopped into the chair next to hers. "Yes, ma'am. Quinn and I were there the day she was killed. I'm surprised the police haven't questioned us yet. Or— well, maybe not."

"That's what I'm here to ask you about," Clare said. "I understand from Quinn the two of you saw a car in the Van Alstynes' driveway that Sunday."

"Yes, ma'am, but don't ask me to tell you what it was. It was little and Japanese, that's about all I can remember."

"Quinn was able to give us the make and the license number—" Clare began, but Vicki interrupted her.

"Babe, what's this about Quinn's parents not wanting you to hang out with him?"

Aaron's display of confusion was almost theatrical. "What?"

"That's what Quinn said, when Chief Van Alstyne questioned him. He didn't want the chief talking to his parents, he said, because he was with you, and his parents didn't approve of that."

"Ahhh." The boy ducked his head. A thick lock of dark hair fell across one eye, and he looked up at his mother sheepishly from beneath it. "That may be because he's not exactly allowed to have anyone in his truck with him when he's plowing."

"Aaron." Vicki frowned. "You've been going out with him all the time when he plows."

The look on Aaron's face was one of perfect teenaged exasperation. "It's just 'cause his dad's got his nuts in a wad about the insurance. He's afraid if anyone's in the truck and there's an accident, he'll be on the hook. It's a dumb rule, Mom. Really, it's safer with two. One to drive and one to keep an eye out for cars on the road."

"I don't care. If that's Mr. Tracey's rule, you need to talk with him and get permission before you go plowing with Quinn again."

"Yes, ma'am."

His capitulation was impressive. Back when she was a kid, Clare would have whined and pleaded a full twenty minutes longer. Clearly, Vicki MacEntyre was doing something right. "Aaron, do you remember anything else from that afternoon? Anything you might have seen at the Van Alstynes', or along Peekskill Road?"

He shook his head. "No, ma'am. Sorry."

"And what was it you were doing out there that day?"

"We were just driving around." He gave his mother a deliberately mischievous look. "Maybe finding a few icy spots to do doughnuts on."

"Aaron!"

Clare hid her smile behind folded hands. Intentionally spinning a pickup wasn't exactly the smartest thing to do, but considering the range of misbehavior two boys that age could get up to, it fell into the reasonably harmless camp.

"Can I go do my chores now? I want my computer time, too."

Vicki gestured toward Clare. "Anything else?"

"No. Thank you, Aaron."

"Anytime." The boy rose and ambled into the mudroom. After he had closed the door behind him, Clare could hear the rustle of a parka coming off the hook and the thud of boots.

"He's a good kid," she said.

Vicki knocked against the kitchen table. "I could wish he'd spend less time on the computer and more on his homework. But what the heck. So long as he graduates and has enough skills so's the army doesn't stick him on the front lines, he'll do fine. Craig and me never went to college, and we're doing just as well as the Traceys. And they have degrees up the wazoo."

Clare collected her empty mug and spoon and stood up. "What is it you and your husband do?"

Vicki stood as well. "Let me take that." She hooked both mugs on one hand and pointed toward where the enormous barn sat across the road. "Organic meats. Beef and poultry. Guaranteed free range, pesticide- and hormone-free." She opened the dishwasher and set the mugs inside. "We bought this farm from my folks, back when it was all dairy. But, you know, it's damn hard for a small dairyman to compete these days. You gotta have something the big agribusiness companies don't have."

Clare retrieved her coat from the back of a chair. "So you went organic."

"Yep. It can be tough. You gotta get certified, you can't use antibiotics or treated feed, but in the end, we net forty percent over what my dad did on a per animal basis—and that was back when the Northeast Milk Compact kept prices high. We're thinking of expanding into exotic meats. Bison. The restaurant trade is hot for bison."

One of the best meals Clare had ever had had been stewed bison. "Do you sell locally?"

"We butcher stock here for special orders, and we send some poultry to Pat's Meat Market in Fort Henry. Turkeys before the holidays, that sort of thing. But most of it goes down to New York." She gave Clare an entirely different sort of assessment than she had at the door and flicked a card out of a holder. "Here's our number. Smallest order we do is a side or a half steer, but once you've tasted our beef, you'll be glad you have the freezer packed with it."

Clare took the card. "I may take you up on that."

"You can get it cheaper, but you'll never get it better."

Clare pulled on her parka. "Thanks for the cocoa, Vicki. And thank you for letting me come in and pester your son with questions."

Vicki smiled a little. "I got a lot of experience with quirky folks. Craig's great-uncle holds meetings for a group that believes the Cubans are trying to spread Communism through fluoridated water. And my father-in-law down in Florida's convinced a super-macrobiotic diet and sheep embryo injections are gonna keep him alive till he's two hundred. So when you come along wanting to play detective . . ." She shrugged. "Seems like pretty small potatoes to me."

THIRTY-ONE

It was full dark outside now, and the falling snow flashed like a thousand stars in the light from the MacEntyres' garage. Clare was surprised to see Alanna MacEntyre behind the Subaru, stomping her feet and beating on her arms to keep warm.

"My brother would like to see you," she said, jerking her thumb back toward the barn, where a row of cell-like windows glowed with liquid light. "There's something he wanted to say without Mom listening in."

So. She and Russ had been right when they guessed the boys had been up to something more than spinning tires on country roads. "Thanks," she said. "Are you headed back that way?"

"Un-uh. My chores are done."

"And you waited around in the snow to give me your brother's message? You're a good sport."

The girl looked at her disbelievingly. "No," she said. "I'm smart about not pissing my big brother off." Then she shook her head—*grown-ups!*—and disappeared into the mudroom without another word.

Clare crossed Old Route 100 cautiously. The blacktop was whitetop now, even the recent boot prints of the MacEntyre children fading fast as the snow accumulated. The massive tractor- and haywagon-sized doors that had caught Clare's eye when she drove past earlier were, she realized, on the second floor of the barn, atop an earthen ramp that was slick with snow. The row of windows was below it, at waist height. She found the door, an ancient accumulation of boards so low she had to duck to go through it, and entered into a blast of warm air and smells: the musky green of sweet hay and clover, the plowed-earth scent of manure, the acrid methane sting of urine. Once down four steps she could straighten comfortably, although a tall man would still have collected cobwebs in his hair.

"Aaron?" she called. She was in a narrow chute, its wooden walls hung with farm implements that could have doubled for medieval torture devices, its floor crowded by tightly covered galvanized cans. She walked forward and found herself near the midpoint of an aisle stretching from one end of the barn to the other, dividing two long rows of stalls where scruffy red-haired cattle gazed upon her in rumination. Halfway between where she stood and the far wall a low wagon squatted, half filled with a reeking mound of wet straw and manure.

"Aaron?"

"Down here," he called, and emerged from a stall near the wagon leading a steer, which, as Clare got closer, seemed to be the approximate shape and size of an Abrams tank. He clipped the beast's lead to a ring and pulled a pitchfork from where it stood quivering in the muck.

Clare skirted the behemoth and peered over the edge of the stall. "Your sister said you wanted to see me."

"Yeah." With quick, efficient motions, he began pitching the soiled straw out the stall door, grunting with the effort.

While Clare waited for him to continue, she glanced around. The beams and joists showed its age, but like every other working barn she had seen in the North Country, it was meticulously clean. Farmers might neglect their children, their spouses, themselves, but they never neglected their cows. She caught the dark and liquid eye of the stall's inhabitant, and the steer lowed at her. Red freckles dotted its pink nose. It was so sweet-faced, it was hard to imagine anyone turning it into hamburger and ribs.

"It's a Gelbvieh," Aaron said in her ear. She jumped. "Sorry," he said. "Didn't mean to startle you."

"No, no," she said. "I hadn't noticed you'd finished. What's a Gelbvieh?"

"Prinz." As if recognizing its name, the steer thrust its nose into Clare's palm. It was soft and cool and snuffly wet. "It's a German breed known for the flavor of their meat. They have just the right, you know, mix of fat and muscle." He reached up, grabbed a long loop dangling from a trapdoor, and, stepping into the center aisle, pulled it open. Straw torrented into the stall. Clare couldn't tell how much was enough, but apparently Aaron could, as he snapped the door back into place and picked up his pitchfork again. He had his routine down pat. The bedding scattered across the floor without a single wasted motion on his part.

"I told your mother I might think about ordering a side of beef," Clare said.

He emerged from the stall and unclipped the animal, leading it unresisting into its pen. "Prinz here's ready, ain'tcha, big boy? We could do him tonight, let him hang for a few days, and have him all wrapped up for you by next Tuesday." Clare made a noise. Aaron stepped out of the stall and latched it shut. "That's if you want to let it bleed out and age a bit. Tastes best that way, you know."

The steer had found its way to its hayrack and was contemplatively munching its hay. "I don't know," Clare said. "It's a lot harder to think of it as pot roast once you've looked into its eyes."

The boy shook his head. "It's meat. It just comes prepackaged in a way that lets it feed and water itself. Really, it's not any different than a watermelon."

"A watermelon doesn't have a pink nose."

He gave her a look that was sly and a little challenging. "Wanna see where we do it?"

Clearly, he expected her to recoil in horror and decline. "Okay," she said.

He led her back the way she had come, past the narrow entryway and stairs, past the remaining rows of placid cattle, until they came to a door set in a track at the end of the barn. Of necessity, it was low, but wide enough to have let the two of them and Prinz pass through, side by side. Clare half expected to see ABANDON HOPE ALL YE WHO ENTER HERE carved around the frame, but instead there was a permit from the New York State Department of Health, certifying that the premises had passed inspection and that the operators were licensed to process meat for human consumption, etc., etc.

Aaron rolled the door open and flicked on a switch. Fluorescent lights sprang up, mercilessly lighting every nook and cranny of the slaughterhouse. Clare could tell at once they were a recent addition to the barn. She and Aaron reflected blurrily in the stainless steel plating along the walls. Four sides of beef hung from the ceiling, with several hooks free for the taking. The butchering side, identifiable by its steel table, rolls of paper, scales, and an armory of knives, was separated from the—what should she call it? killing floor? abattoir?—by a steel and tile divider. One side was hung with a deep steel sink; the other had two heavy-duty hoses coiled on rubber drums. On both sides of the divider, the smooth concrete floor was centered with a large grated drain.

"It's . . . cleaner than I would have thought," Clare said. Her breath plumed in the chill. "How come it's so much colder than the barn?"

Aaron pointed to a series of narrow vents running along the top three walls. "We keep them open in the winter. Dad installed a thermostat switch, so if the temperature goes above forty-five degrees the AC kicks in."

"It doesn't look that much different from the butcher shop in the IGA." She glanced at the rings on the wall where the unsuspecting animal would be chained. "Except for that, of course."

"We can have 'em both in the same place because we're so small. We don't ever process more than one steer at a time." Aaron crossed the floor to a metal locker and opened it. "In here's the captive bolt gun and the bone saws. See, we cross-tie the steer"—he moved to the rings to demonstrate—"and then Dad uses the bolt gun in the middle of its forehead. The steel bolt punches through the skull, through the brain, the animal goes down on its knees, and then—" He made a slicing motion through an imaginary neck.

Clare looked away. Her eyes fell on the collection of knives, and she moved closer to examine them. "Your dad leaves all this unsecured? That doesn't seem very safe."

"You can padlock the door if you need to. But nobody's supposed to come in here unless they're, you know, working."

She gave him a crooked smile. "Are you telling me you've never brought your friends in here to give them a good creep-out? Or maybe a girl, so she can scream and hold on to your neck? I bet with the lights out, this place is better than the haunted house at the fair."

Aaron ducked his face, but not quickly enough to hide his grin.

"Has Quinn Tracey ever been in here?"

He looked up again. "Sure. He thinks it's way cool. His mom and dad—they just want their meat to appear in little plastic packages at the supermarket. God forbid you see how it actually gets there. But Quinn's not like that. To tell the truth"—he dropped his voice—"he wants my life. He'd love to be a farmer, or a soldier. Of course, he can't tell his *ps*, because they'd have a heart attack if he didn't go to college."

Clare leaned on the stainless steel table. In size and height, it was not unlike the altar at her church. A chill reminder that her God had once required the blood of animals to be spilled before Him as a sin offering. "Aaron," she said. "What was it you wanted to tell me that you couldn't say in front of your mother?"

He folded his arms and stared at his boots. When he finally looked up at her, his face was a picture of indecision. "I'm not sure if I should tell this. Quinn's my best friend, and I don't want to get him in trouble."

"You're a smart boy, Aaron. I think you know that if Quinn's doing something that could get him into trouble, sooner or later he'll be found out." Clare ran her fingers across the surface of the table. She could trace a score of fine lines almost invisible to the eye. The memory of the knife. "The question is, will he be found out before or after he hurts himself?"

"It's not—I don't know that he's doing something." Aaron blew out an exasperated breath. "Okay, this is the thing: We didn't just drive by the Van Alstynes' house. Quinn parked the truck and went in. He said he hadn't been paid. He was in there for a long time."

"How long?"

"I dunno. I listened to maybe half a CD while I was waiting."

"So, half an hour or thereabouts?"

"That sounds right. So then he came out, and he was acting all weird. We drove off, and that was the end of it, right? Except later? At school? He told me that we had never stopped there. We just drove by."

"Did you really see the Honda Civic in the driveway?"

"Yeah, that was there. That was why, after we found out Mrs. Van Alstyne had been killed, I thought we should say something to the police. Then Quinn told me we couldn't, because Chief Van Alstyne had been there at the house."

Clare went very still. "He said he *saw* the chief there?"

"Uh . . ." Aaron's dark eyes unfocused as he thought. "No. The chief had been there, that's what he said. I don't know what he saw, but whatever it was, it scared him."

"Quinn called the police, you know. He gave them the make and license number of the Honda Civic."

"I know. He asked me to back up his story if anyone asked me." The boy's face was a mask of misery. "Have I done the right thing? I don't want to make it sound like Quinn did anything bad. And I really don't want to cause trouble for the police chief."

Clare touched his arm. "You're not. At least some of what Quinn told you was a lie."

Aaron's eyes widened. "How do you know?"

"Because I know the chief wasn't at his house on Sunday afternoon."

THIRTY-TWO

When he joined the force with the ink still wet on his criminal justice degree, Mark Durkee had expected some bad moments. He envisioned nighttime stops, walking up to the driver's window never knowing if the person inside the car was armed, enraged, lunatic. He envisioned facing down the barrel of a gun. He envisioned having to take down guys who were bigger, stronger, and meaner than he was. He sometimes envisioned himself wounded (although ostomy bags, brain damage, or having his good looks destroyed never figured in these fantasies), bearing up under the admiring gaze of his brother officers and his weeping fiancée. (Six years on, the fiancée was his wife, who by that time had seen so many brutal injuries as a trauma nurse that she wouldn't have wept if it had been her own mother on the crash cart.)

The things he didn't envision: the interminable boredom of working the radar gun. Having to shoot a dog. (Its owner, who had almost two acres in marijuana, sicced it on Mark while trying to escape.) Telling middle-aged parents their daughter had died in a one-car crash coming home from Rensselaer Polytech. Being shunned by his brother officers for opening their department to the pitiless gaze of the BCI's External Law Enforcement investigator. Shut out from the work of going back through the phone records and the bills and Dennis Shambaugh's history, but unable to walk away. Useless, friendless, watching through a two-way mirror while his chief sat through an interrogation, unarmed and without a badge, in his own station house.

"We know your wife was killed sometime between Sunday afternoon and Monday afternoon," Jensen was saying. "You were seen buying groceries Sunday right after the IGA opened at noon. After that, you don't reappear anywhere in public until close to five o'clock on Monday, when Officer Durkee picked you up, also at the IGA."

"My wife is not dead," the chief said for the hundredth time.

"We know where you weren't. You weren't at your mother's. Her neighbor across the way noticed her driveway was empty when he walked his dog after the eleven o'clock news." The chief glared up at her. "Yeah, I had your man Entwhistle over there checking things out," she said. "Funny how you and your deputy chief didn't bother to confirm your alibi. Or maybe not. Seeing as you're such"—she leaned over the table, her hands spread flat—"*intimate* friends."

The chief's face scared Mark. For a moment, he looked as though he might tear the leg off the table and beat Jensen to death with it. For the first time, for only a moment, Mark felt his faith flicker. What if . . . Could he possibly have . . . ?

"The neighbor also says your mother's drive was empty, and the snow undisturbed, when he walked the dog before leaving for work Monday morning."

"My wife isn't dead," the chief gritted.

"Did you know your mother lied for you?"

His head jerked up. Mark winced. Margy Van Alstyne had bustled into the station, angry and defensive, demanding the release of her son. As soon as Investigator Jensen started probing for information, Mrs. Van Alstyne swore the chief had been at her house all Sunday and Monday, too. Jensen had smiled like a woman getting a mink for Christmas and thanked her before regretfully refusing to let her see the chief. Mrs. Van Alstyne hadn't wasted any time fuming. She had hightailed it out of the station, headed, Mark guessed, for either a lawyer's office or a gun shop.

"For chrissakes," the chief said. "Just get Emil Dvorak on the phone and see if there are any fingerprints in the woman's autopsy file!"

"According to the secretary at the pathology department, Dr. Dvorak is in Albany today, seeing his neuropsychiatrist. I understand he has a head injury he needs to follow up on regularly." Jensen rubbed her hairline in the same place where the medical examiner's scar split his forehead in two. "And to tell you the truth, I'm a little leery of testimony from an ME who's not only a personal friend of yours but who's brain damaged as well."

"God damn you." The chief braced his elbow against the table and pressed his fist against his mouth. "My wife," he finally said, "isn't dead. You can send somebody over to Kilmer's Funeral Home and print the body right there, for God's sake."

In fact, Jensen had directed the crime scene technician, Sergeant Morin, to head over to Kilmer's as soon as he finished with the Keane house. The BCI investigator might not have believed the chief's assertions, but she wasn't stupid. Mark waited for her to tell the chief, but she simply hung over him, her face as professionally sorrowful as a funeral director's.

"Russ," she said. "You have to help me here. Now maybe, as you say, it wasn't you who killed your wife. Maybe it was one of her lovers. From what I've heard already, it sounds like she enjoyed whoring around with the best of—"

The chief came out of his chair so fast that Mark, watching through the observation window, jerked away involuntarily. Jensen stood her ground, her chin out, her mouth curved in a knowing smile.

"You bitch," the chief growled. His hands were clenched into fists. Mark could see the pulse in his neck. "When we get through with this I'm gonna—"

A racket from down the hall buried the chief's words. Mark was grateful. He didn't want to hear that threat. He didn't want to feel what he did now, the wavering, sick, maybe-could-he running through his nervous system.

It sounded like it was coming from the squad room or Harlene's dispatch center, a cacophony of angry voices, male and female, and Harlene calling for Lyle and the thud of running feet.

Noble burst out of the door and trotted down the hall. He unlocked the interrogation room door without glancing at Mark. "Investigator Jensen!" he called. "You might want to get out here!"

She twitched with annoyance. "Can't your deputy chief handle it?"

"Ma'am, I really think you want to get out here."

Swearing under her breath, Jensen stalked from the room. "Durkee," she said, catching sight of him. "You have the detainee."

Mark's mouth formed the word *Me?* But she had already swept up the hall, Noble hopping out of her way and hurrying to keep up with her.

Mark went to the door. The chief walked over. Looked up the hall. "What's going on?"

"I dunno," Mark said. He looked at his shoes. Shiny. Like always. He prided himself on being a spit-and-polish cop, his crease always sharp, his fade high and tight. Not like the chief, with his hair always in need of a trim and his beat-up old boots beneath unpressed trousers. He looked at those boots now. His throat felt hot and full. "Sir," he said, "Investigator Jensen's sent Sergeant Morin over to the funeral home. To . . . to get prints. I don't know why she didn't tell you."

"She's trying to get me mad enough to confess," the chief said. His voice was almost clinical, as if he were passing along a point of law he picked up at a seminar. "I've probably conducted a thousand interrogations over the course of my career. Hard and soft, sitting in with men a lot more experienced than me and running them on my own. I know most of the techniques, and I know the number one rule, which is, if you don't want anyone to have anything on you, shut the hell up. Jensen knows that I know, and she's decided the way to get me to forget that sound piece of advice is to rattle my cage so bad I'll break down the bars and take a swipe at her."

"Is there . . . I mean . . ." Mark didn't want to know, but he was compelled to ask. "Do you have something you don't want her to know?"

The chief looked at him.

The babble of indistinct voices that had accompanied their talk suddenly sharpened. A woman shouted, "Russell! Russell!"

"That's my mother," the chief said, starting forward. Without thinking, Mark threw his arm across the door.

"You gonna keep me in here, Mark?" The chief's voice was low. "You think I did it after all?"

"No, sir," Mark said, because where would he be if it were true? He dropped his arm. The chief brushed past him and hiked up the hall.

Harlene's dispatch center was jammed with people, cops and civilians alike. Lyle McAuley held Margy Van Alstyne by the shoulder as she listened, pink-faced and trembling, to something he said. That shyster Geoff Burns was in Jensen's face—the first time Mark had ever been glad to see the obnoxious little prick. Noble stood behind the BCI investigator, imitating a wall.

A bleached blonde in a ridiculously skimpy jacket wept with fury, mascara running black down her tan skin, while Kevin Flynn fussed around her, trapped between comforting her and staying the hell out of her way. And Eric McCrea was body-blocking a guy with a goofy tie and a notepad. "Oh, crap," Mark said. He didn't know the man's name, but he recognized a reporter when he saw one.

"What the hell's going on?" the chief said in a voice loud enough to stir the American flag in the front hall.

"Russell!" his mother said.

"Durkee!" Investigator Jensen looked like she wanted to rip him a new one.

Geoffrey Burns broke away from Jensen and shoved through the crowd to reach the chief's side. "Don't say another word until we've had a chance to talk," he said. "I'm your attorney."

"I don't need a lawyer," the chief said.

"Be smart for once in your life, Van Alstyne. Unless you've got your bunk-mate all picked out at Clinton, you need a lawyer."

"Fine," the chief snapped. "I'll call the bar association and ask for a referral."

Burns butted up against the chief. His clipped, dark beard pointed accusingly at his would-be client's chest. "I don't like you any better than you like me, Van Alstyne. But I'm doing this as a favor to Clare. Do you want to be the one to tell her you turned down my representation?"

Mark could hear the chief's teeth click, the hiss of his breath releasing. "No," he said.

"Good." Burns turned toward Jensen. "No more questions until I've had a chance to confer with my client," he said.

"Russell." Mrs. Van Alstyne waded toward them. "The man from the state police came to Kilmer's—"

"They're desecrating my sister's body," the bleached blonde said. Her voice shook with anger. "This bastard killed my sister and now he's sending storm troopers over to pry open her coffin and . . . and . . ." She choked on tears and spittle.

"Goddammit, I didn't kill your sister! That woman—"

"*She* says you can't account for where you were!" the blonde screeched, slashing her finger toward Investigator Jensen. "For almost twenty-four hours! Twenty-four hours! My sister was killed! Where were you, you sanctimonious bastard? Where were you?"

"He was with me." A woman's voice, pitched to carry over the crowd. Heads turned. People pushed each other for a better view. The reporter pivoted, his face alight with interest.

"He was with me," Clare Fergusson said. "He spent the night with me."

THIRTY-THREE

He arrived at the cabin just as the last streaks of orange and red were fading from the sky. He had a bag of groceries in each hand, and he balanced his steps carefully as he crunched up the snow-packed drive to the door. Maple and alder and birch trees cast pale violet shadows on the snow. Behind them, the forest thickened into the darkness of hemlock and eastern pine. He paused, one boot on the deck stairs. Above the cabin's deep-eaved roof, he could see the first star of the evening glimmering through a thin veil of chimney smoke.

She opened the door, spilling golden light. "Hey," she said.

"Hey."

"What are you doing?" She bent down—slipping something on her feet, he guessed—and stepped onto the deck.

"First star," he said.

"Did you make a wish?" He could hear, more than see, her smile.

"I don't know what to ask for."

"Ah." No smile now. "That's the problem, isn't it."

He trudged up the steps. "I brought dinner."

"You didn't have to do that. I overcompensated and carried a ton of food up here with me." She opened the door for him. "Trust me, we could be snowed in until spring and we wouldn't run out."

He paused in the doorway. Looked down at her. "And isn't that a tempting thought?"

He could see her cheeks flush before she turned away. She pushed him into the cabin. "C'mon, don't let all the heat out the door."

He let her relieve him of the groceries as he took off his boots and parka. "This is nice," he said. The cabin was one big room, with an assemblage of living room furniture to his left and a dining table to his right. A glowing woodstove set on a platform of riverstones divided the front of the cabin from the kitchen. Russ followed the line of its broad stone chimney to where it vanished through the roof. "What's upstairs in the loft?" he asked.

"The bedroom," Clare said absently, pulling a box of soba noodles and a jar of natural peanut butter from one of the bags. "What were you thinking of?"

What was I thinking of? Bedrooms. Firelight. Skin. Teeth.

"Pad Thai?" she went on, lifting a clove of garlic.

"Oh," he said. "Yeah. Pad Thai." He shook himself like a dog emerging from a river. "Mom's still on the high-protein, low-carbs diet. I need a pasta fix some bad." He went around the woodstove, shucking his sweater over his head as he did so. There were a pair of spindle chairs pulled up to a small kitchen table, hard against the back of the chimney. He tossed it over the back of one and rolled his sleeves up.

"How is it going? Staying with your mom?"

He grabbed the tray of chicken breasts and ripped off the cling wrap. "It's okay, I guess. It helps that she got that house after Janet and I had flown the nest. If I were back in the same room I had in high school, I think I'd feel like even more of a failure than I do now. As it is, it's more like being a houseguest than like moving back home."

Her hands stilled over the peppers. "Oh, God, Russ. I'm so sorry."

He wiped his hands on a dishrag and took hold of her shoulders. "Listen. I know we have to talk. When you asked me up here, I knew it wasn't a date or an invitation to a seduction. But, dammit, before we get to the part where we tear our guts out, I'd like to enjoy a nice meal with you. How many times have we ever had dinner together?"

"Three," she said.

"Okay." He shook her gently. "Can we put all that other stuff aside for an hour or two? Can we just put on the radio and talk about our jobs and the weather and the idiots in Washington like a real couple would do?"

She nodded. Slowly, she smiled. God, he loved seeing her smile. "So," she said. "How 'bout them Patriots?"

She dug up candles in the pantry. Their light reflected in the glass-front book-case behind the dining table. "I'm worried about Kevin," he was saying. "He has the potential to be a good officer, but he's still awfully immature. He needs to broaden his experience. I think the farthest away from Millers Kill he's ever been was the senior class trip to New York."

She speared a bite of sauce-soaked chicken. "Is there any way you could get him into a more urban police department for six months? Like a temporary de-tached duty?"

"Yeah. Except then I'd lose him. You can't keep 'em down on the farm—"

"Once they've seen Paree."

He poured himself another glass of cranberry juice. "As it is, I give Mark Durkee another year or two, tops, before he jumps ship. The talented ones, the ones with brains and energy, they all go off to bigger and better things. The ones who stay are the ones like Noble, who'd be dogmeat in a larger unit, or like me and Lyle, too old to change anymore."

She snorted. "Yep, that's you. Doddering off to the Infirmary. Don't forget to give my office a call. We'll put you on the visitation list."

"Watch it, youngster. We'll see what you say a few years from now, when your knees have given up the ghost."

"Given it up for the Holy Ghost, more like." She took a sip of her wine. "I think you may be wrong about Mark Durkee, though. His wife has family here, doesn't she?"

"Bains. There are dozens of 'em between here and Cossayuharie."

"And they've got a kindergartner, right?"

"Uh-huh."

"Hard to just up and abandon grandparents and school and all." Ignoring her manners, she propped an elbow on the table. "It's Mark you should get a TDD for. He's got something to come back to."

"And Kevin?"

She picked up her wineglass again and looked at him over the rim. "He needs to broaden his experience, all right. I suspect that there's nothing wrong with Kevin Flynn that getting laid wouldn't cure."

He nearly choked on his noodles laughing.

They washed the dishes together.

"My parents used to do this when I was a little girl," Clare said, scrubbing at a sticky spot where the peanut sauce had scorched on. "Mama would wash and Daddy would dry."

"That's the natural order of things," Russ said, putting a final gloss on a plate before replacing it in the cupboard. "Women wash. Men dry." He picked a glass out of the drainer. He hadn't done this in years. He and Linda ate a lot of pre-pared meals, or he would throw something together out of cans if he got home too late or she was working on an order. The dishes would go in the dishwasher, sometimes hours apart. " 'Tain't natural the other way round."

"And why, pray tell, is that?"

"Women have a mystical affinity to water. It's a tidal thing, you know, the pull of the moon."

"Uh-huh. And men?"

"Oh, men just like the repetitive motion of rubbing something up and down."

Fortunately, his glasses protected his eyes when she sprayed water in his face.

They got down to business in the chairs in front of the woodstove. She had blown out the candles and turned off the lights before they sat down. "Some-times, it's easier to talk in the dark," she said.

Of course, it wasn't dark. They were lit by the leaping red-orange of the fire. But she was right. There was something about the heat of the woodstove, and the shadows dancing off in the corners of the cabin, that unloosened the con-straints of the soul. He wondered if there might not be something to the idea of racial memory, if a thousand generations of humans sitting before a fire were making him feel this way: open, balanced, neither dreading nor expecting what was to come. He looked into the face of the woman sitting opposite him.

Or maybe it was Clare.

"What does your marriage counselor say?" she asked.

"What everybody else does. That I need to make up my mind. Except she says 'I need to discern my inner goals and bring them into congruence with my stated intentions.'" He leaned forward, elbows on knees. "What does your spiritual advisor say? Deacon Wigglesworth?"

"Aberforth. Willard Aberforth. He hasn't been advising me so much as listening to me blather on. It helps to unload some of the garbage that's been accumulating in my heart."

"Garbage?"

She smiled humorlessly. "You think I'm so all-forbearing and even-tempered about this. You have no idea. How many times I've caught myself thinking, *Well, maybe his wife will drop dead of a heart attack* or *Maybe her plane will go down on the next buying trip.*"

He winced.

"I know. It's awful stuff, and I hate myself for it. The times I literally sit on my hands to keep from calling you and inviting you over to my house and into my bed. The nasty, gut-churning jealousy when I think of the two of you doing the ordinary, stupid things couples get to do. Eating together every night. Watching a video." Her voice dropped. "Sleeping together. God, when you two went off for the Christmas holidays, I was a wreck. A total wreck. That's when I knew I had to take this time. I knew I needed to be alone to think and pray."

"Oh, darlin'." He sighed. "That was supposed to be a rekindling-the-marriage trip."

"How did it go?"

"I think it would have worked better if I could have stopped thinking about you for more than five minutes at a time."

She smiled a little.

"Ever since I told her about us, Linda's been trying her damndest to reach out to me. First it was shopping bags full of sexy lingerie and silk sheets and massage oils."

Clare winced.

"Then it was the trip to Montreal, then the marriage counselor. Even kicking me out of the house. I don't think she's as interested in exploring the non-marital side of herself, which is what the therapist recommended, as she is in making me see what I'll be missing."

Clare was silent for a moment. "And will you be missing her?"

"Yes." He knew she was half-hoping for a different answer, but he couldn't be anything less than honest with her. "We've got twenty-five years together. Half my life. That's too much to just walk away from. I stood up in front of my family and friends and promised to stay with her until death. She's kept her promises. Why should she suffer because I couldn't?"

"And you love her."

"And I love her. It's different than the way I love you, but yes."

Clare looked away from the fire. She was quiet for a long time. Finally she said, "I think what you have with her is love. What you have with me is novelty. I'm new and different, and we've been catching bits and pieces of each other over the past two years." He had never known her to sound so bitter. "I expect that if we ever spent any real time together, the infatuation would wear off pretty damn quick."

"Clare." He pushed out of his chair and knelt on the rag rug before her, pinning her in place. "Don't say that." Pain and frustration roughened his voice. "Say what's true. You know things about me that no one else ever will, not in twenty-five years, not in fifty. You know *me*. Goddammit, if I was just looking for a quick thrill, don't you think I would have ended it by now? Do you think I like making my wife cry? Do you think I like lying awake at night, caught between destroying her and destroying myself? 'Cause that's what it feels like when I think about never being with you again. Like I might as well walk up into the mountains and lie down and let the snow take me."

She was shaking beneath his hands, and he realized she was crying. He pulled her against him, tumbling her out of her chair, and they rocked together in front of the hissing fire. "Christ, Clare," he said. "Christ. Tell me what to do. I can't leave her and I can't leave you. For God's sake, tell me what to do."

She was standing by one of the windows, looking out. It was snowing, softly, fat flakes that looked like the paper-and-scissors ones his nieces taped to their windows all winter long. He had gone out to the shed and brought in more wood, triggering the sensor light over the deck, and the snow pinwheeled through the brightness and vanished into the dark.

"We have to end it," she said.

"No." He was sitting on the polished wooden floor, his back to the wall. It seemed appropriate.

"Yes," she said. "I'm not willing to buy my happiness with your marriage. And neither are you."

"I love you," he said. His voice sounded bewildered in his own ears. "Am I just supposed to stop loving you?"

She shook her head. "It doesn't work like that. I wish it did. Then I wouldn't feel as if someone put a stake through my sternum. No. We just . . . go on."

"That sounds like that idiotic Céline Dion song."

"Yeah." She stared at the falling snow. "You know it's a bad sign when the theme song from *Titanic* describes your relationship."

She had taken his seat on the floor, back to the wall, legs stretched out in front of her. He was sitting on the second-from-bottom tread of the stairs leading to the loft. "No lunches at the Kreemy Kakes Diner anymore," he said.

"No," she said.

"I won't drive by the rectory to check things out anymore."

"No."

"But it's a small town. We'll wind up seeing each other. We won't be able to help it!" He suddenly felt wildly, irrationally angry with her. It was his town, dammit. He was here first. She should go. He was happy before she came.

Happy like the dead in their well-loved graves. Unknowing, unseeing, un-feeling.

"How often do you run into Dr. McFeely, the Presbyterian minister?"

"Uh . . . I don't know. Once in a while I bump into him at the post office or the IGA. I've seen him at the hospital a couple times."

"It'll be the same with me, then. Less. I'll start shopping over in Glens Falls."

"You don't want to make that drive in bad weather," he said automatically.

"I don't care!" Her voice cracked. "If it means I won't be coming face-to-face with you buying groceries or mailing letters, I'll do it!" She took several short, jerky breaths, then a deep one. "With luck, we won't see one another more than once a month or so. I signed another one-year contract with my parish in December. Next year, I'll tender my resignation and ask the bishop to reassign me. Or maybe I'll just go home to Virginia." She knocked the back of her head against the wall. "I'm such a screwup as a priest. I should never have left the army."

He wanted to tell her no, she was a wonderful priest, and if he could ever believe in a God, it was when he saw Him shining out of her, but the words were stopped in his throat by the realization that she would be going away. In a year or less. And he would never see her again.

He would get back into his coffin. He would pull the lid down himself. He supposed, after a few years, he might even grow to like it again.

There was an old hi-fi near the sofa and chairs, the kind with a stacking bar so you could put on four or five records in a row. They had turned on the lights in the kitchen and one of the lamps, so she could make coffee while he riffled through the albums. Some of them were probably old enough to qualify as antiques. Lots of mellow fifties jazz and classic American pop. He put on Louis Armstrong.

"Here you go." She handed him a mug. "Hot and sweet, just the way you like it."

"Except I'm usually not drinking it at eleven o'clock at night." He put the mug on the coffee table. "Dance with me."

She smiled a little. Put her own coffee down. Went into his arms. Her head fit neatly beneath his chin.

"Give me a kiss to build a dream on," Louis sang as they swayed back and forth, "and my imagination will thrive upon that kiss."

They were sitting on the sofa staring at the fire across the room. The fifth album was playing quietly. Mel Tormé.

"Your turn," he said.

"Okay. Um . . . sometimes I floss my teeth while watching TV."

"Everybody does that."

"Really? Huh. Well, it still counts as something you didn't know about me. Your turn."

"Okay. I once had jungle rot on my feet."

"Eugh! Gross! I don't *want* to know that about you. When?"

"In Nam. I went for five weeks without a change of socks in the rainy season. To this day I still compulsively sprinkle Gold Bond powder before I put anything on my feet."

"You were right. This is true love."

"Hmm? Why?"

"Because even with that disgusting image in my head, I still find you irresistible."

They were spooned on the sofa, her back on his chest, his arm around her. The lights were off again. The music had ended. He could hear the hiss of the fire in the woodstove and the silence of falling snow all around them.

"I want to tell you something I've never told anyone," he said.

"All right."

"You know how I said I was drafted? I wasn't. I enlisted."

"What?" She shifted around so they were facing each other. "You're pulling my leg."

"I swear."

"In 1970? You enlisted during the height of the Vietnam War? And then lied about it?"

"Technically, 1968 was the height of the war—"

She laid a finger across his lips. "Russ."

"I was desperate to get away from home, but I felt like my mom needed me to be the man of the house after my dad died." He rubbed his fingers along the curve of her waist. "I was eighteen years old, and I could see my whole life playing out in front of me. A job at the mill. Living with my mother until I married one of the girls from my class and then moving next door. Going to the Dew Drop Inn every Friday and to Mom's for dinner ever Sunday. I thought I'd rather go out in a blaze of glory than that." He smiled, fond and rueful of the idiot kid he had been.

"But—the Selective Service office—there must have been a paper trail! How did you keep it a secret?"

"More by luck than design. I paid a visit to the local draft board president. Old Harry McNeil. Used to be the chief of police in my grandparents' day, if you can believe that. Looking back, I'm amazed he went along with it. He did ask me, at one point, if I was sure I'd rather face the VC than my mother." He grinned.

"I know your mother. That's a tough call."

"I guess he sympathized with a young man who wanted to get as far away from Millers Kill as he could. He gave me an official notice to show my mom—they were just form letters, with the info typed in—and I took the bus to Saratoga and enlisted the same day."

"And no one ever found out?"

"Mr. McNeil died before I left. My mother didn't start kicking up until after I was through basic and got my orders. If anybody else from the draft board ever checked the records, I guess they must have assumed old Mr. McNeil's mind had wandered and he had misplaced my paperwork."

"That draft notice turned your mom into an activist. You changed her whole life."

"That's one of the reasons I've never told anybody before. Who wants to find out her reason for living was based on a lie?"

She traced the outlines of his face with her thumb. "I'm glad you told me."

He measured himself. He felt . . . lighter. And why not? She was helping him carry the secret now.

The fire was low. No words now. He framed her face in his hands, stroking her hair, her cheekbones, the line of her jaw. If he were a young man, he might believe he would never forget her skin, or her smile, or the strength of her. But he had learned that the mind didn't always hold on to what the heart demanded. *Remember,* he told his hands. *Remember this.*

He woke up at some point. The embers in the woodstove were a smudge of orange. He lifted himself up on one elbow, careful not to disturb Clare, and looked out the window. The snow had stopped. The stars were blazing with the fierce light that only comes in the hour before dawn. Part of him knew he should go, but then Clare gave a little snore and burrowed closer against him. He drew the knitted afghan from the back of the sofa and tucked it around them. He lay awake for a long time, watching her sleep.

Bright sunlight streamed through the windows when he woke the second time. He was alone, covered in the afghan. The cabin was warm again. He sat up, fumbled for his glasses on the coffee table. The first thing he saw was the woodstove, stuffed with logs, heat rolling off it in waves. The second thing he saw was the note on the coffee table. *My dearest Russ,* it read, *I'm sorry, but I can't say any more good-byes to you. I'm taking my snowshoes and my lunch and I'm going, like Thoreau, to be alone in the woods.* He almost wanted to smile. How many guys got Thoreau quoted at them in a Dear John letter? "Only you, Clare," he said to the empty room. "Only you."

He threw the note into the woodstove. Then he left, to start the rest of his life without her.

THIRTY-FOUR

Inspector Jensen came back into the interview room. "His story jibes with yours," she said.

"That's because we're both telling the truth," Clare said.

Jensen looked at her as if she had just offered to sell the Brooklyn Bridge. "Reverend Fergusson, there's a saying we learn in law school. 'Most crimes aren't witnessed by priests and bishops.' It's a way of explaining to juries why the prosecutor trusts the testimony of some scumbot who's got a record almost as long as the defendant's. But I'm thinking there must be a flip side to that saying. How can there be a crime if a priest or a bishop is a witness?"

"I don't think I follow you."

Jensen sat on the table. Clare had to look up to see her face. "Here you are, a priest. Rector of the local church. And you're alibiing Mr. Van Alstyne. Normally, I'd say, 'Okay, that clears that up! Thanks very much, Reverend!'" She leaned closer. "But you two weren't exactly at an all-night prayer meeting, were you? You were lovers."

"That's . . . not exactly accurate."

"Even more of a reason to help him off his wife. He wouldn't sleep with you while she was still around, so—" Jensen sliced her finger across her neck. "Your church doesn't have a problem with widowers remarrying, does it?"

"That's ridiculous! I wouldn't sleep with a married man, but I'd be okay with murder? That doesn't make any sense."

"One thing I've learned, Reverend, is that most of the time, there is no sense behind killing someone. A sixteen-year-old kills a twelve-year-old because the kid hit him with a water balloon. A guy beats another guy to death outside of a bar because he thought he was hitting on his girl. A couple of drifters drag a grandma behind the shopping center and shoot her for twenty bucks and the keys to a ten-year-old minivan." She shook her head. "A pair of lovers conspiring to kill a spouse so they can be together? Hell, that's not just reasonable. It's one of the oldest stories in the book. David and Bathsheba, wasn't it?"

"Russ Van Alstyne didn't kill his wife."

"Can anybody else place him at that cabin between sunset and sunrise?"

"Of course not! That was the point."

"Hey, I understand. I wouldn't want any witnesses if I was boinking somebody's husband, either."

"I wasn't—" A thought stopped her. "Deacon Willard Aberforth came to visit me on Monday. Around one or two o'clock. I have his number somewhere."

"Did he see Mr. Van Alstyne?"

"No. Russ was gone by the time I got back."

There was a sharp rapping at the door. Noble Entwhistle stuck his head in. "What is it now, Officer Entwhistle?" Jensen didn't sound pleased to be interrupted.

"Sorry, Investigator." He didn't look at Clare or Jensen. "Sergeant Morin's back. He wants to see you."

"Okay." She rose. Glanced at Clare. "We'll continue this in a moment. While I'm gone, I'd like you to think about the vocabulary word of the day: accessory."

Alone, Clare folded her head into her hands. She didn't want to think about the last half hour. Every person in the dispatch room now thought she was sleeping with Russ Van Alstyne. No, everyone in the tri-county area, as a reporter from the *Glens Falls Post-Star* had also been present for her declaration. She would have to leave the country. She could work with the poor in the slums of Calcutta. After twenty or thirty years, the gossip would die down. Not in Millers Kill, of course, where she had probably enshrined herself as a local legend, but there might be somewhere in the United States where she could show her face without shame.

She heard voices outside the door and hastily sat up again. It sounded like an argument. Then the door opened and, to her surprise, Karen Burns, Geoff Burns's wife and law partner, strode in. It must have been one of her days spent working at home and taking care of their toddler—she was in jeans and a sweater that had undoubtedly been hand-loomed by Kashmiri goatherds.

"What are you doing here?" Clare said.

"Geoff called me. Right after you made your announcement. Wish I had been here for that."

Clare covered her face with her hands again.

"Come on, we're getting out of here. You're done answering questions."

"But . . ." Clare stood up. "I don't think Investigator Jensen believed me."

"The woman with the too-tight suit and the Payless shoes? I spoke with her. The archbishop of Canterbury could show up and swear the three of you were playing pinochle all night and she wouldn't believe it." Karen smoothed her already immaculate auburn hair and looked at Clare with exasperation. "Why did you agree to talk with her without a lawyer?"

"Well, Geoff was here."

"Geoff can't help you. He's representing Russ Van Alstyne, and the two of you have adverse interests."

"No, we don't!"

"Come on," Karen urged. "I want to get home to Cody. Then we can talk."

"Oh, my God, you didn't leave him alone to come down here and bail me out, did you?" She let Karen lead her out the door and into the hall. A phone was ringing in Harlene's dispatch board. Voices, indistinct but excited, leaked from the squad room.

"One, you haven't been arrested. No arrest, no bail. Two, I would never leave a two-year-old by himself. Fortunately, the new deacon was over to talk about the capital campaign. She was great. She volunteered to watch Cody for me as soon as she heard what had happened."

"Jesus wept!" Clare peeked into the dispatch room. It was empty, except for Harlene, entering information on a keyboard with furious strokes. Clare lowered her voice. "Please don't tell me Elizabeth de Groot knows about this. Please."

Karen gave her the same look of compassionate contempt her mother had the time Clare righteously walked out on a high school date who had been telling racist jokes and then had to hike five miles home. In heels. "What did you think was going to happen when you told a room full of people that Russ Van Alstyne spent the night with you?"

Clare forced herself not to drop her head like a fifteen-year-old. "I didn't really think." She gave herself a shake. "It doesn't matter. What's done is done. The important thing is that the investigator understands Russ didn't kill Linda Van Alstyne."

"I understand that now." Jensen emerged from the chief's office clutching a manila folder. "Sergeant Morin's just gotten back to me with the oh-so-belated fingerprint report." Geoff Burns followed the investigator into the hall, and behind him came Russ, looking dazed. Thunderstruck. Jensen narrowed her eyes and spoke directly to Clare. "It seems the woman found dead in the Van Alstynes' kitchen wasn't Linda Van Alstyne at all."

THIRTY-FIVE

Clare's mouth dropped open. She clasped her hands so tightly together her fingernails went white. Squeezed her eyes shut. When she opened them, they were bright with tears.

"Oh, thank God," she said. "Thank God."

Russ thought he might never have loved her as much as he did at that moment.

He was still unsure if he had awoken from a nightmare or if he had fallen into a good dream. That Linda was alive again was too much like the magical thinking he had returned to over and over since Monday evening. *Let it all be a mistake. This isn't really happening. She can't be dead.*

"Yep. Looks like Mrs. Van Alstyne's disappearance is simply a case of a grown woman haring off without telling anyone."

That snapped him out of his reverie. "Wait a minute," Russ said. "There's no evidence of that. How can we be sure she hasn't been abducted by Dennis Shambaugh?"

"Who's Dennis Shambaugh?" Karen asked.

Jensen turned toward him. "Your deputy chief told me Mrs. Van Alstyne left e-mails to her sister, bragging about a hot date she was heading out on." She glanced across the dispatch area to the entrance of the squad room. He followed her gaze.

Lyle was standing there. He gave Russ a minuscule shrug. "If she hired a cat sitter, chief, she must have been planning to go somewhere for a day or two."

Jensen went on. "Given her predilections, I'd check and see if any of your officers have been out since Sunday."

He could feel the blood rushing to his face. He balled up his hands, then forced them to relax, knuckle by knuckle. Losing it now wasn't going to get him what he needed. "We have to get a BOLO out on her. We have to get the identities Shambaugh stole into the federal cybercrime database and the Federal Reserve routing system. He's on the run. He's going to use one of those card numbers he has to get money. We have to talk to his parole officer and track down any known associates, and we have to do all that fifteen minutes ago."

Now it was Jensen's turn to flush. "Don't tell me how to run this investigation, Mr. Van Alstyne."

"It seems to me that's exactly what he should do." Geoff Burns flicked his suit coat back and squared his hands on his hips. "What looked like a domestic killing seems to be a case of a falling-out amongst thieves. Shambaugh and Audrey Keane were robbing the Van Alstynes' house, they disagreed, and he killed her. When surprised by Chief Van Alstyne this afternoon, he fled. Under what construction do you continue to abrogate my client's duties as chief of police? The only error in this entire investigation is that of the medical examiner, who is not under Chief Van Alstyne's authority or yours."

"Counselor, that's an entirely reasonable scenario. And"—she nodded lightly to Russ—"I'm proceeding with the investigation with that in mind. Paul Urquhart is speaking to Shambaugh's parole officer, and Officer Durkee is continuing to work on the identity fraud aspect of the case. I've called in a colleague from the state cybercrimes division to help him."

Russ bent his neck in acknowledgment. She was just setting him up for some asinine theory, but he could be gracious. His wife was alive. Alive.

"Now let me propose another scenario for you. A couple having an affair. The only thing standing in the way of their happiness is his wife, who insists on boring things like marriage counseling. And who, incidentally, turns out to be worth considerably more than her husband, thanks to her successful business. This couple decides to do away with her. At some point between Sunday afternoon and Monday afternoon, they drive to her house. For whatever reason, the husband can't or won't do the dirty. So the woman—" Jensen turned to Clare, looking for all the world as if she were going to ask her for the St. Alban's worship schedule or the name of a good coffee shop nearby. "By the way, Reverend, is it true you were in the army? Flying helicopters? And that you had advanced survival training? An experience like that must toughen a woman up."

Russ could see Clare's jaw muscles bunching as she ground her reply between her teeth.

"Where was I?" Jensen said. "Oh, yeah. So the woman goes inside. She sees what she expects to see, an attractive fiftyish blonde. How many times had you met Mrs. Van Alstyne in person, Reverend Fergusson?"

Clare opened her mouth.

"Don't answer that," Karen Burns said.

"Never mind," Jensen said. "The woman sees the blonde. She slits her throat and mutilates the body."

Clare's scowl vanished. She looked, horrified, at Russ. *Oh, darlin'*, he thought. *I didn't want you to know that ugliness.*

"The woman comes out. Tells her lover his wife is dead, because, after all, that's what she thinks. The couple then alibi each other, saying they spent the night together."

"That's bullshit," Russ said. "With nothing to back it up. I can spin just as detailed a story using Lyle's theory of a vengeful ex-con with just as little evidence to support it."

Jensen shrugged. "Evidence is what I'm looking for. Reverend Fergusson, would you consent to be fingerprinted?"

"I don't think—" Karen Burns began.

"Yes," Clare said.

"Would you consent to a search of your house?"

"No," Burns said.

"Yes." Clare looked at her lawyer. "I'm not guilty. I have nothing to hide." She paused for a second. She looked up at Russ, and he could see in her eyes the one thing she had gained with her reckless confession. "I have nothing to hide anymore."

Jensen smiled.

"I expect you to restore my client to full duty as soon as the evidence clears him of any complicity," Geoff Burns said.

"Not if the prime suspect is his girlfriend, I won't." The BCI investigator thumbed open the case file she was holding. She glanced at a sheet of handwritten notes. "According to her own statement, Reverend Fergusson left her little vacation cabin early in the morning and didn't return until two in the afternoon or thereabouts. That's a lot of time unaccounted for."

"I didn't leave until ten," Russ said. Talking about this made him feel as if he had a mouth full of dry gravel. "Clare's car was in the driveway. Dusted over with snow. It hadn't been moved."

Jensen spread her arms. "But what about after? I don't claim to be any expert in the geography around here, so correct me if I'm wrong, but I believe she'd have enough time between 10:00 A.M. and 2:00 P.M. to drive south to Millers Kill, do your wife—I mean, Audrey Keane, but she wouldn't have known that—and be back north in time to appear out of the woods to this other priest guy who came to call. Or am I wrong?"

He glanced at Clare. He couldn't help it. He didn't want to, but the calculations thrust themselves into his head: an hour and a half to Millers Kill plus an hour and a half back left one hour, more than enough time for someone swift, decisive, used to thinking on her feet. Maybe she had started with the intent to come after him. It was a long, quiet drive. Plenty of time to brood. And she had been tired, worn like a rag from too much emotion and too little sleep. Not herself.

He realized he had been silent too long. Clare was looking at him with a dawning dismay. "Russ?" she said.

"Am I wrong?" Jensen repeated.

"No," he said.

Clare opened her mouth, but nothing came out.

"Not about the driving times, I mean," he said, but he could hear the weakness in his own voice, the faltering of his belief.

"Russ," Clare protested.

"Officer Entwhistle, can you escort Reverend Fergusson to the processing room and print her?" Her show-and-tell over, Jensen crossed to where Lyle was standing. "MacAuley, who can we spare to search the Reverend's house?"

Karen Burns frowned. "Clare, I'm going to say it again. I advise you most strongly against allowing an unwarranted search of the rectory."

Clare shook her head. "No. Let them."

"In that case, Investigator, I insist on being present."

Jensen shrugged. "Sure. But you better get in gear. We'll be over there in fifteen minutes."

"Fifteen minutes after Officer Entwhistle finishes with the fingerprints."

"Yeah, yeah." Jensen gestured toward Noble. "Anytime now, Officer Entwhistle."

Noble lurched into action. He touched Clare on the elbow and steered her toward the hall, her lawyer at her side.

Karen Burns paused in front of her husband. "I'm going to drop her off at our house with the new deacon. I want her to stay there until I get back."

"Understood," Geoff Burns said.

And all the time, Russ stood there. Watching Clare. His last sight of her was her face, turned back toward him, as she rounded the corner.

"Listen," Burns said. "From now on, I don't want you talking with her. You can't help her case, and you can only hurt your own. Do you hear me? Van Alstyne?"

A prayer she had told him about chased itself round and round in his brain.

Oh, Lord, I believe. Help thou my unbelief.

THIRTY-SIX

Clare let herself be trundled out of the station like a juvenile delinquent being picked up by her exasperated parents. "Take your car to my house," Karen told her, tugging on a wool beret to protect her hair from the steadily falling snow. "You can watch Cody until I get back from the search of the rectory. Which I still really, really don't like."

Following her lawyer down the steps, Clare made a feeble attempt to assert her independence. "Can't I just go home and wait until they're done?"

"No." Karen turned toward the parking lot behind the station. "In the first place, you do not want to be there when a bunch of jackbooted thugs go through your every possession. In the second place, I've already imposed on the new deacon too much. You can pay off some of your legal fee by babysitting Cody. When I get back, we'll talk. I want to go over everything that's happened up to this point."

"Oh, lord. Karen, I haven't thought to ask what this is going to cost me. I don't even know what you charge."

A smile slanted across the lawyer's face. "I told you. I'm going to take it out in babysitting."

"But—"

Karen flicked the snowflakes off Clare's shoulder before resting her gloved hand there. "You're my priest," she said, "and I consider you a friend as well. Neither of which might get you off the hook, normally. But you saved my baby boy's life. That gives you an unlimited line of credit at Burns and Burns." Then she surprised Clare by pulling her into a hug. "We'll get you out of this," she whispered. "Don't worry." She released Clare and held out her hand. "House key?"

"It's unlocked."

"Okay." She paused at her Land Rover's door. "I'll be back as soon as I can. Go straight to my house. Do not pass Go, do not collect two hundred dollars, and for heaven's sake, don't hang around here waiting for Chief Van Alstyne."

Clare, who had been thinking of doing just that, started.

"I mean it, Clare, I don't want you seeing him or talking to him until we get this thing straightened out." With that final admonition hanging in the air, Karen got into her SUV and started it up. Clare, watching her pull out of the lot, felt rather like Cinderella being warned that her outfit and ride had an expiration date.

She dragged herself over to her Subaru, got in, and drove to the Burnses' on autopilot. Their house, on a broad and affluent old street, could have been Judy Garland's family home in *Meet Me in St. Louis*. Artificial candles still glowed in each window. Clare parked beneath the porte cochere and bent her head forward in a brief prayer that she not make more of a spectacle of herself in front of the new deacon than she already had.

The Burnses didn't have a mudroom, they had a back pantry, where Clare let herself in and kicked off her boots. "Hello," she called, hanging up her parka. "Don't be alarmed. It's Clare."

She heard the thudding of tiny, footsie-clad feet. Cody skidded through the kitchen just as she emerged from the not-a-mudroom.

"Care!" He flung up his arms for a pickup.

"Hey, buddy." She scooped him onto her hip. "Can we do it?"

"Yes, we can!" he shouted.

"How're you doing? Where's Mr. Squeaky?"

"Mistah Squeaky watchin' zuh twuck video." Just as quickly, he tired of being held and wiggled away. He dashed toward the family room. She followed. "Elizabeth?" she said.

Elizabeth de Groot was seated in one corner of an oversized sofa, leafing through a magazine by the light of a ginger jar lamp. She folded it into her lap and looked up eagerly. Cody swarmed up onto the cushion next to her and held Mr. Squeaky out for Clare's inspection. "See?" he said. Mr. Squeaky was a rubbery plastic squirrel whose original colors and features had been almost completely obliterated after two years as a teething-toy-slash-love object. Cody pointed toward the television, where an eighteen-wheeler hummed down a highway to the accompaniment of an upbeat ditty about driving the big rigs. "Mistah Squeaky wuves twucks," Cody said, before glancing back at the screen and falling under the spell of the video.

"I see you've met Mr. Squeaky before," Elizabeth said.

"Oh, you'll get to know him, too. He's a regular attendee at the ten o'clock Eucharist. He tends to make himself known during the homily, but I've grown used to it."

Elizabeth craned her neck, looking past Clare into the dining room. "Is Mrs. Burns with you?"

"No. She has . . . some more business to attend to. She asked me to watch Cody until she got home. Not that she was worried about your proficiency," she tacked on, anxious not to offend. "She just didn't want to impose on you any further."

"It was no imposition," Elizabeth said. "He's a sweet little thing. Besides, as soon as I heard what had happened . . ." She lowered her voice in sympathy. "Are you okay?"

Since the attentive deacon showed no sign of leaving, Clare took the chair kitty-corner to the sofa. "I'm fine," she lied.

"I can't imagine what it would be like," de Groot said. "Accused, arrested, having to bare your most private moments . . . it must have been awful."

You have no idea, Clare thought. Part of her—the part that was still seeing Russ look at her, troubled and speculative—wanted to weep and moan and dump on the nearest warm body. But she didn't have that luxury. She hadn't in a long time. Since becoming the rector of St. Alban's.

"I wasn't arrested," she said. A truth. "I am considered a 'person of interest,' but that's because the police have to clear anyone who was remotely involved." A half-truth. There had been nothing in Investigator Jensen's avid expression indicating she wanted to absolve Clare of anything.

"Mrs. Burns said you were trying to give an alibi to the police chief and so you told the whole department you two had spent the night together. She was quite overwrought."

How did she respond to that? *Yes, I lied to the police* or *No, I really did spend the night with Russ Van Alstyne.* When did you stop beating your wife, Congressman?

"I told the state police investigator, truthfully, that there was no way Chief Van Alstyne could have murdered his wife because he was with me during the established time of death. As it turns out, he had a pretty good alibi anyway. His wife hasn't been killed."

"What?"

"The dead woman was a pet sitter named Audrey Keane. She and her partner were evidently deep into stolen credit cards and identity information. The police think her partner may have killed her while robbing the Van Alstynes', then fled." And if Dennis Shambaugh didn't turn up, she was in the spotlight. A fugitive couldn't remain at large for very long, could he? Her mind helpfully threw up the name of D. B. Cooper, who parachuted into the Oregon wilderness and was never seen again.

"How on earth could they get the identity of the victim wrong?" Elizabeth sounded scandalized.

"They had similar body types and hair. Close in age, too, I'd guess. They're not sure if she was killed because she was Audrey Keane, or if she was killed because someone thought she was Linda Van Alstyne. She was"—Clare passed her hand across her face—"mutilated after she was killed."

Elizabeth glanced nervously at Cody, who, oblivious to the increasingly gruesome conversation, was singsonging, "Big wig, big wig, big wig wide zuh woad," along with the video.

"That's horrific," she said. "And up here, too, in such a pretty little town. What are the odds of that?"

"Surprisingly higher than you would think," Clare said. "Look, you've got a long drive home and the weather's getting worse. Why don't you go ahead and call it a day? I'll watch Cody until his parents get home."

"This has got to be so stressful to you," Elizabeth said, showing no signs of budging from the sofa. "Have you thought about taking some time off? Maybe going on a retreat? I know the diocese would be happy to provide a supply priest, all things considering."

"No. Thank you. I just came back from a sort of retreat. Six days alone in a cabin in the mountains. Now I need work." Work and love, wasn't that what Freud called the ultimate cure?

"Not quite alone in the cabin, surely," de Groot said in a small voice.

"Alone enough," Clare snapped. She breathed deeply. "Alone enough to realize that right now I need to make my parishioners my priority."

"I hope I can help you to do that," Elizabeth said. She sat to attention, very upright and brave. "Although . . . won't it be difficult to concentrate on serving them when you have criminal charges hanging over your head?"

"There are no criminal charges!" *Great. Now I sound like a shrew.*

"Because of this Shambaugh fellow, right. Who's a suspect." Elizabeth paused. "But what happens if—just hypothetically, mind you—whatever sort of evidence they pull together doesn't implicate him? Will they start looking at you more seriously? I mean"—she laughed briefly, a musical ripple that went down the scale and up Clare's nerves—"it's silly, because what reason would you have to kill a pet sitter?"

"I wouldn't have reason to kill anyone!"

"Of course not! I just meant—well, you said the police didn't know if someone killed that poor woman because he or she thought she was Linda Van Alstyne. And it seems as if—and I may have this wrong, this is just the impression I've been getting—you're fairly close to Mr. Van Alstyne."

"Elizabeth, what do you want to know? Did I have sex with Russ Van Alstyne and kill his wife? No and no."

The new deacon's head snapped back toward Cody, but it looked as if the *s*-word didn't interest him any more than the *k*-word had.

"Goodness," she said.

"I'm sorry to be blunt," Clare said, although she could think of several words that would have been a lot blunter. "It's been a miserable day. It's been a miserable several days, and I'm in no condition to play ring around the rosies. So let's just cut to the chase. Did I have a relationship with Chief Van Alstyne? Yes. Was it inappropriately physical? No. Did it cross over the bounds emotionally? Yes. Have I severed our connection?"

No. Never. God, she was an idiot. It was a good thing she believed in redemption through grace. Otherwise, she'd have to say she was simply too dumb to live.

"Yes?" Elizabeth quivered with interest.

"I thought," she began. She had come unmoored, and the words and events of the past four days swooped and fluttered through her head like a pack of cards tossed into the air. "We agreed not to see each other—of course, with his wife dead—but she's not, now. They'll have a second chance to be together. That's good, isn't it. No contact."

"Clare?" the deacon leaned forward. "Are you all right?"

Pull yourself together or the bishop's not going to suspend you, he's going to institutionalize you. "Yes," she said. "I'm okay."

The phone rang in the kitchen.

"Should we . . . ?" Elizabeth asked.

"It might be one of the Burnses," Clare said. She rose from the chair with almost indecent haste and went into the darkened kitchen. The phone's number pad was lit, and it was blinking with messages.

"Burns residence," she said.

"Clare?"

"Karen. Hi. How's it going?"

Karen made a noise that in a less elegant woman would have been a grunt. "Do you own a medium-sized backpack? Purple camo? From L.L.Bean?"

"Ye-e-es."

"When was the last time you carried it?"

"This past week, when I was up at Mr. Fitzgerald's cabin. I used it as a day pack when I went snowshoeing. It should still be packed from my last time out."

"What sort of things would you put in it?"

"What sort of things? I don't know. The usual stuff you'd take when you're heading out into the woods in winter. Matches, gorp, one of those heat-reflective blankets. Why?"

Karen sighed. "Because they've just found a knife inside your backpack. A K-Bar. Which happens to be the same sort of knife that killed Audrey Keane."

THIRTY-SEVEN

Thursday, January 17

"The knife doesn't mean anything," Lyle MacAuley said. "K-Bars are as common as dirt. You can pick 'em up at any army surplus or hunting supply store in the state. Russ had one. I have one. Who else has one?" His voice challenged the squad room.

Kevin Flynn raised a hand. "I got one when I was a kid. I was thinking of maybe going into the marines back then."

Lyle looked at him, surprised, over the rim of his coffee cup.

"It seemed like the cool thing to do at the time," Kevin said defensively. "It made me feel real"—he paused—"deadly." He lapsed into a bad Clint Eastwood impersonation. "Do you feel lucky, punk? Do ya?"

"That was a .44 Magnum," Eric said around a mouthful of doughnut.

Kevin looked horrified. "My mom wouldn't let me have a *gun!*"

"Thank you, Kevin," Russ said. "I think you've made your point, Lyle." He settled himself more firmly on the desktop and planted his feet on two chairs. The familiar position helped him feel less out of place in his jeans and flannel shirt.

"Her lawyer says Fergusson's had it since her army days." Emiley Jensen sauntered into the middle of the briefing area and stood legs wide and arms akimbo, as if to remind Russ that this was her meeting, not his. "Says she took it up to the cabin because she wanted a knife with her when she went snow-shoeing."

"That's just being safe, when you're out in the woods," Lyle said.

"Good woodsmanship or not, she's got a K-Bar. The murder weapon."

"No, *a* K-Bar's been identified as the murder weapon. Not hers specifically. I've got one missing. Dennie Shambaugh's got one." Russ tapped the print report laid on the desk next to him. "And according to Sergeant Morin, his prints are in my house. Clare's aren't."

Jensen hooked her thumbs into her pockets. She was wearing low-slung pants instead of a skirt this morning, with a tight shirt that fell over her waistband and a cushy jacket. If she had been in his department, he would have sent her home with orders to dress like a grown-up instead of an Abercrombie and Fitch model.

"I'm going to remind you, Mr. Van Alstyne, that you're here on sufferance. You're still suspended from duty pending the outcome of this investigation."

Like he needed a reminder. The empty space on his hip where his gun wasn't was like a missing tooth, constantly drawing his hand to test if it was still gone.

"I want a time line based on what we have now," Jensen said, turning to the whiteboard on the wall. "McCrea?"

Eric put down his white mocha latte and flipped open his notes. "There were three phone calls made from Mrs. Van Alstyne's cell to Audrey Keane's cell. The last one was Friday at 6:00 P.M. On Saturday afternoon, Mrs. Van Alstyne spoke with Margaret Tracey from the house's landline. Her son, Quinn Tracey, later witnessed Audrey Keane's vehicle parked in the Van Alstyne driveway late Sunday afternoon, just before sunset."

"Four to four thirty," Lyle murmured.

"We're still waiting on the phone company to fax us Keane's records," Eric continued. "Mrs. Tracey finds the body about 4:00 P.M. Monday. The next significant development is at 2:00 P.M. Wednesday, when the chief surprises Dennis Shambaugh at Keane's house."

"I dug out Shambaugh's case file from seven years back," Lyle said. "Audrey Keane was his girlfriend back then, if anyone had any doubts."

"Was Shambaugh out early on parole?" Russ asked.

Lyle nodded. "He's still got three years to go if he violates. We've got a call in to his parole officer."

"Why was he still there?" Mark asked.

Everyone looked at him.

"I mean, he's out on parole. If he so much as runs a red light, he's going back to Clinton. Why hang around his girlfriend's house for forty-eight hours or more after he killed her?"

"It's his address of record?" Eric McCrea pitched his question to the room at large, pointedly not speaking to Durkee. "If he's not there, he's in violation of parole."

Lyle shook his head. "Address of record is the Lafayette Arms." The Lafayette was a single-resident occupancy hotel in Fort Henry.

"His computer setup, then," Eric said.

"It would've taken him a half hour to unplug everything and pack it into the car." Mark turned toward Russ. "I get why he ran when he saw you, Chief. There's gonna be enough evidence on those computers to put him away for another ten years. I just don't get why he was still there waiting."

"Maybe because Dennis Shambaugh didn't kill Audrey Keane," Jensen said. She took a dry-erase marker and underlined Keane's name twice on the board. "It doesn't make sense if he killed his girlfriend. But if she wasn't the intended target—if Linda Van Alstyne was—then why should he run? There's no report in the news that Audrey Keane has been killed. Maybe as far as he knew, his girlfriend was still alive and kicking someplace."

"After a woman had been murdered in the house where Keane was cat-sitting?" Mark sounded dubious.

"Maybe he thought Keane killed Mrs. Van Alstyne," Kevin suggested.

"She has no record of violence," Lyle said. "No record of any kind."

"Besides," Mark said, "wouldn't that make it more likely he would've cleared out? Before we came knocking on the door?"

"Enough." Jensen raised her hands. "We need Dennis Shambaugh. Family member?"

"A whole lot of 'em," Lyle said. "He was one of seven kids scattered between here and Buffalo. Mary Ann, Mary Beatrice, Charles, Dennis, Eugene—"

"Jesus. They sound like the road company of *Seven Brides for Seven Brothers*. Okay, get on them. Friends? Acquaintances? Anybody he owes money to?"

"We'll start with what we can get from his parole officer," Eric said. "I'll call Clinton and see if they have any visitors on record."

"Good." Jensen let her gaze travel slowly around the squad room, making sure everyone there knew he was in her sights. "We need statements from everybody he and Keane came into contact with since he got out. We need to question this Deacon Aberforth who saw Reverend Fergusson Monday afternoon, and I want a warrant to search her car and that cabin she was staying at. We'll pick this up again tonight at five o'clock. Maybe this investigation will make better progress now we're not all worried about where Mr. Van Alstyne is."

He had written down the names, addresses, and phone numbers of the last five clients Linda had worked with on site. He gave it to Harlene. "I don't expect you'll be able to reach my cell phone much," he said. "A lot of these places are in the mountains. If you hear anything, anything at all, and you can't reach me, try one of these numbers. I put 'em in pretty much the order I'm gonna visit 'em."

Harlene, who had three counties' worth of roads in her head after thirty years on dispatch, looked up from the list. "It's supposed to start coming down hard around lunchtime. Are you sure you want to be out driving around in a storm? Can't you just call 'em instead?"

He pinched the bridge of his nose beneath his glasses. "You know as well as I there are things you find out in person you'll never get over the phone."

She gave him a look that said, *Now pull the other one.*

"I'm useless here. A lame duck." He waved a hand at himself: no badge, no gun, no uniform. "I don't get out and do *something*, I'll go nuts."

She shook her head. "Take care of yourself. Don't make more work for us by wrapping your truck around a tree."

He twitched a smile at her.

Walking down the hallway felt oddly final, as if he were going and not coming back. He paused in the foyer to zip his scarf inside his jacket and heard footsteps behind him. He turned. It was Lyle.

"Where are you going?"

"To find my wife."

Lyle jammed his hands into his pockets. "We got that BOLO out on 'er. Coast to coast. Describes her as a cop's wife, so everyone'll be looking that much harder for her."

Except, of course, the ones who would assume she was running away from the domestic violence that sometimes erupts in police families. He pulled his gloves from his pocket and tugged them on.

"Russ," Lyle began.

He held up his hand. "Don't."

"Come on. You gotta hear me out."

"No, I don't. The only thing I've got to do is keep from smashing your face in." Empty talk. Posturing. He didn't feel like taking Lyle apart. He just felt sick and tired and dirty. And it was only eight o'clock in the morning.

"She's alive. That means you're going to have to deal with it sooner or later."

"Her, I forgive. You can take a flying fuck." He turned toward the marble stairs. Lyle grabbed his arm.

Russ spun around. He had a good five inches and forty pounds on MacAuley, but his deputy chief didn't give an inch.

"I didn't know you then," Lyle said, his voice tight. "She was unhappy and lonely, and the only reason—"

"I don't want to hear this!"

"The only reason we got together was because she was so pissed off at you for bringing her to Millers Kill." Lyle glanced away. "I figured that out later."

"Surprisingly, that doesn't make me feel any better."

"Oh, for God's sake, Russ, get your head out of your ass. You've been so busy telling yourself you're happily married you never opened up your eyes to see what was really going on. And I don't mean Linda using me to flip you the bird seven years ago. Okay, I'm a son of a whore and you got the right to re-arrange my face. I slept with your wife and then I got to know you and respect you and to like you, and I never had the guts to come clean. I'm sorry. Jesus. I can't say it any more'n that. I'm sorry. But you gotta face the fact that there's something wrong with the marriage when a husband and wife act like you two have."

"Not that it's any of your business," Russ said between clenched teeth, "but I know there's something wrong with my marriage. And I'm going to fix it as soon as I find my wife."

Lyle released his arm. He sighed, a flat, defeated sigh. "Right."

Russ turned. Took the top two steps. Turned back. "The thing I don't get," he said, "is why? Even if you didn't know me, you knew I was heading up the department. Why make trouble in your own backyard? Why *my* wife?"

Lyle smiled without humor. "I'da thought you of all people would've figured that out." His eyes slid away from Russ's and looked at some point seven years in the past. "I was in love with her," he said. "I was in love with her, too."

THIRTY-EIGHT

———

Clare refused to look at the paper Thursday morning. She cracked open the front door of the rectory and saw it lying on her porch in its bright yellow plastic bag to protect it from the promised storm, and wondered why she had never seen how much it resembled an unexploded pipe bomb. Or a large, malignant yellow jacket, waiting for her to reach out an unwary hand and be stung. She closed the door. Whatever was in it, she'd find out soon enough.

She dressed quickly, trying not to notice the jumbled disarray in her sweater drawer or the way her skirt hangers had been shoved to one side of her closet. In the kitchen, she opened the pantry door to get out the oatmeal and was so dismayed by the mess she shut the door again, her appetite gone. What had they thought she was hiding behind the canned tomatoes and boxes of rigatoni?

She poured coffee from the coffeemaker into her Thermos. She pulled on her boots and parka. Next to her coat tree, the phone on the wall blinked its red message light over and over and over again. She hesitated, her hand over the play button. Maybe Russ had called?

Then she thought of his face in the station, the distrustful cop mask falling over his features, and anger burst behind her eyes, bitter and salty in her mouth. No. Russ had not called. She left the phone flashing monotonously behind the kitchen door and crunched her way down her unplowed drive toward the church.

She let herself in by the back door, walking through the still-darkened parish hall toward her office. She was surprised, as she drew closer, to hear a voice from the main office. She was always the first one in. Lois didn't show up until nine. She slowed her steps, drawing close to the doorway without entering.

The voice was talking, then pausing. A phone conversation. "I don't know enough to make a recommendation." Elizabeth de Groot. Goodness, she was quite the woman of Proverbs, wasn't she? *She riseth also while it is yet night.* "I thought you should hear it from me first," Elizabeth went on. Clare leaned forward, and the Thermos thumped against her leg. She froze. "No," Elizabeth said. Another long pause. "Well, that's for the police to decide, isn't it?"

Clare suddenly saw herself as she was, lurking in the darkness outside her church's office, eavesdropping on a private conversation. It was not a pretty picture. She retreated a couple of steps, cleared her throat, and called out, "Hello?"

There was a second's pause before de Groot answered, "Hi, Clare! It's me, Elizabeth." Then something quiet into the phone. By the time Clare came through the door, she was setting the receiver into the cradle. "I decided to get in early today," Elizabeth said. "There's so much I have to absorb just to get up to speed."

"Mmm." Clare rested her Thermos on Lois's desk.

"I really think I can make a contribution to the ongoing capital campaign," Elizabeth went on. "Not to mention with the stewardship committee. And I've been thinking more about outreach. I think we can expand it way beyond simply getting people who are already congregants back into the pews."

Clare let the deacon rattle on while she debated asking Elizabeth what her *real* agenda was at St. Alban's. Would the information she got be worth tipping her hand? *When reconnoitering enemy territory,* Master Sergeant Ashley "Hardball" Wright drawled, *the first, second, and last rule is: Don't get caught.* Her old SERE instructor would've flunked her if she blabbed about hearing the phone call or wondered aloud what de Groot was doing for the bishop.

Elizabeth ran out of conversational steam and looked up at Clare with a mixture of sunshine and wariness.

"You'd better think about gathering up what you need and taking it home," Clare said. "They're predicting this storm is going to be one for the record books. You don't want to be trapped on the Northway."

The fine lines around Elizabeth's eyes relaxed almost imperceptibly. "Are you going to close the office?"

Clare shook her head. "Not yet. I've got a couple of counseling sessions this morning. If it's looking bad after that, I'll send Lois and Mr. Hadley home."

"What about Evening Prayer?"

"Let's take a listen to what the rest of the world's doing." Clare switched on Lois's radio. The Storm Center First Response Team was reading off an alphabetical list of area schools that were closed, followed by businesses shutting early and manufacturers canceling shifts. Sounded like the world and his wife were going to stay at home and sit this one out. "Okay," Clare said. "I'll call the snow-closing hotline later this morning and let them know there's no Evening Prayer." Two and a half years ago, she hadn't even known what a snow-closing hotline was. Now she had it on her speed dial.

She left her new deacon to either pull together more information on donor programs or plot her downfall and went into her office. Mr. Hadley had left her wood and kindling in a big iron basket next to the hearth, and she laid a fire in the grate, thankful for the soothing manual task, thankful, once the kindling had caught and flames were crackling up in the strong draft, that she spent her days in a beautiful old building with real working fireplaces. And uneven floors. And drafty windows. And a yearly oil bill that probably paid for the president of Exxon's yacht.

Her first appointment arrived promptly at eight. Chris Ellis, father of three, husband to Dr. Anne Vining-Ellis, had had a panic attack two months ago in his office. His doctor prescribed Valium and counseling. It had taken two sessions for Clare to figure out Chris Ellis's problem: He hated his job. He hated the work, civil engineering; he hated his younger, more ambitious colleagues; he hated the management, which was bent on taking the firm national; and he hated his two-hour daily commute to Albany. In one more session, he admitted he wanted to pursue his true passion, fine furniture making, currently relegated to a basement hobby. Since then, he had been working toward either taking the leap or living with what he had. Clare privately thought he ought to go for it, but with his eldest son at Brown and the second due to start college next year, she could see why he was reluctant to abandon the regular paycheck and benefits.

She was delighted when he told her he'd accepted a paying commission. "It's for four classic Adirondack antler chairs and a matching table. Just like the ones I did for my friend David's restaurant. Get this—the owner of the Algonquin Waters was having lunch at David's, saw my pieces, and asked about them. He wants a set for the hotel!"

"The owner of the Algonquin resort? Was lunching in Saratoga?"

"Yep. Name's Oppenheimer."

"Opperman," Clare said. "John Opperman."

"I didn't actually meet him. He left word with the general manager before he left town, and she contacted me. Apparently, they're very committed to using local craftsmen and material in the hotel."

She blinked. First Linda Van Alstyne, then Chris Ellis. Before they knew it, half the town was going to be employed by Opperman's company. It probably wouldn't do any good to mention her belief that the owner of the Algonquin Spa and Resort had manipulated his two business partners to their deaths. The only other person who shared her opinion was Russ Van Alstyne, and he wasn't about to be propping up her arguments any time soon. It was a moot point, anyway. Businesses killed people every day in some part of the world or another. Though she suspected they did it with less personal involvement than Opperman.

She said something encouraging, and Chris talked for a while about seeing if he could structure a part-time position at his firm, or maybe independently consult for them, and when they wrapped up, she was guiltily aware that she'd only given him half her attention. Encountering the same people, businesses, gossip—that was life in a small town. She thought of Ben Beagle, and his big hog-killing story. It was not a conspiracy to make her see the Algonquin Waters at every turn. It was just where she lived.

The Garrettsons were next. Clare took a large slug of coffee and threw another log on the fire. Tim and Liz were always a bit of an ordeal. They entered either bickering or in a stony silence, which was worse. This morning it was silence.

"So," Clare said. "How are you?"

Liz gazed at her husband with Laser Beam Death Ray eyes.

"She's hacked off about her mother," Tim said. "Again."

Clare picked up her coffee mug. Wished she had thought to pour some whiskey into it first. "Last week we agreed we were going to stay off the subject of—"

"I brought her back from the hospital and her cats were dead!"

"You can't blame me for her dead cats, Liz."

"I'm confused," Clare said. "I thought there was a neighbor who looks after your mother's house when she's away."

"A very responsible neighbor who brings in the mail and the paper and leaves the check for the snowplow and feeds the damn cats," Tim said. "We slip her thank-you money in a card every few months."

"We wouldn't need someone else to help Mom if she were living with us."

"We wouldn't have to worry about any of her needs if she was in the Infirmary!"

"What happened to the cats?" Clare asked.

"The cats are a side issue," Tim said. "There's always something that's going wrong. It'll always be something going wrong until we put her in a home, where she belongs."

"They were killed," Liz said, ignoring her husband. "It was horrible. I went into the barn to get the rock salt to scatter on her walk and steps"—her angry glance at Tim led Clare to guess that was supposed to be his job—"and there they were. Sliced to pieces."

"It was probably a fisher," Tim said.

"A fisher would've eaten them," Liz said. "Not left their little frozen carcasses behind."

Clare frowned. "When I saw her in the hospital, your mother said something about someone trying to kill her cats."

"It's not about the cats," Tim repeated. "It's about the fact that Liz's mom isn't competent to manage her own household anymore." He turned to his wife. "It's going to be one disaster after another until you realize putting her in the Infirmary isn't setting her out on a goddamn ice floe."

Liz gasped. "You didn't do it, did you?"

"Oh, for chrissake, of course I didn't kill your mother's cats!"

"Did you report it to the police?"

Both Garrettsons looked at Clare as if she were crazy. "They were cats," Liz said. "It was awful, but it's not like, you know, Quinn Tracey's mother discovering the police chief's wife's body."

Clare's first thought was, *Oh, good, they haven't read the* Post-Star *yet today.* Then Liz Garrettson's phrasing struck her. "Quinn Tracey's mother?"

The Garrettsons looked at each other again. "We figured . . . you probably had heard about that," Tim said tactfully.

"No, I mean, why call her Quinn Tracey's mother? Instead of Meg Tracey?"

"Oh." Liz's face cleared. "I guess I thought of her that way because we know Quinn. He's the one who does Mom's plowing for us."

Clare normally walked the Garrettsons to the church door to bid them good-bye. This morning, she shook their hands, abandoned them where they sat, and was in Lois's office before they had gotten their coats on.

"Lois, what was the name of the family that wanted me to pray for their lamb?"

Lois was never flustered by Clare's more unusual outbursts. "The Campbells. Abigail Campbell is the mom."

"Can you get me their number? Is she likely to be at home?"

Lois was already flipping through her personal copy of the parish directory, hand-annotated with all sorts of facts not readily available to the general public. "She works at Sheehan Realty in Glens Falls."

Clare grabbed the Glens Falls phone book off the shelf.

Elizabeth de Groot was by now standing in the doorway of her minuscule office. "What's going on? Did I hear you say someone wanted prayers for a lamb?"

"A memorial service, really," Lois said.

The new deacon's winged eyebrows knitted together in a delicate frown. "Is this metaphorical?"

"I assure you, it's quite flesh-and-blood." Clare trapped the number beneath a finger and gestured to Lois for the phone.

"I have to point out it's probably chops and stew meat by now," the secretary said. "Maybe a couple of little legs for roasting."

A bland voice answered the phone. "Sheehan Realty."

"Could I speak to Abigail Campbell, please?"

"May I say who's calling?"

"Her priest."

There was a pause. Then: "Oh! Of course. Please hold."

Clare looked up to see de Groot nervously glancing back and forth between her and Lois. Then the Muzak cut off and she was live.

"Hello?"

"Hi. Abigail? Clare Fergusson here."

"Oh, Reverend Fergusson." The woman on the other end of the line sounded embarrassed. "I'm sorry I left you that message last week. It's just that the kids were so upset, and I was, too, of course, and we were trying to come up with something to make us all feel better, you know, and not so *violated*—"

"I have a question that's going to sound a little odd," Clare said.

"—but we had a sweet do-it-yourself service and we donated his body, as it were, to the food kitchen, so he didn't die in vain—"

"Abigail?"

"—and frankly right now I think that having you do anything, you know, official will just open up the wounds again."

This time Clare waited a moment to make sure she had run down. When she was sure there was nothing else, she said, "No service, then?"

"No service. Maybe we could do something else to remember him."

"Abigail, do you have someone plow your driveway?"

This time, there was a definite pause. "Ye-e-es," Abigail said. "I'm divorced. It's one of those jobs I'm willing to pay someone to do."

"Who does your plowing?"

A longer pause. "A young man named Quinn Tracey. I sold his family their house a few years back. Why?"

THIRTY-NINE

As soon as she got off the phone with Abigail Campbell—Clare agreed to insert the lamb's name in the weekly prayers for the dead—she whipped through the pages of the phone book, looking for the number of the Glens Falls newspaper.

"Who are you calling now?" Elizabeth asked.

"A reporter from the *Post-Star*. The one who's writing about the Linda Van Alstyne–Audrey Keane screwup."

The deacon looked at Lois, who shrugged. Clare found the number, stabbed it in, and, getting an automated directory, punched in the first three letters of her party's last name.

"Hi! Ben Beagle here!" The reporter sounded much too bright and cheery, as if he'd already been up five hours, run four miles, and filed the first story of the day.

"Hi. This is Clare Fergusson."

"Ah! What can I do for you, Reverend?" He didn't sound anything less than happy to hear from her. She really ought to read today's paper. Maybe it wasn't as bad as she imagined. Then he went on, "I have to warn you, the *Post-Star* only prints retractions when a subject has clear and convincing proof that we used false information in a story."

Maybe it was worse than she imagined.

"Actually, I'm not calling about the, um, Van Alstyne business. I had a question about the story you mentioned to me yesterday morning." Was it really only yesterday morning? It felt like a year had passed.

"Shoot."

"The guy whose hog had been killed—what actually happened to the hog?"

"It'd been sliced up. Throat slit, cut open from stem to stern, hacked up a bit around the hams."

"Did you see it? Did he report it to the police?"

"Yeah, he filed a report. I didn't see the pig in situ, but he had taken pictures to show to the cops. A full-grown pig's worth three, four hundred bucks, according to him."

"Can you tell me who it was? The farmer?"

"He isn't a real farmer. He's a pediatrician down in Clifton Park. He has a big old place, raises chickens and a couple pigs every year." In the background, she could hear paper rustling. "His name's Irving Underkirk. Why so interested?"

"A parishioner of mine had a lamb killed last week. It sounded similar to what you described."

"You think someone's out there running a do-it-yourself butcher shop?"

Clare made a noncommittal noise. "Do you have a number where I could reach him?"

"I've got his home and work." Beagle rattled off the numbers. Clare jotted them down in the margin of the phone book.

"ThanksMr.BeagleIappreciatethis," Clare said. " 'Bye."

"Wait—" she heard, but the receiver was already in the cradle.

She immediately dialed the pediatrician's office number.

"Clare," Elizabeth said. "Help me out here. I'm not quite seeing how tracking down dead animals fits in with your pastoral duties."

"She's tackling animal welfare and snow removal at the same time," Lois said. "I think that's very efficient, don't you?"

Elizabeth sidled away from the secretary.

"Clifton Park Pediatric Services," the phone said in Clare's ear.

"I'd like to speak to Dr. Underkirk, please."

"Do you have an emergency?"

"No, it's, um—" Clare had forgotten that it was impossible to actually pick up a phone and speak with a physician. "It's not an emergency."

"Well, then, I'm afraid—"

"Could you put me through to his nurse?"

"We have a triage nurse you can speak to."

"It's not a medical issue at all." Clare breathed in. It didn't do any good to tear the head off the hapless receptionist. "I'm looking into a series of animal killings. I understand the doctor lost a pig—"

"Oh, Lord, yes. We all heard about the pig."

"I need to ask him a question related to the"—animal cruelty? Vandalism?—"incident," Clare decided. "If you can put me through to his nurse, she could relay the question for me."

"Well, that's a pig of a different color, isn't it. He'll definitely want to hear about this. Hang on, you may be on hold for a while."

Muzak again. Clare clapped her hand over the receiver and said, "Lois, would you get on the other line and call Harlene Lendrum at the police station? Ask her if there've been any other reports of animals being killed. Try to get the names and numbers if there have been any."

"This just doesn't strike me as being the church's business," Elizabeth said.

"Business? Mankind is our business," Lois quoted, picking up her notepad and swiveling off her chair. "Mind if I use your phone, Deacon?"

Elizabeth made a wilting gesture toward her tiny office. Lois disappeared inside.

"I'm beginning to understand how you get sucked into these things," the new deacon said. "You let yourself get swept away in the rush of events, and you don't stop to think about whether or not this is something you ought to be sticking your nose into."

Clare was about to admit that was a pretty fair assessment of her character, but the sound of a voice on the line brought her back to the pediatrician's office.

"Hi, this is Dr. Underkirk's nurse, Violet." She had the kind of voice that made Clare think of overstuffed sofas and starchy, nourishing meals. "Marcy tells me you know something about Tom, Tom the piper's son?" Nurse Violet let out a peal of laughter. Clare began to get the idea that his office staff had been less than sympathetic to Dr. Underkirk's plight.

"I'm looking for information, actually. My name's Clare Fergusson, and I'm trying to see if there are any common elements between Dr. Underkirk's case and two others."

"What do you want to know?" Nurse Violet said. "He'll be that happy hearing someone's looking into it. He's had his tail in a twist since it happened. Get it? Tail in a twist?" The nurse giggled.

"Uh-huh." Clare closed her eyes for a moment. "Does the doctor have a snowplowing service, and if so, who does the work for him?"

"That's it?"

"That's it," Clare said.

"Hang on." She heard a clunking sound on the other end. Elizabeth looked at her, frustration and unhappiness thinning her lips, throwing previously invisible lines into relief. *Great,* thought Clare. *I'm causing the bishop's deacon to age before my eyes. Maybe that says something about the way I'm running my life.*

"You still there?" Nurse Violet came on. "Dr. Underkirk says he gets plowed out by one of his patients. A young man named Tracey."

Clare forgot all about Elizabeth's premature decay.

"Thanks," she said.

"You're welcome," Nurse Violet said. "And by all means, let us know if you catch the little porker!" She was still laughing when Clare hung up.

Lois emerged from the deacon's cubbyhole. "Bingo," she said, turning her notepad around so Clare could see her writing on the other side. "Three reports of animals being killed in the past month, according to the dispatcher. One of them was the doctor, one is an old fellow named Herb Perkins who lost a dog, and the last is a couple of professors at Skidmore who lost one of their goats." She pointed to the paper. "Names and addresses right there."

Clare took the notepad. "You're wonderful, Lois."

"I know. And I'm not the only one. Guess who had just gotten off the phone with the dispatcher right before I called?"

Clare blanked. "Who?"

"Ben Beagle of the *Post-Star.*"

"Damn. He's a tad too quick off the mark for comfort." She tried the professors' number first and got their answering machine. She left as abbreviated a message as she could: She was looking into a series of animal cruelty cases, and was their driveway plowed by Quinn Tracey? Herb Perkins, who was home, didn't seem happy to hear from a stranger nosing about his business.

"Yeah, I get my dooryard plowed out," he said in a voice like a crumbling cigar. "Don't see what that's got to do with somebody killin' one of my dogs."

"I'm looking for a common thread between several incidents, Mr. Perkins."

"We like as not all shop at the IGA. You think mebbe one o' them cashiers got it in for us?"

"Probably not, no. Could you tell me who does your plowing?"

She wasn't the least surprised by his answer.

Clare laid the notebook face up on Lois's desk. "Look at this. Perkins, Underkirk, the Campbells, and Liz Garrettson's mother. All of them hired Quinn Tracey to plow for them, and all of them have an animal or animals killed within the last month. Outdoor animals, living in barns. Not house pets."

Lois studied the names and addresses she had written down. "All the roads I recognize here are pretty much out in the country. Nobody living in town."

"Like Peekskill Road," Clare said. "Where the Van Alstynes live."

"What are you saying?" Elizabeth pressed her hand against her chest as if to quell the shock. Lois rolled her eyes.

"I'm saying Quinn Tracey has a direct connection to the locations of four animal deaths and a murder. Russ—Chief Van Alstyne likes to say there's no such thing as coincidence."

"You want me to get the police station back on the phone?" Lois asked.

"Please." Clare opened the Millers Kill phone book to see if Dr. Underkirk's address was listed.

"I should certainly hope so!" Elizabeth said. "Most of the people involved aren't even congregants!"

"On second thought, Lois, I'll call from my office." Clare straightened, tucking the phone book and notepad beneath her arm. "Think of it as a sort of outreach, Elizabeth. Maybe the pediatrician and Mr. Perkins will be so grateful we've solved the mystery of who killed their animals, they'll come to church to thank us. Then we'll snag 'em and make them sit through a nice Evensong. A good choir converts more would-be Episcopalians than any amount of preaching does."

In her office, Clare poured more coffee and then picked up the phone before her nerve failed her.

"Millers Kill Police Department."

"Harlene? Hi, it's Clare Fergusson."

"Clare!" Harlene's voice dropped. "How are you, honey? I just want you to know, no matter what they say, I'll never believe you did it."

"Uh, thanks." She swallowed some coffee and pressed on. "Look, Harlene, I've come across some information that I think might be very important to the investigation. Who should I talk to?"

"Hmmm." Clare could picture Harlene's face furrowing with thought beneath her tightly permed curls. "Well, most all of 'em who investigate are out beating the bushes for this Shambaugh fellow. So you got your choice. Investigator Jensen or Mark Durkee, who hasn't been given nothing to do yet."

"I'm guessing Investigator Jensen is still hot for me as suspect number two?"

"Oh, yeah."

"How about Officer Durkee?"

"I don't think he's so convinced you did it anymore, but nobody's talking to him on account of his bringing Jensen here, and since the reason he got the staties involved was because he thought you were a suspect, he might not be feeling too kindly toward you."

"I didn't ask him to run to the state police in order to investigate me."

"No, but he's not the first person to blame someone else for troubles he brought on his own head."

Clare sighed. "Give me to Investigator Jensen. At least she doesn't have anything personal against me."

The line buzzed quietly for a moment and then Clare heard, "Emiley Jensen."

"Hi, Investigator Jensen. This is the Reverend Clare Fergusson." Her grandmother Fergusson would be rolling over in her grave at Clare using her own full title to introduce herself, but Clare figured at this point, every advantage counted.

"Reverend Fergusson. Do you mind if I put you on speakerphone?"

Clare interpreted that to mean *Do you mind if I tape this conversation?* "Not at all," she said.

The sound in her ear changed. "Can you hear me?" Jensen asked, her voice now distant and tinny.

"Yes."

"So, you wanted to speak to me?"

"I have some information I think is relevant to the investigation." Clare started with what she had observed when she met Quinn Tracey at the high school, touched on her talk with Aaron MacEntyre, and finished with what she had learned this morning. When she was done speaking, there was a long, tinny pause.

"Let me get this straight," Jensen finally said. "You think this teenager might have killed Audrey Keane?"

"I don't know," Clare said. "But I do know it's an awfully weird coincidence that four people have had animals killed recently and all of them are Quinn Tracey's customers. And, of course, the Van Alstynes had hired him, too."

"The murdered woman wasn't Mrs. Van Alstyne, though. Does Tracey have any connection to Audrey Keane?"

"Not that I know of. But maybe it's like the animals. He was in a relatively remote place, no one was around, and so he . . . killed her." Stated baldly like that for the first time, it sounded lame. "There's a well-known connection between sadism to animals and violence against humans," she said defensively.

"I've heard that, yeah. There's also a well-known connection between being an incredibly bored teen trapped in the countryside and dumb, destructive pranks. Do we know for sure all these animals were killed by a human being instead of a predator?"

Someone in the room with Jensen spoke to her. The words were too far away and indistinct for Clare to make out, but after the unknown officer had finished, Jensen's voice came back on. "Okay, I'm told investigation confirmed Perkins's dog and Underkirk's pig were killed by someone. The chief suspect in the dog's case is a neighbor whose favorite snowmobiling course was blocked off by Perkins. The theory about the pig is that somebody wanted it for its meat and got scared off by Underkirk before he could finish the theft."

"But you didn't know about the Quinn Tracey connection then," Clare said.

"No, the department didn't."

"Will you have someone look into it?"

"I'll pass the information along to Deputy Chief MacAuley. He'll put someone on it as soon as he can spare the manpower."

While Jensen had been talking, Clare had tightened her grip on her coffee mug. Now her knuckles showed white. "You can't wait until Lyle MacAuley decides there's nothing more important. You need to investigate this now. Quinn Tracey may have murdered Audrey Keane."

"This kid who has no record—you haven't run into him on anything, have you?" The question was spoken to the anonymous officer. He said something to Jensen. "Okay, he has no record and no encounters with the police," she told Clare. "And according to his guidance counselor, he's bright and hardworking, and he evidently has an involved, caring, educated family. And you think because two of his snowplowing clients had animals killed—crimes which were investigated but didn't implicate him—that last Monday he decided to slash a complete stranger's throat and cut her face off. Is that about it? Your theory?"

When you recognize an ambush, Hardball Wright said, *don't think you can turn tables on the enemy. You can't. Get out while the gettin's good.*

"Thank you for your time and consideration, Investigator Jensen." Clare did her best to sound as if she didn't want to strangle the woman on the other end of the line.

"Thank you for reporting this possible criminal activity, Reverend Fergusson. I'm sure we'll be speaking again soon."

Clare hung up. God. If Karen Burns were here, she'd probably thump Clare over the head for contacting Jensen without a lawyer standing by.

The remaining coffee was cooling rapidly. Better chuck it out and start over again. As she passed the office toward the ladies' room, Lois called out, "What did the police say?"

Clare allowed herself the detour. She perched on the edge of the secretary's desk. "I spoke to Investigator Jensen. She didn't come right out and call me an idiot for conflating a couple of dead cats into a conspiracy theory, but she managed to get her point across."

"Sorry," Lois said.

"She didn't dismiss the possibility that the Tracey boy might be involved in some of the animals' deaths, but she shot down my idea that there might be a connection between them and Audrey Keane's murder. She thinks it's just vandalism gone awry."

Lois tilted her head, causing her strawberry blond bob to swing along one side of her jaw. "She has a point. When my brother was in his teens, he and his friends used to set haystacks on fire for fun."

"You're kidding. You could burn someone's house or barn down."

"There's not a lot to do when you're a kid in the country." Lois gave her a sympathetic look, then perked up as the sedate fox-trot music on the radio gave way to the thunderous sound of the Storm Center First Response Team's theme music. Clare retreated with her cold coffee and her shredded enthusiasm, pursued by dire predictions of snow, snow, and more snow.

FORTY

Humility. That, Russ decided, was the lesson the universe wanted to teach him. Certainly, the value he placed on his wife and marriage first. He would never, as long as he lived, forget the horrible pithed feeling of hearing Linda was dead and the soul-lifting experience of having her resurrected by Sergeant Morin's fingerprint kit. It was almost—not quite, but almost—enough to make him believe in God.

Which is where the humility came in. He had spent the morning visiting all Linda's most recent job sites: a second home for skiing, a mother-in-law apartment, a charming farmhouse trying desperately to be a stately home with curtains swagged and draped and pelmeted up to the not-high-enough ceiling.

In each location, he had to explain that he had lost his wife. That she had left without word and had not contacted him in close to a week. Had anyone heard her mention a man? Or seen her with anyone other than one of her freelance seamstresses?

Humility. Clare would probably say it was good for him. He might have swallowed it with more grace if he had gotten anything other than embarrassed, sympathetic looks and "Sorry, I don't know anything that can help you."

He tightened his hands on the wheel of his truck and flicked on his wipers to rid the windshield of its steadily accumulating snow. Noon. The forecaster hit it dead on. He ought to call Harlene, make sure she got Duane and Tim, the parttimers, suited up for emergency response. If what the weatherman predicted was to be believed, they'd be coming up deep snow and whiteout conditions. He should also—

He caught himself short. He couldn't do a damn thing. He was an acting civilian until Jensen decided to give him back his badge. It was up to Lyle to make sure the department was ready for the Blizzard of the Century or the Killer Storm or whatever theme name the television stations would come up with to describe it. His job was to make it to his last stop. Linda's most recent work site. The Algonquin Waters Spa and Resort. He didn't hold out high hopes. It seemed like every time he came near the place, it was a disaster. The summer it was being built, he had taken off from its helipad in a chopper—the first one he had ridden in in decades—and promptly crashed. This past fall, he had the worst dinner of his life there, seated next to his wife and across the table from Clare. Christ, he was still suffering indigestion from that one. The ballroom and most of the ground floor going up in flames was sort of an anticlimax.

He knew what he was doing, recounting his past miseries at the Algonquin. He was avoiding thinking about what he was going to do if he didn't turn up any trace of Linda. He had no other leads. He had nothing. And the thought of returning to his freezing cold house, with its bloodstained kitchen and the fluttering ghosts of disappeared identities . . .

He shook his head, concentrated on the road. Past the turnoff, the hotel's private road was almost dry, the heavy-hanging pines sheltering it from the early snow. The road switched back and forth, climbing the mountain, until it opened out to the parking area, the wide portico, and the snow-covered, rock-walled gardens. He was surprised to see so many trucks and SUVs parked along the curving drive. While the Algonquin was planned as a year-round resort, it was supposed to be closed for rebuilding until spring.

The answer came when Russ pulled into a spot next to a big Ford 350. DON-ALDSON ELECTRICS was plated to the side. Construction workers. He got out of his truck, tugging his hat on to shield himself from the snow. Management must be in one all-fired hurry to finish the job if they had guys out working on a day like this. Maybe the hotel would put 'em up if they got snowed in?

He stepped through the front doors onto a sea of plastic sheeting. The sweeping wooden floor was covered with the sawdust and grit-spattered stuff, just as the few remaining pieces of furniture were obscured by drop cloths. The two-story stone wall at the far end of the lobby was still scorched and streaked with soot, and the open doorways to the ballroom were hung with dusty plastic tarps. No sign of any workmen or hotel employees, but beyond the canvas-covered reception desk, a light shone through a half-open door.

He crossed behind the desk. "Hello?" he said. "Anybody here?"

"Mmm." He heard something clatter against a desktop. A slim woman in jeans and a turtleneck appeared in the doorway, dabbing at her face with a paper napkin. "Sorry," she said around a mouthful. She beckoned him into the office. "Lunch."

He held up one hand. "No need to apologize. I probably should have called before coming over."

She finished chewing and swallowed with evident relief. "I'm afraid we're closed. As you can see, we're in the middle of a major rebuilding project."

"I'm not here for a room." He unzipped his parka.

"No?" She took a plate holding tangerine peels and the remains of a sandwich and slid it onto a credenza. "Please," she said, gesturing to one of two upholstered chairs across from the desk. She sat opposite him. "I'm Barbara LeBlanc," she said. "General manager."

"I know," he said. "We've met before."

She tucked a strand of dark auburn hair behind her ear and looked at him more closely. Her face lit with recognition. "The police chief! You were here the night of the fire. It's good to see you again . . ."

"Russ Van Alstyne," he supplied. "You have a good memory."

"In the hospitality business, it's a must. We're working with a curtain designer named Linda Van Alstyne. Any relation?"

"She's my wife."

Barbara LeBlanc smiled. "She does wonderful work. You must be very proud of her."

Ms. LeBlanc evidently remembered names but didn't keep up with the news. "I am. Proud." He had been spared having to tell everyone who might not have known that Linda was dead. Thank God for that.

She folded her hands and rested them on the desk. "So. What can I help you with?"

He felt his face getting hot, just as it had the last three times he launched into his spiel. "It's my wife. Linda Van Alstyne. She left our house without a word last Saturday or Sunday, and I haven't heard from her since. I'm hoping you might have some idea where she's gone, since she's still replacing the curtains and stuff that was lost in the fire."

Barbara LeBlanc's pleasant expression didn't alter, but it didn't reach her eyes, which became opaque. "She left Saturday *or* Sunday? You're not sure which?"

He sighed. "We're temporarily separated. I've been living at my mother's house for the past few weeks." Embarrassing as it was, he figured admitting he lived with his mom made him sound less like a potentially abusive husband trying to recapture a runaway wife.

LeBlanc shook her head. "I'm sorry. I've met your wife, of course, and we've spoken about payments for materials and things like that, but I don't have any idea where she could have gone."

She would make a good poker player. He had no idea whether she was telling him the truth or not.

"Is there anyone else she would have worked with here? Besides her seamstresses, I mean?" He had already called the three women who sewed for Linda.

"There's Mr. Opperman, of course. The owner. He makes all the design decisions. And I think she had one or two of Ray's crew help her with some of the heavy work. Installations she couldn't handle on her own."

It looked like he wasn't going to get out of this without speaking to Opperman. Another exercise in humility. "Can I speak to the foreman? And is there a number where I could contact Mr. Opperman?"

"He's supposed to be back this afternoon," Barbara said.

"The foreman?"

"Mr. Opperman."

"Here?" he said. "I thought the business was based in Baltimore."

"He's found it more . . . feasible to live here during the rebuilding. He's been away in New York City for a few days. He was going to drive up today, but I'm not sure if he'll make it, with the storm coming on."

Away for a few days? Oh, God, could it be that simple? "Was he alone in New York? Could Linda have been with him?"

Now he could make out what was behind her eyes. Pity. "As far as I know, he was alone. He's been meeting with travel companies about promoting the Algonquin. I can't vouch for his off-hours, but he's been in touch with me every day, either by phone or by fax."

"But you don't know for sure, do you? Is there any way to find out? If she's there?"

You really have been left behind like a three-legged dog, her expression said. She crossed her arms over her chest and bent her head. Russ sat, literally on the edge of his seat, afraid to breathe for fear of making her jump the wrong way. *Come on, come on.*

"Let me try something." She stood up and went around to her side of the desk. She picked up her phone and punched in a shortcut number.

"Hello," she said. "This is Barbara LeBlanc of the Algonquin Waters Spa and Resort. May I speak to Mr. Sacramone?" There was a pause. Then: "Fine, thanks. And you?" She smiled. "You flatterer. Watch out, one of these days I'm going to take you up on your offer." The flattering Mr. Sacramone went on for a half minute or so. "He has?" She looked at Russ. "He said he'd try to get back today. He can always stop in Albany if the weather gets too bad." A pause. She laughed. "Yes, I'm sure I'll be the one booking him a room in a snowstorm."

More unheard talking from Mr. Sacramone. "That's more or less the reason I'm calling," Barbara said. "Mr. Opperman told me to order flowers for the lady with whom he was staying. He wants them to be there when she gets home, you understand. But I don't have her address. Do you have it for me, by any chance? So I can keep looking like a miracle worker?"

Russ's stomach clenched. Barbara's eyebrows went up. "No? Huh. My mistake, then. I'll have to ask him to clarify for me when he gets in touch next." She looked at Russ, shook her head. "You, too, Emilio. *Ciao, bello.*" She hung up.

"The concierge at Mr. Opperman's hotel says he was alone his whole stay. Which doesn't surprise me. Mr. Opperman is very focused on the business."

He had enough of a sense of humor left to be amused by the fact that he was crushed because his wife hadn't gone off with the owner of the Algonquin. "Thanks anyway," he said. "I appreciate you trying."

"Let's go find Ray," Barbara said, her tone professionally upbeat. "Maybe he'll know something."

Russ followed her out of the office.

"They're working downstairs, in the spa facilities," she said. "The fire didn't spread that far, but we had extensive water damage. Lots of rewiring and retiling."

Broad stairs led down from the lobby to the spa. Once they were below the ground floor, Russ could hear the high-pitched grind of a Skil saw and someone cursing a stubborn coupling wire.

"Ray?" Barbara called. She picked her way past sawhorses and coils of insulated cable. "Ray?"

They entered the work area. Russ could see it had once probably been the fanciest place to soak your feet or get covered with mud between New York and Montreal. Now it was a god-awful mess, like a beautiful woman with a bad hangover and ratty hair. A man in a flannel shirt and suspenders unbent from where he was studying a blueprint. "Whitey! Matt! Knock it off a minute." The Skil saw died away. The big guy crossed the work space toward them. He was as tall as Russ and a good fifty pounds heavier, with the open face of a man who viewed the world as his friend until proven otherwise.

"Hey, Ms. LeBlanc. What can I do you for?"

"This is Ray Yardhaas, our foreman. Ray, this is the Millers Kill chief of police, Russ Van Alstyne."

Ray shook his hand. "We met before. Two summers ago, when we were building this place the first time." He grinned. "First time I ever met someone investigating a real live murder. Impressed the hell out of my wife."

"Ray, we're looking for someone who might have been helping Mrs. Van Alstyne with the curtain installations."

"Mrs. Van Alstyne?" He glanced at Russ. "You mean the curtain lady? Yeah, that'd mostly be Charlie. Why? Has he been bothering her?"

Leblanc frowned. "Is that a concern?"

"Aw, his heart's in the right place, I guess. It's just his mouth's usually in third gear while his brain's still easing off the brake. He's got little hands, though. Good for doing that fiddly sort of work."

"Can I talk to him?" Russ asked.

"He's taking a break." Ray mimed puffing on a cigarette. "He's my crew, though. If he's been up to something he shouldn't, I want to know about it."

Ross shook his head. "I'm just looking for some information." He considered how much to share. "My wife—"

Ray pointed over his shoulder. "Here he is."

Russ turned around.

And saw Dennie Shambaugh walking toward him.

FORTY-ONE

Russ was on Shambaugh in two long strides, his knuckles twisting in the neck of the man's shirt, choking off his air and forcing him to his knees. Barbara LeBlanc was yelling something, but he couldn't make it out over the pounding in his ears.

"Where is she, you bastard?" Russ's grip tightened as his voice rose to a howl. "Where's my wife?"

He was jerked back by a pair of oven-mitt-sized hands wrapped around his arms. "Slow down there, Chief." Ray didn't have to raise his voice to boom. "I thought you just wanted to ask him some questions."

Russ twisted out of Yardhaas's grasp. "That man is under arrest," he said, pointing at the quivering, hacking heap of flannel and denim on the floor. His hand shook. "For information fraud, suspicion of murder, and the disappearance of Linda Van Alstyne." He lunged toward Shambaugh. "Where's my wife?" he shouted.

The man threw up his hands. "I don't know nothing! I don't know nothing!" He peeked through his forearms at Russ, bracing for the blow to fall.

Russ stared.

He grabbed the man's wrists and forced them down.

"Don't hurt me," the man whimpered. "Ray, don't let him hurt me."

It wasn't Dennie Shambaugh.

"Shit," Russ said, releasing his hold. He turned away, struggling to get control of himself. "Christ almighty." He turned back. "I'm sorry." He looked at the man cowering on the floor, at Yardhaas, at Barbara, who was staring at him with dismay. "I'm sorry. We're looking for a man named Dennis Shambaugh. I thought you were him. I'm sorry."

Ray held out a meaty hand and helped his crewman up. "This here's Charlie Shambaugh."

The smaller man shuffled behind Ray. "Dennie's my brother," he said.

Russ removed his glasses and scrubbed his face with one hand. "I'm sorry," he said. "You look a lot alike."

"Yeah, we all do." Charlie Shambaugh's voice was shaky.

"Have you heard from your brother recently?"

"Maybe a month ago. He's in trouble again, huh?"

"Wait a minute." Ray twisted around to look at Charlie. "Was this the brother you brought around when we was rehiring in November?"

Charlie nodded.

"You didn't tell me he was a con."

Charlie shrugged. "He needed a job."

Ray turned to Russ. "I had to get some new guys. Some of my crew had already left for southern work. I didn't know he was a con, though. I don't hire no cons."

"Why'd you pass on him, then?" Russ put his glasses back on.

"I got a simple test if I haven't worked with a guy before. I take him through the site and ask him how he'd tackle five different jobs. Charlie's brother didn't know much more'n how to swing a hammer."

"Charlie, did you try to get your brother a job with my wife?"

Charlie was dumbfounded enough to forget to be afraid of Russ. "Are you kidding? He couldn't sew. The carpentry, I figured he could pick up. That's easy. But sewing?"

Russ's hand twitched. Charlie saw it and shrank back into Yardhaas's shadow again. "I mean pet sitting. House sitting. Whatever he would have called it."

Charlie shook his head. "Pet-sitting's a girl job. His girlfriend pet-sits. Doesn't pay crap, but she loves 'little fuzzy critters' "—Charlie's voice crept up into a falsetto—"and just between you an' me, it's about the best she can do. Dumb as a box of hammers."

"She's dead," Russ said.

Charlie's mouth opened.

"Somebody slit her throat and then sliced her up like so much roast beef."

Charlie's mouth was still open. After a few seconds, he said, "Are you shittin' me?"

"We think your brother did it."

"Nuh-uh." Charlie shook his head. "No way. He's nuts about Audrey."

"That's what a lot of guys who kill their wives or girlfriends say."

"No, not like I'm-a-stalker nuts about her. He, you know"—Charlie looked around as if embarrassed to say the word in front of witnesses—"he loved her."

Russ wasn't in the mood to debate Dennie Shambaugh's emotions. "He assaulted an officer, stole a car, and fled from questioning. Do you have any idea where he'd be?"

"No."

"Charlie. If your brother didn't kill Audrey Keane, he needs to turn himself in and clear himself."

"I don't know where he is. Last time I talked with him was Christmas, at Frannie's house. Our sister. Mary Francis Delacourt. She lives in Fort Henry."

"Is he likely to have gone there? Or to one of your other brothers or sisters?"

"I dunno."

Russ pinched the bridge of his nose beneath his glasses. "If he contacts you, get in touch with the Millers Kill police immediately."

"Sure."

Sure. Russ breathed in. Out. "One more question. Ray here says you helped my wife—the curtain lady—with some of her work."

"Yeah." Charlie bobbed his head up and down in an earnest display of helpfulness. "Nice lady."

"Yeah. Did you ever hear her say anything about traveling, or going on a trip, or getting away?"

"She was going away to Montreal at Christmastime. With her husband." His eyes lit up. "That's you."

Christ. If Charlie thought his brother's girlfriend was dumb, she must have been barely functioning about sponge level. "Besides that."

"Nah," Charlie said. "Sorry."

That was that. The moment Russ had been dreading, when he tapped out his last lead.

"Although," Charlie said.

"What?"

"She did have a bunch of stuff here."

"A bunch of stuff?"

"You know. A suitcase, one of those makeup bags women use. Stuff like that." He glanced from Russ to Ray to Barbara LeBlanc. "Mr. Opperman let her use a room to keep stuff in."

Barbara looked at Russ. "That's the first I've heard of it. Although it'd be easy enough for him to give her a master key. We have a bunch of them already made up. If anyone's working late or gets snowed in, they can stay the night."

"Could she be—"

Barbara was already shaking her head. "I can't imagine it. Between me and the crew and the caretaker, no one could be here for more than a night without tipping us off. Besides, as a guest of Mr. Opperman, she'd have no reason to try to hide from anyone."

"Unless she's not hiding."

"What do you mean?"

"I mean she could be somewhere in here, unable to get out or contact anyone."

Barbara and the two workmen looked up at the ceiling, as if they could imagine what sort of condition Linda would have to be in to disappear within the walls of the hotel itself.

"You say you have master keys already made up."

"Yes," Barbara said. Then she looked at him. "Oh, but you can't mean—" She twitched, uncomfortable. "Surely you can't think she's really here."

"I don't know. But I'm not leaving until I make sure."

The manager pressed her lips together, frowning. Then she squared her narrow shoulders. "I'm coming with you."

"Let's get to it, then. There are a lot of rooms to check out."

FORTY-TWO

B en Beagle considered himself a people person. Mostly. He liked that his job required him to interact with men and women he never would have run across in the normal circle of office, errands, restaurant, home. He liked listening to their confidences and unearthing their secrets, and he liked the idea that every once in a while, something he wrote might affect someone else's life. He even liked their e-mails—profane, grateful, funny, scathing.

But Jesus H. Tapdancing Christ he hated it when they followed him home.

Not that he was home, exactly. The offices of the *Post-Star* were, technically, open to the public, which meant that anyone who had to talk to a reporter right away in person about how his neighbors were running an al-Qaeda cell or about how her local school board was filled with godless heathens could enter the lobby, pester the receptionist, and speak to a reporter. Not in the newsroom. In the lobby. Usually it was one of the interns or, if they had all been sent on coffee runs, whoever had the least amount of work or the most time until deadline. The people who came to the *Post-Star* offices rarely asked for a reporter by name. Probably, Ben thought, because they were the sort of folks who had every edition dating back to 1950 in stacks around the house and couldn't remember who was currently working and who had died in 1976.

Debbie Wolecski, unfortunately, had his name. And number.

"Why aren't you out right now tracking down my sister? I thought this was a big-deal investigation for you!"

Ben glanced out the window, where a hard, dry snow was turning downtown Glens Falls into a ghost town, and quelled the urge to answer, *Because I don't like to drive in this kind of weather.* "Debbie, I told you on the phone. A local small-town police chief killing his wife and covering it up with the help of his force is news. It's about corruption, and the violation of the public trust. A local small-town police chief whose wife runs off is gossip."

She crossed her arms. At least today she was wearing a fuzzy turtleneck instead of that skimpy summer thing she had on yesterday. Florida people. Save him. "What about his affair with that clergywoman? That's something! You barely touched on it in this morning's story."

"It's only something if you're the *Weekly World News.*" He sighed. "I'm sorry your brother-in-law was treating your sister badly. But adultery's not a crime anymore, and we don't write about it unless it's tied in to something else. So, if it turns out Chief Van Alstyne was waiving Reverend Fergusson's parking tickets or using departmental resources to benefit her, then sure, we'll take a hard look at it. But barring that . . ."

"What about the fact that she's under investigation for the murder of Audrey Keane?"

He held out his hands in a placating gesture. "I've spoken with someone at the Millers Kill police twice so far today, and I'm going to call again before I go home. Believe me, the murder story is going to remain front page news." Although the fact that the department refused to officially name anyone as a suspect was going to mean his part of the story would be two inches or less. Ciara French, who was covering the Audrey Keane murder–identity fraud investigation, would be getting the headline tomorrow.

"So that's it?" Her mouth twisted. "Now she's not lying in the morgue, the hell with my sister?"

"Debbie, I don't track someone down unless I have to get a quote from him. Finding missing people isn't my job. According to the woman I spoke with this morning, your brother-in-law is heading up the investigation into your sister's disappearance. I suggest you call him and ask how it's going." Then he thought of her parked in the *Post-Star* lobby, emoting all over her cell phone. "Better yet, track him down and see what you can do to help."

"I thought you *cared!* You were just *using* me!"

Now she was starting to sound like his crazy ex-girlfriend. "I do care. As soon as anyone knows anything, I want to hear about it. Go find Chief Van Alstyne, and I promise you, if he's uncovered any evidence of foul play, it'll be in tomorrow's edition." He looked around for her coat, but of course all she had was the Be-Dazzled jacket she'd been wearing yesterday. "And get yourself something to wear before you freeze."

She let herself be maneuvered toward the door. "What are you going to do?"

"While I'm waiting for word of your sister, I'm looking into another possible story. Not related to the Keane murder."

She paused at the exit, and for a moment he thought she might brace herself against the edges of the door and refuse to leave. "About what?"

"Animal cruelty." On that note, he got her out of the building and his afternoon back on track.

He had called about the animals on a hunch, really. Patterns tweaked at him, and although he couldn't have articulated what he thought was going on when a minister involved in a murder investigation asked him about a pig-butchering because one of her people had a lamb killed, the weird three-sided symmetry of it all had him on the phone to the MKPD almost as soon as Reverend Fergusson had hung up on him.

Names of victims in hand, he started by calling his previous contact, Dr. Underkirk. He didn't get through to the doctor, of course—he wondered who did: spouses? stockbrokers?—but it only took a few remarks and laughing at a few ham-fisted jokes for Underkirk's garrulous nurse to reveal the only thing the minister had asked about: the doctor's snowplowing service.

It didn't take him long to go through the remaining people on the list. Of those he could reach, every one had the same service.

Interesting.

He went on the Internet. It took him fifteen minutes to find Quinn Tracey's LiveJournal, half an hour to read the entries, and no time at all to realize the kid was seriously torqued.

Ben discounted the poorly spelled, ungrammatical complaints about fascist parents, irrelevant teachers, and stuck-up, snooty girls. He had felt pretty much the same way when he was in high school, and it had never sent him out gutting livestock.

He also ignored the tedious recounting of television episodes and the pretentious album reviews. Half the Web sites and blogs on the Internet consisted of people telling you what they liked and didn't like in excruciating detail.

But the other stuff the kid was putting up there—that was different. In a dark and unpleasant way. Spiels glorifying war and pain and the unkillable soldier dealing death at every turn. Rants against terrorists, Middle Eastern-ers, immigrants. Fantasies of claiming vengeance against his enemies, with detailed descriptions of what that vengeance would be. Reading it was like picking through the mind of a skinhead who had seen one too many movies where a lone American hero gunned down a moving-van's-worth of faceless baddies.

Ben knew that young men like to fantasize about the glory of carnage. Some of them daydreamed about martial arts prowess, while others pictured them-selves infiltrating behind enemy lines with the SEALs. Violent but essentially harmless. Some kids acted on it and joined up; most enrolled in college and dis-covered getting laid instead.

Quinn Tracey's stuff wasn't like that. It made Ben want to scrub out his eyeballs.

He sent the entire slag heap to the printer and, as it was purring out into a stack of paper, went to find someone who could confirm what time kids would be getting home from Millers Kill High.

Mina Norris snorted at him. "Don't you pay any attention to anything you're not working on? Today's a snow day. Didn't you notice half the office is out?"

"Huh. It did look a little underpopulated. So, all the high schoolers would be home already?"

"Uh-huh. The only reason I'm here is because my two are old enough to stay by themselves."

He went back to his desk singing, "Oh, the weather outside is frightful . . ." He flipped open his notepad, ready to transcribe first the listing, then the con-versation. There were only two Traceys in the Millers Kill/Fort Henry/Cos-sayuharie directory. One was unfamiliar, the other the number he had called Tuesday afternoon to interview the woman who had found Linda Van Alstyne's body. Well, Audrey Keane's body, but they hadn't known that then.

Beagle's pencil went still over his notepad.

Meg Tracey. That was the name of the woman who had found the body.

Quinn Tracey was her *son*?

His hands shook as he punched in the number.

"Hello?"

"Hello, Mrs. Tracey? This is Ben Beagle, with the *Glens Falls Post-Star*. We spoke on Tuesday?"

"Of course. I remember." The woman laughed. "If you want my reaction to the latest development, it's ecstatic. I can't tell you what a miracle it is, having Linda restored to life like that."

She sounded so emotional, Ben wondered if they were talking about the same "latest development." "Have you . . . heard from her?"

"No, no, but I'm sure it's just a matter of time."

"Ah. Great. I'm happy to get a quote from you, but as it stands, I called on a different matter. I understand you have a son who runs his own snowplowing business."

"Quinn? Yes. He inherited it from his big brother when Seamus went off to school. Why? Do you need a plow?"

Ben wanted to be politic. "No. I'm doing a story, and I was hoping to interview him."

"About his snowplowing? It is unique, isn't it? The thing I like is how eye-catching it's going to be on his college applications. Imagine admissions officers, seeing one fast-food job after another, and then a young man who ran his own business! Of course you can interview him. Hang on."

The earpiece clunked as she put her phone down. Ben realized he was thwapping his pencil at high speed against the notepad. He forced himself to relax.

"Hi . . ." The young man who picked up the other end sounded like some-one who had been frogmarched to the phone to talk with an unloved relative.

"Hi, Quinn. I'm Ben Beagle, with the *Post-Star*. Your mom said it was okay if I asked you a few questions. Is that okay with you?"

"Uh-huh."

"Great. You run a snowplow business, right? Can you tell me how long you've been doing it?"

"This winter's my first one by myself. Last year Seamus and I did it together."

"Getting the experience, yeah. How many customers do you have?"

"Uh . . . twelve regular, and two guys who call me if they're too busy to snowblow their drives themselves. Plus I get a lot of pickups when I'm doing the plowing. Like, I'm doing one of my regulars and his next-door neighbor will coming running out with a twenty and ask me to do his drive, too."

"Sounds profitable. How do you get your customers?"

"Most of 'em Seamus got, and they, you know, just kept calling up in the fall. My mom and dad talk it up, so I get some people who know them."

"What do you use for the plowing?"

"I have an '88 Ford Ranger with a fifty-four-inch Deere plow and cement blocks in the bed to weight it down."

"Is it yours, or do you borrow it from your folks?"

"It's mine. I bought it off of my brother."

"Do you use it just for the business?"

"Naw, it's how I get around. I mean, I don't get great mileage during the winter, with the plow and the weights on, but I never get stuck, so it's a good trade-off."

"Especially on a day like today."

The boy huffed a quiet laugh. "Yeah, I'll be way busy as soon as this lets up."

Ben slid the list of reported animal losses in front of him. "Do you plow for John and Zoë Kavenaugh?" The couple he hadn't been able to reach.

"Yeah." Tracey sounded surprised.

"And Dr. Irving Underkirk."

"Yeah . . ." Surprise turning to suspicion.

"And Herbert Perkins."

"How do you know all this?"

"All three of them have had an animal killed within the last month. Throat slit, body hacked up, but the meat uneaten. So we know it's not a starving coyote or panther coming down from the mountains. I'm thinking it must have been done with a knife."

He could hear fast, heavy breathing across the line. Nothing else.

"That's a strange coincidence. Three of your customers reporting an outdoor animal butchered. And those are just the ones who called the police. I know of at least one other person who had an animal mutilated who hasn't involved the cops. Yet." He should have called Clare Fergusson back and asked for the name of the parishioner she mentioned. He would have had to trade information, but right now he'd give just about anything to have another name to throw at Tracey. "Do you have any comment?"

"I didn't do anything!"

"I didn't say you did. Just that it was strange. And another strange coincidence.

Your mom discovered the body of a woman who also had her throat slit and got hacked up. Just like those animals. Were the Van Alstynes customers of yours as well?"

His answer was the blank buzz of the dial tone.

FORTY-THREE

S torms can come to the Adirondacks from any of the four compass points. Soggy and slow from the south, doily-sized flakes dropping straight as beads on a string from the sky. Canadian clippers from the north, with air straight off the arctic circle and fine dry snow that scours whatever it touches. Rarely, the wheeling nor' easters that pound the New England coastline will fall in tattered remnants over the easternmost edges of New York.

But the storms that wrack come from the west. Massive low pressure systems rumbling out of Canada, crossing five Great Lakes before breaking over the shoals of the Adirondacks. Winds that have gathered speed for a thousand miles come howling through the ancient hills. Snow crystals that may have formed over the arctic regions of Hudson Bay hurtle downward, looking for their namesake river. As the snow falls faster and the winds continue to rise, the truck driver on the Northway and the shopper walking down Main Street may be caught in a whiteout, a spinning, shifting blankness that wipes the world away.

Smart people stay inside, watch through windows as the drifts mount two, five, eight feet against the barn door and rising, and shake their heads when a vehicle rolls down the road. "Damn fool," Margy Van Alstyne says, as an SUV rumbles past her drive. She knows, however, that some folks have no choice but to be out in the storm.

Sergeant Ogilvie would have just as soon put off picking up the Shambaugh computers from the Millers Kill Police Department, but his guys from the state cybercrime analysis team were leaning on him to bring in the hardware. When he stomped through the hallway, shedding snow, he thought the station was deserted, but he found the dispatcher, who sent him downstairs to the evidence room. Durkee, the officer who had been working on the preliminary downloads, was overjoyed to meet him, and Ogilvie could see why: The poor bastard was working inside the small evidence cage to preserve the chain of custody. He had to admire the guy's dedication. The room's heat and lighting system must have been installed a century ago; compact fluorescents screwed into overhead bulbs flickered as if they were about to blow, and Ogilvie could almost see his breath in the cold.

He and Durkee both signed off on the custody sheets, and Ogilvie twisted no-release plastic straps around the CPU and sealed them with his department's lead slug. Durkee helped him tote the things up the stairs, through the building, and down another set of stairs. They ducked heads and raised shoulders and stalked through the driving snow to get to Ogilvie's van, then hightailed it back inside and did it again.

The three CPUs secured in a locker in the back, Ogilvie followed Durkee back inside one more time to get the hard-copy transcripts the Millers Kill officer had prepped and to take him up on the offer of a hot refill for his traveling mug.

"Crappy weather," Durkee said, leading Ogilvie to the coffee machine. "I'm glad I'm not headed down to Albany."

"I'll take it slow. My boss thinks your perp might be part of an areawide identity theft ring. He's practically wetting his pants over those CPUs."

"I hope he finds some leads, then, because when we catch Shambaugh, he's going down for Man One, not fraud." Durkee crossed the squad room to his desk and retrieved a thick plastic document box. "Here's the printouts."

"Thanks." Ogilvie hefted the box one-handed and slipped it beneath his arm. "So . . . word is this guy was ripping off your chief when he sliced and diced his partner."

Durkee frowned. "He was there, all right. We've got the prints. The funny thing is—"

Ogilvie's ears perked up. He did enjoy a juicy piece of information. "What?"

"It's probably because I'm not real skilled in this. I'm sure you guys will

uncover something. It's just . . . I couldn't find any trace of any of the Van Alstynes' information in there. No SSNs, no card numbers—nothin'."

Approaching the red light where Main crossed Route 17, Officer Kevin Flynn
feathered his brakes and wished for the fifth time since leaving the station he
had had the cojones to stand up to Investigator Jensen. Not so much about driving halfway across the township to talk with Quinn Tracey, but about taking his
own truck.

He had just gotten back from interviewing first Shambaugh's sister, and then
his sister-in-law. Jensen called him into the chief's office, where she had just
moved in and set up camp. "O'Flynn," she said, tossing a folder across the desk
at him, "there may be a common thread in these animal abuse cases."

"It's just Flynn, ma'am." He picked the folder up.

"Flynn." She smiled insincerely. "This department has three reported
cases, and I have information that there've been two more incidents that
weren't reported. You'll see my notes. A kid named Quinn Tracey worked for
the five owners."

He looked up from where he had been flipping through the folder. "All
five?"

"Amazingly, the brilliant investigative minds in this department hadn't made
the connection. Get yourself up to date and then get over to the Traceys' house
and talk with the kid."

"Okay if I take my personal vehicle, ma'am? It's better in the snow than the
Crown Vics."

"No, Officer Flynn, it's not okay. You've got a uniform and a squad car. I expect to see you in both."

He glanced out the tall windows. He could barely see the trees in the park
across the street for the snow pelting down. "The chief lets me use my four-by-
four if I'm not on traffic duty." He could see from her expression that mention-
ing the chief had been a mistake.

"Your chief lets a lot of things slip by that are frankly unprofessional. If you
ever hope to get out of this town and move up into serious policing, you need to
change your attitude." At that moment, Mark Durkee sidled through the office
door. "Be more like Officer Durkee. No facial hair on him."

Kevin clutched the seam of his pants to keep from touching his soul patch. "Ma'am," he said. He brushed past Mark without looking at him. Suckup.

So now he was sliding toward Route 17, the squad car shimmying as its tires tried, and failed, to find traction. An eighteen-wheeler rolled into the intersection. He was headed straight for its rear wheels. "Holy St. Christopher, pray for me," he blurted out, an incantation his mother always said when she ran into trouble behind the wheel. Amazingly, the light turned green, the truck roared past, and Kevin slid through the intersection unharmed.

"Wow." He gently accelerated. He'd have to tell his mom. Of course, then she'd get on his case even more about going to Mass.

The Tracey house was set back a ways, and he didn't even try to get the Crown Vic up the driveway. He parked on the shoulder, flipped on his warning flashers, and hiked up to the front porch.

A middle-school-aged girl answered the door. She looked at him suspiciously when he asked to see her mother. "Hold on," she said, shutting the door in his face. He took off his hat and beat some of the snow off his shoulders.

A good-looking soccer mom yanked the door open. "Has there been an accident?" she cried.

"An accident? No, ma'am."

"Oh." Her shoulders sagged. "Thank heavens." She stood there, hand pressed to her chest, until she seemed to realize he was still standing on the welcome mat. "I'm so sorry!" She beckoned him to come inside. "I'm afraid Deidre takes 'Do not let strangers in' a little too literally."

"No need to apologize, ma'am." He tucked his hat under his arm. "Are you Quinn Tracey's mother?"

The look of alarm fell over her features again. "Yes."

"I'd like to ask him a few questions, with your permission."

She looked toward the interior of the house, then back at Kevin. "That's why I asked you if there was an accident. He went tearing out of here at least a half hour ago and took off in his truck. I don't know where he is."

Sergeant Isabel O'Brien of the New York State Police was one of the few members of her troop who actually liked storms. Instead of the mind-numbing tedium of the radar gun, she got to cruise east and west on the Thruway, looking for vehicles in trouble. Instead of being greeted with sour jokes about making the end-of-the-month ticket quota, she was hailed as a hero by drivers who had skidded into the median.

She had just passed the Schenectady exit when her radio squawked. She hit the reception button. "Eight-one-nine here. Go ahead."

"Eight-one-nine, we have a call from the Roy Rogers manager at the Pattersonville travel plaza. He's reporting a suspicious individual, male Caucasian, thirties or forties, hanging around the employee parking area."

"Dispatch, I am responding." O'Brien tapped her computer screen to register the time and bring up an incident log. She turned on her lights and pulled into the passing lane. Traffic to her right, already slow due to the storm-imposed speed limit of forty-five miles per hour, decelerated even further as she swept past.

She was a scant five miles from Pattersonville when her radio lit up again. "Eight-one-nine, be advised the suspicious individual has left the Indian Hill rest station and is headed east in a 1992 Volvo station wagon, dark green."

"Plates?"

There was a pause. "Hold on on the plates."

Huh. That was odd. "Should I pursue?"

"Eight-one-nine, the manager reports the POI may have switched plates with one of his employees. We're trying to get a confirmation on that. Please proceed without lights."

O'Brien turned off the lights but kept her speed at a steady fifty-five, which was as fast as she was going to go, unless this guy turned out to be Osama bin Laden.

"Eight-one-nine, we have a confirmation that one employee's rear license plate now matches that of the stolen car last seen in possession of Dennis Shambaugh."

Her computer screen flashed on with the BOLO for Shambaugh. MILLERS KILL POLICE DEPARTMENT glowed over a mug shot.

"Suspect is wanted for assaulting an officer, GTA, questioning in a homicide, questioning in a Class B fraud. Suspect is not known to be armed, but has a prior felony assault conviction. Units eight-two-oh and eight-one-eight are on their way. Proceed with extreme caution."

Her adrenaline kicked into high gear. She sped up, the powerful engine growling, the windshield wipers slapping hard against the snow that seemed to bullet straight toward her. She passed the Pattersonville travel plaza. She passed car after truck after SUV—what were all these people out for on a day like this?

She came up behind a grandpa who didn't recognize her outline in the swirling, snowy gloom and who continued on his steady forty-mile-an-hour way in the passing lane. She gave him the lights, and eventually he noticed and moved to the right.

She snapped off the red-and-whites and accelerated again. She figured she must be getting close. She divided her attention between the road ahead and the vehicles to her right, a task complicated by the poor visibility. Thank God the perp hadn't stolen one of those Japanese cars that look like fifty per cent of everything else on the road. She could concentrate on picking out the unique boxy shape of the Volvo.

SUV. SUV. Lincoln. Toyota. Mazda. Toyota. 'Burbmobiles and grampmobiles and generics.

Then, just past her right front corner, the outline of a Volvo station wagon. Dark, although she wouldn't have laid money it was green. She flicked on her radio. "Dispatch, this is eight-one-nine. I have a possible match in sight. I can't make out the plate in this muck."

"Eight-one-nine, proceed. Eight-two-oh is ten miles behind you bearing west." And so could continue past her after the suspect if she pulled over the wrong guy.

"Dispatch, I am proceeding." She turned on her video recorder and hit the lights.

The Volvo immediately pulled forward, accelerating into the blowing snow and, as O'Brien stepped on her gas, disappearing.

"Holy crap," she said. "He's turned his lights off." She turned the siren on, gripped her wheel, and hurtled after him, the noise jabbing into her head, drowning out the too-fast beat of her heart. No way he could get away. It was the Thruway, not a country road. No exit up ahead except through the Amsterdam toll, where local police were probably already moving into position.

But what he could do was cause one god-awful accident. How far was her siren going to carry over the howl of the wind and the roar of the blower and the swish of the wipers? "Get off the road," she muttered beneath her breath.

A shape loomed out of the darkness ahead. O'Brien swore and stood on the brakes, her car's rear shaking like a bucking bronco. The red taillights loomed larger, and larger, and she gritted her teeth and braced for the impact, and then the traffic in the right lane opened up and the SUV slid across the lane and into the snow piled by the side of the road.

"Dispatch, vehicle off the Thruway at my mark," she got out, right before a flurry of red brake lights sparked through the gray snow haze. A car in front of her spun into the median. She swerved, clipped a minivan with her rear right quarter, saw the car ahead of it slip sideways *oh God please don't roll* and the minivan crunch into its hood, both vehicles spinning out of control *oh God please* and then ahead of her another car skidded out of the murk and plunged into the median and kept going and going and she registered *no lights* and she registered *box* and she said, "God damn, he's taking the turnaround. He's trying to head east."

A split-second glance in her rearview showed her nothing following in the six feet of visibility she had. She swung the car into the turnaround, struggling to hold it, skidding wide, the tires churning and clutching, the dim shape of the Volvo almost-maybe there in front of her. Her wheels dug down into the snow, caught on sand and gravel, and she surged forward, the frame shuddering, only to slam on the brakes as she went past the Volvo, went past its nose, which wasn't where it should have been, and realized it hadn't been able to keep the turn and had instead skewed backward, down into the hollow of the median.

"Suspect has come to a halt," O'Brien said, not realizing she was shouting until the words rang in her abused ears. She turned the siren off. "I have at least three vehicles off the road in addition. At least one collision."

"Ambulances on the way," Dispatch said.

She unholstered her weapon and wrenched open her door. The wind and snow beat against her face. She kicked through the churned-up mess of snow and earth and then waded into the median, her gun in position. She stopped to the right of the driver's door. She could see the man inside, pale-faced and dark-haired. Thickset and terrified-looking. She kept her sights on him. "Get out!" she screamed against the wind. "Keep your hands where I can see them!"

He unlatched the door and listed out, one hand in the air. "Both hands up!" He flopped his wrist, and she could see that there was something wrong with his other arm. Out of the corner of her eye, she saw a whirl of red and white. Her backup.

"Dennis Shambaugh," she yelled. "You're under arrest."

FORTY-FOUR

Clare sat at her desk and watched the snow fall past the diamond-paned windows in her office. It made a beautiful picture, like an illustration from a Snow White storybook she had as a girl. She could imagine herself opening the casement and pricking her finger, the red against the snow. *Hair black as ebony, skin white as snow, lips red as blood.*

Blood on snow. She wrenched her gaze away from the window and forced her attention back to the papers in front of her. She had done all she could reasonably do. She had called the people who had lost animals, and then she had called the police. Why weren't they the ones who had seen the pattern, anyway? She was a priest. Why did she have to do their legwork for them?

She flashed on a long-ago conversation with Russ.

Legwork? he had teased.

Well, that's what they call it on TV.

She smacked the papers with the flat of her hand. No more of that. She was going to get her work finished and go home. Make some soup and put in a DVD and say her prayers and go to sleep. And that would be the end of the first day of never seeing Russ again.

She sank her head in her hands. That was the blood and blackness in her picture. She had already done this, just last Monday, and been whipped from pillar to post in the past four days. His wife was dead, then she wasn't. He was a suspect, then Clare was. He needed her, relied on her, leaned on her. Then he weighed her and found her wanting. Yesterday morning he sat here, right here in this office, and let her hold his heartbreak in her hands. Now they couldn't talk to each other.

No wonder she was distracted. She was waiting for the next blow to fall.

The phone rang.

She eyed it. When Lois had left an hour ago, she had set incoming calls to ring to the rector's office. If Clare didn't pick up after ten rings, it went into voicemail, to be dealt with when they had all dug out from underneath the storm.

Clare picked up the receiver. "St. Alban's Church."

"Hey, Reverend Fergusson."

"Harlene? Why are you whispering?"

"The Wicked Witch of the West asked me to get you on the phone. But I had to pass on some news first. The state police have Dennis Shambaugh in custody. Eric McCrea and herself are meeting up with the arresting officer at Troop G headquarters for the interrogation."

"Holy cow!" Clare whispered. She cleared her throat. "Does Russ know?"

"I left a message on his cell. He's been hauling all over the North Country today, talking to Linda's customers. If he hasn't headed home already, he's probably still at the Algonquin. Oops." Harlene reverted to her normal voice. "Hold please." There was a click.

"Reverend Fergusson?" The woman on the other end of the line didn't sound happy.

"Hello, Investigator Jensen. What can I do for you?"

"You can stop blabbing police business to the press."

Jensen must have finally read the *Post-Star*, which was more than Clare was going to do. "I never spoke to the paper. Whatever the reporter got he got from hanging around the police station."

"I'm talking about Quinn Tracey," Jensen snapped.

"What?"

"Officer Flynn went to his house to question him. The boy's mother said a reporter had called and asked to talk to the kid. After the conversation, the kid took a powder."

"He's gone?"

"You have information or suspicions? Call us. And then trust that we'll handle it. Don't go yapping to the *Post-Star*."

"I didn't!"

"It was the same reporter who's covering the Keane murder, Reverend. Do you want me to believe that's a coincidence?"

"It—well, not exactly, but I didn't—"

"Look, I don't have time. I'm heading down to Loudonville. If we can't turn the Tracey kid up, I'm holding you personally responsible. Have a nice day."

Clare was left holding the receiver, her mouth open to ask another question. *What do you want Quinn Tracey for?* Jensen's level of vitriol seemed way overblown for someone who had dismissed Clare's findings as over-the-top pranks. Unless Jensen had decided there was something more to the string of animal killings. Something like . . .

Audrey Keane.

Where would Quinn run to? Almost before the question had formed itself in her mind, she knew the answer. She reached for the phone book and flipped through the pages until she found MACENTYRE, CRAIG AND VICKI.

She dialed the number. It rang, and rang, and rang, and when the answering machine picked up she wanted to scream. Instead, she said, "Aaron? This is Clare Fergusson. We spoke the other day about your friend Quinn. Would you—"

"Hello," Aaron said.

"Oh." Clare felt foolish. "You're home."

"My folks aren't here. When I'm home alone, I'm supposed to listen to see who it is before I answer." His voice was different. Flat.

"Um . . ." She didn't want to alarm him with something out of a summer scream fest. *Get out of the house now!* "When are your parents getting home?"

"I don't know. They and my sister went shopping in Albany. I can take care of myself if they have to stay, due to the weather."

Aaron sounded as if he were far away, talking about someone else entirely.

"Are you okay?" Clare asked.

"I'm fine."

"Is your friend Quinn there?"

"Quinn?"

She sighed. "Aaron, the police very much want to question him. If he's there, or if he shows up, you need to call them and let them know right away."

"Call the police and let them know. Okay."

She was past exasperated and into worry. "Is he there right now?"

"No."

"Would you tell me if he was?"

"Yes."

She couldn't think of anything else. It wasn't like she could crawl through the line to keep the boy safe. "It's not a game. Call the police if he contacts you in any way."

"I will. Good-bye, Reverend Fergusson."

She hung up. Looked out the window at the snow. Now what? She picked up the phone and dialed the police station again.

"Millers Kill PD."

"Harlene, it's Clare. I'm sorry to bug you, but I have an idea where Quinn Tracey might be."

"Is this official? Okay, hang on, I'm going to record it. Go on."

Clare explained about the boy's friendship with Aaron MacEntyre, and the phone call she had just had.

"So, you're thinking because he seemed funny over the phone, that maybe the Tracey kid was already over there?"

"Yeah."

"You ever talk to Aaron MacEntyre on the phone before?"

"No."

Harlene made a noise. "Never mind, I trust your instincts. I'll send someone over there as soon as I can, but I have to tell you, we're real shorthanded right now."

Clare hesitated. *I have done all that I can reasonably do.*

No, you haven't.

"I'm going to head over there myself," she said.

"Reverend, I don't think—"

"I need to do it. I'll have my cell phone with me." She rattled off the number to the dispatcher.

"You know, the chief isn't going to like this one bit."

Clare paused for a moment, to make sure there was no trace of bitterness in her mouth. "I think the chief has more important things to worry about than me."

FORTY-FIVE

By the time he stepped inside the last of the Algonquin's three hundred rooms, Russ didn't want to see another poofy quilted coverlet, mahogany armoire, or fringe-bedecked armchair in this lifetime. He and Barbara LeBlanc had worked their way from the Presidential and Honeymoon suites through the executive suites, junior suites, deluxe rooms, superior rooms, and standard rooms without finding any sign that his wife had ever been here.

He had gotten an eyeful of John Opperman's current living quarters—in the Presidential Suite, of course—but the only thing that revealed about the president of BWI, Inc., was that he kept stacks of business magazines in the bathroom and that he had really dull tastes in music—unless the Three Tenors and Classical Light CDs stacked by the built-in stereo system came with the room.

As they descended the stairs—the elevators were still offline while the electricians worked on the system—he heard a woman's voice yelling from the lobby.

"Hello! Anybody here? Russ?"

Barbara LeBlanc shot him a glance. "You're certainly livening up the place today."

He took the remaining stairs two at a time and emerged, knees twinging, into the canvas- and plastic-covered lobby.

He saw a blonde in a familiar red peacoat, and his heart nearly jumped out of his chest, but in the next moment, he recognized his sister-in-law, who must have appropriated one of Linda's coats.

"Debbie?"

She turned. She actually looked relieved to see him, which meant she must have really been worried she was stuck up here in an empty hotel with a storm raging outside. "What are you doing here?" he asked.

"I've come to help search for my sister." Her defiant tone wobbled. It had probably been a bad drive up the mountain.

"You can help by staying put. The last thing I need is to be hauling you out of a snowbank."

She narrowed her eyes. "It figures you'd say that. It's a lot easier to claim you've been moving heaven and earth to find her if no one else is around as a witness, isn't it?"

"Oh, for God's sake," he started.

"Hi." Barbara glided up beside him and extended her hand to Debbie. "I'm Barbara LeBlanc, the manager."

"Debbie Wolecski." She bent her wrist and took the manager's hand in the kind of grasp no guy would ever attempt. "Linda Van Alstyne's sister."

"Ah."

"Has *he* told you that she's missing?"

Barbara smiled crookedly. "We've just finished searching the hotel for her. I've seen parts of this place I didn't even know existed."

Debbie looked from the manager to Russ. "Nothing? No sign of her?"

He shook his head.

"Nothing from any of the places she worked at?"

"How did you know I was visiting her work sites?"

Debbie made an impatient gesture. "I spoke to the dispatcher at the police station. *She* told me I should stay put, too."

Russ dragged one hand through his hair, feeling tension knots kinking through his shoulders. "You should leave your rental here and come back into town with me. I'll run you back up tomorrow after they've plowed out." He glanced at Barbara. "That'd be okay, wouldn't it?"

"Sure. Our caretaker will plow our drive and the private road down to Sacandaga Road. You can leave your car here as long as you like."

Russ fished in his back pocket and pulled out a creased business card. "Best way to reach me will be my cell phone for the next few days," he said, handing it to her. "Please call me as soon as Opperman gets back from his business trip. It's probably a long shot, but he might know—"

The front door inched open, admitting a gust of frigid air and a swirl of snowflakes. A man, angular and anonymous in a black wool dress coat and a scarf, banged his suitcase against the door, forcing it wider.

"Speak of the devil," Barbara LeBlanc said cheerfully.

A woman staggered through the door, clutching her valise in one hand and the neck of her coat with the other. The man let the door swing shut behind her. She plucked the hat from her head and shook out her blond curls. Her eyes widened as she saw the three onlookers.

"Russ? Debbie!"

The man—Opperman—unwound his scarf, scattering snow on the plastic sheeting.

"What on earth are you doing here?" Linda Van Alstyne asked.

FORTY-SIX

Debbie burst into tears. She covered her mouth with one hand and groped toward Linda with the other, shaking so hard from her sobs she could hardly walk.

Russ couldn't move. Couldn't move, couldn't breathe, couldn't take his eyes off his wife, off her confused, red-cheeked, *alive* face.

"Debbie, what's wrong?" Linda dropped her suitcase and hurried toward her sister. "What are you doing here? Is it one of the boys?" She opened her arms and Debbie fell into her embrace, still unable to speak.

"We thought you were dead," Russ said hoarsely.

Linda looked up at him, strands of her sister's hair clinging to her jaw. "What are you talking about?"

He found he could move again, and he was on her in two strides, wrapping his arms around both sisters, squeezing them so tight Linda squeaked. "We thought you were dead," he repeated, and Debbie nodded her head, smearing tears and snowmelt over Linda's shoulder.

"If you had bothered to stop by and check, the house sitter I hired could have told you where I'd gone." Linda's voice was amused.

Russ reared back enough to look her in the face. "Audrey Keane was murdered in our kitchen. Her throat was cut, and her face was so disfigured we couldn't tell it wasn't you."

Linda's big blue eyes got wide and her perfectly shaped mouth dropped open. "You're kidding me."

"We thought it was you!" Debbie wailed. "Until last night, we thought it was you! I had to go to your house and pick out an outfit for you—for you—for the—" Her tears got the best of her again.

"But . . . my God, that's horrible!"

"Where. Were. You?"

Linda flinched at the anger in his voice. She glanced away from him to where the Algonquin's owner was stripping off his coat and gloves. "John let me use his house on St. Croix."

Once, as a kid, Russ had spent the afternoon wading through the swift shallow waters of the upper Hudson, amusing himself by sending stick canoes over the edge of the nearby waterfall. He came home slimy from falling between the slick stones, and his mother had screamed at him and shaken him and swore if he ever did that again he'd be grounded for a month, and he didn't understand why until later, when he found out two kids had drowned after they lost their footing and swept over the falls into the boiling rapids below. His mother told him she was furious because she loved him, but he didn't understand why, if that was so, she didn't cry and hug him and treat him especially nice, instead of sending him to bed early with no dessert and no TV.

Now he knew. He gripped Linda's shoulders hard, so hard he could feel her sinew and bones beneath the heavy wool of her coat. "You were on a beach in the Caribbean while I was listening to your goddamn autopsy report?"

"I'm sorry! Next time I'll take out an ad in the paper!" She twisted, but he held on fast, fingers digging in. Hurting her, the way she had hurt him.

"How the hell did you get there, anyway? Your passport was at home! All your makeup and stuff was at home!"

"You don't need a passport. It's a U.S. territory. And if you don't know by now that I have a travel kit of makeup and toiletries . . ." She let out a puff of air that said, *You're hopeless.* "Please let go of me."

He released her, clenching his hands into fists against his thighs. Debbie relaxed her grip on Linda's other side and began patting her pockets for a tissue.

Linda looked across the lobby. "John gave me a lift to New York, and then he let me use his private jet."

Opperman made a deprecating gesture. "Not mine. The company leases it."

"That's pretty damn generous," Russ said. "Don't those things cost something like a thousand dollars an hour? What did you get in exchange? Free consultation on your curtains?" He knew he was being an asshole, but he couldn't stop himself. Linda drew in an outraged breath.

Opperman looked at him coolly. "I'm sure given Linda's skills, it would have been worth it. As it happens, we were flying several potential investors to BWI's St. Thomas resort, so it was easy to drop your wife off on the way."

"That's why I did it," Linda said. "I had been talking about how badly I needed to get away, and John told me about the investors' junket. One of the men who works for him had a girlfriend who was a pet sitter—" She caught her breath and touched her fingers to her lips. "Anyway, it all came together in a rush."

Debbie's search for a tissue had come to the attention of Barbara LeBlanc. The manager retrieved a box from beneath the reception desk and handed them to the wet-faced woman. Debbie blew her nose. "I can understand why you didn't tell *him* what you were doing"—a jerk of her head toward Russ— "but why didn't you let me know?"

Linda looked down at the toes of her boots. Through her blond curls, Russ could see her face coloring. "I knew if I told you you'd want to come along. And I wanted this treat to be just for me."

"That's why I suggested she stay at my vacation home instead of the resort," Opperman said. "Complete privacy."

"And no access to international phone calls?" Russ snapped.

"Chief Van Alstyne." Opperman stepped toward him. "It's not my responsibility to see that Linda maintains contact with you. Maybe next time *you* can take your wife to the Caribbean."

Russ wanted to plow his fist into Opperman's smooth, rich face. Having no reason or excuse only made the urge stronger. Instead he strode across the floor to where Linda had dropped her suitcase and picked it up. "Let's go."

Linda looked at her sister. Debbie paused from blotting her face. "Do you want me to drive you? I have a rental."

"If it's all right with you, I think Russ and I need some time alone right now." Linda shot him a look, half warning, half disappointment.

"Okay. I'll follow right behind you."

Linda stepped toward Opperman and held out her hands. He took both of them and smiled at her.

"Thank you so much," she said. "For everything. And I apologize for—" She cut her eyes toward Russ.

"No apologies needed, dear lady. Shall I see you on Monday?"

"Fabric swatches in hand." Linda smiled brilliantly at him, then hooked her arm through her sister's and walked to the door. Russ followed, like an ungainly bellboy.

"Thanks for your help, Ms. LeBlanc," he said over his shoulder.

"My pleasure," she said. "I'm glad it all ended, um, happily."

Russ paused. The gust of wind from the door closing behind Linda and Debbie ruffled his hair and sent snowflakes shivering down his neck. "Would you do me a favor and call the Millers Kill Police Department? Let them know my wife's been . . ." Restored? Returned? "Found."

"I'm right on it," LeBlanc assured him, heading for her office.

Russ cast one more malevolent glance at Opperman, who smiled and waved good-bye.

Outside, the wind and snow buffeted him. He tucked his chin into the collar of his coat and trudged toward his truck. Linda, he saw, already sat inside, waiting for him. Debbie, parked next to the pickup, was trying to clear her windshield with her wipers. He rapped on her window.

"They're frozen in place," he yelled over the wind. "Hold on and I'll knock the snow off for you."

He jumped into the cab, fired up the truck, and got his brush out. He scraped and brushed his sister-in-law's rental car first, then got the snow off his own windows and head- and taillights.

He rapped on Debbie's window again. She cracked it open. "Stay a good three, four lengths behind me," he said. "Go light on your brakes. These kinds of conditions, you'll skid if you brake too hard." He looked up and down her car. "Are you sure you don't want to ride with us?"

"On that little Band-Aid of a backseat? No, thanks. Where are we headed?"

Good question. His house was still an unheated crime scene. "My mother's," he decided. Debbie made a face. "She's got two guest rooms, and she's a lot closer than the motel you're staying at. We're going to go down the mountain onto Sacandaga Road, then left onto Old Route 100. Follow it along the river, over the bridge, up a few miles into the mountains again, and there you are."

"Over the river and through the woods?"

"Something like that. If you get stuck or anything, flash your lights. I'll be keeping an eye on you."

She nodded. He climbed into the truck's cabin, now toasty warm, and stripped off his coat.

"What was that all about?" Linda said.

He put the truck in gear and backed it up. "I told Debbie to follow us to Mom's." He watched out his side window, making sure his sister-in-law didn't get stuck. Getting out of where you were parked was often the most difficult part of driving in the snow.

"Why your mother's? Why not go home?"

"I could ask you the same question. How come Mr. Sandman there was checking you into the hotel instead of taking you to our house?"

"Because he wasn't sure if his sports car would make it all the way to our place and back here. At the hotel"—she glared at him—"we could each have separate rooms without crowding together like we would've if he had to stay at our house."

Russ grunted. The Algonquin's unplowed driveway was indistinguishable from the gardens on either side, and he edged forward, waiting for the thump that would tell him he'd misjudged and driven over one of their low stone walls.

"And what do you mean, Mr. Sandman? Were you reading my e-mails?"

"We were investigating a homicide. The whole department's seen your e-mails by now. Not to mention all of our bills, financial records, and phone calls." He glanced in the rearview mirror. Debbie was right behind him.

"You really thought I had been murdered?" Linda's voice was so low, he could barely hear her over the hot air blasting from the defroster.

"I really did. We all did."

She rested her hand on his forearm. "I'm sorry."

The pines lining the private road swallowed them. There was less snow on the pavement, and he could see farther despite the gloom of the forest.

"Did you have any suspects? In my, um, murder?"

"Me, for one." He risked a glance at her. "There's a state investigator come in to run the case. I've been relieved of duty. The staties and the aldermen thought either I had done it or I was fouling the investigation to protect whoever did do it."

"That's ridiculous. Who would want to murder me that you'd protect? Your mother?" She laughed, then fell silent. "No. Not your mother." Linda turned to him. "Clare Fergusson. They thought your lover did it."

FORTY-SEVEN

W here are you going?"

Clare jumped. "Good Lord." She turned to see Elizabeth de Groot next to Lois's desk, arms akimbo, her ash blond hair and dark clericals limned by the lamplight falling from her own door. At two o'clock, the feeble, storm-grayed daylight barely penetrated into the interior of the office. "You startled me," Clare said. "I thought you left when Lois did."

"I considered it. Frankly, given everything that's been going on here, I felt you needed me to stay. Are you headed home?" It was a reasonable question, given that Clare was booted and suited up in parka, hat, and gloves.

"Uh." Clare had a pretty good idea that lying to her deacon wasn't conducive to a good working relationship.

"So where are you going? Is there a pastoral emergency?"

Clare sighed. "Not exactly." She pulled her hat off. "Are you going to try to make it all the way back down to Johnston?"

Elizabeth wasn't thrown off the scent. Arms crossed, face expectant, she looked uncannily like Clare's mother, waiting for a confession. The only thing missing was her mother's syrup-sweet voice saying, "You might as well tell me now, because I *will* find out."

"I spoke with Quinn Tracey's best friend a little while ago. He sounded very strange. So I'm going there to check things out."

"Why? Is he one of ours?"

A question designed to make Clare snatch out her hair. She fell back on St. Luke. "The lawyer, seeking to justify himself, asked Jesus, 'Who is my neighbor?' "

The deacon had the grace to look abashed. "All right," she said, "that wasn't well put. But even the Good Samaritan might have let the trained professionals handle things nowadays."

"I've called the police and let them know. They're sending someone over as soon as they can."

"Then why do you have to go?"

"Because I'm afraid that Quinn Tracey is a very disturbed young man. And his best friend—his only friend—is home alone. How is he going to handle it if Quinn shows up and says, 'Hide me' or 'Give me money' or 'Let's run away together?' "

"But the weather . . ."

Clare dug her keys out of her pocket. "I have all-wheel drive. I can get over there and back without too much difficulty."

Elizabeth made a noise that would have been a snort in someone less lady-like. "All right. But I'm coming, too."

"No, you're not!"

The deacon ignored Clare's protest. She crossed to her tiny office and emerged with her wool coat slung over her arm.

"There's absolutely no reason for you to go," Clare said.

"I don't think there's much of a reason for you to go, either, but you've convinced me it's a pastoral call. All right. I will accompany you on the pastoral call."

Clare opened her mouth to argue. Elizabeth speared her with a look. "If you're going to argue that it's not safe for me to come along, you'll have to include yourself in that assessment."

Clare shut her mouth.

The ride out to Old Route 100 was harrowing. The wind picked up the already fallen snow and whirled it in the air to mix with the stuff pelting down from the leaden clouds. Three times, Clare had to take her foot off the gas and let the Subaru roll to a near stop because she couldn't see two feet past the hood of the car. Other vehicles appeared out of the spidery whiteness, headlights blossoming, then winked away into the storm.

Then there was Elizabeth de Groot.

"Have you considered applying to a more urban parish?" she asked. "Perhaps in a more stimulating environment, you wouldn't need to keep throwing yourself into risk-taking experiences like you do here."

Clare didn't answer.

"You know, the bishop thinks very highly of you. But let's face it, on the overall balance sheet, have you been an asset or a debit to the diocese as a whole? What do you think?"

Clare gritted her teeth and leaned closer to the windshield.

"In the short time I've been here, I can see how much you care for your congregation. But don't you think the members of St. Alban's have a right to expect their rector to keep her focus on them?"

Clare snapped the radio on. "Traffic reports," she said.

Later, de Groot mused, "Maybe you're meant to be back in the military. A military chaplain. Travel. Adventure. Lots of eligible young men."

"A church of one," Clare muttered.

"Hmm? Do you think that might suit you better?"

Clare knew responding would only encourage her, but she couldn't let that one stand. "The army spent a lot of time and money training me to fly helicopters. If I ever went back, I'm pretty sure that's what they'd want me to do."

"Really? How do you think you've handled the move from such a dangerous profession to such a peaceable one?"

And so the psychoanalyzing went on, until Clare was ready to drive the two of them into a ditch. The sight of the MacEntyres' massive barn was more welcome than she could have dreamed. There was something different about it this afternoon. She slowed almost to a stop and squinted through the gray-and-white blur. A gust of wind tore open the storm's veil, and for a moment she could see clearly the double doors at the top of the ramp, open, and the rear of a pickup truck inside. Then the wind reversed and everything vanished again.

She drove up the driveway a car length or two and parked. She didn't want to get stuck reversing out. "Bundle up," she said, turning off the engine. With the blower and wipers off, she could hear the storm beating against the car, the wind whistling and thumping, the snow hissing and tapping.

Hearing it still didn't prepare her for steeping out into it. A cold gust clouted the side of her head, and she tugged her hat down deep over her ears and eyes. Elizabeth emerged from the other side of the car with her scarf wound around her head and across her face.

At least it'll keep her from going over my career prospects, Clare thought. She headed down the drive.

"Where are you going?" Elizabeth pointed behind them. "The house is that way!"

"I saw a pickup parked in the barn," Clare yelled. "I'm not sure, but I think it might be Quinn Tracey's."

Elizabeth, either bowing to Clare's wisdom or eager to get out of the storm, nodded. She followed in Clare's tracks. They waded across the road and up the ramp, entering the barn along with the wind and the snow that was coating the truck's bed. Clare walked far enough forward to get out of the worst of it.

"Is this his truck?" Elizabeth asked, tugging her scarf beneath her chin.

Clare pointed to the attached plow. "I don't know, but I'm willing to guess so."

"Where do you think they are?"

Clare walked farther in, until there was nothing but wide wooden flooring beneath her feet. Straight across from them, another double door was firmly closed against the weather. Just as in the cattle pens below, a transverse aisle ran the length of the barn. The remainder of the barn, two levels strutted with dark, hand-cut beams, was filled with hay. Hay in tightly rolled, spiraling bales. Hay in silvery-green mounds.

Elizabeth sneezed.

Clare looked toward the east end of the barn. Nothing there but a two-story-high wall pierced with five windows at irregular intervals. The window glass, rippled and melting with age, was crusting over with frost. The barn was, Clare realized, shaped very much like a church.

Elizabeth sneezed again. "Where do you think they are?"

"There's a poultry barn and an equipment shed out back, but I doubt they're there," Clare said. "I suspect the downstairs is the hangout of choice. It's the cattle pen, and it has to be a good twenty degrees warmer than it is up here."

"Sounds good to me. How do we get there?"

Clare swiveled around. "There's a door outside, but when I was here last time, I saw a ladder coming down from the west end, there. Look." Sure enough, they could see two grainy supports and three rungs sticking up out of the floor.

Elizabeth sneezed. "It better be nailed in place."

"Do you have allergies?"

Elizabeth looked at her with watery and red-rimmed eyes. "Yes. The sooner I can get out of here, the happier I'll be."

"Do you want to go back to the car?"

"Doh." The deacon was as grim as Clare had ever seen her.

"Okay. Give me a sec to check the inside of the pickup, and then we'll go down. I want to go first."

"Of course."

Clare couldn't tell whether de Groot was being sarcastic or just prissy. Either way, she'd better hurry. She strode back to the pickup. The wind ripped into her as she stood on the running board and looked inside. She opened the driver's door and slid in on her knees. Maps in the door pockets, three scrapers stuffed behind the seat. She popped open the glove compartment. Insurance and registration, in Quinn Tracey's name. Paper napkins left over from a fast-food joint. Beneath them, two condom packages and a tin box of breath mints. What her brothers used to call their Hope Springs Eternal Kit.

In other words, nothing. No blood smears, no hidden K-Bar. She flipped down the sun visors and was startled by a piece of paper fluttering to the floor-mat. She pawed at it, clumsy in her gloves, until it came up into her hand.

Dear Mom and Dad,
I am sorry. I tried and tried but I could not control my urges and now a woman is dead. My friends tried to help me but no one knows that I am a killer inside. I am responsible. No one else but me. I'm sorry, but this is the only way I know to stop myself.

Quinn

"Sweet holy—" Clare stuffed the typed note into her pocket and slid out of the car. She looked around wildly. "Elizabeth? Elizabeth!"

The ladder. She hadn't waited. Clare sprinted toward the west end of the barn, her boots thudding on the boards, almost skidding into the open square that led downstairs. She grabbed the edges of the ladder and scurried down, jumping the last rungs.

Too late. Elizabeth stared at Clare, eyes wide and terrified, frozen into stillness by the glittering knife held against her throat.

FORTY-EIGHT

R uss kept his mouth shut and his eyes on the switchback he was negotiating. "I should have guessed. Even this comes back to Clare Fergusson. Did she come running to comfort you as soon as she heard the good news?"

He saw Debbie's lights in the rearview mirror. She had made the curve safely.

"Boy, is she going to be pissed off when she finds out I'm still alive."

I'm not going to mention Lyle, he told himself. *I'm not going to mention Lyle.* That was serious, deep-talking, kick-in-the-guts stuff.

Linda was quiet as they went through another turn down the mountain. They were getting close to the public road. He hoped the plows had been through.

"So who do you think did it now? I mean, who would want to kill our cat sitter?"

Ours? It's not my damn cat. "We're looking for Dennis Shambaugh, her boyfriend. His fingerprints were at the scene, and he fled when I went to question him." Linda had never much cared for hearing about the details of cases he worked on. It struck him that this was one of the most detailed discussions of a crime they had ever had. Of course, it was also the first time anyone had been killed in their kitchen.

"I can't believe it," Linda said. "My God, I met him. And then he turns out to be a murderer? I never would have guessed it."

He slowed down but didn't stop at the sign at the bottom of the Algonquin's road. A quick look told him nothing was coming in either direction. He rolled onto the white and featureless expanse of Sacandaga Road.

"Where'd you meet him?" he asked.

"At the house. He dropped Audrey off." She turned in her seat. "Who's been taking care of Bobbitt?"

"Who's Bobbitt?"

"My cat."

"You named the cat Bobbitt? As in, Lorena Bobbitt?" He shook his head. "The responders took it to the county shelter."

"You let them take her to the shelter?"

"I had a few other things on my mind than the damn cat, Linda."

"I can't believe you! You thought I was dead, and you didn't even bother to keep the last living connection to me."

"If you wanted me to have a connection with the cat, you might have tried telling me about it. Or—hey, here's an idea! You get *me* to watch the cat while you're gone instead of hiring a woman whose boyfriend is a convicted felon! Oh, but wait. That would have required you to *mention* that you were going to *disappear* for a week!"

The truck shimmied beneath him, and he realized he was going way too fast for the conditions. He took his foot off the gas.

"I've already apologized," Linda said, her voice barbed. "I don't know what else to say. I can't undo it or make it not have happened." She looked out her window. She didn't say anything else. She didn't have to. He recognized the words. She was throwing back what he had said to her the afternoon he told her about Clare.

"Look," he said, "this is ridiculous."

"It certainly is. You're treating me like I'm one of your criminals. You say you thought I was dead. Didn't you miss me? Aren't you glad to see me?" She held her hands in front of her, as if asking for a higher power to give her an answer.

"Christ on a crutch. Of course I am." He took one hand off the steering wheel and gripped her hand hard. "I was—part of me kept thinking you were going to show up at any minute, and then I'd realize what had happened. It was like getting knocked down by a tidal wave, over and over." He drew their interlocked hands over to his thigh and hammered on his leg. "Now you really are here. I just need a little time to get my feet under me and catch my breath."

"Silly man. Of course I'm really here." She squeezed his hand and smiled at him. "If this helps us realize what we mean to each other, then it will have all been worth it, huh?"

Not to Audrey Keane. No. He wasn't going to go there. He wasn't going to ask Linda to be someone she wasn't. He smiled back at her. She was here. She was back. Of course, that meant all their problems were back.

No. That wasn't fair. He was the one who evidently needed something he hadn't been finding at home. Linda had been perfectly content with their marriage.

Sure. She had gotten it out of her system with Lyle.

His pants pocket beeped loudly. "We must be back in signal range," he said. "Would you grab my phone and see what messages I've got? I don't want to take my hands off the wheel." The snow-covered road blended imperceptibly with the snow-covered farmland, and the barbed-wire fences he knew marked out the pastures running alongside them were hidden by curtains of white and gray.

Linda wiggled his phone out of his pants and dialed his voicemail. She punched in his mailbox number and listened. "It's your mother," she said. "She's worried about you. She wants to know where you are. She loves you. Call her." Linda looked at him.

"Erase it."

She beeped for the next message. "It's . . . Ben Beagle from the Glens Falls paper. Wants to get a statement from you. No, an interview." She frowned. "What's the sensational event that happened at the station last night?"

His stomach lurched. "I'll tell you later." God. He was going to have to explain spending the night with Clare. Linda would never believe they hadn't had sex.

"He leaves you a couple of numbers to reach him at."

"Uh . . . better save it."

She beeped again. "Oh, it's Lyle." She raised her eyebrows. "The state police caught Dennis Shambaugh, and he and . . . who? I didn't catch that. Anyway, they're going to Troop G headquarters for the questioning." She smiled. "He says to call him if you find out anything about me. Isn't that sweet?"

"Erase it." How many times over the last seven years had she mentioned MacAuley with the same dismissive affection? Lyle was right—it hadn't meant anything to her, not even enough to make her get twitchy or avoid the man. Russ didn't know if that disturbed him less, or more.

"Harlene," Linda said. "She wants to know if you're anywhere near 645 Old Route 100 because . . . what? Meg's boy Quinn? What a POI?"

"Person of interest. Linda—"

She frowned and held a hand up, listening. Her face changed. "Oooh. Now I get it. Reverend Fergusson is involved."

He snatched the phone from her in time to hear Harlene's recorded voice saying, "I'm looking for a responder, but we're short, and with the storm and all—well, you know. Give me a call when you get this." He hit repeat.

"Hey, Chief, it's about two o'clock, and I need to know if you're anywhere near 645 Old Route 100. It's the home of, hang on, Craig and Vicki MacEntyre. You know we've had a couple-three animal killings lately? Somehow that Jensen woman put 'em together with two other unreported cases, and now Quinn Tracey is wanted as a POI. Reverend Fergusson thinks the boy may be at the MacEntyres', and she's headed over there. I tried to talk her out of it, I did. I'm looking for a responder—"

Russ stopped the message and hit the return call button.

"I thought you didn't want to take your hands off the wheel," Linda said.

He ignored her. Harlene came on the line. "Millers Kill Po—"

"It's me," he said. "You got anyone over at the MacEntyres' yet?"

"Chief? Someone from the new hotel called and said your *wife* was *back*?"

"Yes. The MacEntyres'?"

"Oh. No. Flynn dispatched, but there was a bad crackup on the way and he's handling traffic."

"Have you heard from Reverend Fergusson?"

"Nothing new."

"Why's Quinn Tracey a suspect?"

"He plowed for all the victims."

"All of them? And we've got a total of five cases?"

"Correct."

"I'm on it. ETA five or ten minutes. I got nothing here, so for God's sake get me backup as soon as you can."

"Will do."

Harlene hung up, and he had a second to appreciate the one woman in his life who didn't argue with him or ignore what he said and do any damfool thing she liked, the one woman who did what he asked and told him what he needed to know in short sentences.

"You are not running off to get Clare Fergusson out of trouble," Linda said. "This is police business."

"The hell you say. I heard that message, too. Quinn Tracey may know something about some animal killings."

"Linda—"

"No! You let me finish! It is not like you have a hostage situation or a five-car pileup or whathaveyou. I know that boy. There's no way he's ever hurt anything in his life. Someone else can respond to that call."

"Linda, we're practically there. For chrissake, we have to go past 645 Old Route 100 to get to Mom's house."

In fact, he had reached the T-intersection. He slowed and put on his blinker. No cars coming in either direction. In his rearview mirror, he could see Debbie getting closer and closer. Too close. He pulled onto Old Route 100 just in time to avoid her front fender. She managed to stop before sliding into the intersection, at least.

"I'll park nearby. You and Debbie can wait. I'll only have to stay until Harlene can get an arresting officer on site."

Linda sat, silent, as the heater blew and the wipers thumped and he hunched closer to the windshield, trying to stay on a road surface he couldn't see. A cluster of rural delivery mailboxes materialized from the scrim of snow. He read the numbers. Not yet.

He drove on another mile, checking out two more mailboxes, until he found 645. The house itself was set far enough back to be all but invisible in the storm, but the dark bulk of the family's barn loomed next to the road, disappearing upward into the ever-increasing gray.

He slowed, stopped, and finally located the MacEntyres' driveway. He turned in, followed by his sister-in-law, but had to stop immediately in order to avoid running into a snow-covered Subaru.

Clare Fergusson's Subaru.

"Wait here," he said, reaching for his jacket.

Linda stared through the windshield. If she hadn't known, the bumper stickers on the car would have given it away. Who else had both the THE EPIS-COPAL CHURCH WELCOMES YOU and MY OTHER CAR IS AN OH-58?

"Listen." Linda unbuckled and twisted in her seat to face him. Her voice was dead serious. "If you do this, I'm getting into Debbie's car and going to her hotel."

"Dammit, don't act like a spoiled brat who's going to hold her breath until she turns blue."

"I mean it, Russ. You choose, and you choose now. It's me or her."

He could see she was upset. Her cheeks were two bright red spots against pale skin, and her jaw was rigid. But he could also see Clare's face, that night. *I'm not willing to buy my happiness with your marriage. And neither are you.*

"I already chose," he said, his voice harsh. "I chose you."

"Then drive me home to your mother's."

He let out a breath of frustration. "This is police business."

"Goddammit! You have never put our marriage first! Never! For twenty-five years I've been the one who has to understand. I've been the one who puts myself and my needs second so the marriage comes first! It's time for you to put your money where your mouth is!"

"You put our marriage first? You mean, like when you threw me out of the house? Like when your entire life became the goddam curtain business? Like when you slept with Lyle MacAuley? Was that putting our marriage first?"

Linda turned white. Absolutely white.

"Wait," he said. "I didn't mean it."

She opened her door and jumped out.

"Linda!"

She flung her seat forward and hauled her suitcase out with such force she spun around in the MacEntyres' driveway. She slammed the truck's door shut hard enough to set his ears ringing.

"Wait." He scrambled out of the cab. "Linda, wait." She waded through the snow, too far ahead for him to physically catch her. She reached Debbie's rental car.

"Linda! Wait!"

The door slammed. He was almost there, close enough to see her snapping out something to her sister. Before he could reach the car, Debbie backed out of the drive.

"Goddammit!" The car's rear wheels spun up twin fountains of snow, then lurched forward, fishtailing back down Old Route 100.

Goddammit. When he found Quinn Tracey, he was going to make that kid sorry he'd ever been born.

FORTY-NINE

D on't move," Aaron MacEntyre said. "Q, tie her hands."

The young man Clare had been worried about held Elizabeth de Groot pinned in place with one hand twisted behind her back and a knife to her neck. Clare stared at him. His eyes were flat. Calm.

"Uh . . . how? With what?"

Clare darted a glance at Quinn Tracey. Unlike his friend, he was a wreck, his mouth slack and twitchy, his gaze skittering first to Elizabeth, then up the ladder, down the long walkway between the stalls, and finally, reluctantly, to Clare. It was then she noticed his hand, barely keeping a grip on the rifle. It must have belonged to the MacEntyres. Quinn held it like someone unfamiliar with and uncomfortable around firearms.

"With one of the stock leads," Aaron said, a touch of impatience in his voice.

Did he mean it? Was Elizabeth really in danger? Clare narrowed her eyes. Quinn Tracey probably outweighed her, but she had no doubt she could knock him and his rifle down and be halfway to the cattle pen door before anyone could react.

She must have twitched. "Don't try anything," Aaron said. He shifted his hand a fraction of an inch and three drops of blood beaded up on the knife he held to Elizabeth's throat. The deacon whimpered and shut her eyes. "Quinn! Secure the prisoner."

Quinn leaned the rifle against a stall door and inched toward her, a woven lead dangling from his hand.

"Chrissake, Q, stop being such a pussy. She's like a nun. She's not going to bite you."

Clare thrust her arms toward Quinn, clasping her hands together. It was the picture of surrender—a picture taken from TV shows. She was betting Quinn didn't know enough to insist he tie her wrists behind her back.

He looked relieved for a second, then lashed the lead around and around her wrists. How could she reach him? She immediately discarded appealing to his humanity. Self-interest? No, that would be MacEntyre. *Always go for the soft target,* Hardball Wright said. *Eyes, balls, throat. Hit him where he's weakest.*

Quinn knotted the lead off three times, leaving the metal clips dangling, then stepped back, straight-backed, arms akimbo. Beneath his puffy jacket, his chest swelled. "Prisoner secured," he said, picking the rifle up.

What an ass. "Very professional," she lied. "You've been training."

"C'mon," Aaron said, ignoring her. He twisted Elizabeth's arm higher, forcing her on tiptoe as she pivoted away from the ladder.

"Was that what the animals were, Quinn? Training? Practicing your technique before trying it out on a human being?"

Quinn opened his mouth. "Quiet," Aaron said, frogmarching Elizabeth up the center aisle. Quinn shoved Clare ahead of him. The smell of hay and manure and warm living cowflesh rose up around them like incense.

"Better do as he says, Quinn. I can see who's the boss in this relationship. I bet you bend right over and take it up the—" The blow to her back sent her sprawling onto the stained cement. She landed hard against the edge of a stall.

"We're partners," Quinn yelled. "I'm just as much in charge as he is!"

"Bull." And hoo-ray for the kneejerk homophobia of the teenage male. "I bet Aaron killed every single one of those animals. I bet you stood there sucking your thumb while he cut Audrey Keane's throat. Then you poked at her a few times with your little knife and thought you were a man."

"That's not true! *I* was the one who thought of going to the Van Alstynes'. I—"

"Shut up!" Aaron whirled around, knife still hard against Elizabeth's throat. The deacon clawed one-handed against him for balance.

"For God's sake, Clare, don't make them angry!" she screeched.

"We're already dead," Clare said loudly. "What does it matter if I hack this loser off? His boss is going to gut both of us anyway." She straightened up, maneuvering herself against the stall door.

"No," Quinn protested. "We're not going to kill you."

"Is that what he told you?"

Quinn looked toward Aaron. "We don't need to kill them, right? I mean, they're our prisoners. They don't know what we're going to do."

Aaron stared at Clare. In his gaze, she saw that she and Elizabeth were not human to him. They were pieces in the game. Figures in his calculations. Assets or debits. She needed to convince him they were the former.

"Take us with you," she said quickly. "We can use my car. No one will remark on two teenagers traveling with women old enough to be their mothers. You won't be able to use our ATM and credit cards, but we can. We can take you where you want to go and leave you with a wad of money once you get there." She searched Aaron's face as he continued to examine her. Nothing moved behind the surface.

Finally, he said, "We can take your car and your money without you. You think she won't tell me her ATM number if I ask her?" Aaron pressed Elizabeth's arm higher.

"Two-one-seven-seven," she gasped.

He gestured to Quinn with his chin. "Get that one up. We're taking them into the processing room."

That was how she knew she and Elizabeth were debits.

Quinn twisted his fist in the front of her parka and hauled her to her feet. Aaron whirled the deacon around and resumed his march toward the doors at the east end of the barn.

Toward the abattoir.

One cow hung her head over the edge of her stall door, her deep brown gaze fixed on the human procession. It wasn't the first time she had seen creatures making the trip to the killing room.

"Don't do this, Quinn," Clare said under her breath. "You're seventeen. You can turn yourself in and testify against him and you'll be out of juvenile on your twenty-first birthday. But if you kill again, there's no way they won't prosecute you as an adult."

"Shut up," Quinn hissed. "You don't know anything about it."

"I know he's eighteen. No matter what happens, he's going to go up against the death penalty. He's trying to suck you in with him."

"Q, for godsakes, can't you control her?"

"How?" Quinn's voice nearly cracked.

"Belt her the next time she talks."

She twisted her head to catch Quinn's reaction. He gawped at Aaron, then frowned in disapproval. If she hadn't been so scared, she would have laughed. Pretending you were some sort of secret warrior and killing in a surprise ambush was okay. Hitting a woman was not.

"What are you going to do when you get caught, Aaron? Do you have a plan for that?"

She gritted her teeth, expecting a blow. He surprised her by turning his head and regarding her disdainfully. "I always have a plan."

"Was that why you took me aside yesterday and told me about Quinn going into the Van Alstynes' house alone? Was that why you said Quinn told you to lie to cover up for him? Was that part of your plan?"

She registered his arm drawing back, Elizabeth stumbling forward with a cry, the knife swinging free, and then Aaron's fist smashed into her jaw and her head snapped sideways in an agony of bone and motion. She reeled, half-blind from the pain pinwheeling through her skull, half-suffocated by the blood and tears and phlegm in her throat.

"God damn! That hurt!" Aaron's voice shrilled with outrage. Clare wiped her eyes with the arm of her parka and spat blood onto the cement. She blinked hard. Aaron was cradling his hand, tears of pain and fury in his eyes, the first genuine expression she had ever seen on his face. "That fucking hurt! I think I broke something!"

The knife.

On the cement floor.

Clare lurched toward Aaron. Unsteady, off balance, the best she could do was throw herself at him. He went down on his backside, with Clare sprawled atop him. "Run, Elizabeth, run!" she screamed, and damned if the deacon didn't finally listen to her.

Aaron was thrashing, swearing, trying to wrestle Clare off him. She couldn't see Quinn, but she could hear him, his noise of protest, a cry of, "Hey! Stop!" then the slap of hands on wood as he tried to get the rifle in position.

"Stop her, you asshole!" Aaron howled. He finally heaved Clare onto the floor and staggered to his feet. She rolled onto her back in time to see Aaron snatch the gun away from Quinn, chamber a round, and fire.

The report tore through the confined space. The pens erupted in a bedlam of clanking, kicking, and confused bawls.

"Damn! God damn!" Aaron slugged Quinn in the middle of his chest. "You let her get away, you stupid waste of space!"

Quinn stared toward the west end of the barn. "Whadda we do now?" he asked in a panicked voice. He rubbed his chest one-handed. "Whadda we do?"

The two boys stared at each other, one desperate and scared, the other desperate and enraged. Finally, Aaron tipped his head toward Clare. "Get her up," he snapped. "I'll take the gun. It doesn't do you any good if you won't fire it."

This time Quinn used both hands on her, dragging her to her feet. Aaron stepped toward her. Put both barrels of the shotgun under her chin. Pressed hard, so she could feel them bite into the soft flesh, smell the tang of oil and metal.

"I could blow your head off right here," he said.

This time, Clare kept her mouth shut.

"Get my knife," Aaron ordered.

Quinn ducked down and snatched it off the cement. "What are we gonna do? That other one's gonna go for the cops, you know she will!"

Suddenly, Clare felt the weight of her car keys like a curling stone in her pocket. Oh, no. *Oh, no.* Elizabeth wouldn't be going for the cops. She wouldn't be going anywhere. The best she could hope for was that the MacEntyre house was unlocked and that Elizabeth would call 911. And then hide.

"Open it up," Aaron said, gesturing to the wide door that separated the warm and living cattle from the cold and sterile processing room. "We'll do her like we did the other one and then we'll take off."

"But . . . but they'll know! That we did it! They'll come after us!" Despite his protests, Quinn released his grip on Clare's coat and started tugging on the handle.

"Grow some balls, will ya? Jesus, this whole thing has been about proving to ourselves what we can do. If I knew you were going to be such a goddam pussy about it, I would have picked someone else to join me."

"No!" The door rumbled open on its tracks. Quinn dashed to one side and snapped on the lights. "I can do it."

Without moving the rifle barrel from Clare's neck, Aaron leaned forward. The intensity in his eyes seemed to suck Quinn toward him. "I chose you, man.

We're brothers in arms." Aaron's voice was low, persuasive. "Don't let me down. All we gotta do is get through this part. Then we'll be on our way."

Quinn nodded.

"We can do what other people only dream of," Aaron whispered. "We're fucking masters of the universe."

"Yeah," breathed Quinn. Face shining, he reached out and tugged Clare across the lintel into the abattoir. "Where do you want her?"

"Right over there." Aaron followed, the rifle never wavering from Clare's head. "This time, you're going to get to do it. The killing cut."

The expression on Quinn's face wavered. "Uh," he said.

Aaron's eyes gleamed. "It's amazing, man. You'll never know what power is until you do it."

Quinn looked down at the knife in his hand. Clare looked at it, too. It came to her that despite her professed belief in the resurrection of the dead and the life of the world to come, she really really really didn't want to die.

O God, she prayed, *a little help here.*

"Hey," came a voice from the barn. They all looked. Russ Van Alstyne stood in the doorway, relaxed and unhurried, hands open and unthreatening. "What say we talk about this?"

FIFTY

H e had already been heading across the road toward the barn, after a
fruitless search through the house, when he heard the rifle shot. He
reached for his service weapon, which, of course, wasn't there.

Cursing under his breath, he waded through the snow that was drifting
deeper and deeper into the leeward side of the road. He was struggling up the
ramp when a body hurtled out of the barn straight toward him.

He could feel, as soon as he caught her, that it wasn't Clare. She screamed.
He clamped a gloved hand over her mouth. A terrified woman looked up at
him. Tears were freezing along her cheeks.

"I'm Chief Van Alstyne of the Millers Kill Police Department," he said.
"What's going on? Where's Clare?"

"Downstairs. With the cows. Hurry, please hurry! They have a gun and a
knife!"

"How many?"

Her brow knitted up into confusion.

"How many bad guys?" he clarified.

"Two. Um . . . Quinn Tracey and his friend."

"How do you get there?"

"There's a . . . there's a ladder through the floor at the end of the barn." She
pointed.

"Clare?"

"She's . . ." The woman started weeping again. "I don't know. He hit her so hard he knocked her over. That's when I ran."

Like a buzz bomb, her words exploded along his forebrain, whiting out every thought for a split second. He hitched in his breath. Focused on the woman. "You drive a standard?"

"Yes, but—"

He slapped his keys into her hand. "Get into my truck. It's at the end of the drive. Head toward town. Go slow. If it gets bad, pull over and wait. Got it?"

She nodded jerkily. "She's crazy, you know. What kind of woman jumps a man with a knife? She's crazy."

"Yeah. I know." He pushed her in the right direction and thrashed his way up the remainder of the ramp into the barn. He pulled his cell phone out. Flash-dialed Harlene's direct number.

"Harlene here."

"Van Alstyne here at 645 Old Route 100. We've got a hostage situation with gunfire. I need backup."

"You got it," she said, her voice even. Then, before he could sign off, "Chief?"

"Yeah."

"Aren't you unarmed?"

"Yeah."

"Then wait for the backup. That's the smart thing to do."

"I can't. I"—*Clare*—"can't. Van Alstyne out." He clicked off the phone.

He padded between the haymows, his good sense reining in the part of him that wanted to charge, berserker-like, to Clare's defense. His parka rubbed, arms against body, creating a papery noise. He frowned, took the coat off, and laid it on the floor next to the trapdoor opening to the lower level. He laid down on his belly and elbow-walked to the edge. Heard agitated cows and faraway voices from what sounded like the other side of the building. Took a chance and hung his head and shoulders down.

It was the other side of the building. He waited until the figures disappeared into the fluorescent-lit room, then dropped down the ladder. He hurried down the walkway between the stalls, conscious that at every moment he was framed and lit like a shooting-gallery target. Approaching the door, he slowed. Took a deep breath. Heard one of the boys say, "It's amazing, man. You'll never know what power is until you do it."

He felt sick to his stomach. "Hey," he said, stepping forward. "What say we talk about this?"

A dark-haired kid turned with the fast-twitch reflexes of the young, and Russ was staring down the barrel of a .308 Remington. Behind him, Quinn Tracey brandished a wicked long butcher's knife toward Clare's throat.

Clare. Russ felt his gut tighten around an urge to hurt whoever had touched her. She'd been banged around hard—her parka torn and smeared with manure, her jaw and cheek purpling, blood coating the inside of her lips and threading down to her chin.

The Tracey kid recognized him. His mouth sagged open. "Oh, shit," he whispered.

"Hey, Quinn," Russ said. "Good to see you're okay. Your folks are worried about you, taking off in the middle of a storm like that." He shifted his attention to the other one. "You must be Aaron MacEntyre. I'm Russ Van Alstyne. Chief of police."

Something flashed in the young man's eyes. Panic? Anger? Russ couldn't tell. "I've already called in a hostage situation," he went on, using the same easy voice. "This place is going to be swarming with cops soon."

The corner of MacEntyre's mouth curved up. "In this weather? I doubt it."

"You can't get away, Aaron. Your best bet is putting the weapons down and cooperating." Russ turned to Tracey. "I'm here to talk. The guys following me will be here to shoot. Let's not let it get to that."

Tracey looked terrified. "Aaron?" he asked.

"Finish securing her to the wall ring, Q," MacEntyre said.

Tracey awkwardly grabbed a length of chain and slipped it around Clare's badly bound wrists. The kid had to juggle the knife he was holding as well as keep the chain from slipping and reach for a D-clip. Clare looked at him, then at Russ. He could see the question in her eyes.

Should I take him?

Russ glanced at MacEntyre. His aim hadn't wavered. He was still perfectly lined up to gut-shoot Russ. "Don't be afraid, Reverend Fergusson," Russ said. "We'll have you out of there soon enough."

"Is she secure?" MacEntyre asked without turning his head.

Tracey rattled the chain. "Yeah," he said.

"Come here, then."

Tracey hurried to MacEntyre's side. Behind them, Clare immediately began twisting and rotating her hands. MacEntyre dug into his jeans and fished out a rag. He carefully wiped down the barrel, bolt, trigger mechanism, and stock of the Remington. "Hold this," he told Tracey when he was done. "Keep your finger on the trigger. If he moves, shoot him."

Tracey frowned but took the gun. Everything about his stance and his handling of the gun proclaimed his inexperience. Russ considered rushing him, but he could see a round chambered and the safety off. Five-year-olds had been known to kill people under those conditions.

MacEntyre crossed to the rear of the tiled chamber. He opened a battered locker and rummaged around inside for a moment. When he turned back toward Russ, he had on translucent latex gloves, the kind worn by cops handling evidence. And by butchers handling raw meat.

He strode back toward Tracey and retook the Remington.

"Why'd you wipe the gun down?" Tracey asked.

"It prevents a positive gunpowder test," MacEntyre said. "The cops won't be able to tell this rifle was recently fired."

What the hell? That was the screwiest thing Russ had ever—

"He's lying," Clare said.

"Put the knife to her," MacEntyre said. "If she talks, use it."

Tracey walked toward Clare. He brought the knife up.

"He wiped the gun down so you'll be the only person whose fingerprints are on it. He has a plan." She raised her voice. "You said you always have a plan, didn't you?" She dropped her voice and looked directly at Tracey. "Actually, he's had two plans. The one he told you was that the two of you were going to go away together and, what, rob banks?"

Tracey shook his head. "Join up with mercenaries," he said, his voice sounding younger than his years.

"Shut up, Q. You don't tell the enemy your plans."

Clare stared into Tracey's eyes. "The second plan's the one he hasn't told you about. That's the one where he kills you, makes it look like a suicide, and blames it all on you."

Tracey recoiled. "That's a lie!"

"Feel in my coat pocket," Clare said. "I took something out of your truck upstairs. Take it out of my pocket and read it."

"She's trying to trick you," Aaron said. "Who are you going to believe? Her or me?" He couldn't turn and confront Tracey directly without taking his eyes off Russ, but he backed up until his hip checked against a stainless steel table. His eyes flickered toward his friend. "You and me, man. We took a sacred vow." His voice was almost seductive. "We're not going to be drones like the rest of them. We are going to be kings of the earth."

"I thought it was masters of the universe," Clare said.

"Shut up, bitch! Before I blow your head off."

It was probably the first time in his life Russ wanted a gun pointed at him, if only to prevent MacEntyre from making good on his threat. "Were you in it with Dennis Shambaugh?" he asked quickly.

"Who the hell is Dennis Shambaugh?" MacEntyre said.

"The guy whose girlfriend you killed."

MacEntyre gave him a look of withering scorn that was so typically teenaged it was almost a put-on. "You don't get it, do you. Who the target is is irrelevant. What matters is taking the power. Getting the blood on your hands. Being a wolf instead of a sheep."

Russ blinked. "You didn't go to my house to kill Audrey Keane?"

"We went to *a* house with *a* woman alone without a dog or neighbors nearby. We didn't give a flying fuck if we offed somebody named Keane or Mrs. Santa Claus. Right, Q?"

Tracey seemed frozen in place.

"Just take the paper out of my pocket," Clare said. "That's all."

The kid peeked over his shoulder at MacEntyre, then reached into Clare's pocket. He came up with a crumpled sheet of paper. He shook it out, one-handed. As he read it, the knife in his other hand started to shake. He lowered the paper. Stared at MacEntyre. "This is a suicide note. With *my* signature!"

MacEntyre sighed. "She must have written it."

Tracey stalked toward his friend. "Why the hell would she have written a suicide note for me? Why the hell would this be in my truck?" He snapped it in MacEntyre's face. "It says I'm responsible for everything!"

"When it comes down to it," Russ said, "there's only room for one king of the earth. Everybody else is support staff."

"Shut up," Tracey snapped. "Aaron? I'm waiting."

MacEntyre sighed again, a deep, defeated sound. "C'mere," he said, sliding around to the front of the table, the rifle steady on Russ. "Smooth it out here and let's take a look at it."

Tracey stomped over to where MacEntyre stood.

"Get in front of me so you're not in my line of fire."

Tracey glared at his friend but did as he said. He bent forward and laid the paper on the scratchy surface of the butchering table, putting down his knife and smoothing the sheet with both hands.

MacEntyre seized the knife and plunged it into Tracey's back.

Clare screamed. Russ surged forward, but MacEntyre swung the Remington straight into his abdomen. Russ skidded to a stop, the rifle barrel digging into his gut. "Walk," MacEntyre said, and pushed the barrel in. Russ backed away. MacEntyre followed, indicating with his head where he wanted Russ to go. The young man backed him against the white tile half-wall that divided the room into two parts. From the other side of the wall, Russ could hear Tracey's high, skittering moan and gasping breaths. Over MacEntyre's shoulder, he could see Clare, tears spilling down her cheeks, silently working her wrists back and forth, loosening her bonds.

"You've really pissed me off, Reverend Fergusson." MacEntyre stared at Russ while he spoke. Something glinted in his dark eyes, but it wasn't anger. It was excitement.

Russ's stomach lurched with nausea.

"In fact, I may even bring you with me instead of taking care of you right here. So I can show you just how much you piss me off."

Unseen by MacEntyre, Clare yanked her hands free.

"You got any money in there?" MacEntyre nodded toward Russ's jeans. His practicality was even more gruesome laid over the sound track of his friend's slow and rattling death.

"In my parka," Russ said. "Up next to the haymow."

Over MacEntyre's shoulder, he watched as Clare took one step. Then two. "You're not going to get away with this," he said loudly, letting the fear show in his voice.

"Oh, please. Q kills you, kills the lady, and in a fit of remorse puts the end of the rifle against his heart and pulls the trigger. Conveniently obliterating any signs of being stabbed. I go back to school on Monday. Probably score with the girls because I'm all broken-hearted and shit."

"He was your friend! Doesn't that mean anything to you?" Bizarrely, Russ's mind flashed on Lyle for a second.

"I told you. Two kinds in this world. Wolves and sheep." MacEntyre sighed.

"I did what I could for him, but I guess you can't change what you are. I'm a wolf. Q was a sheep."

From the corner of his eye, Russ could see Clare reaching for something in the locker. Jesus God, he hoped it wasn't a knife. MacEntyre'd have his intestines splattered across the room before Clare could get close enough to strike.

"What am I?" he asked MacEntyre, desperate for time.

The young man smiled his cool, curved smile. "I have you pegged as a wolf. Which is why this conversation is at an end."

Clare whirled, leaping toward them, a thick metal tube shaped like a light saber in her hands. She had her fingers clamped over some sort of switch.

"Drop the rifle, Aaron," she said. Her eyes were huge, and her face, where it wasn't purple and bloodied, was stark white. But her voice was hard. "I don't want to hurt you, but I will."

MacEntyre looked bored. "You can't hurt someone with a pneumatic bolt stunner, Reverend. You can only kill someone. And you're not going to do that."

"Put the gun *down*, Aaron."

MacEntyre's lips twitched. He glanced toward her. "Sheep," he said. His head turned, and Russ knew. This was it.

Clare jammed the stunner into the bare skin of MacEntyre's neck. The charge igniting in the chamber made a muffled crack. Russ threw himself out of the way of the gun, but he needn't have worried. The rifle dropped to the floor. MacEntyre gurgled. A wet, bloody hole blossomed beneath his Adam's apple. Clare yanked the stunner away, an expression of horror on her face, as the young man fell over, eyes wide, blood and air spuming out of his neck. The abbatoir stank of urine and feces as his bladder and bowels let go.

They both watched him for a moment, lying on the floor. A dead thing. Then Clare cried out and hurled the stun gun into the farthest corner of the room. "Oh, my God," she said, covering her face with her hands. "What have I done?"

Russ knew she wasn't speaking to him, but he stumbled to his feet and went to her. He wrapped his arms around her and held her as tightly as he could.

"You did what you had to, love," he said. "You did what you had to."

FIFTY-ONE

Ironically (she thought later, when she began to be able to think about it), it was Quinn Tracey, not Russ Van Alstyne, who saved her from descending into a paralysis of guilt and horror. Over Russ's voice, soothing and supporting her, she heard another gasping rattle.

"He's not dead yet," she said idiotically, replaying the Monty Python joke.

"He is, darlin'. I'm sorry, but it was him or me, and he's dead and I'm not."

She pushed against Russ's solidity. "Not . . . him." She couldn't say his name. "Quinn."

He wasn't. Russ stayed with him, compressing his wound, because he was heavier. Clare went back outside and stood in the road, buffed and battered by the wind and snow until she felt scoured raw and she saw the headlights of what turned out to be Kevin Flynn's cruiser. Noble Entwhistle was right behind him, and, thank God, a Glens Falls ambulance that Harlene had diverted. She showed them where to go and then retreated to her car. She turned the heater on full blast and listened to Tal Bachman's melancholy voice: "I was there all the time—even I couldn't find me. So how did you see? What made you believe?" She refused to think of anything. She leaked tears. After a while she achieved a passable state of numbness.

Then the passenger-side door opened and Russ climbed in. He slammed the door shut behind him and looked at her. He touched her jaw with fingers as light as a drift of snow. "You should get in the ambulance and let them take you to the hospital. You ought to have that checked out."

She shook her head. "Nothing broken. I didn't lose any teeth."

"Clare—"

"Hold me," she said, her voice breaking despite herself. "Please."

He leaned toward her and gathered her in an embrace. He rocked her awkwardly over the stick shift while she cried. When she had wrung all the salt out of her body and her face was hot and puffy, she sat back. He let her go but kept hold of her hand. He rubbed her knuckles with his thumb. "Holding on," he said.

"Not letting go." She smiled a watery smile. "Hey, we're talking. Our lawyers won't be very happy."

"Like I was ever going to listen to what Geoff Burns said."

Her smile faded away. "Tell me something good. Please."

"Dennis Shambaugh's in custody. Jensen's gone to Loudonville to interview him. Kevin says that Harlene says that the Loudonville dispatcher says that Shambaugh didn't even know his wife was dead until the news broke in the paper. Supposedly he went back to our house to pick her up, saw all the cop cars, and kept on going. He was waiting around to hear from her when I showed up."

She leaned her head back and closed her eyes.

"I don't know how good you'll think this is."

His tone of voice tipped her off. She looked at him. "You've found out where Linda is."

"More like she found me." He shook his head and huffed half a laugh. "She showed up at the Algonquin right after I finished turning the place upside down looking for her. Turns out she had gone to St. Croix, courtesy of John Opperman."

"And he finally gets revenge on you for destroying his helicopter."

"I was just along for the ride. You were flying it."

She squeezed his hand hard. "I'm glad she's back. And I'm truly, truly happy she's alive and well. I want you to be happy. More than anything, I want you to be happy." Her voice was quavering, so she shut up.

"I want that for you, too, love."

She drew her hand out of his and laid it in her lap. Looked at both her hands. Hands she used to greet parishioners, soothe the sick, comfort the mourning. Hands that cradled the holy mysteries of the Eucharist. "I've killed a man," she said. "With these hands, I killed a man. How can I hold the body and blood of Jesus in these hands?"

He reached over the stick shift and enfolded her hands in his own. "I love your hands," he said.

She shook her head.

"I love you," he said.

She hiccupped a laugh. "Let's not start that again."

He didn't let go. "I'm going to have some sorting out to do. Linda's royally ripped at me."

That was enough to distract her from her failings. "She was the one who left without a word. How can she be mad at you?"

"She was with me when I got Harlene's message about you being here. She heard every word. Told me that if I left her sitting in the truck cooling her heels while I swanned off to rescue you, she was leaving with her sister. I wouldn't back down, so off they went."

"Oh, God." Clare leaned forward and bumped her head against the steering wheel. "I'm sorry."

"I'm not. I told her, it was police business."

She looked at him. "Uh-huh."

"I was driving right by here on my way to Mom's."

"So you had to stop right after she reappeared from the dead? And you would have done the same if it had been, say, Ben Beagle from the *Post-Star* who was chasing down Quinn Tracey?"

"Well . . ." He shifted in his seat. "Maybe I would have taken her and Debbie home and then come back. But I would have come back."

A shape loomed out of the gathering dark and rapped on her window. She unrolled it to reveal Kevin Flynn's eternally cheerful face. "Glad to see you safe and sound, ma'am!"

"Thanks, Kevin."

"Chief, we've secured the scene in case the CS guys want to look it over, but we've got to make tracks. There's been a bad accident on Route 57, and they're calling everybody in. Crap weather. This'll be the fourth accident I've responded to today."

"We'll follow you," Russ said, leaning over Clare. "We have to go that way to get Reverend Fergusson home. You can get us past the tie-up."

Clare turned to him. "We?"

"I'm driving you home." His tone did not invite debate.

"Oh," she said. "Thank you."

"Then I'm going to borrow your car. I gave mine to the woman who was with you."

"My new deacon." She didn't want to think about how today's events would affect her standing in the diocese. And she couldn't think, yet, about how they would affect her ability to pastor. "You may be in luck. She's probably back at St. Alban's, typing up a report to the bishop."

They traded places. Clare sat back, happy to leave the difficult task of driving through a snowstorm to someone vastly more experienced. She kept quiet, letting Russ concentrate on staying on the road, letting herself be hypnotized by the snow whirling out of the darkness into the headlights' beam.

"Kevin's right," Russ said, his voice strained. "This is crap weather." He sighed. "I was going to head over to Debbie's hotel, but I guess I better report in at the station instead."

"Aren't you still suspended?"

He grinned in a way that made Aaron MacEntyre's words echo in her head. *I have you pegged as a wolf.* "With Quinn Tracey in the hospital waiting to confess all? Just let Jensen try to keep my badge from me. Her and her extra *e*. Hah."

"Is he going to be okay, do you think? I mean, healthwise?"

"Tracey? Yeah. He had a punctured lung, but the paramedics were pretty optimistic. Being seventeen helps."

"Do you think he'll get charged as an adult?"

"Dunno. Depends on what we can uncover about MacEntyre. I didn't know him very long, but he sure struck me as a casebook sociopath. Tracey's lawyers'll probably have a pretty good argument that MacEntyre led their client down the road to hell."

"I met him before. That day you asked me to find out—" She shook her head. "Yesterday. It was yesterday. It feels like a year ago. Anyway, I'm just realizing that when he was talking with me and his mother, it was all 'like' and 'seem' about him. As if everything he did, every human interaction, was a performance." She shuddered.

"You don't need to talk about this," he said quietly.

"Sooner or later I do."

"No," he said. His voice was firm. "You don't." He glanced away from the road for a second. "I didn't go into any details about what happened with Flynn and Noble Entwhistle. I said MacEntyre was threatening our lives, and that he'd been killed. As the responding officer, I'm going to write up the official report. I can make it so that I did it."

She sat, silent for a moment. Thinking about changing history with a few keystrokes. "Thank you," she finally said. She smiled a little. "I love you for making the offer. But I can't accept."

He snorted. "Kind of thought you'd say that."

Ahead of them, Flynn's cruiser's brake lights flared red. Russ stepped on the brakes, muttering something under his breath that Clare figured she didn't want to hear. The Subaru fishtailed. "Hang on," he said, steering them into the skid. He got control of the car, and they slowly inched forward, following Flynn, who had turned on his red-and-whites. Emerging out of the darkness, they could see flares, and the whirling lights of squad cars and tow trucks and emergency vehicles, and then the intersection. A truck had T-boned a small car, crumpling it around the Peterbilt grille like a wet napkin draped over a fist.

Clare crossed herself, then folded her hands against her mouth. *Dear Lord God*, she prayed, *show Your mercy to all whose lives will be changed tonight.*

"Wait," Russ said. He slowed even more. "Wait." He pulled off the road. She thought. It was hard to tell.

She was about to ask if he was needed when he opened the door. In the overhead light, his face was a death mask. He slipped out, slamming the door behind him.

Alarmed, she tugged her hat and gloves on and followed him. In the blur of the storm, the rescuers and responders were anonymous, bulky figures in parkas and rip-stop pants, their faces hidden behind skin-saving balaclavas. She lost Russ immediately. She headed toward the accident, where brilliant halogen lights cut through the snow's unending assault.

"Hey!" A masked figure caught at her sleeve. "No one allowed in there, sorry."

She pushed her hat back and her parka collar down.

"Oh! Reverend Fergusson!" The man let go of her sleeve and peeled his balaclava away. It was Duane, an EMT and one of Russ's part-time officers. "I'm afraid they don't have any need of you now, Reverend." He raised his voice to be heard above the wind. "Better say your prayers for the rest of us, that we don't get frostbite sortin' this mess out. It's ugly."

"What happened?"

"Rental car skidded through the red light right into the path of the eighteen-wheeler. The driver says he tried to stop, but . . . He's pretty shook up."

"He's okay?"

"Oh, yeah. It's the other two that bought it."

A sick and terrible weight ballooned in the pit of her stomach. "I have to get in there," she said.

Duane shrugged. "Stay out of the way," he advised. Clare skirted an ambulance—sitting there, both EMTs waiting patiently in the cab, no rush to the hospital for them—and sloshed through a well-churned morass of snow toward the accident.

Four members of the Millers Kill volunteer fire department were attacking the remnants of the car with torches. Cutting away the tortured metal to take out what was left inside. Two fire trucks flanked the scene.

"Russ!" she yelled. She skirted the edges of the light. "Russ!"

A firefighter crossed in front of her, toting a rolled hose. "Excuse me," she shouted. "Have you seen Chief Van Alstyne?" The man—woman?—paused, then pointed to the other end of the intersection.

Clare hurried, slipping and sliding, dodging cops and firefighters, rushing, the panic and dread growing, frantic to find Russ and not wanting to see him at all.

She spotted him standing apart from anyone else. He was facing the remains of the car head-on. The closer she got, the more slowly she walked, until she was too close not to see his face.

Then she knew.

"They . . ." he said, in a voice that had aged a century. "They . . ." He pointed to the intersection. "You can see. From the tracks." She looked. Whatever he saw in the patterns in the snow was unintelligible to her. "And . . . from the angle. They were coming back."

She didn't want to see him like this. She didn't want to ever see such pain in anyone's eyes ever again. If it had been within her power, she would have switched places with the woman in the passenger seat. Just to erase what she saw when she looked at him.

"They were coming back. The hotel. Was that way. They were coming back." He stared at Clare. "And I—" His voice cracked, and he crumpled beneath an enormous cry that tore out of his chest. "Oh, God! What I said to her!"

Clare stepped forward, opening her arms, offering whatever she had.

He turned away.

He stood there, in the snow and the light and the darkness, drowning with the first bitter waters of grief, and she waited, and she waited, until she realized he wasn't going to turn to her. Ever. She stepped back. She stepped back. She stepped back and back, out of the light, past the fire trucks and the EMTs and the squad cars, until she had vanished into the storm.

And she was lost again.

Midway this way of life we're bound upon, I woke to find myself in a dark wood, Where the right road was wholly lost and gone.

EPILOGUE

I t is a cliché that there are no secrets in a small town. It is also true. Despite the fact Kilmer's Funeral Home had no visiting hours for the late Mrs. Russell Van Alstyne and her funeral had been unlisted in the *Post-Star*, the Center Street Methodist Church in Fort Henry was packed. The pews at the front of the church were so crowded, Mayor Cameron had to squeeze in next to Wayne and Mindy Stoner in the third-from-the-last row.

Mindy, who had been in Russ's class at MKHS, sighed when she caught sight of him. "Poor man. He looks awful."

"You speaking today?" Wayne asked Cameron.

The mayor shook his head. "I'm keeping a low profile. The aldermen and I met yesterday and told him he's getting six weeks off whether he likes it or not. Poor bastard just sat there and nodded. I don't want to give him the chance to change his mind."

"Can't say I'd like to sit home and think about it if my wife got turned to jelly in a car wreck."

"Wayne!" Mindy elbowed her husband.

"Why d'you think it's a closed coffin, hon?" He turned back to Jim Cameron. "Where's the other one? The sister?"

"Florida. She had a couple of grown kids who brought her remains back." Cameron shook his head. "What a mess. This is going to screw up our state highway fatality rating for the rest of the year."

Wayne relayed the news about Russ Van Alstyne's leave of absence to Scotty McAlistair at the Agway feed store the next day, and Scotty, in turn, told his daughter Christy at dinner time. When Christy arrived at the Free Clinic for an appointment she thought her father knew nothing about, she was disappointed to find out the nurse pratictioner had already heard that the chief of police was off duty for the next month and a half.

"Yeah, Lyle MacAuley's acting chief," Laura Rayfield said, helping Christy sit up. She snapped off her gloves and popped open a cupboard door.

"Oh. Well, did you hear that Quinn Tracey's already been charged? He's in the Glens Falls hospital, but nobody's allowed to see him. He's like, locked down in intensive care. We had an assembly about what happened with him and Aaron. They had a counselor there and everything."

"I hadn't heard, but I can't say I'm surprised." She handed Christy three boxes. "I want to make it very clear these don't prevent STDs," she said. "You should have your partner use a condom each and every time to protect yourself."

Christy grimaced. "There won't be very many times," she said. "My boyfriend's in the marines. He's going off to California for advanced training."

Laura Rayfield wouldn't have dreamed of talking about Christy McAlistair's sex life, but she had no qualms passing along the information about Quinn Tracey when she met several nurses at the Main Street yarn shop for their weekly stitch and bitch session. They, in turn, told her that one of their colleagues was in the market to sell her house.

"She's spitting mad about it, evidently," Laura said to Roxanne Lunt at lunch the next day. "The husband's taken a new job with the state police in Middletown. Alta Brewer, who's the senior charge nurse and who hears everything, said it was very last minute. He had to do it. No one at the police department will talk to him, evidently."

Roxanne's passion was preservation, but selling houses paid her bills. "Have they signed with a Realtor yet?"

"I don't think so. You should call them. Until they sell the house, he's got one godawful commute."

Roxanne fished her Palm Pilot out of her purse. "What's the name?"

"Rachel Durkee. Mark and Rachel Durkee."

Roxanne was delighted with the house. It was, she told the Durkees, in "move-in shape," and the only fix-up she recommended was a new coat of paint in the kitchen. She was thinking about possible buyers when she got a visit at the historical society from St. Alban's new deacon, who had broadened the reach of the church's fundraising.

"I know you're the mover and shaker behind the historical society, Ms. Lunt." Elizabeth de Groot shook Roxanne's hand warmly before taking a seat. "I feel that your organization is a natural to help us in our efforts to maintain one of Millers Kill's most architecturally significant buildings." She spread several photos of the church from the 1800s on Roxanne's desk.

"I think most of these are originally from our collection." The director smiled. "I think we might be able to make a grant." The niceties observed, Roxanne leaned forward. "Now let me ask you, you're commuting from the Schuylerville area, is that right?"

"Yes. Although after the terrible tragedy on Route 57, I have to admit I'm a nervous commuter."

"Have you thought about relocating up here? I can guarantee you your equity will go a long, long way in Millers Kill. And I've just listed the sweetest little Greek revival farmhouse."

"Well," the deacon said, "I do have reason to believe I may be needed at St. Alban's even more in the future than I am right now. I suppose it's something to consider."

Roxanne raised her eyebrows.

"At the suggestion of our bishop," Elizabeth dropped her voice, "Reverend Fergusson is enlisting—or is it enrolling?—well, never mind. She's joining the Army National Guard."

No one from Millers Kill was around when Clare signed the papers in Latham. It took them a while to figure out exactly what she was doing there. Eventually the recruiting station's major came back from lunch and she was handed over to him.

He looked over her service record. "Not to discourage you, Reverend, because God knows, we need qualified combat support pilots, but how come you aren't querying the chaplaincy corps?"

She sat stiffly, her back not touching the chair. Funny how the body language came right back. "I've spoken to my bishop about this. He . . . agrees that the diocese and the army would be best served by my keeping a hand in my former profession. As it were."

The major steepled his fingers. "Keeping a hand in? You do realize there's a strong likelihood of the 142nd being called up at some point. Even if we don't see action overseas, we have a history of responding to natural disasters. Is your, uh, church prepared to deal with your absence?"

"Yes, sir."

He slid the papers across the table toward her. "Okay, then."

She signed. The major stood. Clare stood. She raised her right hand. She pledged to support and defend the Constitution of the United States against all enemies, domestic and foreign.

The major saluted. She saluted. He smiled at her and shook her hand. "Welcome to the 142nd Aviation Battalion, Captain Fergusson."